"Master of the Quebec thriller."

Praise for the Victor Lessard Thriller *Never Forget*

Never Forget will leave you bloodless, and I mean that in the nicest possible way.

> — Alan Bradley, author of the Flavia de Luce Mysteries

A raucous crime thriller.

> — *Publishers Weekly*

[An] immersive thriller full of darkness, loathing, and vengeance.

> — *Montreal Review of Books*

A fine crime novel featuring a cast of well-delineated characters and a plot that demands the reader's undivided attention.

> — *Booklist*

Never Forget is a crackerjack read. Michaud artfully constructs the world of the Montreal police and a broad cast of characters while keeping his eye steady on ways to ratchet up the tension at every turn.

> — *Quill & Quire*

Martin Michaud is a master at twisty storytelling and compelling atmosphere. This kept me on the edge of my seat from start to finish. I can't wait to read Lessard's next case!

> — Catherine McKenzie, author of *I'll Never Tell*

Michaud is at his best recalling … fraught times through the cooler lens of our present day. It's great to see Canadian history used to such good effect in a story that resonates as well today as when it happened.

> — Margaret Cannon, *Globe and Mail*

Why settle for Scandinavian crime writers when we have in our midst a masterful author who can justly be celebrated as the new star of Quebec crime fiction?

— Martine Desjardins, *L'actualité*

Novelist Martin Michaud has produced a thriller that's solid, fastmoving, intelligent, and enlivened by moments of sharp humour and political insight.

— Marie-France Bornais, *Journal de Québec*

With its breakneck pace and flawless storytelling, this is Michaud's best novel. A thriller — to remember!

— Norbert Spehner, *La Presse*

A VICTOR LESSARD THRILLER

WITHOUT BLOOD

Victor Lessard Thrillers

Without Blood
Never Forget

MARTIN MICHAUD

WITHOUT BLOOD

A VICTOR LESSARD THRILLER

Translated by Arthur Holden

DUNDURN
TORONTO

Originally published in French under the title *Il ne faut pas parler dans l'ascenseur*, © Martin Michaud, 2010, Les Éditions Goélette.

Publisher: Scott Fraser | Editor: Shannon Whibbs
Cover designer: Sophie Paas-Lang
Cover image: istock.com/Instants
Printer: Marquis Book Printing Inc.

Library and Archives Canada Cataloguing in Publication
Title: Without blood / Martin Michaud ; translated by Arthur Holden.
Other titles: Il ne faut pas parler dans l'ascenseur. English
Names: Michaud, Martin, 1970- author. | Holden, Arthur, 1959- translator.
Description: Series statement: A Victor Lessard thriller ; 2 | Translation of: Il ne faut pas parler dans l'ascenseur.
Identifiers: Canadiana (print) 20200168460 | Canadiana (ebook) 20200168495 | ISBN 9781459742093 (softcover) | ISBN 9781459742109 (PDF) | ISBN 9781459742116 (EPUB)
Classification: LCC PS8626.I21173 I413 2020 | DDC C843/.6—dc23

We acknowledge the support of the Canada Council for the Arts and the Ontario Arts Council for our publishing program. We also acknowledge the financial support of the Government of Ontario, through the Ontario Book Publishing Tax Credit and Ontario Creates, and the Government of Canada.

We acknowledge the financial support of the Government of Canada through the National Translation Program for Book Publishing, an initiative of the Action Plan for Official Languages – 2018-2023: Investing in Our Future, for our translation activities.

Care has been taken to trace the ownership of copyright material used in this book. The author and the publisher welcome any information enabling them to rectify any references or credits in subsequent editions.

The publisher is not responsible for websites or their content unless they are owned by the publisher.

Printed and bound in Canada.

VISIT US AT

 dundurn.com | @dundurnpress | dundurnpress | dundurnpress

Dundurn
3 Church Street, Suite 500
Toronto, Ontario, Canada
M5E 1M2

For Antoine and Gabrielle

PART ONE

What does it matter what kind of reality stands outside me,
so long as it has helped me to live, to know that I am
and to know what I am.

— Charles Baudelaire

MARCH 31st, 2005

QUEBEC CITY

Darkness.

Behind his eyelids, he tried to re-create a mental image of the face, but the vision kept slipping away.

For a fraction of a second, he thought he saw the outline of the eyebrows, then everything went blurry. However hard he tried, he couldn't visualize the eyes.

When the eyes absorb death, they reflect only emptiness. I can't find a way to picture that void.

He shook his head. All that remained of his life was a dream, buried in another dream.

Waiting.

Tapping steadily on the tiles.

The rain ended a little before 8:00 p.m.

Crouched in the darkness behind the kitchen counter, he re-inspected the arsenal arrayed in front of him: a hockey bag on wheels, a metal suitcase, a pile of towels, and a bottle of all-purpose cleaner. He was invisible from the entrance. All he would have to do was charge forward to get the man.

Two hours ago, he had parked the car on the street and disabled the alarm system. Before leaving the vehicle, he had slipped his laptop into a knapsack and stowed it under the back seat.

He had proceeded methodically. Everything was in its place.

He stroked the handle of the knife strapped to his ankle.

Soon, he would extract death from death.

He knew the well-regulated life of the man he was about to kill, down to the slightest detail. This being Thursday, the man would leave work at 8:30 p.m. He'd stop off at the supermarket for a frozen dinner. When he got home, he'd microwave his meal and eat it in front of the TV, sprawled in an easy chair.

He had slipped into the house several times while the man was out.

He had looked over the row of DVDs on the man's bookshelf and noted with disdain that they consisted entirely of American TV shows.

People dull their minds with crude, derivative entertainment.

He had also remarked that the immense, luxurious house was at odds with the frugal habits of its owner. He had noticed a marble chess set in the living room. He had observed the detailed ornamentation on the finely carved pieces.

A house like this should have been home to a family with children, not one person living alone. People were losing touch with real values. The cult of the individual, of every man for himself, disgusted him.

People don't take responsibility for their actions anymore. They think they can let themselves off the hook by pointing fingers at others whose actions are worse than their own.

This man would pay for his mistakes. He would see to it.

He heard the car's engine outside, then a key sliding into the lock. The door opened softly and a hand groped in the darkness, searching for the switch.

A final doubt assailed him. He brushed it aside.

His plan had no obvious flaws, apart from the possibility that a third person might be present. The man lived alone and didn't seem to have any relationships outside his work. The fact that the house was isolated provided a degree of extra protection in case a problem should arise. It would be unfortunate to have to eliminate an innocent victim, but sometimes collateral damage was unavoidable.

He held his breath, tensing his muscles, ready to burst out of the shadows.

He'd been waiting a long time for this moment.

As soon as he'd spotted the photograph of the young woman, as soon as she had resurfaced, he'd done his utmost to avoid attracting attention.

He had forced himself not to buy more than a few items in each store, seeking out the anonymity of large retail outlets. He'd been compelled to visit a dozen different establishments, all located outside a two-hundred-kilometre radius from his home. He had never asked a store clerk for assistance.

Once his purchases were made, he had removed the labels and eliminated all markings that made it possible to trace the items.

These precautions had struck him as elementary.

On March 20th, his birthday, he had loaded up his old truck and set out for the hunting lodge at Mont-Laurier, north of Montreal.

Since the lodge was inaccessible by road, he had transported his materials using the snowmobile and utility sled that he kept in the town's storage warehouse. The warehouse had a separate access door. No one had noticed him coming or going. In any case, it wouldn't have been unusual to encounter him in the area at this time of year.

He had decided to transport his victims by night, to minimize the risk of being seen. Not wanting to leave anything to chance, he had made this advance trip to the lodge in darkness. There would be no room for error when he had actual bodies to deal with.

That night, he had put away the food before going to bed. With the cupboards full, he could count on several days' autonomy before needing to resupply.

He'd spent most of March 21st sleeping and recovering his strength. In the evening, he had gone snowshoeing in the forest and heard a solitary wolf howling at the moon in the frigid darkness. It had occurred to him that he was like that wolf: the last prophet on the hill. He, too, would stand alone and howl out his gospel to the world.

The next day, he had carried out the necessary modifications. The lodge was divided into three sections: a main space, a private room, and a dormitory.

He had emptied the dormitory of its four bunk beds, which he had disassembled and stored in the shed. Next, he had boarded up the windows with slats of plywood. Using chains, he had affixed metal manacles to the wall at the end of the room. Then he had tested the apparatus. Once locked, it was escape-proof. Finally, he had installed the projection system.

Two freezers purred in the main space. Each one was big enough to hold a body.

The hunting would be good.

On March 23rd, he had returned to Quebec City, eager to begin.

The alarm system didn't emit its usual beep. The man entering the house was surely wondering why it wasn't working.

The light blinded the hunter for a moment, but he blinked without concern. In a few seconds, his eyes would adjust and he would kill his prey. The old man would have been proud of him.

The old man's been drinking in the truck all morning. Suddenly, a door slams. The boy feels a hand on his back. He's expecting to get hit, but the blows don't come. The old man hands him a rifle with a telescopic sight. The boy knows how to find his way in the woods. He knows how to track a moose. But at this particular moment, all he wants to do is cry. He has no desire to venture into the forest alone. "Quit whining like a baby. Do your father proud." He heads off with an ammunition clip, his hunting knife, a canteen, and a knapsack containing a few sandwiches.

He leaped from his hiding place before the man, who had picked up the telephone, could call the alarm company to report the outage.

For a second, everything seemed suspended, frozen, as though time were folding in on itself.

He drove the knife into the rib cage with a quick, brutal motion. The victim staggered backward. The killer pulled out the blade and struck twice more, two blows as rapid as they were lethal.

He was surprised at that moment to discover how easily the weapon pierced flesh, severed muscles, sliced organs.

A sound of splintering bone confirmed that he had perforated the sternum.

With distorted features, the man gurgled like a bathroom drain.

"We all have to pay for our mistakes," the killer said in a soft, almost compassionate voice.

It's bizarre how the brain works.

The victim didn't even wonder why this fate had befallen him.

Instead, he reflected on the fact that he would never meet the baby his sister was expecting in May. He also thought about the lakefront property that he'd wanted to buy, though he had never taken concrete steps to make his wish a reality. With a hint of panic, he realized that he would miss an important meeting and that he wouldn't be able to take out the garbage.

And finally, his life ended on a question mark: Who had spread that plastic sheet on the floor?

At that moment, the killer drove the knife blade upward, causing irreversible damage to the internal organs.

The man collapsed onto his attacker. Their foreheads came together, giving them the brief appearance of grotesque Siamese twins. They stared at each other wordlessly.

The hunter saw only surprise and distress in the horrified gaze of his prey. On the threshold of death, the man's lips parted as though he were about to say something, but a final spasm emptied him of breath.

The killer slit his victim's throat, and the lifeless body slid gently to the floor.

A jellyfish of blood spread over the plastic sheet.

It had all happened so fast that he barely had time to grasp what he had done.

He opened the metal suitcase and took out a Nikon digital camera. He photographed the body from every conceivable angle, taking several close-up shots of the face and wounds. When he was satisfied with the images, he put the camera back in the suitcase.

He pocketed the dead man's ID cards and rolled up the body in the plastic sheet. As he'd expected, getting the corpse into the hockey bag was the hard part.

Now it was time to clean up. He used the towels to wipe the blood spatter off the tile floor, then scrubbed everything thoroughly with disinfectant.

He removed his gloves and coveralls. He put them in a plastic bag with the dead man's ID cards and the bloodstained items. He put on a pair of clean gloves and rolled the hockey bag to the garage.

After parking his car beside the victim's, he leaned the bag vertically against the bumper. Then he grabbed it from underneath and lifted it until it tipped over into the trunk. Finally, he unzipped it and shoved in plastic ice bags on either side of the body.

Done. No one around.

He downloaded the photographs to his laptop, then erased the Nikon's memory card. He looked at the photographs as one might look at a painting. They were his work of art. The images would be perfect for his blog. And for everything else.

He burned the photographs onto a blank disc, then attached a preprinted label to the disc. He slid the disc into a case, went back into the house, and left the case on the counter. On his way out, he reactivated the alarm and locked the door using the dead man's keys.

He started the old black BMW 740i that he'd stolen the day before from the long-term parking lot at Quebec City's Jean Lesage Airport. Insurance companies spent a fortune each year on theft prevention, but some drivers were simply stupid. If you knew where to look, you could easily find a hidden duplicate key. The BMW's owner had shown exceptional consideration in leaving the parking stub on the dashboard.

Despite his excitement, he forced himself to drive slowly. After a few kilometres, he started to relax. Everything was going according to plan. His victim lived alone and wasn't expected at work until the following Wednesday. Barring unforeseen circumstances, no one would miss him before then, which meant there was ample time to carry out the rest of the plan.

He would stop somewhere for a fast-food meal. Not the healthiest choice, but this evening he was prepared to make an exception. He didn't want to fall behind schedule.

Should he take the body directly to the lodge or get some rest on the way?

He considered the matter.

If he drove at a reasonable speed, he could expect to reach Mont-Laurier around 3:00 a.m. Taking out the snowmobile, loading the sled, and making the trip in darkness would require at least another hour. Everything would depend on how tired he was.

He'd been driving for twenty minutes when a dull thud shook the car. He looked in the rear-view mirror and saw nothing out of the ordinary. He had probably rolled over a pothole.

In the middle of Highway 20! This country is going to hell.

By the time he was five kilometres out of Saint-Hyacinthe, the adrenalin rush was starting to wear off.

He stopped in the town for a bite to eat and took the opportunity to have another look at the photographs on his laptop. Then, in a vacant lot, he burned his victim's personal effects and the soiled items. He dispersed the ashes with the tip of his shoe.

He was struggling to stay awake by the time he saw the glow of Montreal in the distance.

On the Champlain Bridge, with the skyline in view, he decided that it would be wiser to get some rest in the city. He didn't want to risk falling asleep at the wheel.

Then he remembered a motel on Saint-Jacques Street where he'd stayed in the past. It was the sort of establishment that took cash and didn't ask for ID. If he remembered correctly, there was also a pharmacy nearby. Perfect. He'd kill two birds with one stone.

He parked in the motel lot. Knowing he'd be back in Montreal in a few days, he paid for a full week. He stowed his belongings in the dingy room and walked unhurriedly to the pharmacy.

After pulling a ski mask over his face, he drew a hammer from the folds of his coat and smashed the front window. The alarm went off instantaneously. He'd have to work fast. A police car would be there within minutes.

He used the hammer to disable the two security cameras, then walked quickly to the prescription counter. He broke the lock on the cabinet containing restricted medications, took thirty seconds to find what he was looking for, then grabbed several vials and a syringe. He sprinted out into the deserted street. After a minute, he slowed down to catch his breath.

In the distance, he heard a siren.

He strolled back to the motel. Walking helped him put his thoughts in order.

He was ready.

Tomorrow will be a great day.

The label on the disc was dated March 31st, 2005. A web address was printed on it.

So were two words and eight digits.

Error message: 10161416.

APRIL 1st, 2005

1

Montreal

As far as I can remember, there was no sunshine on the morning of April 1st, only the grey drizzle of a late-breaking day. A sheet of dirty ice clung to the pavement in front of my apartment on Saint-Antoine Street.

Caught up among the torrents of snow that the plows had been shoving aside since December, discarded papers lay in a mosaic on the sidewalk.

April.

It's the time of year when, as though recalling a forgotten promise after a long winter, the residents of Montreal start looking forward to blue skies, to buds on the trees and a warm wind on their faces. It's also the time of year when Canadiens fans begin to dream about the Stanley Cup.

Though the district of Saint-Henri was manifestly under-privileged, its fortunes had been looking up lately. Contributing to this trend were the renaissance of the old Atwater Market, the revitalization of the Lachine Canal — where empty factories were being converted into high-end condos — and the creation of a bicycle path linked to the market by a pedestrian bridge.

Unlike the trendy Plateau Mont-Royal, Saint-Henri would never be a tourist destination. It wouldn't become a mini Soho or Greenwich Village. But still, a growing number of young people were moving into the area.

That's precisely how it was with me. I occupied a five-and-a-half with crumbling plaster walls, though I only used the three rooms that were fit for habitation.

My clock radio went off for the first time at 6:45 a.m. I automatically hit the snooze button, giving myself ten minutes' grace. It was the same routine every morning until my official wake-up at 7:15 a.m. But for reasons I'd be hard put to explain, that's not how things worked out this particular morning.

I woke with a start at 8:45 a.m., emerging from an awful nightmare in which a car was about to run me down. I lay in a daze for a few seconds, staring at the clock's liquid crystal display. No doubt about it. The time really was 8:45 a.m. I was going to be seriously late.

Leaping from my bed, I hurried into the shower. I didn't pause to enjoy the scalding caress of the water, a pleasure I usually prolonged until the tank was empty, which generally took less than three minutes.

I had turned thirty-three the previous week. My best friend, Ariane, had given me a green wool sweater, which I now threw on after grabbing my jeans off the floor.

To celebrate the occasion, we'd had dinner in Chinatown. We'd gotten decidedly tipsy and closed out the evening in a seedy karaoke bar on Saint-Laurent Boulevard, where, to my own surprise, I'd launched into a delirious rendition of Cyndi Lauper's old hit "Girls Just Want to Have Fun."

I walked past the mirror and pushed back a few unruly locks of red hair. My face was freckled. As for the rest of me, it was neither ugly nor beautiful. Ordinary, but not boring. Makeup was something I never wasted time on. I grabbed a beanie off the coat rack to keep my hair in place and threw on my old coat.

As I was opening the door, a caramel-coloured furball darted through my legs into the street.

Stupid cat!

I loved to hate that animal, which fled from me every time I set foot in the apartment. But I couldn't bring myself to get rid of him.

I had come home one morning to find him on the doorstep. He had probably belonged to the previous tenant.

A survivor, like me.

By 9:12 a.m., I was running toward the bus stop on Atwater.

After slipping discreetly into my cubicle, I collapsed onto my not-even-slightly-ergonomic chair, which squeaked as I sat down.

I looked at my watch: 9:50 a.m.!

Maybe nobody noticed.

The first thing I did was check my emails. I opened a few messages and noted that there were no new developments in the file that I was supposed to be overseeing.

My tension level rose when I saw an email from the boss, sent a few minutes ago and marked "Important." The company was small, and Flavio Dinar ran it like a dictator. He hated lateness, but I desperately needed this job. My cheeks flaming, I clicked the email.

Date: Friday, April 1, 2005, 9:20 am
From: flavio.dinar@dinar.com
To: simone.fortin@dinar.com
Attachments: Fundraiser(text).doc, Fundraiser(photos).gif

To all employees:
I was delighted to see everyone participate so enthusiastically in this year's "Software Fights Poverty" fundraiser.

I'm proud to inform you that thanks to your commitment, your hard work, and the generosity of our donors, we surpassed our fundraising objective for 2005, collecting the record sum of $16,000.

I want to thank you all for the excellence of your contributions, which reflect the high standards of Dinar Communications.

I've attached some articles and photographs that
appeared in various newspapers some weeks ago.
Cordially yours,
Flavio Dinar

I let out a sigh of relief. The email had nothing to do with my lateness. Since I'd participated actively in the fundraising event, which had been held in a reception room at the Saint-Sulpice Hotel, I opened the file and looked over the media coverage.

Each employee had created a fun piece of software for the event.

My nonsense-phrase generator wasn't particularly brilliant, but it had attracted the highest bid of the night, three thousand dollars. That didn't really come as a surprise. The bidder, a bald, middle-aged man, had been watching me all evening long like a drug user eyeing his stash.

Following the event, Flavio Dinar had hosted an after-party in two connecting hotel suites that he'd booked for the evening. When it came to preserving close ties with major clients, the man knew what he was doing. There were even whispers that over half the company's revenue came from the federal government through the back channels of the scandal-ridden sponsorship program.

As a result, the entertainment laid on by the boss included champagne, cocaine, and high-end escorts. None of which was likely to raise an eyebrow among those familiar with the public-relations business. In that line of work, moral rectitude doesn't count for much.

I had put in my usual perfunctory appearance at the party, but left before it degenerated into a bacchanal. I had decided to leave the event as Dinar, blind drunk, was preparing to offer up a public display of his personal charms, stumbling onto the dance floor in a hypnotic trance.

On my way out, I had run into the bald man. A good-looking young blond was on his arm. Gazing eagerly down my décolleté, he had invited me to join him and his companion for a drink somewhere else. Politely but firmly, I had declined.

Opening the file that contained the photos, I noticed that most of the images were of Dinar employees and inebriated donors. In one of them, I saw the bald man and the blond in a smiling embrace. The blond's gaze seemed unfocused.

On the caption accompanying the photo, I read: *Jacques Mongeau.* The name seemed familiar, but I couldn't place it. Then I forgot about it.

I should have remembered him, but I didn't. Even if I had, I don't think it would have changed anything. More than seven years had passed since the last time I'd heard the man's name. I'd spent those years trying to put a very painful chapter of my life behind me.

Despite all the precautions I'd taken, I saw my own face in the background of another photograph. Not only that, but my name was listed on the caption accompanying the picture. All of which was very upsetting. But at that moment, I had no inkling of the chaos the photo would unleash.

I was starting to feel distinctly anxious when Ariane stepped into my cubicle.

"You're late!"

Her voice was loud and cheery.

"Keep it down," I whispered. "No one noticed."

She threw herself onto the visitor's chair, which let out a groan.

"It's not like you make a habit of it. You haven't taken a day off in two years."

"You know I can't stand being late." I reddened. I was still prone to blushing, even at my age. "A lot can go wrong in five minutes."

I gathered up some loose papers and placed them in a neat stack on the corner of my cracked melamine desk. A lot really could go wrong in five minutes. I knew from experience.

Ariane jumped to her feet.

"Coffee?"

"Are you nuts? I just got here!"

●   ●   ●

10:05 a.m.

Had she used her legendary powers of persuasion, or was I just in the mood for coffee? Whatever the reason, three minutes later we were on our way down to the ground floor.

The question occurred to me the very first time I stepped aboard: Why don't people talk in an elevator?

I must have been six years old, accompanying my father to his office, when I first noticed this phenomenon. Not only were all the passengers studiously avoiding eye contact, but in the steel cage carrying us from one floor to the next, an almost funereal silence reigned, noxious and unsettling.

I asked my father about the reasons behind this puzzling fact, and he answered, "When human beings feel trapped, they retreat into themselves and keep their mouths shut."

Ever since then, with his dictum in mind, I've done like everyone else. I've kept quiet whenever I stepped into an elevator.

But this time, because I was alone with Ariane and she was trying to get an answer out of me, I broke my habit.

"You know," she said, "Jorge's been asking about you again. He's shy, but he's also kind of sexy, don't you think?"

Jorge was a charming guy, but I'd grown accustomed to my solitude.

"Ariane, you really need to stop trying to set me up. How many times have I told you that I like being on my own?"

"Well, if he was interested in *me*, I wouldn't hesitate. He's so sincere, so passionate ..." Her expression was lascivious. "I'll bet he's great in bed. Who knows? He could change your life."

Ariane was an inveterate sensualist. They say opposites attract. Perhaps that was why she was the only person I trusted.

The *G* on the panel above the elevator doors lit up in orange. A synthetic voice said, "Ground floor."

The doors opened.

"Forget it, Ariane. Sartre was right when he said, 'The only person who can change your life is you.'"

Only much later did I realize how incredibly wrong that statement was. Which is why I now live by a fixed rule. It may not be entirely rational, but it's a rule that serves me well, and I think everyone would be wise to follow it.

Never talk in an elevator.

We were crossing the lobby when a phone rang.

"It's mine," Ariane said, searching in her bag. "Hello?" She rolled her eyes in irritation. "Did you try going through the administrator menu?" She turned to me, putting one hand over the mouthpiece, and mouthed, "What a moron." Then she barked into the phone: "Don't think about it, nitwit! No! Don't move, I'll be right there."

"Problem?" I asked.

"It's Hogue. He can't get into the main database. If I don't go back to help him, he'll bring down the whole system. I'll join you in five minutes."

"Okay."

I walked to the building entrance and opened the glass door. I stepped aside to let an old lady go by. Looking at her, seeing her gnarled hands, I suddenly felt sad and ugly.

In the street, a taxi driver and a motorist were yelling at each other. I shook my head. I'd recently seen a news report about road rage. It was a phenomenon that mystified me. A man had beaten someone to death for cutting him off at an intersection.

How was it possible to lose your self-control so completely?

I went around the taxi and stepped off the sidewalk. The café where I spent too much money on lattes was in the building across the street.

I looked to my left to make sure no cars were coming. Did I have enough cash? I opened my bag and found my wallet.

Just then, I was struck by a realization.

Shit. I had forgotten to leave the bathroom window half-open so the cat could get in.

I had to smile.

I cared about that dumb animal more than I was prepared to admit. I opened my wallet and saw two five-dollar bills.

Without being aware of it, I'd gone two steps past the yellow line that ran down the middle of the street. I looked to my right. A black sedan was speeding straight at me. I froze in horror. Collision was inevitable.

I held my breath. My muscles tensed.

The air around me seemed to contract. Other sounds evaporated, leaving only the low, terrifying growl of the oncoming engine.

I felt a sudden impact on my lower body, then I lost my balance and went tumbling forward. The rear wheel lost its traction and skidded over something. At the last instant, I raised my elbows reflexively in front of my face.

A jolt of pain shot from my shoulder to my right ankle, drilling its way down my spinal column.

I heard the rumble of the engine as the car raced away, then a loud squeal of tires, then nothing.

Nothing but silence.

His sleep was deep, dreamless, restorative.

He woke up around 5:00 a.m., feeling clear-headed, and went over his plan.

Before setting out for Mont-Laurier, he would first gather some information about the habits of his second target, Simone Fortin.

At this stage, it was crucial to work out every detail of the operation in advance. Having spent more than six days tailing his first target, he thought he might need even more time for this one. The project certainly had its share of complexities. He had decided to hold the young woman captive, which meant taking her alive.

Whether or not he was satisfied with the results of his surveillance, he would leave Montreal around 3:00 p.m.

That way, he'd avoid the rush-hour traffic and reach Mont-Laurier in darkness, facilitating the trip to the hunting lodge with the body that now lay in the trunk of the BMW. After storing the corpse in one of the freezers, he might give himself a day's rest in the wilderness before resuming his surveillance.

That remained to be seen.

He took a long cold shower and got dressed. Then he stopped in at a service station, where he bought some bags of ice, a newspaper, a cup of coffee, and two banana muffins. He paid in cash and manoeuvred the BMW so the clerk couldn't see the licence plate.

Was he paranoid?

He didn't think so. Better to be cautious.

In the empty parking lot of a shopping centre, he placed the newly purchased bags of ice around the body.

At 7:00 a.m., he took up a surveillance position near Simone Fortin's office building and began his watch. A black notebook and pen lay on the dashboard, in case he wanted to take notes.

The wait had begun.

The dense forest swallows him. At the lake's mouth, he hears a noise, a snap of branches to his right. The animal is moving deeper into the thick brush. He hesitates to advance along the trail. It's already midafternoon. He doesn't want to spend the night in the forest, but he's not about to go home empty-handed. The old man might get annoyed, and when the old man's annoyed, he hits hard. He follows the moose's tracks. Fearing he might have lost the trail, he climbs a tree and sees the animal down below, near the water, at a distance of over seven hundred metres. A makeable shot for a good sniper, but not for a beginner like him. He edges forward, one step at a time, crouching to stay hidden in the high grass. Another fifty metres and he'll try his luck. Suddenly, the animal stamps its hooves and flees.

He started having doubts around 9:15 a.m.

Had he missed her?

That seemed unlikely. There was only one entrance, and he hadn't taken his eyes off the door for a second.

Had he gotten the address wrong? He rechecked the slip of paper on which he'd noted it. He was in the right place.

At 9:40 a.m., a police car pulled up behind him. He relaxed when he saw one of the two cops in his rear-view mirror sipping coffee.

They were on their break.

He started the BMW and pulled out to go around the block. He didn't want to risk attracting attention.

At 9:57 a.m., he parked a hundred metres from his previous observation post and resumed his watch. The police car had disappeared.

Still no sign of the young woman. Something was wrong.

10:20 a.m.

It had all happened so fast!

He had seen Simone Fortin come out of the building. She'd held the door for an elderly woman and stepped out into the street. She had searched for something in her purse.

Without pausing to think, he'd driven straight at her.

He banged repeatedly on the steering wheel, enraged. He'd knocked her down!

With that single act, he had wrecked the plan that he'd put together so patiently. What had gotten into him? Why hadn't he been able to control himself?

He replayed the scene in his head.

It was the young woman's smile as she crossed the street that had provoked him.

That intolerable smile.

He breathed deeply to calm himself and stop his hands from shaking. His mind was racing. He needed to improvise, to put together an alternative plan. Above all, he had to act fast.

Time is always the decisive factor. He knew that.

You can't fight against time and hope to win.

He'd have to go back to the scene and blend in among the bystanders.

As long as she's still alive!

In his fury, he hit the steering wheel again.

What had he been thinking?

He parked the BMW on an intersecting street, Forest Hill Avenue, across from a pharmacy. He grabbed his coat from the back seat and put it on. He pulled a toque over his grey hair and put on a pair of sunglasses. Finally, he took his knapsack.

Had there been witnesses? How long could he leave the BMW unattended?

He got out of the car and locked the doors.

He saw an Asian man in a lab coat standing at the pharmacy entrance, smoking. Despite the situation, he couldn't help thinking that it was inappropriate for a pharmacist to be smoking.

It sets a bad example for young people.

He made an effort to walk at a normal pace, to avoid attracting attention. He melted into the group of gawkers standing around the ambulance.

The group included a mother holding her child by the hand; two students on their way to the University of Montreal, one of whom had covered Simone Fortin with his coat; and an old man with a dog on a leash.

A reverential silence reigned over the scene. From where he was standing, he couldn't see his victim's face as the gurney was loaded onto the ambulance, but he heard the old man tell one of the students that she was breathing.

He let out a long sigh of relief.

All was not lost!

The ambulance sped away, its siren blaring.

The bystanders were going their separate ways as he wrote down the ambulance number in his notebook.

I let myself drift for a few seconds.

Then I heard something. Indistinctly.

A voice? Yes. It was a voice.

Someone was speaking to me.

Lying on the ground, I opened my eyes. I saw an opal sky and, upside down, the face of a stranger bending over me.

A man.

I felt the touch of his hand on my arm and a tugging sensation as he raised my body toward his own. In a moment I was on my feet, facing the man who had just saved my life.

The street was as quiet as a broad desert of white sand.

I looked him over quickly: late thirties, black hair, brown eyes, short beard, fine features. Quite an attractive guy, actually.

I heard that overlay of sound once again and saw that the man's lips were moving.

I had to make an effort to concentrate.

"Pardon me?" I said.

"Was it your cell?"

"My cell?"

"That you were trying to find in your purse …?"

Suddenly, everything cleared up. I remembered starting to cross the street, looking into my purse and freezing when I saw the car. Clearly, the man had grabbed me by the coat and thrown me to the ground.

"I was going to buy a cup of coffee and … it's so stupid. I was searching for my wallet."

I began to feel dizzy. My legs gave out. The man caught me as gracefully as Humphrey Bogart in his prime.

"I don't know how to thank you," I said, trying to steady myself.

The man smiled, revealing straight white teeth.

"Let me buy you that cup of coffee. I know a place not far from here that's perfectly quiet."

As we walked, we encountered no pedestrians or cars.

It was a little surreal to be walking in silence with a stranger. Now and then I'd sneak a glance in his direction. He didn't seem at all bothered as he strode along with his hands in his pockets.

The rain had left a fine film on my face. Because of the unseasonable warmth, I opened the collar of my coat. Exhaling threads of mist into the humid air, we turned onto Blueridge Crescent.

I couldn't tell if it was the rain, the blackened snow on the sidewalk, or the day's pale light making the whole city seem sleepy, but as I walked beside my guardian angel, I felt disconnected from things, as though I were frozen in a Riopelle painting.

I took a few deep breaths, trying not to give in to the sluggishness that was overcoming me. Something was troubling me. Something I couldn't put my finger on.

The man lifted his chin toward the façade of an old building decorated with carved stone gargoyles. One of the winged demons caught my eye.

"I love the gargoyles," I said.

They reminded me of the time my parents had taken me to visit Notre-Dame Cathedral in Paris, long ago, in happier days.

"They're pretty," he answered. "In the old days, craftsmanship mattered."

He pushed open the wooden door and led me inside. A circular counter stood in the middle of a narrow, dimly lit room. Chairs were upside down on the tables. Other pieces of furniture were covered in white sheets, as though the place were just emerging from some kind of hibernation.

"If it isn't Miles Green!" a heavy-set man exclaimed as he came toward us.

I suddenly realized that my good Samaritan and I had never introduced ourselves. So his name was Miles.

The proprietor had slicked-back hair and a thin moustache that crossed his plump, shining face. His shirt was too tight around the waist.

"Hi," Miles said.

The two men hugged briefly.

"Aren't you going to introduce me?"

"Oh, sorry. George, this is …"

Miles turned to me, wearing the desperate expression of a schoolboy who doesn't know the answer to the teacher's question.

"Simone Fortin," I said.

"It's a pleasure," the proprietor said, kissing my hand ceremoniously.

"Some maniac almost ran her over a few minutes ago. A black car. The driver didn't even stop."

"That's the trouble with this damn city. They'd give a driver's licence to a donkey if it could squeeze behind the wheel of a car."

The joke hit me like a whiff of laughing gas.

"Have a seat. I'll get you some coffee."

We took off our coats and went to the only table that was set for customers, to the left of the bar. Miles sat down facing the window. I still couldn't figure out what was bothering me.

"Do you work in the neighbourhood?" he asked.

"Right in front of the spot where the car almost hit me."

George came back and placed two cups of steaming coffee in front of us.

"I added a finger of cognac, to boost your spirits."

He went behind the bar and resumed wiping glasses with a dishcloth.

I took a sip and made a face.

"George must have awfully thick fingers," I said in a low voice.

We both laughed.

"What do you do for a living?" Miles asked.

"I'm a web designer for Dinar, an advertising agency."

"What does that involve?"

"Basically, I design and build websites for our clients."

"Do you enjoy it?"

"More or less. What about you?"

"I'm a horticulturalist. I work not far from here, at the Notre-Dame-des-Neiges Cemetery."

George approached us once again, walking like an old cowboy with hemorrhoids.

"Need anything else?"

"We're good," Miles replied.

"I've been working in the neighbourhood for several years now," I said, after George moved away, "but I never noticed this place before."

"It's a well-kept secret. An oasis of peace for those of us who know about it."

Suddenly, something clicked. I realized what had been troubling me.

How could I have forgotten last night's dream, in which I was being run down by a car? I told Miles about the dream.

"Did you wake up before the impact?"

"Yes."

"Strange," he murmured.

"I'll say."

Without noticing, I had torn my paper napkin into shreds.

"Do you believe in synchronicity?" Miles asked.

"You mean Jung's notion that coincidences are sometimes more than mere chance?"

"Yes."

"I don't know. You?"

"I find the idea intriguing."

I put down my cup. Its white bottom was visible through the thin film of remaining coffee.

"Simone ... would you spend the rest of the day with me? Who knows ... maybe synchronicity brought us together."

2

I preceded Miles onto the porch of his apartment, a red-brick duplex on Côte-des-Neiges. I climbed the half-dozen stairs cautiously, leaning on an unvarnished wooden handrail. A splinter went through my woollen glove and lodged in my forefinger. Shit!

"Go right in," he said, joining me on the porch. "It's open. I never lock the door." I pulled out the splinter with my teeth.

Stepping into the apartment, I glanced around at the décor: white walls, dark hardwood floors, galley kitchen, circular table, several chairs, and a couch covered with a sheet that Miles hurriedly pulled off to reveal an aging chestnut leather surface. There was no sound system, no sign of a TV. Later, I would discover an austere bedroom and an immaculate bathroom.

He took the coat that I held out to him and hung it on a hook. I went to the only window. Beyond a rusty overpass, I saw the cemetery, with its bare trees, its headstones emerging from the blanket of white, and a single red bouquet lying like a bloodstain on the snow.

I thought with sadness of my mother, who'd been struck down by a ruptured aneurysm twelve years ago. I still caught myself occasionally thinking she was still alive, in her garden, surrounded by her flowers. As for my father, that was a whole other story. Our relationship, already strained after my parents' divorce, had been snuffed out forever at the very moment when I needed him most desperately. He'd only ever thought about himself and his damn company.

"Have you been living here long?" I asked, still gazing out into the distance.

"Quite a while, yes," Miles answered.

His voice made me jump. He was a couple of steps behind me.

"Victor Depocas lies buried there," he said, pointing at the bouquet of roses. "He was an architect. A woman comes and lays flowers on that spot every morning."

"Do you know things like that about all the graves?" I asked.

"No!" he exclaimed, laughing. "There are nearly nine hundred thousand people buried on those grounds. But when my workday is over, I like to walk along the paths. A cemetery is like a library. Every resting place contains a unique human story."

Ever since my childhood, I'd always been fascinated by cemeteries. Whenever I visited my mother's grave, I ended up wandering through the grounds, trying to imagine the lives of the people whose names were carved into the stones all around me.

"Hey, do you like jazz?" Miles asked out of the blue. I said yes without thinking, although my knowledge of the subject came from a single second-hand album purchased in a drab bookstore. Miles took a broom out of a closet and banged four times on the ceiling. Almost instantly, I heard the plaintive wail of a trumpet coming from upstairs.

"Four knocks is our signal," Miles said. "My neighbour, Jamal Cherraf, is a talented jazz musician."

I felt suddenly unsteady. Trying not to be conspicuous, I put a hand to my forehead.

"Are you okay?" he asked.

"A little light-headed."

"You've had a shock. The adrenalin is wearing off."

I groped for the right words. "Miles, what you did this morning … you were very brave. That car could have hit you, too."

"My instincts took over. When I shoved you aside, I ran the risk of hurting you very seriously."

"I don't see how."

"If I'd pushed you too hard, you might have broken your neck or fractured your skull against the pavement. Luckily, I didn't have time to think about it."

"You did the right thing. If you hadn't intervened, I'd have probably been killed."

He gave me a wry smile.

"I was lucky. The line between a good decision and a bad one is sometimes very thin."

Upstairs, the trumpet fell silent.

I went back to the window while Miles made coffee.

The street outside was deserted.

It occurred to me that I should call Ariane and ask her to cover for me at the office. I hesitated between two possibilities: pretending to be sick or simply admitting that I had agreed to spend the day with a complete stranger.

I settled on the first option. I had no desire to face the prying questions Ariane would be sure to ask if I told her the truth.

But when I pulled out my cellphone, it didn't work. It had probably been damaged when I fell.

I asked Miles for permission to use his phone and was hardly surprised to learn that he had neither a cell nor a landline.

Oh well.

Ariane might worry a little, but she'd understand. It isn't every day you come within a hair's breadth of getting killed.

My life had been stagnating for too long. I was going to live this day intensely.

I can't say how long I was standing there, lost in thought, but when I turned around, Miles wasn't in the room.

He had probably gone to the bathroom.

I waited a few seconds before advancing quietly along the hallway. I stopped to listen, but heard nothing. I knocked on the bathroom door. When no one answered, I opened it.

Without giving it much thought, I noticed that the white-tiled space was entirely bare. There were no toiletries, no towels, not even any toilet paper.

I came back out of the bathroom and walked to the bedroom, where the door was ajar.

"Miles?"

Hesitantly, I stepped through the half-open door. The room's only contents were a mattress on the floor, covered by a white quilt; a wooden chest of drawers; and, pinned directly to the wall above the chest, an unframed painting. I stepped closer and opened the drawers. They were empty.

The painting was of a stone wall covered in graffiti. I was able to make out six words written in red: *Run, late, elapse, lid, me, tee.* One of the stones had come loose from the wall and fallen to the ground. Through the gap, the staring eyes of a man were visible.

Fascinated by this morbid work of art, I gazed at it thoughtfully.

The creak of the apartment's front door startled me. I tiptoed out of the bedroom and crept back along the hallway.

"Did you find the bathroom?"

I wasn't about to admit to Miles that I'd been searching his bedroom.

"Yes," I lied.

"Sorry for leaving you here all by yourself. I went up to Jamal's place to get some milk."

"No problem. He plays really well, by the way."

"We'll pay him a visit a little later, if you like. He's quite a guy. Sugar?"

"Just a drop of milk."

He handed me a tiny cup. I brought the steaming coffee to my lips and took a small sip. The liquid had a gently calming effect.

We stayed where we were, at the counter, and drank our coffee in silence. When we were done, Miles rinsed the cups and put them in the sink.

"Feel like taking a walk?"

"Sure."

"I'll show you around the cemetery. There's something I want you to see."

"You can point out the graves of famous people," I said, with an eager note in my voice.

We entered the cemetery through the Côte-des-Neiges entrance, a wrought-iron portal flanked by twin gatehouses topped with verdigris.

We walked up the path, skirting the central island, which, Miles pointed out, "is covered in hydrangeas in the summertime." A monumental cross and a pair of smaller angels stood in the middle of the island. As we went by, I noticed the inscription carved into the white marble — *O crux ave spes unica* — which, if I remembered my spotty high school Latin correctly, meant "Hail to the Cross, our only hope."

Miles led me along a path that bore left. We passed a chapel and were soon walking west on a rising slope.

Apart from a few sparse mounds of snow, the paths were clear. The rain had stopped and the air was mild; the temperature must have been fifteen degrees Celsius. Miles took off his jacket and knotted it around his waist. We came to the top of the rise.

Stepping forward among the gravestones, he guided me to a black granite monument that wasn't visible from the path. On it, in white letters, I read:

Alice Poznanska Parizeau
1930–1990

"Do you recognize the name?" Miles asked.

"Yes," I said. "She was a writer and the wife of a former Quebec premier."

"Clearly, you're something of an expert."

"I hardly deserve any credit. My mother was the one who loved literature. I've read one of Alice Parizeau's novels: *The Lilacs Are Blooming in Warsaw*."

We stopped at the grave of actor Guy Sanche, creator and star of the much-loved children's program *Bobino*, and we stopped again at the resting place of famed composer and pianist André Mathieu. Then we turned our steps eastward. I gazed up at the trees that lined the path, the filaments of their branches stretching across the sky as Miles pointed.

"That's a birch. Next to it is a Colorado blue spruce. To the right, you can see a Norway maple and, behind the maple, an Austrian black pine."

We crested a low hill and approached a series of vaults that had been built into the sloping earth. Miles approached one of them, its stone façade decorated with four columns. He read aloud the inscription emblazoned on its iron door.

In memory of
Thomas D'Arcy McGee
The most eloquent voice of
The Fathers of Confederation
1825–1868

"How did he die?" I asked.

"One evening, he made a passionate speech in the House of Commons in support of national unity. When he got home that night, he was shot on his doorstep."

"Did they find the killer?"

"Yes. He was hanged."

We walked to the cemetery's main avenue and turned north. When the avenue split into narrow paths, Miles went a few steps ahead of me and stopped in front of a monolithic gravestone.

"Do you like poetry?" he asked.

"I don't really know much about it," I said.

He cleared his throat and recited:

"The lakes are ice-locked, silent, dead.
Where do I live? Where shall I go?
My soul is ice-locked, silent, dead,
Another Norway, deep in snow,
From which the golden skies have fled."

"That's lovely," I said. "Did you write it?"

"No," Miles answered. "He did."

He stepped aside so I could see the name on the stone.

Émile Nelligan
Poet
1879–1941

"Is this what you wanted to me to see?"

"No. We're almost there."

I closed my eyes and let the soft wind caress my face. I felt relaxed, serene. The surroundings were deeply soothing.

The peace was immense, the tranquility absolute.

In this place, only memories lay ice-locked, silent, dead.

I was enjoying Miles's company. The worries I'd experienced earlier, when he asked me to spend the day with him, had dissolved. There were no feelings of embarrassment between us, no awkward silences.

He led me to a modest headstone in the shape of a cross.

"Here we are," he said.

I read the epitaph.

Étienne Beauregard-Delorme
1993–1998

My heart stopped. I began to shake.

"You knew him?" I asked, feeling my emotions rise.

"No."

I was struggling not to burst into tears.

"Who sent you to find me?"

His answer came without hesitation.

"No one."

I hadn't been in touch with anyone since running away a few months after the boy's death. As a precaution, I had leased my apartment under my mother's last name. I had cancelled my credit cards, closed my bank account, and deliberately failed to renew my passport, health insurance card, and driver's licence. My cellphone number was confidential. I'd gone off the grid. Disappeared from circulation. Or so I had believed.

"Was it Stefan? My father?"

Miles was looking into my soul. His expression was desolate.

"No one sent me, Simone. No one."

He was speaking the truth. I couldn't say how, or why.

But he *knew*.

Leaning against a tree, I stared into the distance. The tear stains were probably still visible on my face.

Hoping, perhaps, for comforting words from Miles, I had revealed my secret to him. I had shone a light into the dark place where I'd been hiding for too long.

Was I right to confide in him?

As I spoke, he simply nodded, not saying a word. It was only when we started walking again that his hand touched mine, gentle as a butterfly.

The daylight was starting to fade.

A bird was singing somewhere, by rote, without conviction.

We came out through the gate on Camillien-Houde. We hadn't seen a living soul during the entire walk.

I felt vaguely nauseated, disoriented, unsteady on my legs. I was finding it hard to get over the shock I'd just experienced. My mind was reeling, struggling to assemble explanations. I didn't know what to think. I needed to understand.

"Miles, when you talked earlier about the thin line between a good decision and a bad one, did you really mean that?"

He looked at me with intensity. "Yes."

"And the headstone you showed me — you're not going to claim that was synchronicity."

He bowed his head. "No."

Night had fallen. A large scarlet moon was sailing across the sky like a fiery balloon. We walked under the overpass and came back to the apartment.

"Everything I just told you about that little boy ... you already knew, didn't you?"

3

For Detective Sergeant Victor Lessard of the Montreal Police, it was shaping up to be a good morning.

He had sent off his reports at 8:00 a.m., then he'd participated in the patrol officers' briefing, giving directives and reviewing unsolved cases.

Apart from a car-theft ring that was proving hard to track down, things were generally going well at Station 11 in the Côte-des-Neiges district.

He answered his phone messages in a hurry, leaving himself time before lunch to go online and learn more about Banff National Park. He had closed his office door deliberately. He didn't want to be disturbed.

As he clicked on his web browser, he was aware of how much better he was feeling. He hadn't touched a drop of liquor in three months. Okay, yes, there was alcohol in his mouthwash, but ever since his teenage years, he'd been careful not to swallow the stuff.

He still needed to lose a little weight, but overall, his life was back under control. He was working out again: a half-hour jog first thing every morning, followed by a short weight-training session. He'd even signed up for a salsa class.

Little did he realize that the events of the next few days would plunge him back into hell.

The hardest part, even now, was living without Marie and the kids. He'd stopped in front of the house the previous evening.

Through the kitchen window, he'd seen his ex-wife and his daughter laughing as they went about their tasks. As usual, his son, Martin, wasn't around.

He bitterly regretted having pushed her.

Marie had put up with all kinds of misbehaviour in the past, wanting to support him in his time of trouble. But that evening, he had stepped over the line. Despite the flowers, the gifts, the numerous pleas for forgiveness, and the attempts to blame everything on the professional trauma he'd been through, she was implacable. If he didn't move out, she'd press charges. Worse still, she had forbidden him from having any further contact with the kids until he'd been dry for a year.

And she was right.

He'd been dragging them down with him. His influence on his children's development had become harmful. These days, he knew nothing about them, though he did occasionally follow them to find out who they were spending time with. There were so many traps they could fall into. Especially Martin, who was just emerging from adolescence.

When Marie realized that he was spying on the kids, her outrage had prompted him to promise that he wouldn't do it anymore. But there were evenings when he couldn't help himself.

The salsa class he'd joined was helpful: it alleviated his solitude. The idea had come from a woman he'd talked to at an AA meeting. But he never mentioned it at the station. It might have raised questions about his masculinity.

It saddened him that, even today, he was forced to hide his vulnerability for fear of being marginalized. Others might see things differently, but he believed the police force still harboured a deeply macho culture.

And he had paid a steep price for that culture. It was only when he'd hit rock bottom and Marie had thrown him out of the house that he'd finally made up his mind to consult the police psychologist.

He hadn't yet forgiven himself for the deaths of two of his men the previous year. But he had gained a clearer sense of how powerfully that event had affected him, and, above all, of why he had sought refuge in alcohol. He was still fragile, of course, but now he felt better equipped to deal with situations that might trigger him.

At forty-three years old, after a dark time in which he had even contemplated suicide, he was finally making plans for the future again. When July came around, he would have a talk with Marie.

Whether or not he'd been dry for a year, he would insist on joint custody. And at the end of the summer, he and the kids would go camping in the Rockies.

He took a sip of coffee.

He was about to launch a Google search when he heard a knock. Nadja Fernandez appeared in the doorway.

"Sorry to bother you, Victor."

"Mmm?" Lessard growled, not looking up from his screen.

"Dispatch is reporting a hit and run on Côte-des-Neiges Road."

"Any deaths or injuries?"

"I don't know. Apparently there's a witness at the scene."

"Patrol cop."

"Excuse me?"

"Send a patrol cop, Fernandez."

"Nguyen's on a domestic violence case. Chagnon's in the east end dealing with a detainee transfer, and Thibodeau's giving a crime-prevention talk at a school in Notre-Dame-de-Grâce. That leaves only Vinet for emergencies. Everyone else is helping out on the Jacques Cartier Bridge."

"Fathers for Justice again?"

"Yep. There's a huge traffic jam."

For the third time since the beginning of the year, a man in a superhero costume had climbed the bridge and was holding law enforcement officers at bay in the name of the militant paternal-rights group. Despite his own strained family situation, Lessard felt no sympathy for the group, whose tactics he disapproved of.

The real problem, he thought, had deeper roots. It was too hard to raise kids in Quebec these days. Driven by globalization, people's work schedules had followed the American model and become inhuman. Jobs were being lost to countries where production costs were lower and workers were exploited. Lessard had closely followed the last provincial election campaign, two years earlier, during which the struggle to balance work and family had become a political issue for the first time.

As far as he was concerned, the heart of the problem lay there. If he hadn't been so caught up in his work, he might have had more time to devote to his family. Quebec needed radical changes. Everyone was always talking about health and social programs. But what did any of that matter, if nobody paid attention to society's nucleus, the family? The good intentions had ebbed away when minimal concrete measures were taken in the wake of the election.

Although values on the police force were evolving, Lessard didn't generally talk about these things. But he'd recently surprised his colleagues on the detective team by coming to the defence of Chris Pearson, a young cop on the squad. Pearson had become the father of a baby girl at the beginning of the year, and his late arrival at a meeting had prompted sarcastic comments from Detective Sirois. In response, Lessard had said that they needed to give more thought to family issues at union meetings. Coming from a guy who was widely known to be an inveterate workaholic, this declaration had provoked an awkward silence.

"Send Pearson or Sirois."

"Their shift starts at one o'clock," Fernandez said.

"Damn."

"Do you want me to transfer the call to another station?"

"No!" he said, his voice rising.

The Station 11 team would handle its own calls. The last thing Lessard wanted to do was give Commander Tanguay an excuse to deliver another of his sermons on honour and integrity.

There were times when Lessard ran out of patience with the latest methods. Police work had been tough enough under the old system. Nowadays, with neighbourhood stations in place, he got the sense that maintaining customer relations counted for more than getting results. The higher-ups were too concerned with the force's public image, and not enough with sound investigative work.

He wasn't a politician or a bureaucrat, for God's sake. He was a cop! He'd been trained to catch bad guys, not to reassure city councillors or comfort senior citizens' groups. Why couldn't they leave him alone? Especially now, when he had to deal with staff cuts.

"Another pain in my ass," he muttered, standing up and grabbing his black leather jacket.

"Thanks, Victor, you're a doll," Fernandez said, smiling.

"Mmm."

The man who had witnessed the accident was very old. He had a dog on a leash. His glasses were so thick that Lessard wondered whether he could see anything more than a few metres away.

Perhaps he'd imagined the whole thing. Too often, solitary elderly people called the police simply because they were starved for human contact.

The detective sergeant approached the man and shook his hand.

"Victor Lessard, Montreal Police."

"Hilaire Gagnon."

"Can you tell me what happened?"

"I was walking my dog. Butor has a bad leg, but he still needs to get out regularly."

Lessard backed away from the animal, a yellow Lab. It ignored him. He couldn't stand dogs.

"I was strolling along the sidewalk when I heard a car moving fast behind me. Then I heard a noise of crumpling metal. That's when I turned around."

"What did you see?"

"A black car, driving at full speed. It raced around the corner with its tires squealing. Then I saw someone lying on the ground."

"The victim?"

"The young woman, yes. I went to her. She looked like she was asleep. I put my ear to her mouth. She was breathing."

"What happened next?"

"Other people came over. One young man called an ambulance. Another young fellow covered her with his coat. The ambulance took her away a few minutes before you arrived."

"And then?"

"That's it."

"Did you hear the car hit the brakes before the impact?"

"No."

"Did you get the licence number?"

"Sorry, no. My eyes aren't as good as they used to be. But it was a luxury car, I'm sure of that. Probably a Mercedes. My grandson has a Mercedes. He works for a bank. Acts like he owns the world. Young people these days, they think they know everything."

"A Mercedes. Are you sure?"

"I think so," the old man said. Lessard suppressed his impatience. He wasn't going to get much out of this witness.

"Recent model?"

"Fairly."

The detective sergeant sighed. He wrote the information down in his notebook.

"What about the headlights? Were they round? Rectangular?"

"Now that I think about it, maybe it was a Lexus."

Impatiently, Lessard handed his notebook and pen to the man and asked him to write down his contact information.

While the old man complied, the detective sergeant approached the spot where the impact had occurred. No blood, no skid marks. Strange.

Probably another drunk driver.

As he was jotting down notes in front of the café, a panic-stricken young woman came up to him. She was speaking so fast he could barely make out what she was saying.

"Calm down, miss. Take your time."

She took a deep breath. "Was that Simone they took away in the ambulance? Was there an accident? Oh, God …"

Lessard rubbed his chin.

"Simone?"

"Simone Fortin. My best friend. I had to go back up to the office for a few minutes. We were supposed to meet in the café. But she wasn't there. Then I saw the ambulance drive away. Tell me she isn't dead!"

"What does she look like?"

The young woman gave him a quick description: age, height, weight, hair colour.

"And your name is?"

"Ariane Bélanger."

She looked at him anxiously. He would have liked to be able to reassure her. But what could he say? He knew nothing so far.

"A woman was just hit by a car, Ms. Bélanger. I don't know her identity."

Ariane put her hand to her mouth, horrified.

"Is she …"

"Dead? No. But for the moment, I don't have any other details."

The young woman began to cry. Lessard put a hand on her shoulder. At that moment, he wished he could be anywhere else, but his voice was reassuring.

"It may not have been your friend who got hit. That often happens with missing persons. Everyone thinks they're dead, then they turn up safe and sound. Your friend may already be back at the office by now."

Ariane called the Dinar receptionist. Simone hadn't returned.

Regretting that his attempts at encouragement had failed so quickly, Lessard pulled out his notebook.

"Where do you live?"

He took down her address on Doctor Penfield Avenue.

"Phone number?"

Lessard was old school. He'd never gotten used to the obligatory standard-form incident reports. When working on a case, he had preserved the habit of scribbling down whatever he could: impressions of the scene, contact information for witnesses, weather conditions — anything that caught his attention.

He hesitated. "I've forgotten your first name."

A lock of hair had fallen in front of her eye. She blew it aside. "Ariane."

Lessard wrote it down, then called Fernandez. As he brought the phone to his ear, he dropped his notebook. A man wearing sunglasses who was standing at the nearby bus stop bent down to pick up the notebook and handed it to him. The detective sergeant gave him a wave of acknowledgement.

"Nadja, I spoke to the witness. He says the ambulance left a few minutes before I got here. Call Urgences-santé and find out which hospital the victim was taken to. White female, early thirties, red hair, about five foot five, a hundred and twenty pounds. Her name may be Simone Fortin. I'm with Fortin's best friend, who's trying to locate her."

"I'm on it, Victor. Let me see what I can find out."

"Oh, and Fernandez, put out an alert to all patrol units. We're looking for a black sedan, Lexus or Mercedes. No plate number."

"That's not much to go on."

"I know. There's no blood at the scene. I'd be surprised if there's any on the car, but the body's probably dented."

"Got it."

"Call me as soon as you have something, okay?"

"Sure."

"Nadja?"

"Mm?"

"You're an angel."

"I know."

He ended the call and turned to Ariane, whose features were tight with anxiety.

"How about a cup of coffee?" Lessard said, opening the door to the café.

"Okay," she stammered.

"Don't worry. We'll figure out where she is, and I'll take you there. Everything's going to be fine."

He reddened. When it came to lying, he was hopeless.

Standing at the bus stop, the man wearing sunglasses watched Victor Lessard and Ariane Bélanger step into the café. He had heard their entire conversation. Calmly, he pulled out his notebook and wrote down the young woman's name, address, and phone number.

That information might come in handy.

He still regretted having strayed from his plan, but there wasn't time for second thoughts, and anyway, his foray had yielded more information than he'd expected.

First of all, he had confirmed the fact that mattered most: Simone Fortin was still alive.

He had also learned that the police were looking for a Lexus or a Mercedes, which meant he had some leeway. Finally, he had gotten the address of his victim's close friend.

There was no reason to hang around.

The man set off in the direction of Forest Hill Avenue, where he had parked the BMW near a pharmacy. He would store the car in a safe place, then he'd call the ambulance service, Urgences-santé.

Dressed like a wannabe rapper, the kid was working under the BMW's dashboard.

"Come on, man," urged Jimbo, a pimply youth in a baseball cap. "We don't have all day."

"Chill out," Snake answered.

Modern security systems were easy to defeat for an experienced car thief like Snake. Stealing a 1994 BMW 740i that wasn't even equipped with an antitheft device almost felt like an insult to his intelligence.

The engine started.

"How'd I do?"

"Thirty-two seconds," Jimbo said. "You rock, man. You totally rock!"

With a screech of tires, they sped away from Forest Hill Avenue and headed east. Bypassing downtown Montreal, they drove for fifteen minutes before arriving at the abandoned garage that served as their hideout.

"Gimme that. Come on!"

"Whoa. Chill out, man."

"Leave some for me."

"Relax, will ya?"

Snake handed over the joint and sank back into the leather seat. The weed was starting to kick in. Nothing super crazy, though. Since his overdose last year, he'd been cautious, sticking to cannabis and maybe a little cocaine now and then.

The outline of Jimbo's face was crystallized in a clearer image, his eyes becoming pinholes and his lips an infinitely fissured highway. A fit of laughter suddenly seized Snake and held him in its grip for a full minute. He calmed down gradually and felt the buzz go up another notch.

He was really high.

"Chill out, man."

Snake had a single ambition: to gather enough money to go to Florida and open a skateboard school with Jimbo.

Skateboarding was his life. He could do amazing things on a board, weaving past obstacles like a serpent.

Hence the nickname.

And Florida was awesome, with its sunshine, its girls, its beaches. He'd probably miss his mother and sister. But not his father. His father had abandoned them. He was a scumbag.

Snake and Jimbo had been stealing vehicles for six months, supplying them to a local car-theft ring. They got a hundred and fifty dollars apiece for new models, up to five hundred for the most popular makes.

Since starting out, they'd earned about thirty-five thousand dollars and spent a little more than half of that. Snake figured they'd need at least a hundred grand before they could head south.

The acrid aroma of the marijuana hung in the air, making his throat tighten. He was floating.

He looked down at his heavily tattooed arms. Was there room for one more?

"Yo, Snake!"

"What?"

"You reek, man. It's gross."

"The hell I do. Your nose must be too close to your mouth."

"I mean it. There's a weird-ass smell in this car."

"So what?" Snake said. "We'll unload it tomorrow. Tool's gonna give us two hundred for it."

Jimbo started playing with the car radio, switching from station to station.

"Hey, Jimbo, listen."

Snake farted loudly.

"Aww, man, you're disgusting. I knew it was coming from you."

4

To his own surprise, Lessard found the right words to reassure Ariane Bélanger. He also convinced her to go back to her office. He promised to call as soon as he located the hospital to which her friend had been admitted, adding, "It shouldn't take long."

She was a nice person. Generously curvaceous and pretty. He hadn't seen a wedding ring. Was she single?

Ahh, why even think about it? As though anyone would be interested in him. He didn't have what it took to charm a woman anymore. Still, he couldn't help wondering how long it had been since he'd talked to someone so interesting.

He searched his memory and failed to come up with an answer. If his phone hadn't been humming incessantly, he might even have risked suggesting that they have lunch together.

But during the fifteen minutes they'd spent in the café, Commander Tanguay had called three times. Tanguay had unfortunately decided that now was the best time to request an update on the car-theft case. The commander pointed out to Lessard that the mayor was losing patience.

The detective sergeant almost retorted that the mayor should be focusing on more important matters, like repairing potholes and cleaning up the filth that was piling up all over the city. But he kept his mouth shut. This job was all he had left.

By rights, he should have handed off the hit-and-run case to a junior officer. He was a detective, after all.

But the station was woefully short of personnel, and Lessard couldn't bring himself to let cops from another district intrude on his territory.

Instead of going straight back to the office, he decided to stop by his apartment and take a quick shower before his AA meeting.

He turned left from Sherbrooke Street onto Oxford Avenue, where he'd been living since his separation.

Lessard loved the Notre-Dame-de-Grâce district. The English-style cottages and mature trees created an island of comfort in which it was easy to forget how close it was to downtown Montreal.

A new generation of homeowners had come into the district since the turn of the millennium, most of them young families.

Children played in the alleys and schoolyards, couples pushed strollers along the sidewalks, and the area teemed with life, even in winter.

Monkland Avenue, the commercial thoroughfare that ran through the district, had also been revitalized. Cafés, bars, restaurants, and shops were flourishing.

Sherbrooke Street was undergoing a similar renaissance. Korean, Middle Eastern, Chinese, and Thai grocery stores had sprung up, delighting Lessard, who was gradually improving his rudimentary culinary skills.

But all was not perfect; far from it.

On Sundays, when he went running through NDG Park, too many scraps of paper littered the ground. That came as no surprise to Lessard. City workers, protected by a gold-plated collective agreement, weren't doing their jobs.

Parked cars lined both sides of the street. Lessard drove past his building, looking for a free space. He was going too fast and had to slam on the brakes when a father and his child burst out from between two parked vehicles. The furious father brought a fist down on the Corolla's hood. Lessard shrugged apologetically.

He rubbed his face, and his fingers touched a bit of tissue that he'd stuck to his chin after nicking himself with the razor that morning. He'd been walking around with toilet paper on his face ... what a crappy day.

His thoughts strayed to his sister. He hadn't spoken to her since December, when he had passed out, dead drunk, at her dining-room table in the midst of Christmas dinner. He really should give her a call.

Lessard stopped behind an elderly lady who had just gotten into her car. Finally, a parking space. He waited for a long minute, then the lady got back out of the car and walked into a nearby building. Lessard swore.

He gave up the search for a space and double-parked. As he was emerging from his car, he slipped on a patch of ice and came down on his backside.

A group of passing children saw him fall and couldn't help laughing. He shook a fist at them.

"Little shits!"

He turned his key in the front door lock, stepped into his apartment, and saw his dirty clothes piled up on the couch.

He had completely forgotten to do his laundry.

He swore to himself. There was nothing he hated more than putting on dirty underwear after a shower.

Discouragement welled up in him. He wasn't going to make it. He thought about taking refuge under the covers with a glass. One little glass.

Don't screw up, Lessard.

The killer took off his sunglasses and frantically scanned Forest Hill Avenue, but he knew he hadn't mixed up the location.

The BMW had vanished! How the hell was that possible?

Unable to suppress his frustration, he kicked a brick wall

repeatedly. When a passerby gave him a look, he made an effort to compose himself. He couldn't afford to lose control.

Not now.

He saw that there was no parking restriction in the spot where he'd left the car. In any case, the car wouldn't have been towed away for a simple parking violation. Try as he might to consider the problem from every angle, he kept coming back to the same two hypotheses: either the police had discovered the vehicle, or it had been stolen.

He decided to walk into the pharmacy and question the employees. They might have seen something, perhaps a tow truck in the street, or maybe the police. But he changed his mind at the last moment.

This time, he would think before acting.

Deep in thought, he kept walking until he reached a restaurant that he'd noticed earlier. He chose a table at the back and ordered a cup of coffee.

At first glance, there was nothing that linked him to the first victim. But if the police had managed to get their hands on the vehicle so quickly, that didn't bode well. Even though he'd taken every possible precaution, a single oversight on his part might be enough to put them on his trail.

Those police bottom-feeders never fail to come up with some clue.

He scoured his memory. Had he forgotten any compromising items in the car, anything at all that might make it possible to identify him? He didn't think so.

But how could he be sure?

The hypothesis that the car had been stolen presented fewer short-term risks.

After discovering the body, a car thief would surely abandon the BMW on a quiet street, taking care to wipe off any fingerprints. As improbable as this hypothesis might seem, it was the one he favoured. He had heard the detective giving orders over the phone. The police were looking for the wrong make of car.

If he was right, the theft offered him a brief respite, perhaps a few hours before the car was back on the street, and a couple of days at most before the smell of the corpse caught the attention of some passerby.

Anger surged through him. He had prepared everything to the last detail, and now his plan lay in tatters. He smacked the table with the palm of his hand. Conversation in the restaurant stopped. A few diners turned to look at him.

He pretended to have bumped his elbow.

When he was calm again, he took stock of the situation. There was now a significant risk that the BMW would be found and traced back to him before he could carry out the rest of his plan.

He would have to improvise.

He didn't give a damn about what might happen if he was arrested afterward. The only thing that mattered was getting it done.

A fallback plan was slowly taking shape in his mind.

She must see.

Barring a miracle, the first body was lost. But he still had the photographs. He realized that retaining possession of the third target's body would complicate his task and increase his chances of getting caught.

Before dying, she must see.

The scenario he had originally conceived was no longer possible, but with the photos, he would be able to present her with a slide show. And add material to the blog.

All was not lost.

He drew up a mental inventory. What had he left in the car?

He had stored his clothes in the motel room, and his laptop was in his knapsack, so the only items he had lost were his photography equipment and the vials he'd stolen from the pharmacy the previous night. The photography equipment wouldn't be a problem. He could go to any store and buy a cheap camera. Replacing the vials, on the other hand, was going to be a lot trickier in broad daylight. Breaking into another pharmacy was out of the question. He left a five-dollar bill on the table and walked out of the restaurant.

On the off chance that he'd missed something, he walked back to the pharmacy, scanning the street for any sign of the BMW. It was gone. But the pharmacist was standing outside, smoking a fresh cigarette.

You must really be weak-willed if you can't quit.

He made up his mind to go back to the motel and get himself organized. He was about to walk away when the smoker called out to him.

"Are you looking for something?"

"No, I ..."

His initial reflex was denial, but on second thought, if the pharmacist had noticed him, maybe he had also observed something related to the car theft.

As it turned out, the pharmacist hadn't seen the BMW or noted any suspicious activity. He offered to call the police.

"Thanks, it's already taken care of."

His mind was racing. He decided to take a chance. "My antidepressants were in the car. Would you be able to help me out?"

"Sure. Do you have your prescription?"

"No. It was in the car, too."

The pharmacist stubbed out his cigarette against the brick wall and tossed it in the snow. "Step inside, I'll look you up on the database."

He had foreseen this. "The trouble is ... I live in Ontario."

The Quebec pharmaceutical database was unlikely to provide

information on an out-of-province prescription. The pharmacist hesitated, looking at the man's honest, respectable features.

"What's the medication?"

"Amytal. It's a barbiturate."

The pharmacist shook his head. "I wish I could help you. If it were a different drug, I might have been able to tide you over with a couple of doses. But for Amytal, you're going to need to see your doctor."

"I understand," he said in a voice devoid of expression. When he had walked some distance down the street, he hailed a taxi.

A parking ticket was waiting on Lessard's windshield when he got back to his car. In his annoyance, he punched the dashboard, which accomplished nothing apart from making his knuckles sore.

His late arrival at the AA meeting earned him a scolding from his sponsor. Discipline was very important, the sponsor pointed out. It might save him from giving in to temptation someday. Lessard wanted to smack the guy in the head to stop the drivel. But he restrained himself.

After the meeting, he went home for a bite to eat. He was thinking of reheating some of the lamb couscous he'd made the night before. Over the last few months, Lessard had discovered the pleasures of cooking. He'd gotten into the habit of trying out new recipes that he received from friends or dug up on the internet.

He'd found an Iranian grocery store in the neighbourhood: Supermarché Akhavan. He enjoyed going there to shop for ethnic foods. On December 31st, he had stopped off at the spice counter and exchanged significant looks and smiles with the salesgirl, whose amber eyes had haunted him through the night. He'd gone back two days later, hoping to invite her out for a drink, but she hadn't been there.

Since then, he'd been returning every week with clockwork regularity, his pulse quickening at the thought of meeting the young woman. He didn't want to leave a message. The mystery and hope of his unfulfilled wish did more for his spirits than any practical action ever could. Now and then he would tell himself that an exciting romance with the young woman lay just around the corner, and he'd savour the thought that nothing had been settled, anything could happen, the future was still wide open.

Deciding that couscous would be too filling, he made himself a cucumber-and-tomato salad, which he ate while watching a documentary about Muhammad Ali that he had previously recorded.

The legendary heavyweight had become Lessard's new passion. He wasn't a boxing fan, but he never wearied of watching the fighter rally to defeat his adversaries, even when the whole world thought he was beaten. Lessard envied Ali's strength, his determination, and his absolute faith in his own abilities.

The salad didn't satisfy him. Without thinking about it, he munched crackers during the entire bout against Sonny Liston. He'd have to get things back under control tomorrow.

But would he have the willpower?

Lessard was driving back to the station when his phone rang. He considered letting the call go to voice mail, but answering the phone is second nature for a cop.

"You're not going to believe this," Fernandez said. "The Urgences-santé dispatcher can't seem to track down the ambulance that picked up the hit-and-run victim, Simone Fortin."

"Nadja, I'm not in the mood for April Fool's jokes."

"I'm not joking. The dispatcher says they didn't have any vehicles in that sector at the time of the accident."

"He's mistaken. There were witnesses who saw an ambulance take the victim away. Call around to all the hospitals."

"Sirois's already on it."

Fernandez's unfailing competence was something he too often took for granted.

"Okay. Keep me posted." He hung up, baffled. This case wasn't making any sense.

5

Étienne Beauregard-Delorme.

I was shaken. The memories that Miles had revived were still painful. Yet I was also relieved. Was it because I had opened up to someone who wouldn't judge me? Or was it perhaps the words he had spoken that morning?

The line between a good and a bad decision is sometimes very thin.

I'd told myself the same thing many times over the last seven years. Why was it so much more convincing when it came from a stranger?

I had led an ascetic life since the little boy's death, a cheerless existence in which I had taken refuge in a fortress of solitude, cutting all connections with my past. I'd done these things out of necessity, driven by my survival instinct, like a mammal caught in a trap. Now, for the first time in years, I was taking an interest in another human being. I wanted to know more about Miles.

We were sitting side by side on the couch. I drained my third glass of wine with a smack of the tongue. I hardly recognized myself.

"Are you married?"

His expression darkened. "I was. She died of leukemia."

One more question like that and he'll kill himself on the spot.

I plunged onward. There could be no turning back now. I was hell-bent on squashing myself like a bug against a windshield.

"I'm sorry. You must have loved her very much."

"With all my heart. We had a son. He was five years old when she died."

"How old is he now?"

"Last time I checked, he was twenty-two."

"You have a twenty-two-year-old son!"

Miles laughed. "I was only twenty when he was born."

Which put his present age at forty-two. I would have guessed he was in his thirties.

"He isn't living with you anymore?"

"No. Actually, I haven't seen him in some time."

"Why not?"

"Things have been hard for him lately. When he's unhappy, he has the unfortunate habit of seeking comfort in alcohol. I try to get in touch with him regularly, but he's closed himself off. The harder I try, the more he shuts me out."

"He'll get over it."

"I hope so. When he's sober, he's an amazing person. I think you'd like him." Miles paused. He seemed lost in his memories. "He was a shy boy, very bright, with a passion for word games. At seven, he was writing me coded messages in the form of anagrams. His school years were difficult. He was a solitary kid, lacking in social skills. You know what I mean?"

I kept silent, unsure of how to answer.

"He was so loveable. I have wonderful memories of his child-hood. One time, at our chalet in Trois-Pistoles, we filled a small treasure chest with mementos and buried it. We were going to dig it up together in the year 2000."

As Miles spoke, his voice became choked with emotion. It was clear that he and his son had never kept their resolution.

I got up to go to the bathroom.

As I walked up the hallway, my vision became blurred. I suddenly felt faint. Though I'd always told myself that it was silly to worry, each time a migraine came on I found myself fearing that I might die the same way my mother had, struck down by an aneurysm. I leaned against the wall for support, but my legs gave out. I lost consciousness.

I felt an oppressive weight suffocating me. Someone was immobilizing my arms, preventing me from moving. Hands were palpating me, opening my mouth. I felt the cold metal of an instrument being forced down my throat.

I was struggling, kicking in the emptiness.

As a precaution, he asked the taxi driver to let him off a few blocks short of the motel. He went the rest of the way on foot, without haste.

He took off his shoes and put his knapsack on the bed.

He'd done well to take the room for the week. He had made the place his own, and now he felt at home here.

He turned on the TV and selected a twenty-four-hour news channel, setting the volume on low. It was a habit he'd gotten into several years ago, to enliven his solitude.

He scribbled a to-do list in his notebook.

First of all, he needed to contact Urgences-santé and locate Simone Fortin. Next, he would have to get his hands on a car and come up with a way to replace the lost vials of Amytal. Finally, he needed to work out a plan for getting the young woman out of the hospital without attracting attention.

He already had some ideas on that score. He was glad he had brought along a few accessories to help him alter his appearance.

He was feeling surprisingly calm. The challenge was great, but he was up to it.

Before getting started, he decided to have a drink. He went to the mini fridge in which he'd placed a bottle of rum. He never drank more than a glass a day. He was proud of his moderation. He opened the fridge door and stopped dead.

The Amytal vials!

He had completely forgotten that he had put them in the fridge to preserve them.

For once, he allowed himself a smile.

I screamed in terror and sat up with a start on the bed.

"You gave me quite a scare," Miles said, handing me a glass of water.

Still disoriented, I took a few gulps.

"I'm sorry. I was out of it."

"Feeling better?"

"Yes. It was probably just a drop in blood pressure. I don't usually drink so much."

I glanced around the bedroom. What was happening to me? Fainting at the drop of a hat was hardly my style.

I took another few seconds to collect my thoughts. My gaze fell on the painting that hung above the chest of drawers. Once again, the graffiti in the picture caught my attention.

Run, late, elapse, lid, me, tee.

So strange. So beautiful.

"I'm no expert," I said, "but I love that painting. Who did it?"

"Me," Miles said shyly.

"Seriously? It's terrific."

"Thank you."

"What does it mean?"

"I don't know," he said, shrugging.

"Do you paint a lot?"

"Not really, no."

I spent another few seconds contemplating the work, then I got up.

We climbed the stairs to the upper floor.

"Are you sure you're strong enough to do this?"

"Definitely. I'm really in the mood to hear some jazz."

•   •   •

Jamal Cherraf was a small man, Moroccan-born, about sixty years old. He greeted us warmly. After leading us into his living room, he disappeared for a few moments to make tea. When he came back, he was carrying a tray.

He talked to us about his service in the Moroccan army, his participation in the Saharan conflict against Spain in 1975, and his subsequent immigration to Canada. He spoke with an accent, and there was great humility in his voice.

"Jamal, would you play something for us?"

"With pleasure, my friend. How much do you know about jazz, Simone?"

"Not a lot. The truth is, I only have one album at home."

"Which one?"

"*Kind of Blue* by Miles Davis."

"That album ought to be everyone's first experience of jazz. You know more than you realize."

Jamal got up and reached for his instrument.

We were sitting on a thick Persian rug strewn with cushions. The room was bathed in the flickering glow of a three-arm candelabrum.

Jamal launched into the opening bars of "So What."

I let the music carry me away. The trumpet's warm voice thrilled me. Without thinking, I put a hand on Miles's knee. He didn't flinch.

After thanking Jamal warmly, we went back downstairs to the apartment.

"Did you enjoy yourself?" Miles asked.

"Very much. I'm now officially a fan. I'm going to buy myself a boxed set of Miles Davis CDs."

"What about your dizziness?"

"All gone," I said, stifling a yawn.

"Listen, it's been a long, intense day. I put clean sheets on the bed earlier. I'd like you to spend the night here."

"No need for that. It's super easy for me to go home and ..."

I was only arguing to be polite. I had no desire to go home.

"I insist. I've put out a towel and a robe in the bathroom. There's a toothbrush still in its wrapper on the counter."

I took a long hot shower, letting the water dissolve the day's accumulated tensions. I used the towel to wipe away the fog from a corner of the mirror, then dried my hair. Finally, I put on the white robe and brushed my teeth.

Before turning the door handle, I parted the lapels of the robe slightly to reveal the curve of my breasts. I felt my pulse accelerate. It had been a long time since I had desired a man this way.

Miles was looking out the living-room window when I entered. He half turned and gave me a smile.

I don't know what came over me at that moment. The impulse was irrational. I approached until our faces were only a few centimetres apart. With an expression full of desire, I drew close to him. My lips brushed his mouth. Our tongues curled around each other. A tingle of adrenalin ran up my spine. I pressed myself against him.

With infinite gentleness, he broke the embrace.

"Miles, I —"

"Shh," he said, putting a finger to my lips. He took my face in his hands and kissed my forehead.

"Sleep well."

Easier said than done!

Alone with my longings, I had a troubled sleep.

I dreamed that I was being hit by a speeding car. I saw my limp body flying through the air, over and over again.

Lessard closed his office door and sat down at his computer.

Time was slipping away!

With a cup of coffee at his elbow, he was ready to start the research that he hadn't gotten around to that morning.

While he was opening his browser, Fernandez walked in, interrupting him once again. He threw up his hands, exasperated.

"Can't a guy get two minutes' peace around here?"

"Sorry, Victor. I just got a call from the Urgences-santé dispatcher. They've tracked down Simone Fortin."

"Where is she?"

"The emergency ward at the Montreal General. Do you want me to notify Ariane Bélanger?"

Lessard reacted with embarrassment. "No, I'll handle it. Why did it take them so long to find her?"

"The EMTs who picked her up were at the end of their shift. They only reported the case when they got back to headquarters."

Lessard called Ariane's number and made an effort to sound professional.

"Ms. Bélanger? This is Victor Lessard. I … yes, we've located her. I can swing by and pick you up." His expression changed. "Great. I'll be right over … Ariane."

I looked around the sparsely furnished room. The chest of drawers seemed forlorn in the morning light.

I lay there, disoriented for a few seconds, before remembering that I was in Miles's bedroom.

I looked at my watch.

Strange. The hands were stopped at 10:20. I tapped the glass with a finger. Nothing. Must be the battery.

No matter. I was going to be late for work again. Only this time, I didn't care. All I wanted to do was stay with Miles.

I threw back the quilt and sat at the edge of the bed for a moment before putting on the bathrobe. I walked to the kitchen, which was filled with the aroma of coffee.

Miles was busy squeezing oranges.

"Sleep well?" he asked.

I stretched lazily.

"Mmm-hmm. But I had the same dream again. Except this time, the car actually hit me."

"Really?"

He handed me a cup.

"How about some coffee? I also have fresh-squeezed orange juice." His T-shirt was soaked with sweat.

I thanked him and took a sip. I noticed a set of weights in the corner.

"How about you? Did you sleep well?"

He winked. "Me? I never sleep."

I walked over to the window. The sky was grey.

"Is it as warm out as it was yesterday?" I asked.

"Not quite. Around eight degrees."

Breakfast consisted of fried eggs and toast, which I ate with gusto. Though not normally talkative, I chattered happily through the entire meal. I was in such good spirits, feeling so light and care-free, that I chalked up Miles's sad expression to the bad night he'd had.

Outside, raindrops started to fall against the window.

While I was showering, I thought about how much I wanted to spend the day with him. I decided to call the office and let them know I wasn't coming in. Then I'd bring him to my place. It was irrational, I knew. But I hadn't felt so alive in a very long time.

When I walked into the living room, I found him on the couch, looking heartsick.

"What's the matter?"

"Our time's up, Simone."

"Right. Do you feel like going for a walk? We could stop off at the Atwater Market and pick up a few things, then hide away at my place. I have to feed my cat and ..."

"That's not going to be possible."

I froze, humiliated. He wasn't attracted to me.

"I get it," I said. "You have other plans."

He didn't speak.

"Am I moving too fast?" I asked. "Is that it?"

"No, Simone. You need to ... *leave*."

I raised my hands. It was all a misunderstanding.

"Don't worry, I'll call the office. I'll let them know I'm taking the day off, then I'll ..."

But as I was speaking, a wave of excruciating pain struck the back of my neck. I collapsed onto the couch, unable to finish the sentence, my eyes rolling back in my head. Before I lost consciousness, I felt a dull throb in my right ankle as hands seized my arms and probed my throat.

I sank down, down, down ...

6

This evening, it will all be over. He left the key on the counter. He wouldn't be needing the room anymore. The motel desk clerk was busy on the phone and didn't turn around. If he had turned, would he have noticed the change in appearance? The killer stepped outside. The cold air slapped his face. In the parking lot, he saw an old Buick Regal. He'd have no trouble hot-wiring the vehicle, as he'd seen the old man do so many times with his truck. A few minutes later, he was at the wheel of the car, pulling out onto Saint-Jacques Street. As he drove, he made sure to respect all the rules and stay within the speed limit.

First, he had called Urgences-santé.

Inexplicably, those idiots hadn't known which hospital Simone Fortin had been brought to. Next, he had tried the Royal Victoria and Saint-Luc hospitals, both without success. His ruse was simple: his daughter had been hit by a car on Côte-des-Neiges that morning. Had they admitted her?

As he waited for the traffic light to turn green, he couldn't help laughing. He had hit the jackpot with his third call: Simone Fortin was at the Montreal General Hospital. At first, he hadn't believed it. He'd made the switchboard operator confirm the information twice. Everything happened for a reason, but even so, this was an exceptional stroke of luck.

Simone Fortin had been brought to the very hospital where Jacques Mongeau was executive director.

Jacques Mongeau, that arrogant son of a bitch, that low-life bastard, was also his third target.

Only a few hours ago, he had been cursing himself for straying from his plan. Now the mistake was working to his advantage.

Things were moving fast, but he had made up his mind to let himself be swept along by the flow of events. He would have to act in haste, with minimal preparation, but he knew he couldn't fail.

As he reflected, he saw that this was no coincidence.

It was a sign from God.

An acknowledgement that his cause was just.

It was a strange sensation, like trying to see through a veil. The space around me was murky, except for a circle of light to my left. I blinked a few times, the way you do when you're trying to get something out of your eye. Then I saw a flower in a vase.

What had happened to me?

I tried to lift a hand. I couldn't. I made an effort to shift my legs. In vain. A terrified panic seized me, similar to the feeling I would get as a child when, roughhousing with playmates, I suddenly found myself trapped under their weight.

Was I paralyzed?

I wanted to cry out, but no sound came from my parched throat.

As my eyes opened more fully, the circle of light around the vase grew wider. I saw the corner of a table, a chair, monitors, and tubes snaking off in all directions.

As far as I could tell, I was lying on a bed, unable to move. There were curtains on either side of me, serving as partitions. I saw outlines moving like shadow puppets on the yellowed fabric.

Where was I?

A lab? A hospital?

A human figure stirred on the chair.

Miles?

I listened and heard a murmur, distant, almost imperceptible. The circle widened some more. I saw a face.

Ariane.

What on earth was she doing here?

I wanted to say something, but despite my strongest intentions, my eyelids drooped.

Everything went dark.

When I came to, I felt like I'd swallowed a lump of sand.

I cleared my throat.

A man was standing in front of a lamp. I could only see his silhouette as he spoke to Ariane.

"Don't worry, she's waking up gradually. Everything looks good. We had to intubate her briefly, but she's okay now."

In a corner of my brain, neurons received and processed this information. I'd been intubated. That explained the sore throat.

"Is there any permanent damage?"

"It's too early to say for sure, but I don't think so. She may be a little confused or even incoherent for the first few hours."

"I understand. Can you take off the straps?"

"Yes. She's calm now. I'll send someone to take care of it."

I wasn't quadriplegic! I'd been placed in restraints. But why?

"Thank you, Doctor," Ariane said.

"You're welcome."

What were they talking about? What was going on? Water! Someone please bring me some water!

Everything went dark again.

• • • •

Warm breath on my cheek.

Like a half-melted wax mask, Ariane's face was hovering a few centimetres above my own.

"Her eyes are open. Can she hear me?"

"I think so," the nurse said.

"Simone, it's me, Ariane. Can you hear me?"

I tried to answer, but my throat refused to produce any sound.

"Oh, sweetie, you gave me such a scare."

"Thhh … thhh … thirsty."

"What's she saying?"

"I think she's thirsty. I'll go get some ice chips."

Yes, that was definitely a nurse. I couldn't see her, but the tone of voice clearly marked her as a medical professional. I knew from experience.

"Wh … where's … Mi-iles?"

"What?"

"Mi … le … Miles."

I was still pretty woozy, but I could see the puzzlement on Ariane's face.

"Miles?"

The nurse spoke.

"A little confusion is normal."

"Dr. Pouliot mentioned that."

Ariane stroked my cheek with the back of her hand.

"Try to rest, honey."

I only half listened to their babbling. My thoughts were taken up by a single question.

What had happened to Miles?

Snake's gaze took in the flat grey sky, the parallel rows of parked cars, the buildings that stretched down the street. He buttoned his jacket and set out on foot. The BMW was parked at the corner of Saint-Joseph, but he preferred to walk along Mont-Royal.

He enjoyed strolling through this artsy neighbourhood, rubbing elbows with the colourful residents of the Plateau, walking past the trendy boutiques and the little bistros crowded with regulars. He was a familiar customer at a few second-hand bookstores, where he had a knack for unearthing rare editions of comic books. He also spent long hours rummaging through their stacks of used CDs in search of musical treasures.

As he walked back in the direction of the car, he passed a man holding a sleeping child in his arms. Seeing the man, Snake was reminded of his father, but he quickly chased the thought out of his mind. There was nothing to be gained from false hopes. His youth wasn't like a once-cherished CD rediscovered on a shelf. It couldn't be replayed.

Jimbo and Snake had established a schedule that never varied. They started work at 7:00 a.m. each day, breaking off at noon when the streets became busy and things got too risky. Their second shift began around 5:00 p.m. and sometimes continued late into the night.

Between the two shifts, Snake would often go home for a nap. But he had to be careful. A month ago his mother, thinking he was at work, had come home unexpectedly. He'd had to pretend he was sick so as not to raise suspicions.

This morning, there had been another confrontation.

He had come downstairs in his underwear around 5:45 a.m. and found her struggling agitatedly with the toaster, which was spewing billows of greyish smoke.

Defiantly, he had opened the fridge and taken a swig of orange juice straight from the carton, a practice he knew she detested.

"Morning, Mom."

Still busily poking at the toaster's innards with a knife, she hadn't turned around.

"What time did you get in last night?"

"I can't remember."

She had finally succeeded in extricating a charred crust of bread from the appliance.

"I went to bed at midnight and there was no sign of you."

In her indignation, her voice had gone up an octave. "I'm not putting up with this! I don't have time to discuss it now, because I have to get your sister to school. But you and I are going to have a talk tonight, young man!"

Arguing was pointless when she was in angry-mom mode.

Now that she thought he was employed in a garage, he had a little more latitude. But he still had to figure out a way of taking afternoon naps without getting discovered.

Anyway, with the money he was saving, it wouldn't be long before he could leave town and open that skateboard shop.

He had given his mother an obedient nod that would have made Ferris Bueller proud.

"Yes, Mom."

And he had stepped out into the cool morning in fine spirits.

The day was shaping up to be a good one.

He and Jimbo had stolen three cars this morning. They could expect to get three more tonight. With a little luck, they'd pull in over a thousand dollars.

He parked the BMW on Pie-IX, near the iconic structure of the Olympic Stadium, the widely disliked colossal half shell that had been built for the 1976 Games.

It had a seating capacity of over seventy thousand.

Like many Montrealers, Snake thought the stadium was ugly, elegant, and glorious, all at the same time.

His grandfather, while he was alive, had been fond of saying that the stadium's designer, Roger Taillibert, was either a genius or a nutcase. But as Snake beheld the looming concrete bowl, he couldn't help thinking that the French architect was clearly both: a genius *and* a nutcase.

A memory came back to him.

He and his father had taken the funicular to the observatory at the top of the stadium tower, where they'd been able to gaze out at the city and surrounding suburbs. On a clear day, you could see nearly eighty kilometres out.

He shook himself out of the reverie.

His father was nothing but a hypocrite, a lousy traitor.

Holding a bag that contained two bagels, he rang the doorbell and entered the apartment without waiting for an answer.

An old lady's voice came up the hallway.

"Is that you, my boy?"

"Yes, Mrs. Espinosa. I brought you something to eat."

A very elderly woman approached along the linoleum floor, moving spryly. Bluish veins were visible under her papery skin.

She patted him on the shoulder.

"You're a fine boy. A fine boy."

Six months previously, Snake had snatched Mrs. Espinosa's purse in a metro station. In his haste to flee, he had jostled her. The old woman had fallen.

The next day, overcome by guilt, he had found her address in the purse and returned it to her. She hadn't been injured, but he'd gone back the next day anyway.

Since that time, they'd developed a ritual. Snake would drop in three times a week. Occasionally, if she had errands to run, he'd drive her. Like his mother, she believed that he worked in a garage.

Nobody knew about these visits, not even Jimbo. Snake had often asked himself why he kept going back. Maybe it was because the old lady was happy with what he had to offer.

"Would you like me to take you for a ride, Mrs. Espinosa? I just finished repairing a BMW. We could drive around the city, maybe stop in at Saint Joseph's Oratory. What do you say?"

"Good heavens, my boy, you can't be serious!" The old lady liked to be persuaded.

I heard footsteps and a clink of metal on metal.

"Ms. Fortin, can you hear me? I'm Dr. Pouliot. You're in the intensive care unit of the Montreal General Hospital. Can you tell me what day it is?"

I tried to speak, but nothing came out of my mouth.

"It's April 1st, 2005. Do you understand what I'm saying, Ms. Fortin?"

I nodded.

"You were brought in by an ambulance around eleven o'clock this morning. You'd been hit by a car in front of your office building. Do you remember?"

Unable to speak, I nodded again.

"You have a sprained right ankle and some contusions. You may be experiencing soreness or discomfort. Are you in any pain right now? I can give you something for that."

I wasn't in pain.

The doctor paused, as though catching his breath. Then he continued hesitantly.

"Ms. Fortin, you've also sustained a head trauma. We're going to keep you under observation for a while. You were unconscious for several hours, and we want to be sure you're okay. A nurse will stop by regularly to check your vital signs and neurological condition. You may have some difficulty remembering what day it is or where you are. You may even briefly have trouble recognizing loved ones. But don't worry. With time, everything should gradually get back to normal."

I didn't react. I was in a state of shock.

An immense orderly with a long ponytail was pushing my hospital bed down a corridor, blazing a trail among the gurneys that lined the walls. I saw a toothless man lying on his side, spitting blood into a bowl, his emaciated body visible through his open hospital gown. Another man was shuffling along, step by tiny step, grimacing with effort as he dragged his IV pole behind him like a ball and chain. A woman lay on her back, her face a mask of pain as she filled the hallway with terrifying screams.

But I paid scant attention to the landscape of human misery through which I was travelling. Something the doctor had said was troubling me.

You were unconscious for several hours.

What was I supposed to think?

I knew that short-term memory could be affected by head trauma. Patients sometimes became confused, describing events that seemed plausible to friends and family, but turned out to be false. Was that my situation? Was I confused?

I knew very well that the brain was a complex mechanism. Even so, when I considered the matter from every angle, I couldn't bring myself to believe that Miles was simply a figment of my imagination.

Could I really be so incoherent that I had dreamed up the whole thing?

The orderly rolled my bed into room 222. Ariane was already there, putting a bouquet of flowers in a vase.

"How are you feeling?" she asked when we were alone.

I swallowed painfully.

"I feel like a brick was jammed down my throat. Have you been here long?"

"About an hour. You had me in a total panic."

"Sorry," I said with a weak smile.

"What happened?"

"I was crossing the street, and then … bam. It's a total blank."

"The doctor says that's normal. Your short-term memory will come back little by little."

I didn't say anything. I didn't want to worry Ariane. But my memory hadn't been affected all. I remembered exactly what had happened. I hadn't spent the day unconscious on a bed. I had spent it with Miles.

If only he were here to back me up.

7

Having resolved to fetch ice chips despite my sworn assurance that I didn't need them, Ariane was raising hell in the corridor, bellowing like a madwoman.

Despite the racket, I was feeling better.

In fact, if it hadn't been for the bland green walls reminding me that I was in a hospital, I could almost have denied reality and pretended that nothing had happened at all, that I had dreamed the whole thing.

But I knew that wasn't the case.

Something had indeed happened. Something I couldn't explain.

It may seem stupid, but when an inconceivable event takes place, we tend to fall back on concrete considerations. In anguish, I wondered whether there was a history of mental illness in my family — a history my parents had hidden from me. Maybe I was simply in the early stages of degenerative psychosis.

But, as Cyrano de Bergerac famously observed to Christian, "You're not a fool if you're aware of being one." Did a similar logic apply in my case? Can a person really be crazy if she's sane enough to wonder about her sanity?

Another kind of person might have sought explanations in mysticism or paranormal phenomena, but I didn't believe in ghosts, or reincarnation, or out-of-body experiences. And I certainly had no faith in God. If there was a God, he'd missed out on some fine opportunities to reveal himself. As for the devil, I'd have happily offered him sexual favours in return for a timely intervention, but Lucifer, too, had been a no-show.

And, just for completeness's sake, I was only too happy to mock anyone who believed in astrology. My attitude on the subject was so absolute that it bordered on pedantry.

Without knowing why, I found myself remembering a young man I had once ridiculed at a party after he suggested shyly that if the moon could influence ocean tides, then perhaps the stars were capable of affecting our lives. I felt guilty now as I recalled the flush in his cheeks when I made fun of him. What had become of that young man? I couldn't help wondering whether I had inadvertently played a decisive role in his life by inflicting permanent damage on his self-confidence.

But these vague regrets had no effect on my convictions. I was certain that there was a rational explanation for what I'd been through. And I would find it.

There's a logical reason for everything.

Ariane swaggered in like a conquering heroine, holding a bucket of ice chips and a plastic water pitcher that hardly inspired confidence.

"Here you go, sweetie. Ask and ye shall receive."

"Thank you," I said politely, as she poured out a glass that I would never drink.

I hesitated.

Even if Ariane was one of the few people in the world I could rely on, I wasn't sure whether I should tell her about my encounter with Miles. If I was having trouble making sense of my own experience, what was she liable to think?

"You okay, sweetie?" she asked, as though picking up on my indecision. "You seem preoccupied."

What choice did I have?

I took a deep breath, conscious of the possibility that I was about to make myself look ridiculous, or worse, unhinged. I imagined

Ariane fleeing down the corridor in terror and coming back with Max von Sydow in his priest outfit from *The Exorcist*, ready to banish the demonic spirit that had possessed me.

"Can I trust you?" I asked.

"What kind of question is that?" she demanded indignantly.

"There's something I need to tell you. You're going to think I've lost my mind."

With that, I began telling her the story of my twenty-four hours with Miles.

Humming Charles Trenet's classic song "La Mer," he pressed the elevator button.

The doors opened on the sixth floor, where the administrative offices were located.

His hair was dyed black. He was wearing a charcoal pinstripe suit and steel-rimmed glasses and carrying a fine leather briefcase. He looked like a banker.

I am a chameleon.

He straightens up to make a mental note of the spot where the animal entered the forest. Suddenly, he hears a growl. He turns. A large black bear is glaring at him. One of the old man's favourite pieces of advice comes back to him: "Melt into the environment like a chameleon." The animal approaches to within a few centimetres, sniffing his hands like a dog. He forces himself to hold still and stifles the scream rising in his throat. Even if he wanted to, he wouldn't have time to raise his weapon and fire. The bear swats him hard with one paw, its claws lacerating his back. When he turns around, he sees that the animal has made off with his knapsack. Despite himself, he starts to cry.

Securing an appointment with the executive director of the Montreal General Hospital had turned out to be child's play.

He had called Jacques Mongeau's office.

Giving a false name, he had told Mongeau's secretary that he represented a private trust that was interested in donating money to the hospital foundation. If the executive director had a few minutes to spare this afternoon, he'd like to meet him and discuss the matter.

After being informed that Mongeau couldn't fit him in today, he had insinuated that the planned donation was substantial, and that the trust was having second thoughts about giving it to the hospital. The secretary had put him on hold.

Jacques Mongeau himself had come on the line a few seconds later and proposed that they meet at 2:30 p.m.

If everything went as planned, he would eliminate the man in the afternoon and arrive at the lodge in Mont-Laurier with his captive that night. His scheme for abducting Simone Fortin was audacious, but he felt like fortune was on his side.

I left nothing out.

From Miles's providential rescue to our walk through the cemetery, from Jamal's improvised concert to my waking up in the hospital, I told Ariane the entire story.

But I made no mention of Étienne Beauregard-Delorme or the dark secrets of my past. It wasn't easy to speak of things I'd worked so hard to conceal for so many years. I didn't have the strength.

Not now.

Ariane's face was full of compassion. "What a fabulous story. So romantic."

"You believe me, don't you?"

"Of course! Your unconscious was probably churning the whole time."

"Ariane, I'm not talking about my unconscious. I was there!"

"Sweetie, Dr. Pouliot says it's normal to —"

"What? Be confused? Incoherent?"

"You were in a coma."

"Ariane, please. You think I'm delusional?"

"That's not what I said!"

I made myself take a dispassionate view of the situation, and what I saw wasn't good. Having barely regained consciousness, I was now describing otherworldly experiences.

"I don't know what to think, or what to do," I said. "But there has to be a rational explanation."

"Why don't we bring it up with your doctor? I'm sure he —"

Despite myself, I became agitated. "No! Not a word to the doctor! He'll think I have brain damage."

What had I been expecting from Ariane? Approval? She thought I was disoriented. But getting to the bottom of this mystery had become imperative. My sanity depended on it.

"You need to get some rest, honey. They're keeping you under observation tonight. If everything's okay tomorrow, they'll let you leave."

"You're right," I said. "I should rest."

I wasn't the least bit sleepy. I knew the risks, but I had made up my mind. Waiting until tomorrow was out of the question. The only way to figure out what had happened was to get out of this bed and find Miles as soon as possible.

And I wouldn't be able to count on Ariane for help.

Which meant I had to get her out of the room.

He knocked three times. A woman with a pinched face came to the door and let him into a windowless anteroom. An aging computer stood on a small desk. After offering him a cup of coffee, which he declined, she gestured toward a faded couch.

"Please have a seat. I'll let Mr. Mongeau know you're here."

She walked to a padded door and opened it slowly, without knocking. "Mr. Tremblay has arrived."

"Thanks, Jeannine. Show him in."

She stepped aside to let him pass.

A bald man of about sixty shook his hand. "Jacques Mongeau."

"Pierre Tremblay," the man answered.

The executive director turned to his secretary.

"You can take the rest of the day off, Jeannine. I won't be needing you until tomorrow."

"Thanks, Mr. Mongeau."

She closed the door behind her. Then she picked up her coat and left. By way of introduction, the executive director launched into a little speech about the virtues of private giving. Without donations, hospitals like this one would find it hard to maintain their standards of care.

Jacques Mongeau expounded on the subject with practised assurance. His tone was warm, his arguments compelling. *I'm making a strong case*, he thought with a tingle of pride.

With his lower body hidden by the desk, the killer took advantage of the executive director's focus on his speech to unsheathe his knife. His expression had hardened.

Jacques Mongeau was too vain and self-obsessed to notice that his visitor wasn't listening. He didn't have time to react before the man drove the knife into his chest, near the heart.

"We all have to pay for our mistakes," the man murmured into Mongeau's ear, twisting the knife in the wound.

In a final effort to dislodge the blade that was ripping his flesh, the executive director grabbed the knife handle with one hand while, with the other, he tried to push his attacker away. His legs failed him and he collapsed to his knees, but he managed to get back on his feet. His physical strength was impressive.

As he felt his resistance ebbing away, Jacques Mongeau couldn't help thinking about the breasts of the youthful waitress who had cleared his table after lunch. He had only one regret. If he had known that this was his last meal, he would have stepped forward and kissed them. Was there a more stirring sight on earth than the curve of a young woman's bosom?

The executive director's last impulse was to cry out for help, but all he could manage was a feeble croak.

The killer cut his throat with a single stroke.

After a few gasps and a final spasm, the mortal remains of Jacques Mongeau fell with a clatter onto the pale maple-wood desk, which quickly became as red as mahogany.

The killer laid the dead man's right hand flat on the desk and cut off the index finger, which he inserted into an aluminum tube. He had given up on his plan of transporting Mongeau's body to the hunting lodge. In his eyes, the finger wasn't so much a substitute as an artifact, bearing witness to what he had done.

Next, he opened his briefcase and took out a digital camera that he'd paid for in cash at an electronics store.

A quartz desk clock spattered with fine droplets of blood indicated that it was 2:50 p.m.

A young blond nurse came into the room. Without being aware of it, she achieved precisely the outcome I was hoping for.

"Ms. Bélanger," she said softly, "visiting hours are over. Your friend needs to rest."

Ariane stiffened, wanting to protest, but I intervened.

"She's right, Ariane," I said. "Besides, you've got to pick up Mathilde at school."

Ariane had adopted the little girl from Guatemala a few years ago. I loved the child like she was my own.

"I was going to call the daycare service," Ariane said. "They can keep her an extra hour."

The nurse spoke gently.

"I'm sorry, but the rules are clear. You really have to go. You can come back this evening at seven-thirty."

The nurse retreated to the door.

"I'll give you five more minutes."

Ariane nodded reluctantly, and the nurse walked out.

"I'll be fine," I said reassuringly.

"Promise?"

"Go on, get out of here."

"Is there anything you need?" she asked as she put on her coat.

A "no" might have seemed suspicious.

"Uh … could you bring me some reading material?"

Ariane perked up. Being useful raised her spirits. "Sure! How about some magazines? *Cosmopolitan*?"

"Whatever you like."

"I'll bring Mathilde this evening."

"Great idea."

Ariane took me in her arms and squeezed so hard I thought I might pop. I felt guilty for lying to her, but I needed to get out of here at all costs. When the door closed behind her, I took a deep breath, relieved that she was gone. I loved Ariane, but what I was about to do would require my full concentration.

At the admissions desk, the man said he was a relative of Simone Fortin's. He was informed that the patient had just been transferred to room 222. He thanked the receptionist and walked up the main corridor toward the laundry area.

He was now wearing a wig and round glasses that transformed his appearance, giving him a vaguely intellectual air. The way ahead was clear. This time, whatever happened, he would be patient.

•   •   •

His injury isn't serious. He can feel the forest lowering its opaque veil over him, but he's not afraid anymore. The old man will see that he's no weakling. He's survived a bear attack. After nearly an hour's hiking, he sees the moose grazing a hundred metres away. He looks around, searching for a steady location from which to take his shot. He rests the rifle barrel on a branch and adjusts the scope. The animal is directly between his crosshairs. It turns, exposing its right flank. He releases the safety catch and slowly caresses the trigger. The blast shatters the silence. The forest reels under the deafening noise. The moose jumps, then starts to run. Making a mental note of the animal's path through the trees, the boy straightens up.

The direct approach had served him best until now.

Why change a winning formula?

He strode into the hospital laundry area, looking confident and authoritative. A woman was ironing sheets with an industrial press.

"Hello, I'm Dr. Hamel," he said smoothly. "I'm in a bit of a bind. You see, it's my first day here. I'm supposed to be in surgery in ten minutes, and I've forgotten my scrubs."

The woman gave him a conspiratorial look.

"I really shouldn't be doing this, but Dr. Bourque sometimes leaves his scrubs with me for ironing. If you go to that closet over there in the back, you'll find a pile of surgical tops and pants. He's about your size."

"You're a lifesaver. What's your name?"

"Claire."

"I won't forget."

He picked up a set of scrubs.

"If everyone were as competent as you, we'd be able to do something about the waiting lists that afflict our hospitals. I'm really grateful to you … Claire."

Unaccustomed to receiving praise, the woman blushed deeply.

"Thank you, Doctor."

He went out as regally as he had come in.

Now, there's a gentleman! she thought to herself as she went back to work. *Not like those young know-it-alls, fresh out of medical school.*

Only later, when the case was closed, would Claire recognize the photograph in the newspaper and read in shock about the man whom the media were calling a monster.

8

The Montreal General Hospital cafeteria was full to bursting.

Lessard drank the remains of his coffee and pushed away his newspaper. He'd finished reading the sports and entertainment sections. He stood up and stretched.

A young woman in a white blouse approached, carrying a tray.

A club sandwich!

He hadn't eaten french fries in ages. He was sick of healthy diet choices. He picked up his empty cup and yielded his seat to the young woman, grumbling.

He looked at his watch. He had dropped off Ariane Bélanger at the emergency ward some time ago. He decided to check in on the hit-and-run victim and see if she was well enough to talk. If she was, he would take her statement and go back to the station.

He was stepping off the elevator when his cellphone rang.

A nurse scowled at him and pointed to a sign that showed a cellphone with a big red X through it.

Lessard shrugged and showed the nurse his badge.

"It's Fernandez. I just wanted to let you know that Simone Fortin's been transferred to room 222."

"Okay. I'll head over."

Lessard scanned the wall, looking for a directory.

The nurse came back into the room a few minutes after Ariane's departure.

"How are we doing?" she asked with a cheery expression on her young face.

She started checking my vital signs and entering the results meticulously in a notebook. I looked straight at her, doing my best to appear as sharp as a Swiss army knife.

"My name is Simone Fortin. Today is April 1st, 2005. I'm at the Montreal General Hospital, in room 222. Since being brought in at eleven o'clock this morning, I've received treatment for a sprained ankle, various contusions, and a traumatic head injury. I'm not feeling any numbness and my vision isn't blurred."

The nurse stared at me.

"That's what you wanted to know, isn't it?" I asked.

She frowned, clearly impressed.

"Do you have medical training?"

I hesitated. "Sort of."

"Is there any pain in your ankle?"

"It's bearable."

"Do you want painkillers?"

"Don't need them."

"Any nausea?"

"No."

"Gaps in your memory?"

"Apart from a few seconds just before the accident, no."

"Perfect."

She did some more scribbling in her notebook.

"Would you please ask Dr. Pouliot to come and see me? I'd like to talk to him."

"He'll come as soon as he's finished his rounds, which should be in about fifteen minutes. Do you need anything in the meantime?"

"Not at the moment, thanks."

"If Dr. Pouliot runs late, I'll let you know."

I reacted with a start. "I'm sorry," I said, "what did you just say?"

"If Dr. Pouliot runs late," the nurse repeated, "I'll let you know."

Run, late.

"Do you have something I can write on?"

"Sure."

She tore a page out of her notebook and handed it to me, along with her pen. Hastily, I wrote down the six words that were blazing in my memory.

Run, late, elapse, lid, me, tee.

I shuddered.

Could I really be so confused that I was imagining these details?

The detective walked right by without noticing him. For the killer, it was a strange feeling. The cop was oblivious of the fact that he had the power to defeat the killer's murderous intentions. Even so, the killer bore him no ill will. They were both simply doing their duty. Under different circumstances, they might even have been friends.

It occurred to him that he hadn't had a friend in a very long time. Oh sure, he'd made a few acquaintances here and there; he'd had some pleasant colleagues at work. But a true friend? Someone he could confide in? He hadn't had one of those in years.

He tried to recall the precise moment when he had withdrawn from the world of the living and slid into the shadowlands. But he shook himself out of his reverie. None of that mattered.

Watching as Victor Lessard stepped into the hospital room, he was finally able to put his finger on what he felt for the police officer.

Respect.

The faded curtains separating the beds, the incessant to-and-fro of the hospital personnel, the sporadic moans of patients unable to bear their pain, the merciless glow of the fluorescent lights, the battered furniture, the chipped paint in the corners — all these jumbled, long-forgotten images were coming back to me when I heard a knock at the door. A man wearing a leather jacket walked in.

"Hello. I'm Victor Lessard. I'm a detective with the Montreal Police. May I come in?"

"Of course."

What did the police want with me?

He drew a chair close to the bed.

"How are you feeling?"

"I'm okay, thanks."

"Do you know why I'm here?"

"The accident?"

"To start with, I'll need your personal information. Name, address, phone number, age, and occupation."

He pulled a notebook and pen from his pocket. I wasn't happy about having to reveal these things, but what choice did I have? Reluctantly, I gave him my information.

"Okay, now tell me what happened. Even the most seemingly trivial details may be important."

I told him what I remembered. I'd been crossing the street to go to the café. I had looked down for a moment to find something in my purse. After that, my memory was blank until the moment I woke up in the hospital. I didn't mention my encounter with Miles. I wasn't about to tell a police detective about my unhinged delusions.

"Did you notice the make or colour of the car?"

"No."

"Did you see the driver's face?"

"No."

"Do you remember whether the driver hit the brakes?"

"I think I shut my eyes."

"Did you hear the tires squeal?"

I tried to concentrate, but I couldn't remember a thing.

Detective Lessard was all business as he questioned me, but his voice was gentle, as though he wanted to compensate for his bluntness. I found him likeable. It pained me that I couldn't be more helpful.

"I'm sorry," I said.

"That's all right. We're not flying completely blind. A witness heard the car hit you and gave us a good description of the vehicle. It's a black Mercedes. According to the witness, the car didn't brake or swerve to avoid you. And there are no skid marks on the asphalt."

What was the cop getting at?

"The car struck your legs. You were thrown some distance. The doctor believes your head hit the pavement when you landed. In cases like this, we're often looking at a drunk driver."

That surprised me.

"So early in the morning?"

"It happens more often than you might imagine. A lot of the time, we're able to track down the driver because of the dents in the car's body."

For the first time since our conversation had begun, he looked straight at me.

"To be honest, I can't guarantee that we'll ever catch the person who did this."

But my mind was elsewhere. At this point, I didn't much care whether the police caught the driver. I had no memory of the impact, and even if the facts seemed to prove beyond any doubt that it really had happened, all I could think about was finding Miles. The detective's phone rang. Without taking his eyes off me, he cut off the call.

"Thanks for trying," I said.

"That's my job," he said. As he stood up, he handed me his business card.

"In case something comes back to you."

He placed the chair against the wall.

"I almost forgot … is there anyone who might have a reason for running you over?"

"You mean … on purpose?"

"It may seem weird, but sometimes —"

The detective's cellphone rang again.

"I'm sorry. I'd better take this."

He pressed a button. "Lessard."

His face suddenly turned red. He hurried to the door. He seemed to be on the verge of tears.

"Is something wrong?" I asked.

He rushed out without answering, letting the door slam behind him.

Looking like he'd seen a ghost, the police officer ran down the corridor and disappeared around a corner. The killer watched him go.

Have they already found the body?

There were no more obstacles in his way. His goal was within reach. As he advanced toward room 222, he consulted his notebook. He would only need a few seconds. The door was ajar. Through the gap, he glanced furtively at the young woman.

An adrenalin rush hit him.

Instinctively, he patted the pocket containing the vials and syringe that he'd stolen from the pharmacy. He would speak to her calmly as he injected the liquid into the catheter. He knew exactly what he'd say. *It's just something to kill the pain.*

When the drug had taken effect, he would roll the bed into the vacant examination room that he'd noticed earlier. Getting her there wouldn't be a problem. He had watched how patients were shuttled from one room to another.

Then he would dress her and place her in one of the wheelchairs that was already in the examination room.

With the drug in her system, the young woman would be unable to speak or move. He would go out the main entrance and walk through the indoor parking area to the Buick.

From there, he would make his way unhurriedly to the hunting lodge in Mont-Laurier and carry out the plan that he had crafted specifically for her.

He was about to open the door when a sudden thought stopped him.

Why not follow the detective?

Why not pay a visit to the sixth floor? Why not walk past that office and see how much trouble *his* work had caused for the police?

Was he taking too many risks? He smiled, realizing that he'd let himself slip into a common fallacy.

These days, everything is reduced to a single consideration: risk management.

He despised the empty catchphrases that everyone was always spouting in contemporary culture: vacuous expressions like "value added," "sustainable development," "knowledge management," and "growth of human capital." Just so many trendy buzzwords, bereft of actual meaning.

Why was it that the stupidest ideas always came out on top?

It was the con job of the century. The triumph of unrestrained capitalism had given rise to a popular belief that it was possible, even natural, to do more with less.

Wiping the beads of sweat from his forehead, he composed himself. There was no point in getting upset. He needed to focus on the task at hand: neutralizing Simone Fortin and getting her out of the hospital without attracting attention.

On the other hand, he would only be gone fifteen minutes. And in her present condition, it wasn't like she'd be leaving anytime soon.

He turned and headed for the elevators.

Fernandez had notified him that the executive director of the hospital had just been found murdered in his office.

Lessard was in no mood to go through another bloodbath like the one at the Polytechnique.

Ever since that mass shooting, the response protocol had been clear. The top priority was establishing a secure perimeter.

As he ran up the stairs, he unholstered his Glock.

If the son of a bitch who'd done this was still in the building, Lessard wouldn't think twice before gunning him down.

He had made lethal use of his weapon before. Doing so had caused him all kinds of problems, but he wouldn't hesitate to do it again.

He sprinted along a corridor jammed with metal trolleys and went past a group of nurses.

One of them saw his pistol and shrieked.

"Police!" he yelled. "Step aside!"

He was running hard. Fuelled by adrenalin. He came to the floor where the administrative offices were located. He released the safety catch.

He was exultant.

Total anarchy had taken hold in the corridor. The police officer was out of breath. A red-faced security guard was pacing back and forth uncertainly as he kept watch at the door.

A few of Mongeau's colleagues were standing around in horror. One woman was crying intermittently. A man seemed to be in shock.

A group of people returning from a wine-soaked lunch were coming up the hallway. The laughter suddenly died in their throats. The news was spreading.

The executive director had been murdered …

The man blended into the gathering crowd. Through the open door, he saw the police officer vomit into a wastepaper basket.

They couldn't understand.

He alone knew, and that gave him a heady sensation of power.

The boy reaches the spot where the animal disappeared. He sees no trace of blood. Could he have missed his target? Bearing left, he skirts a dense stand of conifers. The animal is lying on its side in front of him, one eye still open. Is it dead? He's seized by a mixture of fear and excitement. He approaches the creature, nudges it with the barrel of his rifle. It doesn't move. The boy lets out a loud whoop. Using his hunting knife, he guts the animal. Plunging his hands into the still-warm innards gives him a strange sensation. He marks the spot with fluorescent tape, picks up his rifle, and sets off. Night falls.

He wanted to step closer, but he restrained himself.

He watched the scene for a short while, then walked to the stairwell and went back down to the second floor.

He took a deep breath. The moment of truth was finally at hand: his prey was a few steps away, unaware and unprotected. She would pay for her mistakes.

He pushed the door open and walked into the room.

Instantly, he knew something was wrong. The bed stood in the middle of the space, unmade and empty. He opened the bathroom door. No one!

When Dr. Pouliot came in, the tube was hanging down from my IV bag. I was dressed and ready to go.

"What do you think you're doing?" he demanded angrily. "You're in no condition to leave."

"My vital signs are normal. Ask the nurse."

"You only regained consciousness a couple of hours ago. Do you have any idea what kind of risk you're taking?"

He was right. This was very foolish.

"I know what I'm doing."

"I won't permit you to walk out of here unless you sign a refusal-of-treatment form."

At my request, the nurse had brought me that very document a few minutes ago.

"It's already taken care of."

Disapproval twisted his mouth into a bitter smile.

"Fine. Suit yourself."

Dr. Pouliot left without another word.

I stepped into the corridor, determined to solve the mystery.

What was going on? Where was Simone Fortin? Had she been transferred to another room? Suddenly, he became aware of a presence behind him.

"Can I help you?"

He spun around, ready to reach for his knife. A nurse had entered the room. He hesitated for an instant.

"I'm Dr. Hamel. I was to examine the patient who was here."

"You work with Dr. Pouliot?"

"Uh, yes."

"She left a few minutes ago. From what I was told, she refused to stay under observation."

He froze for longer than he would have liked.

"Do you know where she went?"

"Home, I guess."

"Do you have her contact information?"

"The other nurse took care of the paperwork before her shift ended."

"May I see the forms?"

The nurse frowned irritably.

"I'll have to find them. That's going to take some time. Is it urgent?"

He was taken aback. "Well, it's just …"

"Let me get my patient settled in, then I'll see what I can do. What extension can I reach you at?"

He couldn't afford to wait around and run the risk of being noticed. The hospital would soon be crawling with police.

"Forget it. I'm sure I have the information on file."

He hurried out.

He stepped outside and looked around, trying to spot the young woman among the passersby. He had let her get away again! An uncontrollable sensation of panic gripped him. He was on the verge of exploding. He'd made another unforgivable mistake. He had let vanity get the better of him. He went back to the parking area.

Inside the car, he bit down on a fist to suppress the howl of rage that was rising in his throat. He started beating his head against the dashboard, but stopped himself instantly.

He was losing his grip.

It took him several minutes to get his emotions under control. When he had calmed down, he wiped his forehead with a handkerchief.

He needed to concentrate, to come up with a new plan.

What were his options? Where did she live?

He felt the anger starting to rise once again. He'd been unable to get her phone number, which was surely confidential.

Suddenly, he had a flash of inspiration.

Though he didn't know where Simone Fortin lived, he knew exactly where to find her friend Ariane Bélanger.

He took out his notebook and checked the address. Simone Fortin had vanished, but she would surely get in touch with her friend. The way forward was clear. He would watch Ariane Bélanger. Sooner or later, she would lead him to his target.

And this time, he wouldn't miss.

9

Trois-Pistoles

The temperature had just fallen below freezing.

A dozen chalets stood along the shore of the Saint Lawrence, separated from Route 132 by two kilometres of snowy fields.

This area was a popular summer destination for city dwellers seeking wide horizons, starry nights, and tranquility. But in the winter, it was bleak and practically deserted.

Pale smoke was rising from the chimney of one of the houses.

The interior consisted of a bedroom, a bathroom, and a large main space that served as kitchen, dining room, and living room. A fire was crackling in the cast-iron stove.

The floor was littered with empty vodka bottles, and the air was thick with rancid odours of sweat and decay. The white spruce-panelled walls had clearly seen better days.

A man was sprawled on a couch, fast asleep, when the phone started ringing. He answered on the fifteenth ring.

"Hello?" he groaned.

"Laurent? It's Nicolas."

He lay there in silence. The caller spoke again.

"Are you coming to work tomorrow?"

"Uhh … no," the drunk finally managed to answer. "I'm still sick."

"Laurent, it's been five days. I can't keep covering for you like this. Not without a doctor's note."

"I'll get better soon, I promise."

"Laurent?"

"Yes?"

"You're really starting to piss me off."

Laurent dropped the handset.

He groped for the bottle that stood on the side table, but his fingers touched the cold metal of a pistol.

He seized the weapon and released the safety catch.

Do I finally have the guts?

He cocked the gun and closed his lips around the barrel, his finger tickling the trigger.

Through the bay window, he saw the distant silhouette of an oil tanker moving up the Saint Lawrence.

In the end, Laurent replaced the gun barrel with the spout of a bottle. He'd spent the whole day indoors watching a soporific billiards match on TV.

His only meal had been a can of beans eaten straight from the container. There was no food left in the house. He'd have to go out soon. He hadn't showered in three days. He was in a tailspin. How had it come to this? Even he couldn't explain why he'd fallen off the wagon.

The phone rang again. Laurent picked up.

"I'm feeling better, Nicolas," he said, trying to sound sober. "I'll be there tomorrow."

"Laurent, this is Kurt Waldorf. It's good to hear your voice."

"Leave me alone, Waldorf!" he shouted.

"You never called back. Did you get my letters?"

"What letters?"

Laurent had gotten them, but he'd thrown them in the fire after reading them. What Waldorf was suggesting was madness. The man was out of his mind.

"Laurent, we need to talk about your father."

"Fuck off! I don't know what you're trying to do, but it's sick."

"Stay where you are, I'm on my way."

"If you set foot in my house, Waldorf, I'll shoot you!"

A thick blanket of fog off the river had enveloped the house. The silence was broken now and then by a dry cracking noise as the rising tide compressed the ice floes and broke them up. The sound of the 4x4 approaching along the snowy road failed to rouse Laurent. He didn't see the imposing figure of the man in the doorway. Nor did he hear the noise of the coffeemaker being turned on.

He was dreaming.

Trois-Pistoles
1998
Under full sail, the vessel is scudding across the cold waters of the Saint Lawrence. The wind is blowing hard from the north, dispersing the fluffy clouds. Two large herons are following them, flying above their foaming wake. The boat runs headlong into a wave, sending a spray of water into his face. He's pumped on adrenalin, yelling at the top of his lungs as his father keeps a firm grip on the tiller. Laurent looks to his right. He sees the steeple and four shining turrets of the church, built in 1827. Farther east, he can see the outline of the hospital. They've been sailing since sunrise. After going around l'île Verte, they stopped for a picnic lunch on l'île aux Pommes, a well-known attraction for birdwatchers. Now they're coming home. They cruise past a couple of dozen houses standing on stilts at the waterline along the Chemin du Havre, and Laurent sees the place they've rented. He observes a tennis game in progress on the court where they often play. At his father's request, Laurent starts to bring in the sails. Charlène is waiting for them on a bench beside the walkway that runs around the wharf. She gives them

a wave, and Laurent waves back. The two men begin to execute docking manoeuvers, and the boat is soon at rest beside the wharf. Laurent gives his father a pleading look. "Tie us up," his father says, laughing. "I'll handle everything else." Laurent knots the dock lines in a hurry, then goes over to Charlène. They share a long, long kiss. Laurent's father smiles as he watches them walk off toward the Rue Notre-Dame. He looks out across the water and inhales the iodine-tinged salt air. The sun is setting fast, illuminating a golden path across the water. Wanting the boat to be ready for their next outing, the man scrubs the deck. At last, he removes the perishable foods from the refrigerator and stows them in a bulky metal cooler, which he picks up. Gripping this burden, he puts one foot on the wharf and, with the other, pushes off from the sailboat's gunwale. But instead of providing the resistance he needs to get safely onto the wharf, the boat shifts away abruptly. Thrown off balance, the man falls between the wharf and the boat. His head strikes the concrete edge and he goes down like a stone. On the wharf, people are scrambling to provide assistance. Laurent and Charlène have gotten as far as the rectory. The towering silver steeple of the church fills the sky. Charlène's mouth tastes of mango and honey. Her hair smells of lavender. A man walks toward them, looking grave. There's been an accident. The moment Laurent reaches the wharf, he realizes that something isn't right. He didn't properly secure the boat's rope to the cleat.

"Laurent! Wake up."

He spluttered. A dangerous-looking man had just thrown a glass of water in his face. Laurent tried to get up, but he fell back onto the couch, unable to hold himself upright. The stranger put a cup of coffee on the table.

"Drink."

Laurent swept his arm across the table, sending the cup and its contents flying.

"Idiot," the stranger said, grabbing him by the collar. He was in his midforties, dressed in black, and had angular features and a long scar running down the right side of his face.

"Waldorf?" Laurent asked.

"Who else?"

The young man looked around for his gun.

"Don't even think about it. I took your weapon."

"Get the fuck out of here, Waldorf, or I'll call the police!"

He reached for the handset, but it wasn't there.

"I also hid your phone."

Laurent glanced around the room. The bottles and trash had disappeared. Freshly washed dishes were drying on the counter. The ashtrays were empty.

An icy wind was blowing in through the open windows.

"Thanks for dropping by to clean the place up, Waldorf. I'll mail you a cheque."

"Shut up and listen to me —"

"Go fuck yourself! Who do you think you are, some kind of fortune teller?"

"No, just a man who honours his word. I made a promise to your father, and I'm going to keep it."

"Even if I believed you, what could I do?"

Waldorf pulled out the pistol and pointed it at Laurent.

"Get in the bedroom."

"What is this, a joke?"

Waldorf cocked the weapon.

"Fine," Laurent said scornfully, raising his hands.

He entered the bedroom with the barrel nudging his back.

"Lie down on the bed," the visitor ordered.

"Sorry, Waldorf, but you're not my type."

"Stop messing around!"

With one hand aiming the gun at Laurent, Waldorf used the other to pull out two pairs of handcuffs, which he locked to the bedposts, then to Laurent's wrists.

"What are you doing?" Laurent asked.

"Keeping my promise," Waldorf said.

He found a glass in the adjoining bathroom, filled it with water, and fished some pills out of his shirt pocket.

"Open your mouth," he said, holding the pills in front of Laurent's face.

"Forget it! You're going to drug me."

"No choice," Waldorf snapped, waving the pistol under Laurent's nose. "Open up."

"What are you giving me?"

"Benzodiazepine and acamprosate. They'll help. I'll give you a shot of vitamin B1 later."

Reluctantly, Laurent swallowed the pills. Waldorf was closing the door behind him when the young man called out.

"What the hell is wrong with you? What do you want?"

"To convince you," Waldorf answered.

"Of what?"

"The fact that I saw Miles."

PART TWO

I do not believe in an afterlife, although I am bringing a change of underwear.

— Woody Allen

10

Limping, I went out to the hospital parking area and made my way to the taxi stand. My arrival interrupted a conversation among several drivers. From what I could gather, they were talking about *The People's Almanac* and its weather forecasts for the coming summer.

Stepping around a sheet of ice, I got into the first car in line.

I gave the driver the address of Miles's building and sank back into the seat. I wasn't surprised that I had remembered the address. I've always had a photographic memory for numbers.

The driver sped away from the taxi stand. He spent the entire trip alternately flooring the accelerator and slamming on the brake. By the time we reached Miles's place, my heart was in my mouth.

The fare came to less than seven dollars, but I gave the man both five-dollar bills that were in my wallet. I was touched by the picture of his two young daughters taped to the dashboard.

I had spent the brief cab ride thinking about the events of the last few hours.

What had *really* happened?

If there was a logical explanation, I was hoping with all my heart that Miles would be able to supply it.

I looked up.

The building was wreathed in a fine mist. I struggled up the front stairs, leaning on the handrail for support. As though to highlight my disability, a squirrel was scrambling up the building's façade as nimbly as a spider.

Reaching the doorstep, I knocked twice, then turned the door handle without waiting for an answer.

The door was locked.

Strange. Miles had told me that he never locked the door.

I was about to knock again when a wrinkled old lady opened up. Her white hair and thick glasses were in stark contrast to the trendy tracksuit and running shoes that she was wearing.

"Yes?" she said.

I was briefly dumbstruck by this unexpected apparition. Did Miles live with his grandmother?

"Can I help you?" the woman asked.

"Uhh … I've come to see Miles."

The woman's surprised expression wasn't encouraging.

"There's no one by that name living here."

She was going to close the door, but I blocked it with my forearm.

"It's important, ma'am. I need to see him."

Her aged eyes peered at me suspiciously, as though I were a weirdo. "You've got the wrong address, miss. I don't know anybody named Miles."

As I raised my hand, I realized that I was trembling. Even so, I managed to point into the apartment.

"This may seem silly, but would you mind if I had a look around?"

The old lady studied me. I could well imagine what was going through her head. Was I one of those junkies whose syringes occasionally turned up in the cemetery?

"It'll only take a minute," I said.

Could she sense my distress? After a moment's hesitation, she let me in.

Inside the apartment, a terrible shock awaited me.

The living room had been completely redone.

The walls had been painted a dull shade of green. A frayed carpet lay on the floor, and a couple of old shelves were sagging under the weight of a variety of knick-knacks. In the middle of the room, a worn-out couch faced an antiquated TV set. A game show was on.

I had been in this place only a few hours ago. I recognized the configuration of the apartment. The living-room window offered an identical view of the cemetery.

Yet someone — I didn't know why, or how — had figured out a way to rearrange the interior.

"Is something wrong, dear?"

"I need to look in the bedroom," I said, determined to get to the bottom of this.

Without waiting for permission, I went up the hallway. I opened the bedroom door and found myself looking at an aging four-poster flanked by mahogany bedside tables. My eyes swept the room, searching for Miles's painting.

All I saw was dusty yellowed wallpaper on the walls.

I headed straight for the bathroom.

Once again, a bitter disappointment awaited me.

The room was full of towels, perfumed soaps, creams and ointments of all kinds. There was no sign of the spartan simplicity that had reigned in Miles's bathroom.

I looked at myself in the mirror. I was in a sad state, with purple rings under my pallid eyes and tangled hair flying in all directions. I heard the old lady behind me.

"What do you think you're doing?" she asked, nettled. "Come, I'll see you out."

A perfect stranger had walked into her home and started searching the place. Who could blame her for being annoyed?

I followed the woman back to the front door, scanning the living room once more in the hope of finding some indication, however small, that Miles had been in the apartment.

I saw nothing.

Could I have gotten the address wrong? No, I knew I hadn't. The old lady opened the door. I gave her a timid smile.

"I'm sorry I bothered you, ma'am," I murmured.

Despite the woman's obvious sincerity, I couldn't quite convince myself that I had made a mistake. Before walking out, I gave in to temptation and asked the question I was burning to ask.

"Forgive me for prying, but how long have you lived here?"

"Since July 1st, 2002," she said. "I remember the date because it was one year to the day before my husband's first heart attack."

The response was out of my mouth before I had time to think.

"That's impossible. You're lying!"

Watching her expression darken, I instantly regretted the outburst.

"Get out," she said sharply, "or I'll call the police."

I must have been a sorry sight.

After wiping my eyes, I blew my nose noisily.

"Take another one."

The old lady held out her box of tissues. The tears had come in a rush, and I'd been helpless to stop them. The woman had been taken aback, but she'd recovered her composure and sat me down on the couch.

Her anger was gone. Now she was holding my hands between arthritic fingers.

"You really are a mess," she sighed. "What's got you so upset?"

"I … it's kind of complicated."

"And you don't think I'd understand? You remind me of my daughter. She thinks I'm feeble-minded. She hasn't called in a month."

Poor woman. I looked at her with sympathy.

"It's this fellow Miles you're all worked up about, isn't it? You don't need to explain. I know what it's like to be in love."

"He was just a friend. The truth is, I hardly knew him."

"Considering the state you're in, I'm guessing he was more than a friend."

She was right. Miles had awakened something in me that had been asleep for too long. Desire, certainly, but this went deeper than sexual longing. After the little boy's death, I had withdrawn from the world. I had walled myself in, preventing anyone from touching my heart. Miles had made me want to live again. Thanks to him, I was ready to take off the mask.

"The truth is, I thought this was his apartment. That's why I reacted so strongly when you said you'd been living here since 2002."

"My husband and I took the place over from my sister-in-law, after she moved to Brussels."

She paused before speaking again.

"Maybe your friend lived here before her."

"How long was your sister-in-law in the apartment?"

"Lucille? I'm not sure. Twelve years, maybe."

"That can't be," I whispered. "It can't be …"

"I only mention it because you're not the first person who's asked for permission to look around."

"What do you mean?"

"A young man came to the door one time. He said he'd lived here years ago. He insisted on looking around, kind of like you."

"Do you remember his name?"

"He never mentioned it."

"What did he look like?"

"I hardly remember. He was quite tall. Youthful."

I gave her a quick description of Miles.

"Yes, that could be him."

"When was this?"

"More than a year ago," she said without hesitation. "My husband was still alive at the time."

"Did he come here yesterday, by any chance?"

"If he had, I'd have noticed."

She patted my arm.

"I know how upset you are, dear. But when two people love each other, their paths are bound to cross sooner or later. Your story reminds me of that American couple who were separated during the war. She got remarried, believing he'd been killed, but it turned out he was in a German hospital the whole time, being treated for amnesia. Then, three years later ..."

I wasn't listening anymore. All I could hear was the harsh drumming of my heartbeat in my ears.

"Good heavens, you're so pale!" the old lady said. She winked. "Let me pour you a glass of gin. That'll put things right. Oh, and since you're here, why don't I bring out my wedding album? Wait till you get a look at Alfred. He was such a handsome devil ..."

My brain felt like it might explode.

Everything the woman had said was impossible.

I had retreated to the front door. The old lady was sweet, but I was in no mood to look at her wedding pictures. Despite her evident good will, there was nothing else she could do for me.

"I'm sorry, but I have a pressing engagement," I lied. "I really must go."

Her expression was so disappointed that I almost relented.

"Thank you for everything," I said, clasping her shoulders.

"You'll find him, dear. You just have to believe."

I left. Outside, the daylight stung my eyes. A whirlwind of information was spinning in my head. What had I learned? The old lady had said that she didn't know Miles, and that she'd lived in the apartment since 2002. She had also claimed that a young man answering Miles's description had insisted on looking around the place some time ago.

Unless she was a stellar actress, she was telling the truth.

I went down the front stairs and started walking along Côte-des-Neiges. I crossed the street and approached the cemetery gate.

A funeral procession was going up the main path, led by a black limousine. As I watched the cars rolling along, I was struck by the thought that life is no more than a brief intermission.

I stood there, lost in thought.

The procession disappeared at the end of the path.

As I gazed at a headstone, the puzzle confronted me in all its contradiction. On the one hand, I had no reason to think the old lady was lying. On the other, I couldn't shake the sense that someone had altered Miles's apartment.

Which forced me to weigh a hypothesis that was painful to consider, but nonetheless inescapable.

Had Miles orchestrated the whole thing?

If so, why?

And an even greater question was haunting me.

Where had he gone?

11

Lessard holstered his weapon. The killer wasn't in Jacques Mongeau's office. A hospital security guard had arrived on the scene before the detective sergeant. Lessard instructed him to move back the crowd of gawkers gathered at the office door.

He would remember this day as one of the longest and most difficult of his career. When death strikes, the body that's left behind is like a remnant of the past, paltry and grotesque. Hanged, drowned, heads blown off, bodies shattered by car accidents — Lessard had seen them all.

As a cop, he had learned, more or less, how to cope with this aspect of the job. But his initial response was always the same. Something in him couldn't accept the abjection of death.

It had happened again just now. He had thrown up into the wastepaper basket.

He started noting details of the crime scene. The man was sprawled in his office chair, his chin resting on his chest. His throat seemed to have been cut. Another wound near his heart had left a large pool of blood on the floor. His right hand lay palm upward on his thigh. The visitor's chair had been overturned.

Suddenly, the detective sergeant spotted a detail that made him wonder for a moment if he was seeing things. The man's index finger had been cut off.

It was a clean cut. Judging from the marks on the wood, it had been done on the desk.

Had it been inflicted post-mortem?

Next to the blotter lay a transparent plastic CD case. The disc inside bore a label showing a date, a web address, and a line of text:

Error message: 10161416.

Had the disc been left there by the murderer, or did it belong to the dead man?

There were no other signs of violence in the room. The pastel walls, faded carpet, and melamine furniture suggested that the place hadn't been redecorated since the 1980s.

A photograph on a shelf caught his eye. It showed the victim with his wife and two sons.

Lessard sighed.

The family would have to be notified. At this moment, they were going about their lives, unaware of what had just happened. In a few hours at the latest, a police officer would bring them the terrible news. Lessard himself had carried out this grim task too many times. Nothing was worse than the anguish of family members and the helplessness he felt on such occasions. He did his best to behave appropriately, but he never knew what to say.

After violence has spoken, what's left to add?

Not having any gloves, Lessard took a tissue and used it to extract the victim's wallet. Inside, he found some cash and a driver's licence with a photo. The corpse sprawled before him was, beyond any doubt, Jacques Mongeau.

The name rang a bell. Was he well known?

Lessard opened a drawer and found an agenda, a packet of stamps, a toothbrush, a tube of toothpaste, and a few condoms. No great surprise there. The man wasn't the first or the last to have enjoyed a little action on the side.

He heard approaching footsteps and voices calling out. Fernandez and Sirois entered the office, followed a moment later by Pearson, who handed him a cup of coffee and a pair of latex gloves. Constable

Nguyen was in the corridor, cordoning off the area with police tape. The entire sixth floor would now be a crime scene.

Fernandez and Pearson both reacted with brief revulsion when they saw the body. Sirois was impassive.

"The technicians are on their way," Fernandez said.

"Who are they sending?" Lessard asked.

"Doug Adams and his assistant."

The detective sergeant nodded. Adams wasn't exactly the world's most exciting guy, but he was conscientious and trustworthy. He knew his work, and he was unfailingly discreet.

"Who took the call?" Lessard asked.

"I did," Fernandez said. "It was his secretary who found him. She's being treated for shock."

"I want to see her as soon as possible."

While the conversation continued, Pearson and Sirois were examining the victim's wounds.

"Find out who came in here before I arrived, apart from the secretary. Did the security guard touch the body?"

Fernandez was scribbling in a notebook.

"Has anyone checked for surveillance cameras on this floor?"

"I just did," Pearson said. "Negative."

They observed the crime scene in silence. Sirois was idly fiddling with his ballpoint. Fernandez and Pearson were taking notes. Lessard tried to reach Commander Tanguay. He left a message on his voice mail. It dawned on him that the others were waiting for him to speak. What should he say? He tried to organize his thoughts.

"Okay," he said, "what do we know?"

"Jacques Mongeau was the executive director of the hospital," Sirois began. "He was found dead by his secretary."

"There's a severe wound in Mongeau's chest," Lessard continued. "His throat's been slit and his right index finger has been cut off. Adams should be able to confirm this, but it looks like the injuries were caused by a knife."

"The stab wound is deep and irregular. I'm guessing the weapon was a commando knife," Pearson said. He had served in the army before becoming a cop.

"So the killer may be in the military," Fernandez suggested.

Lessard took a sip of coffee and continued.

"We don't know the murderer's identity, or his motive. Apart from the overturned chair, there are no signs of a struggle, but it's clear that Mongeau was killed in this room." Lessard took a step toward the window. "It doesn't look like he tried to escape. Did he feel safe? Did he have an appointment with his assailant? If so, did the secretary see him? Was the office searched? Is anything missing?"

The questions hung in the air.

"We can rule out robbery. The victim's cash and credit cards are still in his wallet."

"What I don't get is the severed finger," Sirois interjected. "It's like some kind of ritual, or the settling of a score."

"I was coming to that. Why cut off the man's finger? Why the right index? Was the injury inflicted before death? Should we be reading something into it?"

"There's another possibility," Fernandez suggested. "Maybe he was tortured. The assailant may have been trying to get information out of him."

"His screams would have been heard," Sirois said.

"I'm not so sure," Lessard said. "There's padding on his office door."

"What if the information was the finger itself?" Pearson mused.

"What do you mean?" Lessard asked.

"Fingerprint recognition," Pearson said.

Everyone was silent for a few seconds.

"That's a lot of unanswered questions," Fernandez sighed.

Though still confused, Lessard knew the detail was an important one. It would be crucial for the medical examiner to determine whether the finger had been cut off before or after death.

Pearson knelt down and looked under the desk.

"Nadja, dig into the guy's past. We don't know what we're looking for, but we need to find the key that unlocks all this. Who was he? Did he have enemies? A mistress?"

"Which amounts to the same thing," Sirois said. No one laughed at the joke.

"Check his bank records. Have any large amounts gone in or out lately? Find out whether his fingerprints are on file. Did he own a safe with fingerprint recognition? You get the idea."

Fernandez was already striding toward the door.

"Pearson, I want you and Adams to go over every inch of this office. Lift any fingerprints you find. See what's in the guy's computer, look at his emails. I noticed an agenda in the right-hand drawer. Go through it. I also want to know what's on that disc lying on the desk. And check the web address on the label."

"You got it."

"I'll send over the secretary as soon as possible," Lessard added. "She can let us know if any files or other items are missing. Have Nguyen draw up a list of hospital staffers whose offices are on this floor. He should start taking witness statements. We can't rule out the possibility that the killer works here."

Pearson was already leafing through the agenda.

"Sirois," Lessard continued, "you'll notify the family. Bring along the psychologist, if you want. I'll join you as soon as I can. You know the drill. Get whatever information you can, but don't press. Were there any recent changes in his behaviour? Money problems? Gambling? Drugs? Alcohol? And don't forget the safe."

"What do we do about the hit and run?" Sirois asked. "Did you get any information from Simone Fortin?"

Lessard swore. It had completely slipped his mind.

"No, nothing. Let's put that on the back burner for now. The murder comes first."

A small man in a police windbreaker entered.

"Hey, Doug," Lessard said.

"Hello, Victor," the man said, extending a bony hand.

"Pearson will bring you up to speed. I have to go, but give me a call as soon as you find something."

Adams nodded and started unpacking his equipment. His assistant, whose name Lessard could never remember, walked in carrying two heavy cases.

The detective sergeant was on his way out the door when he stopped short. "Pearson, I almost forgot ... what about the medical examiner?"

"It's Berger. He's on his way."

Lessard made a face.

Condescending and capricious as a rock star, Berger embodied most of the traits that the detective sergeant liked least in a person. But his work was meticulous.

"I want his preliminary findings as soon as possible. Especially regarding the finger. We need to know whether the injury was inflicted before or after death."

"Got it, Victor."

"Oh, and Pearson ..."

"Mmm?"

"Thanks for the coffee."

A long, dreamless sleep.

Death might well be a deliverance. Lessard had thought about the matter a few months ago, when he'd considered ending his life.

His cellphone rang. It was Fernandez.

"The secretary's name is Jeannine Daoust. She's in intensive care. They're expecting you."

"What about the security guard? Did he touch anything?"

"No. He stayed in the doorway."

"Do you believe him?"

"Yes. He was shaking like a leaf."

Lessard shuddered.

He'd been physically present in the hospital when this terrible event had occurred, this catastrophe arising from nowhere, this act so senseless that, by rights, it should never have happened at all. And yet he knew there was no reason to be surprised. Human beings had been preying on one another since the dawn of time.

His phone rang again.

His superior officer, Commander Tanguay, had just heard the news. Lessard gave him a brief rundown.

"Do you think you can handle the situation, Lessard?"

Tanguay was clearly referring to the personal problems that had led to the collapse of the detective sergeant's marriage the previous year.

"Yes, sir."

"Do you know who Jacques Mongeau was?"

Once again, the name rang a bell, but Lessard couldn't place it.

"Uh …"

"Until recently, he was a top fundraiser for the Liberal Party of Canada. A very influential man with close ties to the former prime minister. Do you understand the implications, Lessard?"

"The case will get a lot of media attention."

"Exactly. Journalists will be watching your every move. I've called a press conference for seven o'clock this evening, and I'd like you to be there. We need to get out in front of this and establish clear guidelines for sharing information with the media."

Lessard sighed. He had no problem facing the cameras, but he knew he'd have nothing useful to offer journalists at seven o'clock. What Tanguay was really saying, indirectly, was that he wanted results in a hurry.

"Another thing, Lessard. As you know, there's still some debate at headquarters regarding the effectiveness of neighbourhood police stations. We don't have much wiggle room. If your team doesn't come up with a solid lead by tomorrow, there's going to be significant pressure to transfer the investigation to the Major Crimes Unit. So let's be clear. I'll hold them off as long as I can, but you need to move fast."

The detective sergeant swore silently. Tanguay's message was unmistakable. He wasn't about to stick his neck out on this. If he thought things were getting hot, he would step aside and let the heavy hitters from Major Crimes take over the investigation. Lessard had no desire to go through the humiliation of seeing his case handed over to his former colleagues. He hadn't spoken to any of them since being transferred out of the Major Crimes Unit in the wake of a blunder that had cost two of his men their lives the previous year.

"Any questions, Lessard?"

"No."

Tanguay hung up before he could add anything. Stepping into the elevator, Lessard realized that he still hadn't done his laundry. Discouragement took hold of him. He was sure that he would screw up the investigation.

As he walked through the intensive care ward, he saw a woman who reminded him of his sister. He called her phone number but hung up after two rings.

Not now. He lacked the strength.

Lessard drew up a chair beside the bed.

Under her oxygen mask, Jeannine Daoust had a chalky complexion, but she was doing better. He introduced himself.

"Ms. Daoust, I know you've just been through a terrible ordeal, but I need your help."

The woman began to sob. He spoke in the gentlest voice he could manage.

"In murder cases, the actions taken during the first few hours after the body is discovered often determine whether the investigation succeeds or fails."

Jeannine thought of the dead man's widow and two sons. How would they react if she was unable to help the police?

She took a deep breath and dabbed her forehead with a crumpled tissue. Her eyeshadow had run, creating ghoulish Alice Cooper smudges under her eyes.

She sat up straighter and pulled down the oxygen mask. For the first time since Lessard had walked into the room, she looked at him.

"You're right," she said, her voice trembling. "I'm sorry."

"Thank you. I gather you saw the murderer. Tell me what happened."

"A man named Pierre Tremblay called this morning, asking for a meeting. There was no room in the schedule, but he insisted. He said he wanted to make a large donation."

"Do you get a lot of calls like that?"

"No, but they're not unheard of."

"Do you know the name of the organization he represented?"

"He didn't mention it."

"Go on."

"The boss got on the line personally and gave the man an appointment at two-thirty. He told me to cancel a meeting that he'd scheduled for that time, so I did."

"This Pierre Tremblay … what did you know about him?"

"Nothing. He had never called before."

"Did he arrive on time?"

"Yes."

"Then what happened?"

"I offered him a cup of coffee. He said no. I left him in the anteroom and went to tell the boss that he'd arrived."

"Did the man seem nervous or excited?"

"No," she said after a few seconds of thought.

"What did you do next?"

"I opened the door and announced the visitor. He went in."

"Did he sit in one of the chairs facing the desk?"

"I assume he did."

"And then?"

"Mr. Mongeau said I could go home. I turned off my computer and left, closing the door behind me."

"Did you overhear their conversation?"

"No."

"Why did you come back?"

"My daughter's on vacation in Provence. Earlier in the day, she'd sent me an email with pictures of the Pont du Gard." Her eyes lit up a little guiltily. "For years, I've been trying to convince my husband to book a trip to the south of France. I had printed the pictures using the boss's colour printer. As I was standing at the bus stop, I realized I'd forgotten them. So I went back." She wiped her eyes and stifled a sob. "When I walked back in, the office door was still shut. I thought the boss must still be in his meeting, but I wondered why I wasn't hearing anything. The door is padded, but over the years, I've learned how to pick up the vibrations that come through the frame. Before leaving again, I thought I should check to make sure he didn't need anything, and that's when ..."

She started crying again. She needed to take a long pause before continuing. Lessard made an effort to be understanding, but he was burning with impatience.

"Describe the man."

"Not very tall, I'd say five foot five. Trim. He was wearing a dark pinstripe suit, nicely cut. His hair was very black. And he had glasses, I think."

Lessard was scribbling some of her answers in his notebook.

"What about his face? His eyes? Was there anything noticeable about him? Did he have a beard?"

Jeannine Daoust frowned, concentrating. "I think he had brown eyes. His face was ... ordinary. Clean-shaven. He might have had a moustache, I'm not sure."

"And his voice?"

"What do you mean?"

"Did he sound educated? Any accent?"

"Courteous. Polite. No accent."

"How old was he?"

"Hmm … hard to say."

"What would you guess?"

"In his fifties. Late forties, maybe. I don't know."

A fresh crying fit struck Jeannine Daoust. Lessard doubted that he'd get anything useful from her today.

He was constantly having to deal with this kind of situation. Some people had difficulty recalling anything on the spot, but if you gave them a few days, they'd offer up a flood of details. This time, unfortunately, Lessard didn't have the luxury of being able to wait.

"Would you recognize the man if you saw him?"

"I think so, yes."

"A police officer will come by later and show you some pictures. We'll also ask you to help create a composite sketch. Later on, you'll go back to the office with one of my colleagues and check to see if anything's missing."

A look of distress contorted the woman's face.

"The body will have been taken away by then," Lessard added. That seemed to reassure her.

"Is there anything else you remember? Even the tiniest details could turn out to be useful."

Unconsciously, the secretary smacked her tongue twice as she pondered. "He was carrying a briefcase."

"Soft or rigid?"

"Rigid. Dark leather. Black. Yes, it was black."

Lessard scribbled.

"One last question. To your knowledge, did your boss have a safe with a fingerprint-recognition device?"

She was visibly taken aback.

"You mean like in spy movies?"

Lessard suddenly felt ridiculous.

"I guess you could put it that way ..."

"No, I don't think so. There's no safe in his office. Not even a file cabinet with a lock on it. Actually, I used to scold him about that."

"Here's my card. If anything comes back to you, give me a call."

There were too many possibilities. A short man in his forties or fifties with brown eyes and black hair, carrying a leather briefcase, wearing a dark suit and glasses. Maybe.

Even if the killer had given his real name, which Lessard very much doubted, he and his fellow cops wouldn't be that much further along in their hunt. The Montreal phone directory probably contained three hundred entries for Pierre Tremblay.

Lessard suddenly felt weary and a little discouraged in the face of the immense task before him. This investigation was going to be difficult. What could he tell the commander and the media? He and his colleagues knew nothing.

And at the moment, he really needed a cup of coffee.

12

I am schizophrenic, and so am I.
— What About Bob

In hindsight, it's clear to me that the sensible thing to do at that point would have been to give up and go home. Not only was I needlessly putting my health on the line, but my visit to Miles's apartment hadn't brought me any closer to finding him. And I had no additional clues to help track him down. If I had abandoned the search then and there, might it have been possible to prevent everything that happened afterward?

From the cemetery, I walked south on Côte-des-Neiges. Lacking any other clues, I decided to go back to the scene of that morning's near-fatal accident. After all, wasn't that where I had met Miles? Wasn't that where the whole thing had started?

As I advanced slowly along the sidewalk that borders Mount Royal, I stepped aside to let two joggers in form-fitting outfits go by. Though the ground rose quite steeply on this stretch of Côte-des-Neiges, the two men were talking as they ran, seemingly without difficulty.

I wasn't finding the climb so easy. By the time I passed the 2nd Field Artillery armoury, I was out of breath and my throat was dry.

I went into the first convenience store I saw. With the change that remained in my wallet, I bought a chocolate bar and a bottle of water, which I drank right there on the sidewalk.

I tossed the empty bottle in a trash can and slipped the chocolate bar in the back pocket of my jeans before continuing on my way.

Something was eluding me in this business.

If Miles was behind the whole thing, how had he managed to transform the apartment so quickly? The change had been striking. Had Miles received outside help?

And what about the old lady I'd spoken to? Had he manipulated her without her knowledge? Another crucial question: Had this entire affair been staged for my benefit?

Though my thoughts were still confused, an idea was taking shape in my head. I had never met Miles before, yet he seemed to know about the little boy's death. Perhaps someone had decided that it was time I paid for my mistakes. Perhaps Miles had been given the task of punishing me. But then, he had seemed sincere when he said no one had sent him to find me.

I patted the pockets of my jeans and coat, trying to find the chocolate bar. It had probably fallen out as I was walking. I turned around to retrace my steps.

The movement was barely perceptible, but I could have sworn that as I turned, a man in a duffle coat ducked behind a phone booth at the street corner.

The man had moved fast, as though not wanting to be seen.

Without thinking, I hurried toward him.

"Miles?"

My voice was strangely high-pitched and louder than I had expected it to be. A passing pedestrian turned his head reflexively. I went by him without a glance. My gaze was fixed on the phone booth.

"Miles?"

Other passersby looked at me curiously. The sight of a young woman shouting in near hysteria was bound to attract attention.

"Miles?"

Without letting me see his face, the man in the duffle coat came out of the phone booth and hurried around the corner.

"No, wait! Miles! Wait!"

My nerves had been a mess since my visit to the old lady's apartment. Something broke inside me when I saw that the man had disappeared. Without thinking, I started to run. My ankle was hurting terribly. Tears were running down my cheeks.

The world was whirling by, faster and faster. Trees, cars, and buildings were blending into an undifferentiated blur on my retinas.

Gasping for breath, I kept running until my legs gave out and I collapsed to the ground. I was weeping by now, yelling at the top of my lungs.

"I'm not crazy!"

How long did the fit last? A few seconds? Several minutes?

I don't know. When I came to my senses, I was in the cemetery, lying beside the grave of Étienne Beauregard-Delorme.

Are we haunted all our lives by the wrongs we've committed?

If so, I was condemned. There would be no redemption.

Deciding to cut across the cemetery to reach the street, I set off along a sodden path, my feet sinking into mud up to my ankles. Instantly I felt water seeping into my socks. Within a few seconds, my feet were soaked.

I could see the street beyond a row of evergreens. Trying to make my way between two fir trees, I tripped and fell into the mud. I swore and got back on my feet.

Finally, I succeeded in escaping from the cemetery. When I was safely on the sidewalk, I looked down at my clothes. My jeans and coat were covered in mud. I sighed. I had stopped caring.

I tried to get a grip on myself, to empty my mind of negative thoughts. I did my best to focus on my surroundings: shop windows, people's clothes, the colours of passing cars.

This was my method for reconnecting with reality and overcoming the anxiety that afflicted me. Little by little, it began to take effect. After a few minutes, I was calm again.

● ● ● ●

As I walked toward the spot where the accident had occurred, I was
mentally replaying the events of the day, trying to make sense of
them. One: I had been struck by a car and had lain unconscious for
several hours. Two: An old lady was living in the apartment where
I had spent time with Miles. Three: The apartment had been dra-
matically transformed. Four: A man resembling Miles had asked to
visit the place a year ago. Five: Miles had disappeared.

I had to face facts. My loss of consciousness and my encounter
with Miles were irreconcilable. The most plausible explanation?
Our meeting had been a hallucination, invented by my unconscious mind in the aftermath of my brief coma.

But this logic didn't explain everything.

Although the décor was completely different and Miles was
nowhere to be seen, how was it possible that I had found the apartment? If Miles only existed in my mind, who had visited the place
previously?

I couldn't help wondering whether, like a schizophrenic, I was
living in several parallel realities at the same time.

I had never missed my mother so desperately. I had so many
things to tell her, so much anguish to overcome.

During the months that had followed her death, I wished someone could have helped me to understand my fits of teenage apathy,
my ingratitude, my sulks. I had lost my mother before reaching
adulthood, before I was ready to face the hardships of grown-up
life.

After Étienne died, the sensation of emptiness had plunged me
into a state of misery that obliterated my emotional resources. I
had emerged from that ordeal alone and liberated; I had overcome
paranoia, the sickness that destroys minds.

The events of the last few hours were troubling. They threatened
to wreck the delicate balance that I had taken years to establish. I
didn't want to sink back into that abyss.

It's only when a person is dead that you realize how many things you wanted to say. *Oh, Mom, if only you were here.*

I was close to the spot where the car had hit me. Fearing that I might run into someone from work and be obliged to talk about the accident, I turned left onto Blueridge Crescent, thus avoiding my office building.

After I'd walked a few metres, the back of my neck began to tingle disagreeably. Something wasn't right. I could feel it.

I spun around. Once again, I saw the man in the duffle coat. I could have sworn that he looked straight at me before melting into the flow of pedestrians.

Was it my imagination, or was he following me? This time, I would find out. A city bus was coming up the street. I waited for it to approach, then darted into the street in front of it. The driver honked at me, but I got safely across. On the far sidewalk, I spotted an apartment building that had a canvas awning over its front entrance. From this vantage point, I'd be able to conceal myself from passersby.

If the man in the duffle coat was following me, my sudden change of course would certainly provoke a reaction. He would have no choice but to reveal himself.

I scanned the opposite sidewalk. A heavy-set woman carrying several plastic bags lumbered onto the street, followed by a little boy. Two teenage girls came next, passing a cigarette back and forth.

There was no sign of the man.

Come on, Miles, show yourself and let's clear this whole thing up.

I squinted. Where was he? I left my observation post for a few seconds to make way for a young couple leaving the building. Then I went back to my position and resumed the search. Still nothing. Disheartened, I emerged from my hiding place ten minutes later. The man had vanished once again.

. . .

I started walking again, with rage in my heart.

What are you playing at, Miles?

Stepping around an orange trestle that blocked a section of collapsed sidewalk, I went by the front window of a health food store. I looked absently at the displays offering a variety of dietary supplements. The longer I walked, the stronger my sense that I was straying away from familiar territory. I felt as lost as a musician without a score.

That thought brought back a distant memory.

When I was a child, my father had insisted that I take violin lessons. Despite the fact that I didn't particularly like the instrument, I had forced myself to master its basics, only allowing myself to quit at last after several years of instruction.

Another memory, even more distant, came back to me.

One Christmas, my father had given me a pair of gloves. It was usually my mother who purchased Christmas presents, but this particular holiday season, I knew my father had picked out the gloves himself. And although I would have preferred to receive a doll, and despite the fact that the gloves weren't the right size, I hadn't shown any hint of dissatisfaction. I had proudly worn those gloves for the rest of that winter, as well as the following three. That's how oversized they were.

I had spent my entire childhood offering my father similar gestures of unspoken consideration, because I was afraid to disappoint him or to hurt his feelings.

When would I finally have the courage to reconcile with him?

I stopped short. Something had snagged my attention. I wondered briefly whether I'd caught another glimpse of the man in the duffle coat. I looked around, studying the faces of the passersby. A slender woman in a poorly tailored wool outfit was walking along distractedly, moving her lips. A few steps behind, a girl was rummaging through her bag, trying to locate a ringing cellphone.

I turned my head.

No, it's something else.

It was some nearby object that had stood out, somehow, as I walked distractedly past the storefronts.

I turned around and went back the way I had come, with my senses on high alert, swivelling slowly as I tried to scan as much of the street as possible. But despite my efforts, I couldn't identify the object that had caught my eye.

A man strode by and gave me a smile. I wanted to scream in frustration. Suddenly, I froze in front of the health food store.

The gargoyles!

Atop the building's façade, I saw a winged demon.

I was trembling.

This is the building where I had a cup of coffee with Miles.

13

Sitting alone in the hospital cafeteria, away from the other tables, Lessard was going over his notes, trying to spot connections and establish patterns. He wanted to proceed methodically, but he kept doubling back, worried that he might have overlooked some important element. The coffee he'd bought was the worst he'd tasted since puberty. He was about to complain to the attendant when the hum of his cellphone brought him up short.

"Lessard."

"It's Berger."

"Thanks for calling, Jacob. How are you doing?"

There was a long, weary sigh.

"Same old, same old. People think it's cool being a medical examiner. If they only knew how much useless paperwork is involved …"

Lessard had to make an effort to restrain his temper.

"I appreciate your coming in so quickly. Have you finished?"

"Initial findings, yes. I'll still need to do a full autopsy in the lab."

"And?"

Berger sighed again, sounding like a lovesick teenager. "Death occurred a few hours ago, no more. It was caused by stab wounds to the chest, three or four in all, inflicted with a knife."

"The slashed throat didn't kill him?"

"It would have done the job, but I don't think that was the fatal wound."

"Why not?"

"Unless I'm mistaken, the man was already dying when the killer cut his throat. The internal organs were a mush, Victor. Hemorrhaging was massive."

"What kind of knife was used?"

"I'll have a better idea after the autopsy, but at first glance, I'd say it was a hunting or survival knife. One edge smooth, the other serrated."

Lessard pulled out his notebook and started writing.

"What about the severed finger?"

"It was cut off post-mortem."

"Are you sure?"

"Positive."

Lessard didn't speak for a few seconds. If the finger had been cut off after death, that ruled out the possibility that the victim was tortured to extract information.

Unless they found proof to the contrary, they had to presume that the killer had sliced off the finger for a specific reason. The idea of a device equipped with fingerprint recognition was suddenly much more interesting. The team would need to look into this.

"In your opinion, Jacob, what are we dealing with here?"

"Well, the killer knew what he was doing."

"What do you mean? Someone with a medical background?"

"Possibly, but not necessarily. The killer knew where to strike to cause the greatest damage with the fewest blows."

"So, a doctor? A soldier?"

"Could be anyone, really. These days, there are websites that'll teach you how to build a bomb. I don't know if you've noticed, Victor, but it's a sick world out there."

Lessard wasn't about to argue with that. He'd seen his share of horrors over the last ten years.

"Yes, I've noticed. Call me if you come up with anything else."

After hanging up, he put on his leather jacket and went out to his car. The conversation with Berger had given him an idea.

•   •   •

The wind had risen, gusting from the north.

Lessard drove east along Doctor Penfield, turned down De la Montagne and went south as far as Notre-Dame, then headed east again. He parked his Corolla in front of Baron Sports, a hunting and fishing store, and slid a few coins into the parking meter.

He knew the store from having come here to buy a rod and reel for Martin. They'd been planning a father-and-son fishing expedition, but the souring of their relationship had scotched that plan. Things had gone from bad to worse after the separation.

He walked into the store. It was empty.

The detective sergeant approached a sales clerk who was bent over a crossword puzzle. He asked to see some hunting knives.

"Ungoverned chaos," the clerk said. "Seven letters. Any ideas?"

Lessard shrugged.

"Sorry."

Slender as an altar boy, the clerk set aside his puzzle with reluctance and, moving unhurriedly, led Victor to a glass case. Lessard saw a few dozen blades on display: daggers, survival knives, hunting knives.

"I'm looking for something sturdy, smooth on one side, serrated on the other. What have you got?"

"Depends on what you want to do with it."

Without going into specifics, Lessard explained that he was working on an investigation. This seemed to motivate the clerk, who laid out five different models of survival knife on the counter, all of them meeting the detective sergeant's requirements.

Lessard picked one up, a black-and-silver weapon with a set of immense teeth running along its upper edge.

"That's the knife from *Rambo*," the clerk said.

"The movie?"

"Yes."

"Is it well made?"

"It's manufactured by a reputable company that puts out lots of products. If you're looking for a good survival knife, they don't come any better than this one. It'll slice an arm in half or cut firewood. There's a compass in the handle. It even has a compartment for matches."

"Is it popular?"

"Yes, it's a steady seller."

"What kind of people buy these knives?"

"The occasional *Rambo* fan. Hunters love them."

"Are they easy to come by?"

"Any store like this one would carry them."

"I'll take it."

The clerk drew up a bill of sale.

Above the cash register, two mounted caribou heads on the wall were gazing down at Lessard. He took out his wallet and gave the clerk his credit card. He would put in a request for reimbursement later. Just then, as his phone began to ring, it came to him.

"Anarchy."

"Excuse me?"

"Ungoverned chaos. Seven letters. Anarchy."

The clerk thanked him, stepped behind the counter, and went back to his crossword. With a last glance at the caribou heads, Lessard pressed a button on his phone and took the call.

Built in Italian Renaissance style, the dome of Saint Joseph's Oratory overlooked the city. "It's the biggest in the world, after Saint Peter's in Rome," Mrs. Espinosa had explained to Snake. When it came to churches, the lady knew her stuff.

They had taken the BMW right up to the oratory entrance, avoiding the hundreds of steps that true believers still climbed on their knees on Christian feast days.

They went inside.

Snake, who had never visited the place before, was surprised by the modern, unadorned style of its interior. He was no expert on architecture, but as he looked up at the arching golden-hued ceramic ceiling, he estimated that the sanctuary must be as big as two football fields.

While Mrs. Espinosa was lighting a votive candle in memory of the oratory's founder, Brother André, Snake walked to the end of the apse. There, behind a monumental grille, he saw the Saint-Sacrement chapel, the most richly decorated section of the building.

Mrs. Espinosa knelt and began her prayers, which generally went on for about ten minutes. Snake looked over an information pamphlet that he'd picked up at the entrance. With a yawn, he read that the oratory was among the largest religious structures built in the heart of a major city, ranking behind only Saint Peter's in Rome and Sacré Coeur in Paris.

The old lady was right. But Snake didn't care. He was nodding off when she gave him a little shake and informed him that her prayers were done.

They got back in the car and drove along Queen Mary to Victoria Avenue, then headed south. Reaching Côte-Saint-Luc Road, Snake turned onto the entrance ramp to the Décarie Expressway.

He took Mrs. Espinosa to a shopping centre near the Blue Bonnets raceway.

During the drive, she pointed out that there was an unpleasant smell in the car. She was right. Luckily, he'd be handing off the BMW to Tool later in the day.

At the shopping centre, she bought a variety of soaps and skin creams, a striped dress that she wouldn't be able to fit into unless she lost twenty pounds, and a thousand other useless toiletries. Poor Mrs. Espinosa. How could she be so intent on making herself pretty when a single glance in the mirror should have been enough to convince her that it was a lost cause?

Maybe that's what happens when people get old, Snake mused.

He offered to carry the old lady's packages. Loaded down like a
mule, he had to struggle to make it to the car. Placing the packages
on the ground, he unlocked the passenger door and helped Mrs.
Espinosa get settled.

Then he opened the trunk to stow her purchases.

A stench of putrefaction billowed up into his face. He slammed
the trunk shut, threw the packages in the back seat and sped out of
the parking lot.

"What's the matter, my boy? You look like you've seen a ghost."

What he'd seen was worse than any ghost.

There was a hockey bag in the trunk, with a lock of blond hair
sticking out through its closed zipper. Snake had never seen a dead
body before, but the smell made it clear that he'd been driving
around with one all day.

He needed to drop off Mrs. Espinosa as quickly as possible and
then call Jimbo.

He was doing a hundred kilometres an hour in a fifty zone.
He eased up on the gas pedal. The last thing he needed was to be
stopped by the police.

The old lady had been staring at him since they'd left the shopping centre.

"What's wrong, my boy? You're white as a sheet."

Lessard was still on his phone as he walked to the car.

"What we have so far is still very preliminary," Fernandez said.
"Mongeau started out as a general practitioner in the South Shore
of Montreal. Then he got interested in politics. During the 1984
federal election, he was a Liberal candidate in the constituency
of Taschereau, where he lost. From 1986 to 1994, he was principal secretary to the prime minister. He was known to be a man of
influence, heavily involved in party financing. He was named executive director of a hospital in the Quebec City area in 1997. He held

the job until last year, when he took a similar post at the Montreal General Hospital."

"Do we know why?"

"Apparently his wife pressured him to come back to Montreal. She was tired of only seeing him on weekends. I talked to the chairman of the board at the General. According to him, Mongeau was an excellent manager, well respected by medical staff, very hard-working. He had a reputation for being fair and, above all, very well connected."

"Any criminal record?"

"No, but I found a complaint for sexual harassment dating back to 1978. It seems to have been dropped. It's the only blot I've found on his record so far."

Lessard opened the door of his rust-covered Corolla and got behind the wheel. They would have to go on digging. They needed to find an opening.

"Nice work, Nadja. Keep searching. If there's a chink in the guy's armour, we need to know what it is. Have you checked his bank records?"

"Not yet, I haven't had time. But I did speak to the president of Atlas, a company that specializes in biometrics."

"And?"

"He says the fingerprint-recognition market has been growing like crazy since the late 1990s. Apparently, there are all kinds of uses for the technology. It's incorporated into safes and strongboxes, but also into more common items like computer mice and cellphones."

Lessard was suddenly seeing his ancient Nokia in a new light. "Is it really that widespread?"

"The market is exploding. Several of these applications are readily available."

"We'd better widen our search. If I'm hearing you right, the victim's index finger could be used to open a safe, to get into a computer, or to access a cellphone."

"Among other things."

This wasn't good news. They were already groping in the dark. The fact that the commander had called a press conference for 7:00 p.m. didn't help matters.

Lessard felt a bout of heartburn coming on, as he did whenever his stress levels rose. "Okay. Stay focused on the guy's bank records. As for biometrics, I'll have Sirois question Mongeau's wife. For now, that'll be our starting point."

He hung up and spent a few seconds scouring his memory. He had a nagging sense that he'd forgotten something. But it faded away. He put his key in the Corolla's ignition.

Killing a man to get his finger.

What kind of messed-up world are we living in?

14

Lessard stopped off at a convenience store and bought four cups of coffee. Arriving at Mongeau's office, he gave a cup to Pearson, one to Adams, and one to Adams's assistant.

Was the guy's name Perron or Charron?

He could never remember.

He took a gulp of coffee that scalded his tongue and the roof of his mouth. He brought a hand to his lips, swearing like a sailor. "Aaargh! What do they make this stuff with, a goddamn blast furnace?"

Pearson was still working at the computer.

"Hey, Victor. Check this out."

Lessard stepped behind his colleague, who scrolled through a series of photographs of the victim taken from various angles.

"Are these the pictures Doug took?"

"No, they're from the CD that we found on the desk. This answers your question. The disc was left here intentionally by the killer."

Lessard licked his lips reflexively.

Why had the murderer taken these photographs? Was he sending them a message? If so, what was it?

"Is that all?"

"I checked the URL on the label. It's a blog, created from a public IP address."

Lessard knew almost nothing about the digital world. Pearson might as well have been speaking Chinese.

"A what?"

"A blog. It's like a personal website where you can post online content for free. There are millions of them out there, on subjects as varied as curling, the Kennedy assassination, and erectile dysfunction."

"Are you telling me anybody can create one of these things? Like, for instance, I could build a site devoted to Muhammad Ali?"

"Or your vacation on Lake Pohenegamook."

Lessard had taken his family there two summers ago. Their last ceasefire before everything went to hell.

"Hey, show a little respect. Lake Pohenegamook is really nice."

"Sure," Pearson said, grinning. "It even has its own monster."

Lessard ignored the jibe. "If there's a website, then there's got to be some kind of electronic trail. We should be able to track down the person who set it up, right?"

"If the blog came from a private computer, yes. But in this case, it originated on a public network."

"Meaning?"

"It was created at an internet café in the Quebec City area."

"Okay. Are there security cameras at internet cafés? Registration requirements?"

"None."

"So we have no way of knowing who's behind this blog?"

"Barring a stroke of luck, no. I've put in a call to the café. I'm waiting to hear back from the manager."

"If you go to the website, what do you find?"

"That's the weird part. You don't find anything, except the same text that was on the label of the CD: *Error message: 10161416.*"

"Maybe the site is where the killer plans to publish the pictures that are on the disc. What do you think the error message means?"

"Typically, an error message appears when an operating system or program runs into a problem. The number usually indicates the nature of the problem."

"Does the number on this message refer to a well-known type of problem?"

"No. I checked the standard error messages that are used on current systems. None of them matched this one. I thought it might be a reference to an anniversary or a phone number, but there are too many digits."

"What if it's the combination to a safe?" Lessard asked.

"A safe equipped with fingerprint recognition? Interesting idea. But in that case, why would the murderer be giving us the combination?"

Lessard was silent for a moment.

"Honestly, I don't know," he said at last. "But it's too soon to be ruling out possibilities. Keep looking through the pictures. Maybe they hold some message or hidden meaning we haven't figured out yet. The killer's trying to tell us something, that's for sure. Otherwise he wouldn't have left us the disc." Lessard picked up Pearson's Coke can from the desk and took a sip. "Find out from the manager of the café if it's possible to identify the person who created the website. And check with Adams to see if there are any prints on the disc, and whether he can say what kind of camera the pictures were taken with."

"He's already working on that."

"Good. Anything else?"

"Yeah. I found something pretty interesting. Have a look."

Pearson clicked on a file and an image came up on the screen. It showed the victim, Jacques Mongeau, kneeling on an earthen floor, his hands manacled and chained to a wall. He was stark naked. A woman in skin-tight latex pants stood over him brandishing a riding crop. The dominatrix's pendulous breasts hung a few centimetres from Mongeau's mouth. Lessard had seen this woman before. Where? The staging was very suggestive, very hardcore.

Lessard stared in astonishment.

"BDSM?"

Pearson nodded.

"Who's the woman?"

Pearson pointed to the family photograph on the windowsill.

"His wife."

Lessard made an effort to overcome his surprise.

"Are there others?"

"Fifteen pictures in all. Based on lighting and framing, I'd say they were taken by an amateur, using a digital camera. It's just the husband and wife in some shots. In others, additional couples have joined in."

"Swingers?"

"Sure looks like it."

Lessard hesitated. What did this mean?

"Did you recognize any of the other people?"

"No. Most of them are masked."

"How twisted do the photos get? Any animals? Children?"

"No, no. As far as I can tell, it's just consenting adults."

Lessard frowned, perplexed. Was this a real lead, or just another dead end? He had trouble imagining the prime minister's former counsellor bound to a bed, getting whipped by a latex-clad dominatrix. But the pictures spoke for themselves.

"Was this stuff well hidden?"

"Not if you know anything about computers."

"Could the killer have copied the pictures?"

"With ease, either by emailing them to himself, downloading them to a USB flash drive, or burning them to a CD. I can tell you right now that they weren't emailed."

"Were they downloaded or burned to a CD?"

"There's no way to know."

Pearson looked at Lessard. "Victor, do you think the killer might post these photographs on his blog?"

"Maybe." Lessard thought for a moment. "Would it be possible to put the blog under surveillance to identify the killer? Like setting a digital trap?"

"Absolutely. But if he's careful and sticks to public computers, we won't have much chance of catching him. Do you want me to request a warrant?"

"No. Let's not waste time on that for the moment. What else have you got?"

"Not much. There are a lot of emails, including some exchanges with the former prime minister, but nothing that hints at a link with his death."

Lessard looked over at a metal file cabinet in the corner. Adams and his assistant were busy lifting prints from it.

"What about physical files? Have any gone missing or been tampered with?"

"I had a look with Ms. Daoust earlier. She didn't notice anything out of place."

Lessard cleared his throat. "So what are we looking at? A guy who's tight with the former prime minister and a fan of kinky sex, who gets murdered and then has his finger cut off. The whole thing is clear as mud!"

Lessard approached Doug Adams.

"What have you got, Doug? Any prints?"

"A ton of them. A ton of fibres, too. That's the problem. The desk, in particular, is covered with prints. If the killer left any and we have him in the database, we'll identify him. But it's going to take time."

Lessard let out a growl. He had nothing definite, nothing he could work with. It was maddening. Tanguay would be only too pleased to hand off the case.

The detective sergeant made a face. This goddamn heartburn was driving him nuts! "Pearson, the commander's called a press conference for seven o'clock. Let's all meet at six-thirty to debrief. Doug, the minute you come up with anything —"

"Yes, Victor. You'll be the first to know."

Lessard walked out, hands in his pockets, scowling. The image of the two caribou heads crept back into his mind. The feeling that he'd forgotten something was nagging at him.

A glass of Scotch would make everything so much simpler.

15

I can't say how long I stood there on the sidewalk gazing at the health food store. It felt like I was rooted to the spot, incapable of the smallest movement, as though an invisible bubble had descended, making me its prisoner.

I scoured my memory and inspected the wall minutely, searching for the slightest difference, but I couldn't find any. Everything was the same — the ornamentation, the colour of the stonework, and, above all, those inimitable gargoyles.

Everything was the same except for one detail: George's bar was nowhere to be seen.

I walked into the establishment.

A young store clerk with a ring through his lower lip was working languidly at the counter. Standing in front of him, a man with a deeply lined face was waiting to be served. I gazed at the shelves, the walls, and the faded linoleum, as though these things might reveal some truth that I hadn't yet thought of.

The dimensions of the space were roughly the same as those of the bar. But the similarity ended there. Though its walls were configured the same way, the health food store, crammed with items of all kinds, bore no resemblance to the minimalist interior of the bar.

Hesitantly, I approached the clerk, who seemed unaware of my presence.

"Excuse me. I'd like some information, please. How long has this store been open?"

The clerk turned and looked at me with a dazed expression. Keen intelligence clearly wasn't his defining trait.

"Huh?"

Impatiently, I repeated the question.

"Uh … since nine o'clock this morning."

"No, I mean, how long has the store been located here?"

"Like, in this building?"

"Yes."

"Since 2000, I think. Before that, we were on the other side of the street."

Which meant they'd occupied the space for more than five years. How could that be?

"What was here before that?"

"I can't remember, exactly. I think it was a dry-cleaning place."

"Are you sure?"

"Uh … yeah."

"It wasn't a bar, by any chance?"

The young man shook his head. I murmured a vague thank-you and left the store. My head began to spin. I sat down on the curb and vomited between my legs.

What was happening to me?

First it had been Miles's apartment. Now it was the bar where I'd had a cup of coffee in his company. In each instance, the space had been radically transformed between my two visits.

These discoveries were forcing me to rethink the whole situation. Changing the appearance of an apartment in a few hours was one thing. Moving one business out of its premises and replacing it with an entirely different business was something else altogether. The task would have been impossibly complex.

I remembered a movie starring Michael Douglas in which an

elaborate scheme had been concocted to make the central character believe that someone was trying to deprive him of his property
and take his life.

Did Miles have the means to pull off a hoax of that magnitude?
This wasn't Hollywood.

Nobody had that kind of power in real life.

Trois-Pistoles

Through the window, Laurent watched as tendrils of mist rose off
the river and dissipated into the air.

Still strapped to his bed, shaking uncontrollably, he had spent
the last few hours yelling.

"Waldorf! Let me go!"

But the son of a bitch wouldn't even answer.

Then a moment came when Laurent couldn't hear anything on
the other side of the door. Was the man still in the house? If so,
what was he up to?

He wished he could free one arm. But despite pouring every
ounce of his strength into the effort, despite tugging in every
conceivable direction, he couldn't do it. Waldorf was manifestly
skilled at restricting a person's movements. Laurent's desperate
struggles had achieved nothing except to flay the skin from his
wrists.

He was dizzy and nauseated.

He knew it wasn't Waldorf's injection that had made him unwell.
No, the problem was that Laurent desperately needed alcohol. Just
thinking about it made his bones ache.

His head was spinning. He began to scream.

"Waldorf! Waldorf!"

•   •   •

In the living room, Waldorf was peacefully immersed in a book. Now and then he would mark a passage with a yellow high-lighter.

Betraying no emotion, he took small sips from a cup of green tea while the screaming ran its course. Only after several minutes of silence did he finally stand up.

Noiselessly, he stepped into the room.

Laurent looked at him with haggard features. A thread of drool hung from his left cheek. Without a word, Waldorf jammed two tablets into the young man's mouth and forced him to swallow some water. A fresh wave of energy washed through Laurent, and he began struggling once more.

"Let me go, Waldorf! You have no right to —"

Waldorf smiled and patted the jacket pocket into which he had slipped the gun.

"On the contrary," he said, cutting Laurent off, "I have every right."

"You want to talk? Fine. Talk!"

"Not yet. I promised Miles I'd wean you off the booze first."

Laurent's eyes narrowed. He hated this man.

"Stop it, Waldorf! You never spoke to Miles! You know that's not possible!"

With a sigh, Waldorf left the room. Would he succeed in break-ing the young man's will?

I no longer had enough strength to think.

What are you supposed to do when reality turns upside down? What are you supposed to believe when all the things you took for granted turn out to be wrong?

I remained seated on the sidewalk, hoping to get over my leth-argy. After a moment, I heard the door of the health food store swing open.

Aware that someone was behind me, I swung around. The man who had been waiting at the counter when I entered the store was now approaching. He bent down. I tried to brush some snow over my vomit, but he glimpsed it.

"Are you okay?"

I wanted to tell him I was fine, but I couldn't control myself. The tears started to flow again. It was my second crying jag in the space of a few hours. Hardly my usual style.

"I'll be all right," I said. "Thanks for asking. I'm just having a really bad day."

Then the weeping started afresh. There was nothing I could do to stop it. The man pulled a checkered handkerchief from his pocket and handed it to me.

"Go on, give your nose a good blow. It'll make you feel better."

I did as he instructed. He waited patiently while I calmed down.

"I'm sorry," I said. "My memory's been playing nasty tricks on me today."

"Oh, I know all about that," he said. "And I have bad news for you. It doesn't get better with age. But in your case, I think there may be hope."

"What do you mean?"

"I overheard your conversation with the cashier. I didn't want to seem like I was eavesdropping, so I didn't interrupt. But you're quite right, there used to be a bar at this location. A jazz bar. It closed down years ago. I wasn't a regular customer, but every so often I'd stop in for a drink. It was run by two brothers, Tom and George Griffin."

I was on my feet in an instant.

Hearing the man talk about the bar and an owner named George filled me with hope. Here at last was proof that I hadn't imagined the whole story, that I hadn't fallen prey to hallucinations.

But as my mind processed everything the man had just said, my spirits fell.

Closed down years ago.

"When did it close down?"

"If I remember correctly, it would have been sometime in the early eighties."

I described the bar in great detail, wanting to be sure there was no confusion.

"Yes, that's it exactly," the man said. "You have an excellent memory. You must have visited the place. With your parents, perhaps?"

I almost replied that such a scenario would have been impossible. I was in kindergarten at the time, my parents didn't like jazz, and anyway, we lived in Quebec City. But I didn't want to contradict the man.

I tried to ignore the strangeness of the situation and focused on the questions I needed to ask. "What happened to George? Where can I find him?"

The man's expression grew sombre. "I'm afraid you can't. George had a serious motorcycle accident in the late seventies. He's surely dead by now. Tom never got over it. He started drinking heavily. That's what led to the bar closing down."

I stared at the man, expecting him to start laughing at any moment. He did nothing of the kind.

I didn't believe in ghosts, but I felt fear creeping into me.

How could I have met George if he was dead?

It took an effort to fight down the anxiety that was threatening to overwhelm me.

If George was dead, then I had lost my only lead. How could I possibly hope to find Miles?

"What about his brother?" I asked.

"Tom? He opened another bar on Monkland Avenue. I think it's called the Old Orchard Pub. But it's not the same kind of place. In the old days, people used to come from all over to listen to jazz here. All the local greats performed at this bar: Sandy Simpson, Jamal Cherraf, Felix Redding ..."

"Hang on. Did you say Jamal Cherraf?"

"Yes. Great trumpet player."

Miles's neighbour!

How could I have forgotten him?

"Have you seen Jamal lately?" I asked.

"No. I don't know what became of him."

I thanked the man warmly and gave him back his handkerchief.

"I'm sorry. It's soiled now."

He put it back in his pocket, unconcerned.

"Aren't we all?"

I considered calling Ariane to ask for help, but decided against it. She'd try to persuade me to go back to the hospital, which was out of the question. I now had two good leads, which, with a little luck, might help me find Miles.

Those leads were named Jamal Cherraf and Tom Griffin.

I walked back down Blueridge Crescent and turned right onto Côte-des-Neiges. The temperature was falling fast. I buttoned my coat and turned up my collar.

As I walked, I kept an eye out.

Was the man in the duffle coat still watching me? At one point, I thought I spotted him, but as I drew closer I saw that it was just a pimply teenager shooting the breeze with his friends.

The red-brick building came into view. The ground-floor apartment, the one Miles had led me into, was entirely dark. I pressed my nose against a window, trying to see inside, but the curtains were drawn.

Had the old lady gone out to run errands?

A light was on in the apartment on the second floor. Slowly, I went up the stairs to Jamal's apartment.

A young olive-skinned woman opened the door. She was holding a plump baby in her arms. She reminded me of a friend I'd had in elementary school, who, after sneaking a peek into my diary, was hurt to discover that she wasn't listed among my best friends — a list I updated regularly back then.

Children can be so cruel.

"I'm sorry to bother you. I'm looking for Jamal Cherraf. He's a jazz musician."

The young woman looked at me strangely.

"If this is a joke, it's in very poor taste."

She started to close the door, but I blocked it.

"I apologize if I've said something to offend you. I certainly didn't mean to. But I need to speak to Jamal. It's a matter of great urgency. If you know where to reach him, please let him know that Simone Fortin is looking for him. He knows me," I added with conviction.

The young woman studied my face.

"You seem sincere. Come in."

My hostess introduced herself as Raïcha and asked me to wait a few minutes while she put the child to bed.

I sat down on the couch and looked around the room.

I wasn't surprised to note that the configuration and dimensions were the same, but the furnishings were entirely different from what I'd seen when Miles and I visited Jamal.

The difference didn't upset me. I was getting used to this.

Raïcha emerged from the bedroom and put on a kettle. Without a word, she gave me a cup of tea and sat cross-legged in front of me.

"So you're looking for Jamal Cherraf?"

"Yes."

"You know him?"

"I met him for the first time yesterday. Here, in fact. He played the trumpet for me."

The young woman laughed out loud.

"I'd be very surprised if that actually happened."

"Why?"

"Because I was just holding Jamal in my arms. He's asleep."

"You mean your son —".

"He's the son of my roommate, Dalila. He's ten months old. I babysit when his mother's in class."

"And his name is Jamal?"

"That's right. Jamal Cherraf."

A child?

Suddenly, the walls and ceiling began to spin.

16

Westmount

Well-kept sidewalks, elegant homes, impeccable (but empty) parks, leafy green spaces, stylized streetlamps, spotless streets unmarred by potholes: the wealthy hilltop municipality of Westmount resembled Nice. Minus the sun, the sea, and the bikini-clad starlets.

Well-ordered Westmount was bereft of pedestrians, unless they were Filipina housekeepers walking their employers' pure-bred dogs. Prosperous Westmount was perfect and luminous, its skin-deep beauty worthy of magazine covers. But you couldn't actually *live* there. Neighbouring Montreal, by comparison, with all its grime, squalor, and disorder, was Westmount's poor relation.

As Lessard parked his car in front of the imposing stone house on The Boulevard, it occurred to him that the division between the two sister cities couldn't have been clearer if it had been marked with a bright red line.

Going up the front walk, he counted the floors of the house. He stopped at four and rang the bell.

A young man of about twenty opened up. His eyes were red. He was one of the victim's sons.

"My name is Victor Lessard. I'm a detective sergeant with the Montreal Police."

"I'm Sacha."

The cop wished he could have found comforting words, but he had to settle for ordinary condolences.

The young man stood aside, and Lessard stepped into a large front hall dominated by an impressive crystal chandelier. Respectfully, he removed his shoes before advancing along the marble floor.

Sasha led him into a luxurious living room, tastefully decorated in subdued tones, with dark leather furniture. A fire was crackling in the massive brick fireplace.

Sirois was seated on a couch, talking to Hélène Lacoursière, the dead man's wife. She stood up to greet the detective sergeant.

She was wearing a dark outfit. Lessard guessed her to be in her early fifties, considerably younger than her husband. Feeling ill at ease, he couldn't resist a glance in the direction of her bosom, which he'd been scrutinizing on the computer screen just a few minutes earlier. Only now did he realize what a beautiful woman she was, with her classic features and distinguished demeanour.

Suddenly, he felt out of place in his socks and worn-out leather jacket.

"Detective Lessard? I'm Hélène Lacoursière. Your colleague let me know you'd be coming."

She seemed to be bearing up well. He took a deep breath.

"I'm sorry we have to meet under such difficult circumstances, ma'am. Allow me to extend my condolences to you and your family."

"Thank you. Commander Tanguay called earlier to offer his support."

Lessard was taken aback, but he maintained his outward composure. By what right was Tanguay sticking his nose into his investigation?

"Believe me, ma'am, we'll do everything in our power to apprehend the culprit as soon as possible."

She looked at him with a determined expression.

"The commander said the same thing. I'm entirely at your disposal, Detective. I want the person who did this caught. And punished."

Her eyes filled with tears, but she kept her composure. Now that the initial shock had passed, she was making an effort to be strong.

"It's my sons who are suffering most. Sacha is coping, but Louis has shut himself up in his bedroom."

Lessard spoke gently.

"These things take time, ma'am."

He led the woman back to the couch, where she sat down beside Sirois, who hadn't moved. Lessard pulled up a Louis XIV chair.

"With your permission, I'd like to ask you some questions. A few may touch on subjects that Detective Sirois has already asked you about. Others may embarrass or even shock you. I apologize in advance, but the first few hours after a crime is committed are crucial."

"I understand, Detective. Go ahead."

"I'd also like your permission to have Detective Sirois look through your husband's things. Did he have an office in the house?"

"Yes. Sacha, would you please take Mr. Sirois to your father's office?"

When the two had left, Lessard pulled out his notebook and sat up straighter in his chair. "First of all, when was the last time you saw or spoke to your husband?"

"This morning, around ten-thirty. I called to let him know I'd bought a new painting. Jacques is ..." She wiped away a tear. "I'm sorry. Jacques was an art lover."

"Did he seem changed in any way? Unlike his usual self?"

"No. We were planning to spend the weekend in the country. He was going to pick me up at the end of the day."

"Did you get the impression, lately, that he was more preoccupied than usual? More anxious? Different?"

"My husband was deeply involved in politics. Jacques was a very active person, full of energy. He played tennis three or four times a week. He was highly skilled at managing stress. In thirty years of marriage, I rarely saw him upset, despite the heavy responsibilities he had to deal with every day. I didn't notice any change in his behaviour during the last few weeks."

"Did he have money troubles?"

Her laugh caught Lessard by surprise.

"Let's put it this way, Detective. If Jacques ever did have money troubles, they ended the day he married me."

Now Lessard remembered the woman. Hélène Lacoursière was the daughter of Charles Lacoursière, the telecom magnate.

"I'm sorry if my questions seem strange, but we don't want to overlook any possible angle. Was your husband a gambler?"

"No. We did travel to Las Vegas occasionally to catch Cirque du Soleil or Céline Dion, but I had to use every trick in the book to get Jacques to join me at the blackjack table."

"Did he drink? Use drugs?"

The woman gave Lessard an offended look. "Jacques was always careful about his health. He drank sparingly, just a glass of wine with meals now and then. And he certainly didn't use drugs."

"Tell me about his career …"

The woman gave Lessard an account very similar to what he'd heard from Fernandez earlier, mentioning nothing that even hinted at a lead. Jacques Mongeau had risen fast in the world, thanks partly to his political connections and partly to the influence of his wife's family.

"Did he have any enemies that you knew of?"

She chuckled drily. "He was a politician, Mr. Lessard. In politics, enemies come with the job. Jacques used to tell me that he couldn't trust anyone, not even the people he was close to, not even his own party allies."

"Do you have anyone in mind? Can you think of someone in particular who might have had a reason to —"

"To kill him? Honestly, nobody comes to mind. It's been a long time since D'Arcy McGee."

Lessard didn't get the reference. History had never been his favourite subject in school. By now, he only had a few questions left, and he was no closer to a solid lead.

"Ms. Lacoursière, do you know anything about biometrics?"

"A little. Isn't that the technology behind retinal scans, things like that?

"Exactly. Did your husband have a safe or a lock that made use of fingerprint recognition?"

Hélène Lacoursière was clearly taken aback.

"We have a safe deposit box at the bank that requires two keys. That's it."

"Could there be some other item you're not thinking of, like, say, a computer or a cellphone?"

She frowned. "No. If Jacques had bought a gadget like that, I'd have known about it. Technology wasn't really his thing. Why do you ask?"

Lessard hesitated. He didn't want to be insensitive. On the other hand, this was the dead man's wife. She had a right to know.

"The murderer cut off one of his fingers, and we're trying to figure out why."

She put a hand to her mouth in horror. Tears began to trickle down her cheeks.

"Good God, how awful! Did he suffer? Was he tortured?"

"The medical examiner believes death occurred in a few seconds," Lessard said with empathy. "He was already dead when the killer removed his index finger."

That did it. The floodgates opened. Hélène Lacoursière could no longer contain herself.

She began to weep.

Lessard wished he could have taken her in his arms and comforted her, but he sat frozen in his chair, looking at his notebook, unable to move.

He decided not to bring up the kinky photographs.

Not now.

Snake parked the car in the disused garage on Hochelaga Street. Jimbo insisted on verifying the truth of his friend's claim. He put on work gloves and partially unzipped the hockey bag. He fell to his knees.

"*Fuck!*"

"What do we do now?" Snake asked.

"Dump the body, then deliver the car to Tool, like we planned."

"Forget it. First of all, Tool will never take the car. The cops have probably already put out a search alert. And second, if we dump the body, we could end up getting charged with murder ourselves. We stole a car. Lots of cars. But we never killed anyone."

"Fine," Jimbo said. "Let's just park it somewhere and walk away."

"Our prints are all over it."

"We'll wipe it down first."

"And risk erasing the killer's prints, too?" Snake asked.

"So what? Not our problem."

"We're talking about a murder, Jimbo."

"Like I said, not our problem."

"We can't just sit on our asses and do nothing while there's a murderer on the loose. That body in the trunk could have been somebody you cared about. What if weeks go by before the cops even notice?"

"If it makes you feel any better, we'll call 911. Anonymously."

"Have you forgotten that our prints are all over the car?"

"I keep telling you, man, this isn't our problem. We don't give a shit."

"I do, Jimbo."

"You do what?"

"Give a shit. I'm not walking away from this."

Jimbo lost his temper and shoved his friend hard.

"So now you're a good citizen, all of a sudden? What do you want to do?"

"Notify the police."

"Are you out of your fucking mind?! They'll throw us in the can! I'm not going back inside, you hear me?"

Snake was silent for a few seconds.

"There may be another way …"

17

This time, I'm the one driving the black sedan. I'm advancing at high speed through a brick tunnel that has gaps in its walls. Menacing eyes glare at me from behind each opening. A man is lying on the road ahead. At the last instant, he turns, screaming. The car squashes him with a noise like a watermelon bursting on the ground. Miles! The car stops. A group of men comes toward me. I'm led into a dark building with barred windows. A mental asylum.

I opened my eyes.

Without moving, I looked out the window. Through the glass, I saw the naked, twisted branches of a tree.

I lifted my head. It took me a few seconds to recognize the room.

I was stretched out on the couch, and Raïcha was dabbing my forehead with a damp washcloth. There was a worried expression on her face.

"Are you okay? You seem to have had some kind of shock."

I didn't deny it.

At this point, the sensible course of action would have been to go back to the hospital. I was feeling confused, and the fact that I had passed out was a bad sign.

"You may not be aware of it, but you were talking while you were unconscious."

"What did I say?"

"You kept repeating two names. George and Miles. Also some words. I didn't catch them all, but I heard 'run,' 'late,' and 'lid.'"

My thoughts were tumbling over one another. I felt like a

prisoner in a world where reality and delusion were locked in a struggle, with my sanity as the battlefield.

"Will Jamal's mother be coming home soon?" I finally asked.

"Dalila? Not for another couple of hours. Would you like to wait for her?"

I accepted Raïcha's offer.

All of this had been so unexpected, so incredible, that I needed time to gather my wits. I also wanted to talk to Dalila and question her about Jamal.

But half an hour later, I couldn't sit still anymore. For one thing, the baby had woken up crying three times. For another, I was getting more and more obsessed with the idea that Tom Griffin might be able to help me track down Miles.

"Do you have a phone book?" I asked Raïcha.

Just then, the baby started to cry again. The stridency of his wails made me wince. Raïcha stood up with a sigh.

"He has an ear infection. I don't think the antibiotics are doing any good." She walked away in the direction of the bedroom. "The phone book is in the cupboard above the sink."

I had no difficulty finding a number for the Old Orchard Pub. I wanted to ask Raïcha for permission to use the phone, but she'd disappeared into the bedroom and clearly had her hands full with the baby. After a moment of hesitation, I pulled out my cellphone and keyed in the number.

"Old Orchard Pub," a woman answered in a nasal voice.

"Hello. May I speak to Tom Griffin?"

"Who?"

"Tom Griffin."

"Just a minute, please," the voice said.

A chorus of conversations was audible in the background. Among them I could hear the woman who had answered. She was speaking loudly to another woman.

"Someone's calling for Tom Griffin."

"Okay, I'll take it."

I heard the handset being picked up.

"Hi, this is Tina. You're looking for Tom Griffin?"

The voice was warm and friendly.

"Yes. I was told he owned the pub."

"He sold it last year."

"Do you know where I can find him?" I asked.

"Hold on. I think I have his number somewhere."

She put down the handset.

I heard her talking to a man, but I couldn't understand what they were saying. A full minute went by before she picked up the handset again.

"This is your lucky day. The bartender gave me an address and phone number. I can't promise that they're still good."

I scribbled down the information in a hurry.

"Thanks very much."

"No problem. Listen, I don't know why you're looking for Tom, but if you haven't met him before, I should warn you that he's kind of unusual."

"Unusual?"

"As in, drunk. All day, every day. He can get pretty nasty. Even violent."

"Thanks for the tip."

I immediately called Tom Griffin's number. I let it ring a dozen times before giving up.

No voice mail. Now what?

Should I wait for Jamal's mother to return or take a chance and go to the address that Tina had given me, hoping to catch Griffin at home?

I made up my mind on the spur of the moment. I'd go to Tom Griffin's place, hoping he could direct me to his brother, George.

I'd already made plenty of bad decisions over the course of this nightmarish day, but I swore to myself that if Griffin couldn't help me, I really would give up this time.

Before saying goodbye to Raïcha, I made her promise to have Dalila call me as soon as she got back. But I had no illusions about the chances that Dalila would be able to help me.

Or Tom Griffin either, for that matter.

Griffin lived in Notre-Dame-de-Grâce. I'd have to take a taxi to his place, but I was out of cash. I walked toward Blueridge Crescent, where I knew I could find an ATM.

Out of habit, I turned into the alley that I took every day on my way to the office. The shortcut would save me a couple of minutes.

Looking up, I saw a dark, moonless sky. Night had fallen.

I had a hundred metres to go before emerging from the lightless alley onto the street. Suddenly, a silhouette loomed straight ahead of me, blocking my path.

The sweep of a distant headlight beam briefly illuminated the duffle coat. An instant later, I was running as fast as my bad ankle would carry me in the opposite direction. In that moment of illumination, I had seen the man's face.

It wasn't Miles!

I didn't know why this stranger had been following me for the last several hours, but I had no trouble imagining the worst possible reasons.

Easily outpacing me, he caught me halfway up the alley.

His hand on my shoulder almost knocked me off my feet. Instinctively, I spun around and hit him in the face with my bag. A few metres away, to my left, I spotted a fire escape and started to climb.

I'd passed the first landing when the man seized my calf. I kicked out hard, catching him in the temple, and continued to ascend.

Desperate for help, I was yelling and banging on doors and windows as I made my way up the fire escape. Finally, I realized that there were no lights on in the building. It was empty. In my haste to flee my pursuer, I hadn't even noticed.

Short of a miracle, there was no chance of anyone coming to my rescue. I tried to kick a door open, but it refused to yield. Hearing the man's footsteps on the metal stairs, I took off again without a backward glance.

My only chance of escape lay above me, on the rooftops. I rushed up to the fourth and final landing.

From there, access to the roof was by means of a rusty ladder bolted to the brick wall. I gave the ladder a tug to test its solidity, then started to climb.

As I swung myself onto the roof, the man was already coming up the metal rungs. When he came within arm's length, I started hitting him with my bag. He wrenched it from me and sent it plummeting to the pavement four floors down.

I set off at a run, blindly clambering over the steel beams that littered the roof's surface. Suddenly I lost my footing and fell hard, scraping my hands badly. Hearing the man panting at my back, I got up and managed to advance a few more metres.

The man was about to grab me when the surface suddenly opened up beneath my feet and I felt myself falling into a void.

I cried out in terror.

The roof had collapsed under my weight.

"Mom, why is Simone in the hospital?"

"I just told you, Mathilde. She was hit by a car."

"Didn't she look both ways before crossing? I always look left and right before I cross the street. Sometimes, I have to wait until the little man lights up. And if I see the red hand, that means I have to stop, right, Mom?"

"Right, sweetie."

"Last week, Axelle crossed the street without looking, and her dad slapped her."

"Jean-Pierre? Really?"

"Yes. Axelle told me. He's meaner than you."

"Ah. Well …"

"Mom?"

"Mmm?"

"Is Simone going to die?"

Ariane smiled and looked at her daughter.

"No, my love. She'll only be in the hospital for a few days."

"Mom! Keep your eyes on the road!"

Ariane was striding along the corridor, holding a pile of magazines in one hand and her daughter's hand in the other. The child was clinging to her cherished stuffed toy.

"I'll let her borrow him, okay, Mom? Until she feels better."

"That's very nice of you, sweetie."

"But she can't keep him. She has to give him back."

"Of course. He's your frog."

"That's right. He's my frog. Mom, why does it smell so weird in here?"

"That's just how hospitals smell, sweetie."

"How come? Don't they clean up?"

Ariane was momentarily stumped. Did illness have a smell all its own?

"Sure, they do. But the building is quite old and … oh, look, here we are."

Ariane gently pushed open the door to room 222. A boy of about fifteen was asleep on the bed, his head wrapped in a bandage.

"Are we in the wrong room, Mom?"

Ariane was a little early, but Simone should be here.

She checked the room number again.

"Come on, Mathilde."

"Where are we going, Mom?"

"To ask the nurse where Simone is."

"I'm tired of walking."

"Come on now, sweetie."

Ariane pulled the child along.

"Did she change rooms?"

"I guess so."

Ariane suddenly had a sense of foreboding.

"But maybe Simone went home, huh, Mom?"

"D-d-don't move."

Braced over the opening, the man had grabbed the collar of my coat and was doing his utmost to lift me back through the gap onto the solid part of the roof.

Making an effort to stay calm, I avoided looking down into the emptiness beneath my feet. I could hear the man grunting and straining. After what felt like an eternity, he succeeded in gripping me under the armpits and hauling me up to safety.

As the man caught his breath beside me, I gazed through the gaping hole. If he hadn't grabbed me, I'd have fallen at least two floors onto a pile of debris. A dizzying surge of fear struck me, and I had to sit down.

We were silent for a while. At last I ventured a glance in the man's direction.

He couldn't have been older than twenty-five. His face was ravaged by acne, and he was dressed like a hobo. This was the man I had mistaken for Miles!

Just then, he turned to me.

"You okay?"

Fear gave way to anger. I threw myself at him, fists flailing. He tried to fend me off as best he could.

"You goddamn maniac! You could have killed me!"

"No, w-w-wait ..."

I gave him a hard kick in the shin that doubled him over.

"What the hell do you want from me?"

I was beside myself. I leaped at him, trying to scratch his face, but he seized my wrists and managed to subdue me.

Kneeling on my forearms, he pinned me down firmly but not roughly. I noticed, not without pride, that I had split his lower lip in the skirmish.

"I d-d-don't want …"

He had a stammer.

"… to hurt you."

I looked into his eyes. He was telling the truth.

The man seemed incapable of the slightest cruelty. Indeed, his bloody mouth almost gave him the appearance of a martyr. He loosened his grip, and I sat up. But I wasn't ready to forgive him quite yet. This nutcase had put me danger.

"What do you want?"

"I d-d-didn't mean to s-scare you. I just wanted to t-t-talk. B-b-but then you ran away."

"What did you expect me to do when I saw a stranger following me?"

"S-sorry."

"Who are you?"

"Gustave. M-m-my name … is Gustave."

The man had such an air of innocence about him that he seemed almost simple-minded. I softened. He had saved my life, after all.

"Why have you been following me, Gustave?"

He scanned the rooftops, looking anxious. "B-b-because you saw them."

"Saw who?"

He became agitated.

"You w-went to the ap-apartment. You went to the b-b-bar. You saw them."

"You mean Miles?"

His haunted eyes were darting in all directions.

"Answer me. Who? George? Jamal?"

"Shhh! You m-m-mustn't say their names."

He drew close and whispered in my ear. "Beware!"

"Beware of what, Gustave? What are you trying to say?"

"They c-can see us. They can hear us. They can c-control our minds."

"Who are you talking about?"

"The m-m-men from the other world. They're am-among us."

He jumped to his feet. Before I could react, he was going down the ladder. I reached the fire escape landing just in time to see him plunge into the shadows and vanish.

The men from the other world?

18

Lessard stopped briefly at his desk, took out the bottle of Pepto-Bismol that he kept in the drawer, and drank half. He put the bottle back in the drawer, then changed his mind and stuffed it into his jacket pocket.

They all sat down at the big table in the conference room. Sirois handed out cups of coffee. This meeting would bring everyone up to speed on the various aspects of the investigation.

Lessard went over his notes one last time and reviewed the medical examiner's report as he tried to marshal his thoughts. He had drawn up a list of points that he wanted to address.

The day was dragging on. He noticed that Pearson, who was the father of a newborn baby, had bags under his eyes. Lessard was sympathetic. He'd been there. He found himself reflecting once again on how hard it was to balance work and family in today's world.

Things were different for Sirois and Fernandez, who were both young and single.

As for Doug Adams, he'd experienced what Lessard was going through. His first marriage had fallen victim to the insidious gulf that separates those who have experienced true horror from those who haven't.

"Seeing so much pain and violence," Lessard had once observed to the police psychologist, "you develop this interior space where nothing can touch you. It's a defence mechanism, but some people perceive it as indifference, or cynicism, or coldness."

Lessard cleared his throat. Everyone stopped talking.

"We'll keep this short. The press conference starts in about half an hour."

He paused to order his thoughts. All eyes were on him.

"Okay," he said with a sigh. "Today is April 1st. Jacques Mongeau was murdered in his office between two-thirty and three-thirty this afternoon. His secretary saw the killer. She's working with Xavier Langevin to create a composite sketch, which should be ready tomorrow." He coughed. "Nguyen has taken statements from Mongeau's colleagues. Since the murder happened during the downtime after lunch, no one remembers seeing the killer." He looked at his notes before continuing. "Berger has determined that Mongeau died of stab wounds to the chest. In his opinion, the killer knew what he was doing. All the wounds were lethal. The murder weapon was probably a survival knife. I've put a similar one on the table. One side of the blade is serrated, the other is smooth. These knives are widely available. They're popular among *Rambo* fans and hunters. Our killer may fall into either category."

"Or maybe military personnel?" Fernandez suggested. "Some kind of paramilitary?"

"Could be," Lessard said. "The index finger was amputated. But Berger is categorical. The wound was inflicted post-mortem. So the killer wasn't torturing Mongeau to get information out of him. Which means we still don't have a motive for the murder, or for the amputation. Our best guess ..."

He stopped talking when the conference-room door swung open. In uniform, Commander Tanguay entered and sat at the table, facing him. The detective sergeant briefly summarized what he'd said so far. Tanguay was wearing his habitual expression of superiority.

Lessard picked up where he'd left off.

"Our best guess for the moment is that the killer needed the finger to open a safe, or to get into a computer or a cellphone equipped with fingerprint recognition."

"Why cut his throat like an animal?" Fernandez asked. "It looks like an execution."

Glances were exchanged. Lessard took a sip of coffee.

"One of these avenues may lead us to the killer," he said. "We need to figure out which one."

"And fast," Commander Tanguay added, speaking up for the first time. "As you're all aware, media scrutiny will be intense. Jacques Mongeau wasn't just some guy off the street."

A deathly silence fell over the group. Lessard glared at his superior officer. It angered him that Tanguay was pressuring the team this way. The cops needed to be encouraged, not kicked in the ass. He tried to repair the damage.

"This is a major investigation, and I know you're all doing your best. Don't get discouraged. We'll find the killer's trail sooner or later. Fernandez, what did you learn from the bank records?"

"I went through the family assets. There's a house in Westmount, a country place in the Eastern Townships, and a condo in the Florida Keys. Four cars. All paid for. Zero debt. I didn't find anything suspicious in their bank transactions. These people are loaded."

"Okay, so we can rule out unpaid debts or some kind of transaction gone wrong. And I'm betting the wife didn't have him killed for the insurance money. She could have bought and sold the guy ten times over. What else did you come up with?"

"Not much. I ran his prints through the system. They aren't on file. He had no criminal record. I found an old complaint for sexual harassment that was lodged while he was still a practising physician. I'd be surprised if there was any connection with the killing. And that pretty well covers it."

"I'll look into the harassment complaint," Lessard said. Fernandez handed him the file folder.

"Don't waste time on that, Lessard," Tanguay interjected. "It's ancient history."

Why was he sticking his nose into this?

Lessard pressed on.

"Mongeau was a former adviser to the prime minister. He was also heavily involved in party fundraising. He was named executive director of the Montreal General Hospital after occupying the same position at a hospital in Quebec City. He was a well-respected manager, but his wife told me that he'd made some enemies in politics. Which raises the question: Was the killing politically motivated?"

"Maybe he was mixed up in the sponsorship scandal," Pearson mused.

Tanguay coughed loudly, as though to register his disagreement. Lessard pretended not to hear.

"Maybe," he said. "Sirois, what have you got?"

"Nothing you don't already know. The victim's wife is Hélène Lacoursière. Her father was the guy who founded the telecom empire. She's extremely wealthy. Does a lot of charity work. She runs her own foundation, which benefits malnourished children. She's ten years younger than her husband. There are two sons: Sacha, a law graduate, and Louis, whose education ended after high school. Louis plays bass in a rock band. He's not very outgoing. I found a small amount of cannabis when I went through his bedroom."

"Which you will leave out of your written report," Tanguay said, "since it's irrelevant to the case."

Lessard was a hair's breadth from blowing up.

"Go on, Sirois."

"Ms. Lacoursière spoke to her husband for the last time around ten-thirty this morning. She didn't notice anything different about him. There'd been no changes in his behaviour over the last few months. He drank sparingly, didn't gamble, exercised regularly. To his wife's knowledge, he didn't own a safe or other device equipped with fingerprint-recognition technology. I also searched his office. He didn't have a home computer. I didn't find anything out of the ordinary among his papers. And that's about it."

"Pearson?"

While Sirois was talking, Lessard had slipped a note to Pearson, who was seated beside him: *Don't mention the kinky pictures in front of Tanguay.*

"As you all know, we found a CD containing various photographs of the crime scene. We're working on the assumption that the killer took them. Doug Adams is trying to determine what kind of camera they were taken with. There was a line of text printed on the disc label: *Error message: 10161416.* We're assuming the killer was trying to tell us something with that text, and we're trying to figure out what it might be. We're going over all the principal error messages that are normally found on computer systems. Also on the label was a web address linked to a blog, which shows no activity so far. We believe the killer may be planning to post the photographs of Mongeau's body on the blog. It was created at an internet café in the Quebec City area. After speaking to the manager and employees of the café, we have no solid information that could help identify the killer. We're thinking about connecting a digital booby trap to the blog, so we can trace the killer next time he logs in."

"Anything else?"

"I checked to see if any of Mongeau's files were missing, and I went through his computer, like you asked."

"And?"

Pearson hesitated.

"Uh … I didn't find anything. I also helped Nguyen take statements from employees who work on the same floor. Most of them have solid alibis. One of the support staffers was celebrating a birthday, so just about everybody had lunch at the same restaurant. We're still looking into the employees who don't have alibis. No suspects so far."

"Thanks, Pearson. Doug?"

Tanguay got up to go. Before leaving, he caught Lessard's eye and gave his watch a significant tap. The press conference would be starting shortly.

"Tactful as ever," the detective sergeant growled.

"We isolated forty-nine distinct prints in the office," Adams said, "in addition to those of the victim and his secretary. We're running them through the database now. So far, no hits."

Lessard poured a glass of water and drained it in one gulp.

"So that's where things stand. We still don't know much. Fernandez, keep looking into Mongeau's past. There may be something we've missed. Sirois, follow up with Berger regarding toxicology results. And show him the knife, ask if it corresponds to the murder weapon. Pearson, tell the rest of the team about the kinky photos. Try to figure out where they were taken and what kind of camera was used. That may prove helpful. But don't mention them to Tanguay." Lessard paused for a moment to make sure everyone got the message. "Oh, and Pearson, call the wife. Tell her we'll be coming by after the press conference. I want to ask her about those pictures."

He ended the meeting and hurried out of the room in a state of excitement.

7:00 p.m.

The media room was full to bursting. All the major dailies had sent reporters. Five TV networks had dispatched camera crews.

Pearson and Sirois were observing from the back of the room. Fernandez had taken a seat among the journalists and was scribbling on a sheet of paper.

Everything was going according to plan. Tanguay hadn't opened his mouth except to kick off the press conference with the usual formalities: a brief outline of the dead man's life, a terse description of the crime, and the approximate time of death.

Lessard was masterfully tight-lipped, using a variety of phrases to convey the same message: he was unable to provide details, because doing so might compromise certain aspects of the investigation.

The press conference ended. Several journalists walked out, knowing from experience that the cop wouldn't reveal anything else. Lessard was about to give a brief interview to a TV reporter when he overheard Tanguay telling another journalist that "Detective Sergeant Lessard had confirmed that he was working on a significant lead and would soon have important information to disclose."

Seething, Lessard marched over to his superior officer. Tanguay ended his interview with a declaration of absolute confidence in Victor Lessard and his team. The detective sergeant pulled him aside. The two men's faces were centimetres apart.

Lessard wanted to flatten the guy, but he forced himself to maintain a semblance of composure.

"What do you think you're doing?"

"Buying you time, Lessard. The Major Crimes Unit is already breathing down my neck. If you still have nothing by this time tomorrow, you can kiss the case goodbye."

Lessard turned around and walked into the changing room. In a fury, he punched a metal locker, which shuddered under the blow.

Tanguay was a gutless fool whose only concern was to cover his own ass. Lessard could already picture the next day's headlines. A fresh onset of heartburn assailed him. Pulling the half-full bottle of Pepto-Bismol from his jacket pocket, he took a swig.

He headed toward Pearson's desk. They needed to question Hélène Lacoursière about those photographs.

Why the hell was he still in this line of work?

19

Trois-Pistoles

Laurent had only one desire: to shed the battered remnants of his body and soul. His spirit had been broken over the course of this pitch-black night, and he understood, now, just how utterly he had wrecked the best years of his life.

Waldorf had returned three times. The first time had been to give him water and additional pills. The second had been to inject him again. The third had been to release him from the bed.

The two men were facing each other across the table. Laurent was handcuffed to his chair. The pistol lay on the table, as mutely threatening as ever. Pale and defeated, Laurent had reluctantly agreed to listen to what Waldorf had to say.

"Miles was a gardener at the Notre-Dame-des-Neiges Cemetery. Your mother's name was Catherine. She died of leukemia when you were five years old. Your family lived in a red-brick duplex across the street from the cemetery. You used to spend your summer vacations at a chalet in Trois-Pistoles that Miles had inherited after the death of his parents. You started sailing when you were four. When you were eight, your father bought you a baseball mitt — it was a brown Rawlings. You rubbed it with lemon oil and shaped it by putting a ball in the web and closing it with a big elastic band. Your first hockey coach was named Raymond Bolduc. You won several medals in cycling. The superhero you liked best was Batman. Your favourite colour was yellow. The name of your first dog was Pico. Every night at bedtime, Miles would walk around the house with you to show you that no one was hiding anywhere. One day, you and he camped out in a cornfield."

A tear rolled down Laurent's cheek.

"Shall I go on?" Waldorf asked.

Summer 1985
Laurent is nine years old. The heat is stifling. And the corn is impossibly high! Flies are buzzing in his ears. He should never have wandered away. Did he come from the left or from the right? Is he walking in circles? He feels panic rising. He's not a baby, he doesn't need help. He keeps walking. He hears a noise that makes him jump. It must be an animal. Or something else. Terrified, he cries out. Miles is there in thirty seconds. "You okay, buddy?"

"I got lost. I heard a weird noise."

Despite himself, he starts bawling like a baby. His father kneels, takes him in his arms, and holds him tight. "Don't worry. It's okay to be scared." Laurent feels better. Miles has always known just what to say to make him feel strong, to help him get past his limitations. He dries his tears, and they head back. He holds Miles's hand as he walks. "Dad, will Mom come back someday?" Miles lifts him off the ground. "She's always with you, wherever you go. She's in your heart."

Waldorf had known Laurent's father; that much was undeniable. He'd listed too many specific facts about Miles's life for there to be any doubt.

But the things Waldorf was saying were even crazier than the contents of his letters. There was something surreal about watching this man speak in such a calm, reasonable voice. How could he seem so stable while saying things that were so obviously delusional? Laurent didn't know what to think. He was still hoping that there might turn out to be a rational explanation for all this.

But what was he supposed to do?

I recovered my bag in the alley and checked its contents. Despite having fallen four floors, my cellphone seemed intact. The same wasn't true of my bottle of cheap perfume, which had shattered on impact. Luckily, it had been almost empty. I tossed the shards in a nearby dumpster.

The men from the other world?

I didn't know how much of the young man's incoherent talk to believe. Was it possible that he had some kind of intellectual disability? Or was Gustave actually Miles's accomplice? I shook my head. The whole thing was beyond me.

I got some cash from an ATM. After that, it took me a few minutes to hail a taxi. The car pulled up in front of a shabby building on Queen Mary Road. I checked the street number beside the door. The driver had taken me to the right location. This was the address that Tina had given me.

The place was a dump.

I stepped into an entrance area lit by a naked bulb. A row of mailboxes lined the yellowing wall. Below these, there was a buzzer for each apartment.

I had no trouble finding Tom Griffin, apartment 312.

Perhaps fortune was smiling on me, after all.

A few seconds after pressing the buzzer, I heard a click as the interior front door was remotely unlocked. I went up the stairs. On the first landing, I had to step over a dog turd and a few used condoms.

As I continued to climb, I remembered Tina's warning. Griffin had a violent streak. I hadn't considered the matter until this moment, but now I couldn't help wondering how he'd react if I told him I'd just spent some time with his brother, who was, well, dead. Best-case scenario, he'd shout insults. Worst case … I didn't want to think about the worst case.

How should I approach him?

It all happened very fast. On impulse, as I was knocking at the apartment door, I decided to try a ruse.

A voice yelled through the closed door.

"If you're another insurance salesman, go away and let me die in peace!"

This was it. Time to find out whether Griffin would fall for my ploy.

"Hello, sir," I said loudly enough to be heard through the door. "My name is Simone Fortin. I work for the City of Montreal. May I have a word with you?"

"What do you want? Get the hell out of here!"

"I represent the elections office. We're updating the voters' list in this district."

A filthy creature opened the door. His stained bathrobe was half-open, revealing a greasy, flaccid torso. His teeth were rotten, his fingernails were encrusted with grime, his breath was appalling, his hair was unwashed, and he stank of sweat.

"I don't give a shit about your list. I never vote anyway. Every damn politician in this city is a scumbag!"

Tina hadn't been kidding. Griffin was clearly volatile. He might slam the door in my face at any moment. I made my move.

"Are you Mr. Griffin? Mr. George Griffin?"

Instantly, he was yelling, advancing on me with a menacing glare.

"You people are complete fucking morons! I can't believe the city actually pays you a salary!"

What he said next made my blood run cold.

"George has been in a coma since August 7th, 1979. So you can stick your list where the sun don't shine, lady, 'cause George isn't gonna be voting ever again."

Feeling weak at the knees, I left the building.

Before I'd had time to process what I had just heard, my cellphone rang. Dalila Cherraf's name appeared on the caller ID.

"I'm warning you, if you come near my family again, I'll call the police."

The voice was harsh and aggressive.

"Wait, I …"

"I don't know how you got our address, you sneaky bitch, but if you know what's good for you, you won't bother us again. Do you hear me? Leave my father alone!"

"Your father? There must be some mistake. I thought it was your son who …"

"Enough with the lies! I know how you reporters work. We have nothing to say to you."

"But I'm not a reporter, I …"

"It was clever of you to come while I wasn't home. And yes, Raïcha was taken in by your little fainting act. But you can't fool me."

I heard Raïcha protesting in the background. Dalila shut her up.

"Listen," I said sharply, so she wouldn't interrupt. "There's been some mistake. This may be hard for you to believe, but like I said to Raïcha, I'm trying to find a man. His name is Jamal Cherraf. He plays the trumpet."

"Stop trying to con me! You know I named my son after his grandfather. What's the angle this time? A feature story for the twentieth anniversary of his attack? An interview with musicians from his band?"

Musicians from his band?

So I'd been right. I really had found Jamal.

"It's not what you think, I …"

"I don't know what newspaper you work for, but you're not the first reporter to come around looking for a story. Only there's nothing left to say. When are you people going to get that through your heads?"

"Dalila, wait, I …"

"Leave us alone! My father's been in a coma since 1985, and he's never going to wake up!"

20

Hélène Lacoursière offered the detectives a cup of coffee. Lessard declined politely. They sat down in the living room, and the detective sergeant decided not to beat around the bush.

"We found some photographs in your husband's computer at the office."

For a fraction of a second, she seemed shaken. He saw her jaw clench. Then she recovered her composure.

"Is that unusual, Detective?" she asked in an emotionless voice.

"No, but these photographs are, well …" He paused, groping for the right word. "They're somewhat particular."

"And how are they connected with his death?"

"We think he may have been the victim of a blackmail attempt."

"What's your question, exactly, Detective?"

Pearson handed her a file folder in which he had placed a few copies of the pictures that had been found in the dead man's computer. She looked at the images of her nude self.

Lessard was expecting her to blow up.

Instead, she lifted her chin slightly. Her lower lip trembled.

"You're nothing but an ill-mannered boor. Please leave."

"I'm sorry, ma'am, but we need your help. We're trying to find the person who killed your husband."

She stood up and walked toward the front door.

"Get out, Detective. And don't come back. You're no longer welcome here."

．　　．　　．

Unable to concentrate anymore, Lessard left the office around a quarter to nine. Pearson had gone home five minutes earlier. The detective sergeant needed a good meal and a shower. He wouldn't be able to sleep right away, but at least he'd be able to relax while screening the documentary on Muhammad Ali that he never grew tired of watching. He'd enjoy seeing Ali take on Joe Frazier once again. As he walked unhurriedly to his car, his cellphone rang. Tanguay's name appeared on the caller ID.

Would he never be allowed a moment's rest?

"Lessard."

"You're way out of line, Detective, sticking your nose into matters that don't concern you."

"I'm sorry, Commander, I don't know what you're —"

"Don't play dumb. Leave the widow alone."

Lessard was stunned.

How could Tanguay have found out so fast? Had Pearson talked to him? Surely not. That left only one possibility. Hélène Lacoursière had called the commander herself.

Why had Tanguay agreed to intercede for her?

"We don't want to make her life difficult, Commander, but this is a promising lead we're talking about."

"Drop that lead immediately, Lessard, do you hear me? If you don't, you may regret it!"

Lessard couldn't believe his ears.

"Is that a threat?"

"Let's just call it a friendly warning."

Tanguay hung up.

Lessard was shaken. He didn't know what was going on in the shadows, but it was clearly something significant enough to prompt this crude intervention from Tanguay.

He walked to the car and stood there for several seconds in a state of shock.

•   •   •

He was driving along Somerled Avenue when the ring of his cellphone roused him from his thoughts. He looked at the caller ID. It
was a number he didn't recognize. He almost didn't pick up, but he
couldn't resist.

"Uhh … hi, Victor. It's Ariane Bélanger. We met this morning.
After the hit and run …"

Of course he remembered her.

He suddenly felt as nervous as a schoolboy at his first dance.

"H-hello, Ariane," he stammered.

"I'm sorry to bother you. It's about my friend Simone …"

It made sense for her to be calling about the investigation. Still,
he felt a twinge of disappointment.

"Is something wrong?" he asked.

"When I went to the hospital to visit her this evening, I was told that
Simone left shortly after talking to you. She signed a refusal of treatment form. I've tried to reach her, but she's not answering her phone. I
was wondering if she mentioned where she was planning to go."

Lessard was taken aback.

How had the young woman managed to get discharged from the
hospital so fast? In any case, at the moment, he had bigger fish to fry.

"No, she didn't say anything to me. But I'm sure there's no cause
for concern. The doctor wouldn't have let her go if he'd had any
doubts. You have nothing to worry about."

"That's what I told myself. Sorry for bothering you."

"No problem." He was about to hang up.

"Victor? I saw you on TV earlier. Tough day?"

"The joys of being a cop," he said, trying to sound cheerful.

"Listen, you're probably exhausted, but I've just made osso buco,
and there's enough to feed an army. So, uh … if you have no plans,
would you like to come over for dinner?"

Lessard hesitated. He'd been intending to put in a call about that
sexual harassment complaint. But it could wait until tomorrow.

•   •   •

Looking up at the palatial home on Doctor Penfield Avenue, he rechecked his notebook. Yes, he had the right address.

At the sight of the mansion, he almost lost his nerve. But he forced himself to go up the stairs and press the doorbell.

Ariane opened up almost instantly, as though she'd been waiting for him to arrive. She was simply dressed, in jeans and a tight-fitting camisole. Her hair hung loosely around her shoulders.

A tingle went through Lessard. She was a lot sexier than she'd been this morning. Here was a real woman with real curves, not one of those Photoshopped stick figures you see glorified in fashion magazines.

"Hi," she said.

He gave her the flowers he'd bought at a convenience store after stopping off at his apartment to shower. He had removed the plastic wrapping that would have betrayed their provenance. Normally, etiquette would have dictated that he also bring a bottle of wine, but he had promised himself not to fall off the wagon. This was the first time he'd accepted a dinner invitation since he'd stopped drinking. He wasn't sure how he would deal with the issue during the meal with Ariane.

She stepped forward to kiss his cheek. He leaned toward her at the same instant, and their foreheads collided.

She laughed.

"Sorry," he said, "I'm a klutz."

"No, no, my fault. Come in."

He stepped into a large white-walled hallway. To his left, a small chapel-like space caught his attention. At the foot of an altar draped in red silk, two candles stood beside a photograph of a middle-aged couple. On the adjacent wall was a photo enlargement of Ground Zero. Ariane noticed his surprised expression.

"Those are my parents. They died in the World Trade Center attack. They were diplomats. They'd been scheduled to attend a

conference on development aid for African countries. Their floor
of the north tower took a direct hit from the first plane. They never
had a chance."

"I'm sorry," Lessard murmured. "That's awful."

"It is and it isn't. My parents led a richer existence than most
people can ever hope for. They were happy every day of their lives.
They turned their dreams into reality. And they died together,
without suffering."

Lessard didn't know what to say.

"I know I sound like an incurable optimist. But it's a lesson I
learned from them. Never lose heart."

This woman intimidated him. He suddenly felt overdressed in
his jacket and tie. He put his hands behind his back to give himself
some semblance of composure.

"Your house is … very nice."

"It was theirs. I haven't been able to bring myself to sell it. I grew
up here. I'd love to see my daughter grow up here, too, but the place
is way too big for the two of us."

Despite his newfound interest in cooking, Lessard was in the habit
of preparing simple meals in keeping with his solitary lifestyle.
Eating Ariane's sumptuous dinner was consequently a delight.

But he swore to himself that he'd resume his diet tomorrow.

He hesitated briefly when she offered him wine, but eventually
declined on the pretext that he had to be at work very early the
next day. For a moment, he wondered whether it wouldn't be better
to tell the truth. But on further consideration, he decided to wait.
Happy young women didn't generally take an interest in recovering
alcoholics.

Over dinner, Ariane described what she'd gone through to adopt
Mathilde, who was asleep upstairs.

During her parents' postings, Ariane had lived in South Africa
and Poland before coming back to Canada.

At the age of nineteen, after a turbulent adolescence, she'd gone backpacking in Central America and had become particularly attached to the residents of one Guatemalan community. She had gone back at twenty-four under the auspices of a Canadian NGO.

With some help from her father's diplomatic contacts, she had adopted a baby from a local orphanage and brought her back to Canada.

That was in 1999, when the child was six months old. Ariane's parents had helped her care for the little girl until their deaths.

Lessard talked about his ex-wife and his children, but he didn't get into the specific reasons for the separation.

When Ariane asked how he'd gotten into police work, he felt comfortable enough to tell her about the tragic events of his youth, but he didn't mention the deep depression that those events had caused.

They also briefly discussed Simone and the hit-and-run investigation. Lessard repeated to Ariane that she had nothing to worry about. They ate dessert in the living room — chocolate profiteroles accompanied by strong espresso. At Ariane's request, Lessard lit a fire in the fireplace.

She shivered and pressed herself against him.

"Warm me up," she said languorously.

Lessard almost choked as he hastily swallowed the piece of profiterole in his mouth. She put a hand on his thigh and raised her face to kiss him.

He barely had time to worry about his coffee breath before her tongue was pressing into his mouth.

He hadn't kissed a woman in a very long time. Ariane tasted of chocolate, and her tongue was sliding over his with the melting softness of a ripe peach.

She pressed herself closer. The young woman's hand moved up his thigh to his zipper, and he felt himself redden.

If she kept going, she would discover his erection.

And why not?

Lessard bent his head over Ariane's throat. He saw a pale blue vein and kissed it. The young woman shuddered with pleasure. Encouraged, he pulled off her camisole while she was frantically unzipping his pants. He cupped her ample breasts in his hands and pressed his tongue against her hard nipples.

An instant later they were naked, flesh against flesh, white-hot.

Mouths and hands moving eagerly in a silent ballet.

Ariane got up to fetch a blanket. She came back and covered Lessard, who had fallen asleep like a baby after checking his phone messages. She liked this man. He was humble, serious, sensitive. He was a good lover, precisely because of his visceral fear of disappointing her. She lay down beside him on the couch and fell asleep. Everything felt right.

He had spent the evening in a dark corner of Mathilde's bedroom, content to watch the child sleep.

He liked her pretty olive complexion.

Latin Americans, Asians, and Haitians have done a good job of integrating into Quebec society. The same can't be said of Islamic fundamentalists. Those terrorists have no trouble slipping through the porous screen of Canada's immigration system. Montreal has become a powder keg. They come here, they keep their culture, and under the protection of our Charter of Rights, they bring hijabs, turbans, and daggers into our schools and institutions. Luckily, in Quebec City, at least, classrooms are still safe.

At first, he had thought the detective's visit was related to the hit and run. When it became clear that that wasn't the case, he had stopped paying much heed to the conversation. Clearly, the young woman and the cop were powerfully drawn to each other.

After they fell asleep, he slipped out through the same basement window that he had forced to get in.

Simone Fortin hadn't shown her face, but there was no point in hanging around. Nothing was likely to happen tonight. He would go to the motel and get a few hours' rest. Then he'd come back and be in position by 6:30 a.m.

He walked to the Buick. The engine started without a hitch.

Good old American know-how.

Snake had promised to wait a few hours before making the call, giving Jimbo time to get out of town. It was now almost midnight. He still wasn't sure he was doing the right thing. But there was no one else who could help him, and he wasn't about to let a murderer get away.

He called his father's cell number.

Lessard woke up with a start, jumped off the couch, got his legs tangled in the blanket, and fell headlong to the floor. He glanced nervously at Ariane. She hadn't woken up.

He picked up his phone on the third ring.

"Lessard."

At the other end of the line, Snake hesitated.

"Dad, it's Martin."

Lessard hadn't spoken to his son in at least two weeks. And the young man wasn't in the habit of calling at this hour.

"Martin? What's wrong? Is there some kind of trouble with your mother?"

"No, listen to me! I'm in deep shit. I need your help."

APRIL 2ND, 2005

21

Did he have any illusions left?

If so, Victor Lessard lost them that night. Afterward, as he reflected on everything that had happened, he would wonder where he had gone wrong. How could he have lost touch with his son so completely?

Not long after the arduous case was finally closed and Lessard's report had been filed, Fernandez would come into his office and find him drinking at his desk, his face grey, his service weapon lying on the blotter. She would sit down without a word and listen while he spilled his guts.

"I thought I knew my kids, Nadja. I watched Martin grow up. I watched him go from one phase where he needed me in his life to another phase where all his efforts were focused on a single objective: to be as little like me as possible. Then, in a moment of distress, he reached out, needing my help. I felt useful again. We were close, just like in the old days. If you only knew how much I regret all the times he wanted to play and I said no, because I was too busy or too tired. And in the end, what does it matter? It's all just water under the bridge."

That evening, Fernandez would drive him back to his apartment and put him to bed. The next day, when they saw each other at the station, he would lay a hand on her shoulder for a few seconds to express his gratitude. They would never mention the episode again. But they would both know that she had saved his life.

•   •   •

When he arrived, Lessard didn't know what to expect. He walked into the filthy garage and stepped over several cardboard boxes full of electronics: music players, game consoles, MP3 players, etc.

He saw a BMW sedan, its trunk half-open.

Looking frail in his oversized sweatshirt, Martin hadn't heard him come in. During the drive, Lessard had promised himself not to be aggressive. But his temper got the better of him.

"For Christ's sake, Martin, what are you doing here? And at this hour?"

Martin turned around. He was wearing a dust mask over his nose and mouth.

"Look in the trunk."

No. It couldn't be.

Lessard was motionless for a moment, then, unable to control himself, he threw up beside the car.

There was a body in the trunk, in a hockey bag.

A corpse.

Memories of key moments in Martin's childhood unspooled in his head like an old Super 8 home movie. Outlandish scenarios tumbled through his mind.

Lessard felt a knot of panic growing in his stomach. He had a sudden impulse to turn around and leave, to flee from a situation he couldn't handle.

Had Martin …?

His own son? A murderer?

He felt unequal to the challenge. How could he cope with the idea that his own flesh and blood had committed the worst crime imaginable?

He wiped his mouth with the back of his hand.

"I didn't kill him, if that's what you're wondering," Martin said. "I just stole the car."

Relieved, Lessard let the air out of his lungs. Without a word, he sat down on a wooden crate beside the boy. To his surprise, his voice was calm.

"What happened?"

Martin raised his chin in the direction of the BMW. "I stole it this morning, off the street."

"What street?"

"I can't remember."

"Make an effort, it's important."

"Forest Hill, I think," the young man whispered. "Yes. I'm sure. The corner of Forest Hill and Côte-des-Neiges."

Lessard wrote the street names in his notebook.

"And then?"

"I was supposed to deliver it to a buyer tonight."

"A car-theft ring?"

Martin's voice was a murmur. His lower lip was quivering. "Yes. I'd noticed the smell, but it was only when I opened the trunk to put in some packages that I ..."

The boy burst into tears. Lessard held him awkwardly until he had calmed down. He wished he could have taken his time, but he had to act fast.

"Martin, I'm going to ask you a very, very important question. Take your time before answering, and tell me the truth."

The boy looked at his father.

"Did you touch the body?"

The answer was swift and unequivocal.

"No."

Lessard looked searchingly at his son. He was being truthful.

"Does anyone else know about this?"

Martin hesitated for a fraction of a second. His father knew instantly that he was about to lie.

"No."

"Who?"

"Nobody, Dad ..."

"Don't fuck with me! Who?"

"Jimbo."

"Who's Jimbo? Does he steal cars with you?"

"Yeah. He's a friend."

"Where is he?"

"His father's house. It's out of town, I don't know where, exactly. I really don't."

The boy was calmer now.

"Did he touch the body?"

"No. I swear to you, Dad, we didn't ..."

"And this friend of yours, Jimbo — can he be trusted to keep his mouth shut?"

Surprised, Martin took a few seconds to consider the question.

"I think so."

"How long have you been stealing cars?"

"About six months."

The detective sergeant thought of the car-theft ring he'd been trying to dismantle.

"Do you work in the Côte-des-Neiges area?"

Martin hung his head. "Yes."

Lessard made an effort to think calmly.

It was obvious that his son wasn't guilty of murder. But he *was* guilty of stealing automobiles. By rights, he should be held responsible for his actions in a court of law. He had committed a serious offence.

Still, Lessard hesitated. On the one hand, a crime had been committed. Morally, he had a duty to do his job.

On the other hand, it was in his power to save Martin from interrogations, legal proceedings, incarceration, a criminal record, and, above all, the inevitable social stigma arising from a conviction.

Lessard's own feelings of guilt tipped the scales. Martin was angry at him. It was no coincidence that the boy had been stealing cars in his district.

Was it as simple as that? And really, what difference did it make?

"Why didn't you just make an anonymous 911 call?"

"My fingerprints are all over the car. Sooner or later, they'd have found me."

"Not if your prints aren't in the system."

"I know."

"So why?"

"We're talking about a murder, Dad. It got me thinking."

"You wanted to be free of all this."

Martin held his father so tightly that Lessard almost lost his balance. For a moment, his son was a little boy again.

"I'm sorry, Dad."

Lessard had to fight back his tears.

"I'm glad you called me, Martin."

As the young man wept in his arms, the cop would have given anything to be able to go back in time and give his son the attention that he himself had never received.

Lessard thought about his own father and the monstrous act he had committed that fateful day. Lessard would have met the same violent end as his mother and brothers if he had come home from school at the usual time instead of walking Marie to her house — the same Marie who would later become his wife.

The newspapers had dubbed it a "domestic incident."

After that, there'd been several years of bouncing from one foster home to another, until he had finally been adopted at age sixteen by a happy family. And yet, with his recent drunken antics, he had been an embarrassment to his adoptive sister, whom he loved more than anything. He thought of his adoptive parents. If they'd been alive, his behaviour would have mortified them. He resolved to call Valérie later in the day.

He had become a police officer in part to prove to himself that his paternal genes had no hold over him. Marie had reminded him of that fact after he pushed her.

"Are you going to do like your dad and kill me now?"

If it had been possible to go back and start over, he would have followed his instincts and become a carpenter. That had been the dream of his teenage years.

Life is a series of choices. Once you're on the wrong path, there's no turning back.

"Marie, it's me ... yes, I know what time it is.... No ... don't hang up!... Listen, Martin's with me. Yes, that's right. I'll explain later. I need you to come and pick him up." He gave her the address. "Yes, now. I'm aware of what time it ... don't hang ..."

He sighed. She had hung up.

Martin hadn't expected his father to handle the case this way. Knowing his principles, the young man had assumed that he'd be arrested and questioned.

They waited in the Corolla, across the street from the garage.

Without giving the kid a sermon, Lessard wanted him to know the matter wouldn't end here.

"Do you understand what I'm doing right now, Martin?"

"Yes, Dad."

"Let's get one thing straight. When my investigation is over, you and I are going to have a serious talk."

"I know."

"I want your word that you'll do what I tell you."

"Yes."

"That's going to include seeing a psychologist."

"I'm not crazy!" the boy protested.

"Martin, you need to understand how you ended up here. Believe me, a psychologist will help. I saw one myself, and it did me a world of good."

"Really?"

"Yes. Also, I'm going to break up that car-theft ring. And you're going to give me the information I need to do it."

The young man reacted instantly.

"I'm not a snitch!"

"Or I can just turn you in. Your call."

"If they know I gave information to the police, they'll kill me."

"Don't worry about that. There are ways to prevent them from finding out. Do I have your word?"

Martin groaned. "Yes."

"One last thing. You're going back to school."

The boy exploded.

"No fucking way!"

"Whoa. Keep your shirt on. If you get your high school diploma, I'll pay for that sound-engineering course you want to take."

"Are you serious?"

"Very. Think it over."

When his ex-wife arrived, Lessard took her aside and explained the situation. She kept her composure, despite having to wipe away a few tears.

"Thank you, Victor. I know what this means for you."

"I'm doing it for Martin." He paused. "And also because I'm to blame for all of this."

She didn't contradict him on that point, but she gave him a brief hug before getting into her car. Lessard watched the vehicle roll away. His heart was heavy with failure and guilt, but he also felt something else.

Hope. Maybe this thing would bring them all closer.

Fernandez answered on the fourth ring.

"I need you to come and meet me. Have you got a pencil and paper?"

She answered sleepily.

"You might at least say you're sorry for waking me up. What's going on?"

Lessard swallowed. He was about to lie to his colleague for the first time.

"An anonymous call came in on my cellphone. There's a body in the trunk of a car."

That snapped her awake.

"Where are you?"

He gave her the address on Hochelaga Street.

"Okay, give me fifteen minutes."

"Call Doug and Berger. No need to wake up anyone else."

"I'm on it."

Lessard went back to the BMW and closed the trunk. He put on a pair of latex gloves and started the motor by connecting the wires that hung loosely under the steering wheel.

He drove out of the garage and parked the car two blocks away. He detached the wires to cut the engine and left the trunk half-open.

He looked up and down the street. No one.

He went back for the Corolla and parked it behind the BMW.

Fernandez and Adams arrived in separate cars twenty minutes later. Adams waved to him and walked toward the trunk, holding a flashlight. Fernandez approached and handed him a cup of steaming coffee.

"Male or female?"

"Don't know. I didn't want to touch anything before you got here. Where's Berger?"

"On his way. Should I have a flatbed bring the car to the garage?"

"Not yet. Let's give Adams and Berger time to do the preliminary work."

Berger pulled up behind them and got out of his car, grumbling. Lessard heard the hockey bag's zipper sliding open.

Adams had already begun to set up high-powered lights so that every corner of the car's trunk was visible. Fernandez established a secure perimeter.

Lessard and Fernandez joined their colleagues beside the BMW. Berger cut through the plastic sheet and freed the victim's head.

His throat had been cut.

Lessard noticed that the man had pale skin and blond hair.

"Late thirties, early forties," Berger estimated.

He opened the plastic sheet to reveal the upper body. There was a dark stain on the corpse's chest.

Dried blood.

Berger cut away a rectangle of shirt cloth to reveal the wound. Lessard had looked at one just like it less than twelve hours ago. Berger turned to him, his face pale.

"Are you seeing what I'm seeing, Lessard?"

"Is it the same kind of wound?"

"It certainly appears to be."

Fernandez gave voice to the thought no one else dared express.

"Sliced throat, stab wound to the chest … could it be the same killer?"

"Too early to say," Berger answered, "but at first glance, there are a lot of similarities."

"Have any fingers been cut off?" Lessard asked.

Berger carefully disengaged the hands from the plastic sheet. Damp with sweat, he turned to Lessard.

"No."

What the hell is going on? Lessard wondered. If it was the same killer, why cut off an index finger from Mongeau, but not from the other victim?

Wasn't there something else he wanted to ask Berger?

Suddenly, the question came back to him.

"Jacob, can you give me an approximate time of death?"

"Not before the autopsy."

"Just a rough estimate, based on your experience."

Berger sighed, irritated. "Hard to say. This plastic sheeting complicates everything."

"Did the guy die before or after Mongeau?"

"Before. At least twenty-four hours before."

"Does he have a wallet?"

"I can't get at it in this position. We'll have to take out the body first."

Fernandez looked at him.

"What do we do?"

"Bring the car in. Call the flatbed. If there's a link between the two murders, we need to identify this body as fast as possible."

Lessard turned to Adams.

"This isn't the scene of the crime. The car was abandoned here, but the murder was committed elsewhere. Take a few pictures, but don't waste too much time."

He was trying to focus his thoughts as Fernandez gave instructions over her cellphone.

Adams took out his photography equipment and shot the BMW from every angle. Then he got down and looked under the car for possible clues. He picked up all the stray items he saw in the vicinity and slipped them into sealed evidence bags — beer caps, cigarette butts, and an old shoe.

Lessard didn't intervene, though he knew that nothing Adams picked up would be of any value.

The situation could hardly have been worse.

His son had stolen a car with a corpse in the trunk. Then he himself had made up a fake story about an anonymous phone call. Now he was discovering that there might be a link between this killing and the Mongeau murder.

He would have to go on making up stories, lying to his fellow cops. He hated to do it, but what choice did he have? He had chosen the wrong path. There was no turning back.

He took a few paces to dissipate the tension. His stomach felt like he'd swallowed a barrel of battery acid.

He couldn't help wondering whether they were after a serial killer. But the severed finger puzzled him.

He was gripped by a sense of urgency, a panicky fear that important details were eluding him. He looked at his hands.

At least I have all my fingers.

How could a thought like that even occur to him?

It wasn't his mouth that needed washing out with soap. It was his soul.

22

The bus was rolling through the cold night, its motor rumbling in counterpoint to the hammering of my heart.

To my right, I saw a campground full of RVs beside the highway and a sign announcing Rivière-du-Loup. It was a little before one o'clock in the morning. We'd been on the road for nearly five hours.

For the hundredth time, I slipped a hand into my pocket and touched the slip of paper on which I'd written the address of the Trois-Pistoles Hospital's long-term care centre.

I was struggling to keep a lid on the emotions that threatened to overwhelm me. Except for the day of the little boy's death, I had just been through the worst day of my life. The information I'd learned a few hours earlier had done nothing to make me feel better. I leaned against the window and watched the raindrops running down the glass.

In my head, I replayed the events that had followed the phone call from Dalila and my conversation with Tom Griffin.

After leaving Griffin's place, I had walked to Monkland Avenue and went into the first restaurant I saw. Not having eaten all day, I had ordered a slice of pizza and a Diet Coke. The polyester-clad waitress had watched in amazement as I scarfed down my meal in a few bites.

Moments later, I was back outside. I bought a pack of cigarettes at a convenience store, spotted a public bench, and sat down for a quiet smoke. I should probably have been full of doubts, struggling to come up with a coherent explanation. But I was unruffled as I sat tranquilly on the bench.

I even lit a second cigarette.

Now I understood what Gustave had been talking about when he referred to "the men from the other world." I decided to embrace a notion that, on its face, was nonsensical. I had spoken to Miles, George, and Jamal while I was in a coma.

Ariane woke up on the couch and looked around for Victor.

She got to her feet, still groggy with sleep. He was gone.

He was a good man. She had known that right away.

Maybe he's too good for me.

She had gone overboard in recent months. She couldn't deny that she had indulged her fantasies. Overindulged, perhaps?

It had all started when she met Diego on a dating site. Gradually, he had initiated her into the pleasures of BDSM.

Was it wrong for a woman to like sex?

Diego had been her master for several weeks. During that time, she had gone along with his every sexual whim, willingly participating in orgies and fucking anonymous partners.

There was a side to Ariane's character that one might call ... adventurous. She enjoyed light domination, being tied up while a man took her hard. Diego had always been respectful. But now she wanted something else, something steadier. Though she didn't believe in the idealized love of romance novels, she thought it might be nice to have a lover who was also a friend.

Someone she could cuddle up with on Sunday mornings, under the covers, laughing. A man who wasn't too macho — but still a little. A man like Victor Lessard.

He was clearly an old-school type of guy. Would he be able to accept her past?

I could have asked Stefan to help me find Miles.

He had the access codes for the various databases in the health-care system. But calling him was out of the question. I hadn't spoken to him in seven years. I wasn't ready to dredge up the past.

I decided to use other contacts instead.

I called the number of Suzanne Schmidt, a person I had trusted implicitly before my sudden departure. There was, of course, a risk that she'd tell Stefan. But I was willing to take that chance.

By luck, she picked up on the second ring.

"Suzanne, it's Simone Fortin."

There was a long silence at the other end of the line.

"Simone? Is it really you? How long has it been?"

She was more emotional than I'd expected her to be. But I didn't want to get bogged down in a conversation about the old days.

"Nearly seven years."

"My God, I can't believe I'm talking to you. What are you up to?"

"Listen, Suzanne, I don't have time to explain. I need a favour. I'm trying to locate a patient who's in a coma."

I gave her all the information I had on Miles. She asked a number of questions, to which I gave the briefest possible answers. Yes, I was doing well. No, I hadn't returned to the profession. No, I hadn't been in touch with Stefan. And no, I wasn't planning to come back.

She agreed to help me, but in return, I had to give her my word that I'd get back in touch soon. In the meantime, she promised not to let Stefan know about our conversation.

"When do you need this information, Simone?"

"Yesterday?" I said, and laughed too hard.

•   •   •

She called back in less than an hour.

What she told me came as no surprise. Miles Green had been in the long-term care centre of the Trois-Pistoles Hospital since June 21st, 1998.

He was in an irreversible coma.

As she was about to get back into bed, Ariane heard a noise in the basement. She went down and saw that a window was rattling.

Ariane Bélanger wasn't the sort of person who got worked up over little things or jumped at the sight of her own shadow. She didn't notice the marks that the crowbar had left on the windowsill.

Her experiences as an international aid worker in Central America had given her great faith in human nature.

It never would have occurred to her that someone might try to break into her home.

With a shrug, she closed the window.

After tucking in Mathilde, she went back to her room and slipped into bed.

After that, things moved fast.

I took a taxi to the bus terminal at the corner of Berri and De Maisonneuve. I bought a ticket from a listless clerk, then picked up a bottle of water, a sandwich, a few fashion magazines, and a short story collection that I happened to spot on the book rack.

There were only a dozen passengers on the bus. I laid out the magazines, book, and food in the vacant space beside me before sinking back into my seat.

The bus pulled out punctually at 8:00 p.m. and arrived in Trois-Pistoles around two-thirty in the morning. During the trip, I had leafed through the magazines, glancing at the articles' titles without reading them. There was one that touted weight-loss gimmicks. Another offered a list of ten ways to please your man in bed. A third promised a surefire trick for finding out whether your boyfriend was cheating on you.

As I unwrapped my sandwich just outside Drummondville, a Jaguar sedan was slowly passing the bus. The car's ceiling light was on. I could see a man and a woman, both in their fifties, having a bitter argument. They didn't know it, but they were entering the phase that precedes indifference. I was something of an expert on the subject. The same thing had happened to Stefan and me before I'd left him.

For the first time in years, I found myself wondering what had become of Stefan. I knew from experience that regrets were pointless, but I was too weary to resist the sadness that came over me.

We were east of Quebec City when I succeeded in reaching the head nurse at the long-term care centre. Despite her initial reluctance, I persuaded her to wait until 3:00 a.m. for my arrival, and to grant me permission for a late-night visit.

After ending the call, I turned off the phone to save battery power.

I couldn't stop thinking about Miles.

Why was I going to his bedside?

Because the man had touched me. He'd gotten under my skin.

As we approached Trois-Pistoles, I began to feel increasingly anxious. When I picked up my book, I realized that my hands were trembling. How would I react when I saw him?

He turned off the TV.

On the news, he'd seen a report about the press conference that Victor Lessard had given a few hours earlier. He was pleased to see that the police were in the dark. They knew almost nothing.

He felt a measure of respect for Detective Lessard. But the senior officer, who was clearly an arrogant man, inspired nothing but contempt.

Not everyone can handle power. Too often, those who have it simply abuse it.

He rose from his chair, finished off the last few drops of rum, and put the glass on the counter. Then, as he had done every evening for thirty years, he went through his stretching routine. He washed up quickly, brushed his teeth vigorously, and got into bed. From under the pillow, he took a copy of Hans Christian Andersen's fairy tales. He opened the book and began to read "The Little Match Girl."

"Miss? We're in Trois-Pistoles."

The driver's voice roused me from my slumber. The bus was empty. I looked at my watch. I'd slept a little. I got out of the vehicle. I could have taken a taxi, but decided to walk instead. The hospital was only a few blocks away.

When I got there, the nurse led me up a long, cheerless corridor, speaking in authoritative tones about "her" patient's condition. As I glanced fleetingly into the darkened doorways, I paid scant attention to the nurse's explanation of what a coma was. I already knew everything she was saying.

The hospital smells, so redolent of discomfort and suffering for most people, brought a thousand memories, a thousand faces, bursting back into my consciousness, like flames from a fire-eater's mouth.

The nurse stopped in front of a half-open door. She had been in the middle of a sentence, but she trailed off, as though suddenly too tired to continue.

"You have fifteen minutes," she said, and walked away.

A man lay behind that door, a mind imprisoned in a body.

A man I had briefly known in a parallel reality, though it was hard for me to acknowledge that fact, even now. A man who had been cut off from the world for so many years.

Could I have loved him if our time together hadn't been so short? I approached the curled-up form and reacted with a start.

It was Miles. There was no mistaking him. Yet he seemed vastly different. His face was emaciated. His bones projected under his thin flesh. His hair was thin and grey. Age, combined with his long coma, had ravaged him.

I noted the presence of a feeding tube.

I was overcome by emotion. Tears rolled down my cheeks like marbles flung by little children. Each time I reached out a hand, a kind of invisible force prevented me from touching him, which was strange, for I had seen death and illness many times.

Only much later did I understand that this life undone in its prime had brought me face to face with my own inability to confront the terrible mistake I had committed.

I stood there in the midst of my doubts, with a troubling sense that death was lurking in every corner. I tried to get my head around the idea that Miles was watching from another world. I was even vain enough to suppose that some logical, palpable reality bound us together. Our encounter couldn't simply have been a coincidence.

I thought of Miles's son, who, after enduring the pain of losing his mother, now had to live with the knowledge that his father was in an irretrievable vegetative state. How would he react if I told him about the encounter that I believed I'd had with Miles? Would he find comfort in the notion that his father inhabited a parallel reality? In asking myself such a question, I realized that I hadn't yet accepted the situation. I couldn't bring myself to acknowledge that the empty shell lying before me and the vibrant man to whom I'd been attracted were one and the same.

What, after all, did I know about reality?

Hadn't I been fleeing it myself for far too long?

If I'd been hoping for a miracle, none came.

Miles remained unconscious while I, submerged in self-pity, wept uncontrollably, unable to do anything.

When my fifteen minutes were up, the nurse, seeing how emotional I was, put an arm around my shoulders and walked me back to the entrance. I stepped out into the misty parking lot, staggering like a drunk.

A man approached. Dressed in black, he looked like a priest.

By the streetlights' wan glow, I saw a long scar on his face and instinctively retreated. Looking at the man, I felt a strange mixture of fear and respect.

"Simone Fortin?"

"Who are you? What do you want?"

"My name is Kurt Waldorf. I'd like to talk to you about Miles."

PART THREE

My interest is in the future because I am going to spend the rest of my life there.

— Charles F. Kettering

23

4:45 a.m.

Exhausted, Lessard headed back to his apartment on Oxford Avenue. As he drove, he thought of the events that had marked this crazy day: Mongeau's murder, the press conference marred by the commander's clumsy intervention, and, finally, the discovery of a second body and the existence of a possible link between the two killings.

His son's indirect involvement in the spiralling situation, combined with his own cover-up of that involvement, had left a knot of anxiety in his stomach.

He needed to prioritize, taking care not to neglect anything. As he drove west along Sherbrooke Street, he tried to sort out the tangled lines of thought in his brain.

First of all, there was the hit and run case. If he wanted to avoid giving ammunition to the higher-ups, he mustn't neglect this ongoing investigation, even if he had two homicides to deal with at the same time. He would ask Constable Nguyen to take the lead on the hit and run.

Then there were the murders.

He would assemble the members of the investigation team to review leads and determine the best way to proceed. But what would he tell them? He mustn't worry about that now. Fatigue was overwhelming him.

He lowered the car window. An icy wind slapped him. His mind refocused.

Ariane had been the only positive thing about this awful day.

He liked her. He would call later to apologize for his hasty departure. And he'd make sure to get her recipe for osso buco.

He stopped on the highway overpass at the corner of Côte-Saint-Luc Road and Décarie Boulevard. A newspaper vendor walked up. Poor guy. How could he stand being outside in the cold and wind every day?

Lessard bought a copy of the day's paper.

The story had made the front page: JACQUES MONGEAU MURDERED. Lower down, Lessard saw his own face. The picture had been taken during the press conference.

There was a second headline: ARREST IMMINENT? INVESTIGATORS HAVE A LEAD.

He threw the paper onto the passenger seat and, with a growl, took another swig of Pepto-Bismol.

This time, he found a parking spot in front of his building. The temperature had fallen to minus fifteen degrees Celsius. Lessard noticed a sparrow hopping blithely along the top of a rickety fence. If someone had offered him the chance, he would gladly have sprouted wings and flown away from this dark world.

He kicked off his boots without unlacing them, threw his coat on the couch, and looked at his watch: 5:45 a.m. He set his alarm for 6:35 a.m. and got under the covers with his clothes still on. The commander's face was among a succession of images that floated through his mind before he fell asleep.

"Don't forget Tanguay," he muttered to himself as he drifted off.

He would need to talk to the commander eventually and tell him about the second murder. But knowing that Tanguay wanted to hand off the case to the Major Crimes Unit, Lessard had decided to wait a few hours.

.   .   .

He was in a car with his son. They were speeding along a foggy tree-lined path. Cresting a hill, they shot out into the clear.

He only saw the wall at the last moment.

6:35 a.m.

The alarm was howling. His sweat-soaked hair was plastered to his forehead, and there was a piercing pain under his left shoulder blade. He dragged himself out of bed and let his clothes fall to the bathroom floor. He took a scalding shower, put on fresh clothes, and gulped down a cup of coffee.

He stepped outside with a crust of bread that he broke into pieces and left on the front porch. Would the sparrow be back? For a few seconds, he looked up at the sky and saw nothing but dull grey clouds. There was something soul-crushing about the unrelenting drabness of the season.

Goddamn winter.

In the car, he made a mental list of subjects he wanted to go over with the team. As he drove past Shäika Café, he resisted the temptation to stop for a croissant. He didn't want to be late for his own meeting.

He spent the rest of the drive thinking about Martin.

He was still finding it hard to grasp how his son had managed to fool him so completely. He felt simultaneously helpless and incompetent as a father. What angle should he take to help Martin overcome his demons? Should he try to be understanding, or should he take the opposite approach and be a disciplinarian? How could he, who was so baffled when it came to young people, find the right words to comfort his boy?

In the parking area of the police station, he met Pearson and told him about the previous night's events, omitting any mention of Martin, of course.

The younger detective frowned.

"Why didn't you get me out of bed?"

"You ought to be looking after your wife and kids, Chris. That should be your priority. Don't wreck everything the way I did."

Pearson didn't answer. But he looked at his fellow cop with the same empathy one might feel at the sight of a sick child.

Lessard poured himself a cup of coffee in the kitchenette. Fernandez was filling in Sirois on the discovery of the second murder victim. A box of pastries lay on the table. Lessard resisted a powerful urge to take one.

"You missed Berger by five minutes," Fernandez said to him. "He's gone home to bed."

Lessard looked out the window. The grey sky stretched away as far as the eye could see. Was it possible for a normal human being to endure an entire lifetime of dreary Quebec winters? Billions were being spent on genome research and stem cells, but had anyone stopped to consider the possibility that dismal weather might be a cause of cancer? Dismal weather and loneliness. Lessard knew a thing or two about that, as well.

"Victor?"

He came back to reality.

"Sorry," he said. "What was the conclusion?"

"The two victims were killed with the same weapon," Fernandez said. "The possibility of error is very low, practically zero. The first victim was killed Thursday, sometime between three o'clock and eleven o'clock at night. Berger should be able to give us a precise time of death after further tests."

"Do we know the victim's name? Did Berger find any ID?"

"No, but his assistant is trying to identify the body by looking for a dental match in the Register of Missing Persons."

"That'll take too long. What else have we got?"

"The toxicology report should come in early this afternoon."

"We need to identify the body as soon as possible, Nadja. Have you seen this morning's paper? If we don't get a breakthrough in the next few hours, Tanguay will take the case out of our hands. He's itching to do it. The vultures from Major Crimes are circling."

"Have you spoken to him?"

"No. I can buy us a little time, but when he hears about the second murder, he's going to hit the panic button."

Putting his hands on his knees, Lessard winced suddenly with pain.

"You okay?" Fernandez asked with concern.

He blinked to signify a yes. He had an impulse to ease his conscience and tell his colleagues about Martin's involvement in the case. What had possessed him to lie to them?

But he kept the truth to himself. His son's redemption hung in the balance. Perhaps, in some small measure, his own did, too.

"Have you found the owner of the BMW?" he asked.

"The car belongs to one Éric Leclerc," Fernandez said. "His alibi checks out. He parked the car at Quebec City Airport on March 12th. He's been in Florida since then. I reached him at his hotel. His story was backed up by his wife and another couple who are down there with them. Unless the guy's an illusionist, he didn't kill our two victims."

"I'd still like to talk to him. Have him stay in his room. Tell him I'll be calling in the next hour. Where's Doug?"

"At the police garage," Fernandez said. "I spoke to him less than half an hour ago. He was about to start examining the car."

Lessard had assembled the investigation team in the conference room. He wasn't sure where to begin. To improve his spirits, he imagined himself with Martin and Charlotte, camping in the Rockies. *A lie is a terrible thing*, he thought. But there was no going back.

"Last night, a call came in on my cellphone. The caller, a male, said he'd discovered a body in the trunk of a car. He gave me an address. I went there and found the body."

Pearson was taking notes.

"Did the caller say anything else?"

"Only that he'd stolen the car around noon on Friday at the corner of Forest Hill and Côte-des-Neiges, and that he had nothing to do with the murder."

"We'll need to look at your phone log. We may be able to trace the call."

"Already done," Lessard said, lying again. "The call came from a pay phone."

"There's no way to be sure he was telling the truth," Pearson said. "Your anonymous informant may be the killer himself."

Lessard had to concede the validity of that point. But what would his colleagues think of him, of his skills as a father, if they learned that the car thief was his own son? He tried to redirect the conversation.

"You're right, but I have a feeling he was telling the truth. In any case, we'll need to question residents and store owners on that stretch of Forest Hill Avenue. Someone may have noticed something."

Pearson raised his hand.

"I'll handle it."

Without realizing, Lessard took a sip from Fernandez's coffee cup. She didn't object.

"We have two bodies. Berger thinks we're looking at a single killer, based on the murder weapon, the stab wounds to the chest, and the fact that both victims had their throats cut. But there are two significant differences. The killer cut off Jacques Mongeau's index finger, and he left a CD on Mongeau's desk."

Sirois got up and mumbled an apology before going to the men's room. Lessard waited until he came back, then continued.

"We don't have much of a timeline. On Thursday, between three and eleven p.m., the killer murders the man whose body we found in the trunk of the BMW. On Friday, between two-thirty and three-thirty p.m., he kills Jacques Mongeau in his office."

There were nods around the table.

"The BMW was parked at the airport in Quebec City. It belongs to a man who was out of the country when the murders occurred. The man's alibi has been checked and corroborated. We can assume that the killer stole the car from the airport. Does it follow that the dead man in the BMW was a Quebec City resident? We'll need to look into that."

"The possibilities are endless," Sirois interjected. "The killer could have stolen the BMW in Quebec City and committed the murder someplace else."

"That would be an excellent way to throw us off the trail," Pearson said.

"Good point," Lessard said. "We'll have to fax a photograph of the body to Quebec City police headquarters. Can someone take care of that without attracting Tanguay's attention?"

"I'll do it," Sirois said.

"What else do we know about the first murder?" Lessard asked.

He waited for someone else to speak, but the other members of the team stayed silent, preferring to let him continue.

"The killer took the trouble to wrap the body in a plastic sheet," Lessard said. "That suggests he was acting methodically. His crime was carefully planned. It was lucky for us that the car got stolen, or it might have been some time before we found the body."

Fernandez opened her mouth to speak, then seemed to think better of it. The detective sergeant noticed.

"What is it, Nadja?"

"Just an idea. We're assuming the killer abandoned the BMW on the street after committing the murder. But there's another possibility."

"Go on."

"The killer may have parked the BMW with the intention of coming back for it."

"Unlikely," Sirois said. "Why would he risk leaving the car unattended?"

"He couldn't have guessed that it would get stolen," Pearson ventured.

"True," Sirois replied, "but you're not going to walk away from a car with a corpse in the trunk unless you have a damn good reason."

Voices were starting to rise.

"Okay, that's enough," Lessard said.

There was a heavy silence. Lessard spoke again.

"The best explanation we have for the severed finger is biometrics. The killer had a specific need for Jacques Mongeau's index finger. We need to figure out why."

He looked around at the members of the team and saw nothing but uncombed hair, unshaved beards, and rings under weary eyes.

"The trouble is, we don't have a motive to guide us. There has to be some link between the two murders. We've got to keep digging until we know what it is. We don't have all the relevant information yet, but we need to work with what we've got, or we won't make any progress at all."

"Knowing the first victim's identity would be a big help," Pearson grumbled.

Lessard turned to Fernandez.

"Nadja, call Berger and find out where things stand with the dental information. He should accelerate the process by sending the records directly to dentists' offices."

"It's Saturday, Victor."

He swore. He had lost all sense of time.

"What about the kinky photographs?" Sirois asked. "Where do they fit in? Should we be looking for a political angle in all this?"

"And let's not forget the CD," Fernandez added. "The killer was clearly sending us some kind of message regarding Mongeau."

They were trying to put together a thousand-piece jigsaw puzzle without having seen the picture it was made from. Lessard could feel a migraine coming on.

"I'm still trying to figure this thing out," he admitted. "But whatever we do, we'd better do it fast, before Tanguay takes the case out of our hands."

The meeting was wrapping up. As the other cops rose to leave the room, Lessard spoke.

"One last thing. We need to cover our asses with the higher-ups and make sure they don't think we're dropping the ball on other investigations. Apart from the hit and run, what have we got going at the moment?"

Fernandez gave him a quick list of active cases. None of them seemed to require immediate attention.

"Nadja, do you think Nguyen could handle follow-up on the hit and run?"

"Sure. I'll talk to him."

Sirois frowned.

"Wasn't the car in question a black sedan?"

They'd been looking for a black Mercedes or Lexus, but given the age of the witness, he could easily have gotten mixed up.

Lessard wondered why he hadn't thought of it before.

As Lessard and Fernandez hurried into the police garage, they saw Adams on his hands and knees on the concrete floor, scrutinizing the BMW's body with a work light.

"Doug, did you find signs of an impact on the car?"

"I found more than that. I was just about to call you."

He walked to a stainless-steel counter and came back with a plastic bag containing a bit of torn fabric. Lessard peered at it.

"What is that?"

"A piece of denim. It was stuck in a gap in the front bumper."

"Do you think the car might have hit a pedestrian?"

"Yes. The bumper has buckled in one spot, and there's a slight dent in the hood."

Lessard thought back to his conversation with the doctor at the Montreal General Hospital. The physician had said Simone Fortin was struck in the legs. That helped explain why the damage to the car was relatively minor.

"Nadja, try to get in touch with Simone Fortin for an identification. Have her come in as soon as possible with the clothes she was wearing at the time of the accident. And call the witness, the elderly gentleman I spoke to yesterday."

"The one who was walking his dog?"

Butor. The only name he could remember was the dog's.

"Right."

As Fernandez left the garage, Lessard pondered. For the moment, there was no conclusive proof that the BMW had struck Simone Fortin. But he couldn't help wondering. If the car had indeed hit her, what did that mean? Probably nothing, except that she'd been in the wrong place at the wrong time.

"I also found some half-smoked cigarettes and joints in the ashtray. I've sent them to the lab. The saliva traces should yield plenty of DNA."

Lessard turned pale. He had no doubt about the smoker's identity. It was his own son.

"Come here," Adams said. "I have something else to show you."

Adams led him to a table where a complete set of photography equipment was arrayed.

"Was this in the car?"

"Yes. Under the hockey bag."

"Was it used to take the pictures we found on the disc?"

"No, but it's top-notch equipment. We should be able to find out where it was purchased. I've already called a few camera stores. And look at this."

Adams pointed at several plastic bags filled with water.

"Ice bags?" Lessard guessed.

"Yes," Adams said. "It seems like someone wanted to preserve the body. And there's something else."

He handed a small plastic evidence bag to Lessard.

"It's a slip of paper I found under the driver's seat. There's writing on it."

"4100 CN. What's CN? Canadian National? The railway company?"

"I was thinking the same thing. It could be the number of a train car or a specific route."

"Or maybe another error code. I'll put Pearson on it."

Lessard's cellphone hummed.

"Yes, Nadja?"

"I just spoke to Mr. Gagnon, the witness. He's at home, expecting your call. As for Simone Fortin, I haven't been able to reach her. She's already left the hospital —"

"I know," he said, cutting her off. "Don't ask how."

He had no desire to tell Fernandez about his torrid night with Ariane.

"Did you leave a message?" he asked.

"Yes."

"Perfect. Tell the old guy we'll be there to pick him up in fifteen minutes. I'll meet you in the parking lot."

By the glare of the work light, Adams resumed his painstaking examination of the BMW, looking for fingerprints.

"Doug, call me if you —"

"Find anything. I know."

Lessard left the garage. Had his luck finally turned? As he walked toward his car, he thought he glimpsed a ray of sunshine. Or was his imagination playing tricks on him?

As he was opening the car door, his phone hummed again. He recognized the number on the caller ID. Tanguay was trying to reach him. That was the last thing he needed. He knew he was taking a big risk, but he didn't answer.

•   •   •

Lessard watched, humiliated, as Fernandez tried to clear the passenger seat so she could sit in it. The Corolla was as messy as his apartment and his life.

"Maybe we should take another car, Victor."

He surveyed the car. He wished he could snap his fingers and get rid of the newspapers, the banana peel, the chocolate bar wrappers, the ancient pair of leather boots, and the umbrella that lay piled on the seat. Not to mention the turntable and the old vinyl Genesis albums that had been lying there since Marie threw him out. He needed to do a proper cleanup, but the mere thought of it made his heart sink.

"You're right," he said, and let out a deep sigh.

While Fernandez went back inside to get the keys to an unmarked service car, Lessard called his ex-wife's number. He felt strange every time he did it, worried that a man might answer. That was a possibility he didn't want to consider. She answered in a whisper on the first ring. He had to argue to get her to wake up Martin. What was the matter with her? Did she think everyone was taking it easy this morning?

"Hey, Dad," Martin said in a sleepy voice.

"The photography equipment in the car — did you and your friend steal that, too?"

"What?"

"This is important, Martin. Don't lie to me."

"It wasn't us. I swear."

Lessard could tell from the boy's tone that he was being truthful.

"And the slip of paper?"

"What slip of paper?"

"4100 CN."

"I don't know what you're talking about."

"Are you sure?"

Martin sighed. "Yes, Dad."

"How about the joints and cigarettes in the ashtray?"

There was a silence. "Yeah, those are ours."

"You and I are going to have a serious talk, son."

"Yes, Dad."

Lessard hung up without saying goodbye, then immediately regretted it. Fernandez opened the driver's door at the same moment. He jumped like a kid with his hand in the cookie jar.

"I've got the keys. You coming?"

Had she heard his conversation?

"You bet," he said, trying to sound cheerful.

"Any news?" she asked casually.

He flushed. "Nope."

Fernandez insisted on taking the wheel. Lessard had a reputation for being a bad driver. More than one colleague had gotten carsick while he was at the wheel. As for Nadja, she drove fast, but smoothly.

"You okay, Victor? You seem preoccupied."

"This goddamn case is wearing me out."

While they were waiting at a red light, he almost made up his mind to tell her the truth about his son, but then he saw the elderly man waiting on the sidewalk.

Lessard helped the man get into the car along with his dog, which promptly started drooling on the seats. God, he hated dogs!

The man spent the entire drive complaining about his various medical problems, while Fernandez listened compassionately. Lessard preferred to stay silent. He had no sympathy for seniors. The idea of having to look after one disgusted him.

He began to daydream, imagining his vacation with the kids in Banff. He would buy a tent, sleeping bags, a camping stove. They'd swim in mountain lakes, go fishing, build campfires, look at the stars, and, above all, get to know one another again. They'd start fresh. With the kids' help, he would become a model father.

Maybe Ariane could join them with little Mathilde.

Slow down, Lessard. How about you give your own kids some quality time before complicating matters?

Fernandez helped the old man out of the service car. They walked into the police garage. Adams and his assistant were off to one side, having sandwiches and coffee.

Lessard lifted his chin in the direction of the BMW.

"Take a good look, Mr. Gagnon. Is that the car you saw in the street?"

The man's eyes narrowed behind his thick glasses. "Sure looks like it. What did I tell you? A Mercedes."

Fernandez spoke up. "It's a BMW, Mr. Gagnon."

"Mercedes, BMW, they're all the same. Believe me, young lady, I know a German car when I see one. When you fought over there, like me, you don't forget. I even blew one up with a grenade, once. At Dunkirk, as I recall. For the life of me, I don't know why they're allowed to sell those things in this country. It's an insult to our veterans."

Lessard and Fernandez traded looks.

"Are you sure that's the car?" the detective sergeant asked.

"Absolutely. Do I look like I'm not sure?"

Repressing the first answer that came into his head, Lessard simply said, "Thank you, sir. My colleague will drive you home."

As he watched the two of them walk away, the detective sergeant wondered how much faith he could place in the old man's answers.

If it really was the BMW that had struck Simone Fortin, had she simply become mixed up in the case by accident or had she been deliberately targeted?

Though the latter possibility struck him as highly unlikely, he couldn't rule anything out.

A ray of sunshine caressed my face. I stretched lazily under the covers. It had been such a long time since I'd slept late! What was I going to do today? For starters, I'd make myself a cup of coffee.

And then?

And then, we'd see.

I reached out to my left. Was the cat curled up in his favourite spot beside the pillow? Still half-asleep, I realized that I wasn't in my apartment. I opened my eyes.

The room was bathed in the harsh light of a neon lamp. I sat up on the bed and looked around.

I remembered that I was in a motel room. The ratty bed, grimy carpet, cheap chest of drawers, melamine table, and two folding chairs all testified to that fact. In a corner, asleep in an armchair, was the man who had introduced himself as Kurt Waldorf.

Between gulps of Pepto-Bismol, Lessard remembered that he was supposed to look into the sexual harassment complaint that Fernandez had discovered. He reread the document dated September 25th, 1978. The yellowing form had been filled in with a typewriter. The complaint alleged that Mongeau had made statements and insinuations of a sexual nature to the complainant in their workplace. The alleged harassment had occurred on several occasions over a period of three weeks. Lessard put the document down on the desk, wondering whether he really needed to look into this. The incident had happened more than twenty-five years ago. It wasn't the sort of crime that might leave the victim craving deadly vengeance so many years later. Even so, after some hesitation, the detective sergeant called the complainant's number, which Fernandez had tracked down.

"Hello, I'm looking for Véronique Poirier."

"Speaking."

The woman had a refined voice. Lessard introduced himself.

"I'm calling about Jacques Mongeau …"

"Uh-oh, what has naughty Jacques done this time?" she asked teasingly.

The last thing Lessard had been expecting was to hear her refer to the man who had harassed her with such cheerful familiarity, as though he were an old friend.

"In the wake of his murder, I have a few questions about your comp—"

He heard a muffled cry at the other end of the line.

Véronique Poirier spoke in a trembling voice.

"Jacques? Murdered … it can't be."

"Haven't you seen today's papers? It's a front-page story."

"I'm sorry, I just got back from the country. I had no idea. Poor Hélène … and the boys. My God, it's a nightmare!"

Lessard's astonishment went up another notch.

Far from the embittered woman he'd been expecting, Véronique Poirier seemed to be close to the family. His investigative instincts told him he needed to follow up on this lead without delay.

"I'd like to talk to you in person, ma'am. I can be at your place in twenty minutes."

24

After ringing Véronique Poirier's doorbell, Lessard froze on the threshold. For considerably longer than good manners would dictate, he simply stared at the breathtaking woman who had opened the door.

She had dark hair and dazzling green eyes. Lessard guessed she was between thirty-five and forty. Given the date of the complaint, he'd been expecting a much older woman.

She invited him in and gestured toward the couch.

"I made coffee. Would you like a cup?"

"Please."

She excused herself and walked gracefully to the kitchen as the detective sergeant admired the sway of her hips.

"How do you take it?" she asked, coming back with a tray.

"Black," Lessard answered nervously. He straightened up on the couch and took the cup from her hands.

She sat down facing him. She'd been emotional over the phone, but now she seemed to have recovered her composure. Her expression was warm and friendly. The detective sergeant had to force himself not to look at her legs.

"So you just got back from the country?" he began.

"Yes, I was in Lanaudière. I have a hideaway in the mountains, where I go to paint."

Lessard's phone hummed. He checked the caller ID. Tanguay was calling again.

"You paint for a living?"

"That's one way of putting it. I paint full-time. But it doesn't pay the bills. In case you're wondering, I inherited this house and the place in Lanaudière when my parents died. Let's just say I've never needed to earn a living wage."

"When did you get back to town?"

"Yesterday, around midnight. If you're thinking I might have killed Jacques, I was with friends all week long. They can confirm my whereabouts." She took a sip of coffee.

Véronique Poirier was clearly a woman of spirit and intelligence. Lessard was doing his best to seem poised, but he felt like an oaf in her presence.

"When did you first meet Jacques Mongeau?"

"May 24th, 1978."

"You remember the precise date?"

"That was the day I received my master's degree in social work. We were introduced by a mutual friend, Flavio Dinar. Jacques subsequently hired me to work with sick children in his practice."

How could she have gotten a postgraduate degree in 1978? She would have been in her early teens.

"Forgive my indiscretion, but how old are you?"

Véronique's laugh spilled out in a crystalline cascade.

"You should know better than to ask a woman's age. I'll be fifty-four next month."

He couldn't believe his ears.

"Seriously," he said, "I'd have put you in your thirties."

"You're very kind. I look after myself."

"So it was while you were employed by Mongeau that you filed the complaint?"

"What complaint?"

"The one in which you alleged that he was sexually harassing you."

She laughed again, more heartily than ever. Lessard's nervousness was intensifying. He wiped his forehead.

"It's been so long," she said, "I'd forgotten all about it. Is that why you're here?"

Lessard nodded.

"He never harassed me, sexually or otherwise. I filed the complaint as a pressure tactic."

"Would you mind explaining?"

"Not at all. I'd been sleeping with him for a few months when I discovered that he was secretly videotaping our sexual encounters. I demanded that he give me the tapes. He was slow to comply, so I filed the complaint."

"And?"

"He handed over the tapes three days later. I withdrew the complaint. Problem solved."

"Did the episode create bad blood between you?"

"Not at all. Jacques was devious. He appreciated that quality in others."

"Did you go on being his mistress?" Lessard asked.

"What an old-fashioned word. We both liked sex, that's all. Now and then, I'd participate in what he liked to call his 'intimate soirées.'"

"Intimate soirées?"

"You never heard about them? My God, you must be one of the few people on the island of Montreal."

Lessard felt ridiculous. This woman intimidated him.

"Jacques used to organize sexual get-togethers," she said, "for his political friends."

An image of Jacques Mongeau was starting to take shape in Lessard's mind, fed by the pictures in the computer and these details about Mongeau's private life.

"You're talking about swingers' nights?"

"Having been to a few of them, I think 'orgies' might be closer to the mark, but you can call them whatever you like."

"He used to take pictures at these events?"

"And sometimes videos."

"Were his guests aware of this?"

"Never. Jacques was a little sneak. He referred to the photos and videos as his insurance policy. They were his way of keeping people honest."

"Who used to come to these soirées?"

Véronique Poirier uncrossed and re-crossed her legs. She was wearing white lace panties. Lessard swallowed with difficulty.

"Local celebrities, Ottawa policy-makers, advertising executives working on the sponsorship program, doctors, lawyers, judges, bankers, businessmen, high-class call girls … I even met a few senior police officers."

Lessard thought of Tanguay. He'd always suspected the man of being a bootlicker. Tanguay was obviously covering for someone. A superior officer? Himself?

"Could you give me some names?"

"I could, but I won't."

"What if I got a warrant to force you?"

"You won't do that."

"Why not?"

"Because you're a gentleman."

The detective sergeant reddened like a teenager. He was under the woman's spell.

"What about the prime … I mean …"

"The prime minister?"

He nodded.

"You'd like to know if he was involved in these little events? Some of his top ministers were on the guest list, but to my knowledge, neither the prime minister nor his wife ever took part in the festivities."

"Was Jacques Mongeau's wife … uh … in the loop?"

"I spent some very agreeable evenings in Hélène's company," Véronique Poirier purred.

"Actually, I was referring to the photographs. Did she know what was going on?"

"I couldn't tell you. Jacques was a discreet man."

"When was the last time you saw him?"

"About a month ago. February 17th, to be exact. It was a gallery opening, and some of my recent paintings were featured. Jacques came with Hélène. So did Flavio Dinar and his wife. We had a glass of wine and … anyway, it was very nice."

She looked at him with a sexy flutter of the eyelids. Lessard gulped.

Mongeau had invited influential business and political figures to his orgies and videotaped them in action, gathering material that he could use to obtain subsequent favours. The whiff of extortion was unmistakable.

Had Mongeau misjudged the reaction of one of his "intimate" guests? There were powerful men out there who would do anything to protect their reputations.

Lessard was discovering a world that made his head spin, though so far he'd only glimpsed the tip of the iceberg. Unless he was very much mistaken, he'd just gotten his hands on a compelling motive for murder.

"In your opinion, was Mongeau using these videotapes or photographs to put the squeeze on people?"

"Jacques was a very good lover. I was very attentive to his private parts, but less so to the rest of him. I always avoided getting mixed up in his activities. He used to say that he was playing a dangerous game. He often told me that his 'collection' was stored in a safe place."

"Do you know where?"

"He'd never have revealed that to me. He didn't trust anyone. Not even Hélène or his sons."

"Did he ever mention having a safe equipped with fingerprint recognition?"

"No."

Lessard decided to explore another avenue. Véronique Poirier might have met the killer without realizing it. Perhaps the encounter was hidden in some half-forgotten recollection.

For thirty minutes, he urged her to scour her memory. He questioned her about the soirées in which she had participated, as well as her personal contacts with Jacques Mongeau. He left no stone unturned, going back over the same ground several times.

Had she observed someone trying to avoid being noticed? Someone who was always there, yet never seen? She did her best to be helpful, but they uncovered nothing remotely resembling a lead. Lessard was convinced that she wasn't hiding anything.

He promised to bring her a composite sketch of the suspect that afternoon. But he wasn't optimistic about how helpful she'd be in that regard. If the murder had been committed for political reasons, a professional assassin had probably been hired.

Having exhausted his questions, Lessard stood up and handed her his card.

"If anything comes back to you, even a small detail, don't hesitate to call me."

Véronique Poirier accompanied him to the front door. He couldn't resist admiring her as she advanced with a light gait, as though walking on air. She turned to him with a grave expression.

"Did he suffer?"

The question caught him by surprise. He lowered his gaze.

"I don't think so."

They stood in silence for a moment.

As he was closing the door, he saw tears on her cheeks.

Outside, the wind had risen.

Still a little dazed by what he had just learned, Lessard walked back to the Corolla. Had Mongeau stepped on the toes of some powerful individual who didn't take kindly to being provoked? If so, had the provocation been sufficient to get him killed? In any case, it was unlikely that the victim of Mongeau's blackmail attempt, if such an attempt had occurred, would have risked doing the job personally.

People like that don't get their hands dirty.

What about the man whose body had been found in the trunk of the BMW? Where did he fit in? What role did Simone Fortin have in the whole affair, if indeed she was involved at all? Had she been a participant in Jacques Mongeau's erotic soirées?

Véronique Poirier's revelations shed a new light on the killer's possible motives. If Mongeau was in possession of compromising photographs and videos, then he had clearly taken the necessary steps to keep them secure. Suddenly, the idea of a safe with fingerprint recognition didn't seem so outlandish. Lessard and his colleagues would need to locate that safe and its contents in a hurry.

And what part did Tanguay play in all this?

Lessard would have to keep an eye on the son of a bitch. Tanguay was intent on interfering with the investigation. Was he covering for someone? If what Véronique Poirier had said was correct, the detective sergeant was stepping into a minefield. There might even be people on the police force who wanted to bury the case. If so, he'd be stymied.

As he started the car, he had a nagging sense of having neglected a vital detail. With one hand on the steering wheel, he called his sister's number, but hung up when the call went to voice mail. As he was slipping the phone into his pocket, it rang. He looked at the caller ID. Tanguay was getting impatient.

Making a face, he decided not to answer.

He woke up soaked with sweat. His sleep had been uneasy.

Was it the omelette he'd eaten the previous evening?

Very uncharacteristically, he'd been dreaming.

In fact, the dream had been about Simone Fortin. It was the first time he'd dreamed about one of his victims. In the dream, she was stretched out on a hospital bed. He pushed open the door and entered the room noiselessly. The young woman's eyes opened just as he was about to plunge the knife into her chest.

His thrust was stopped cold.

Try as he might, he couldn't move the knife, which remained suspended in the air.

He was a superstitious man, but he made an effort not to interpret the dream as a bad omen.

He ate a breakfast of fresh fruit juice, an orange, and two slices of toast with jam.

Armed with a Thermos full of coffee, he took up his surveillance position near Ariane Bélanger's house. Through the clouds, the sun was shining over Mount Royal.

Lessard opened the door for Fernandez and they stepped into the Shäika Café.

The place was eclectically decorated with eighties-style furniture and kitschy accessories. Fernandez ordered a fresh fruit juice while Lessard opted for a sandwich and a café au lait. He sank into a chair covered in orange vinyl. He had given his fellow cop a summary of his conversation with Véronique Poirier. They had also discussed the clues discovered by Doug Adams.

"Do we have the composite sketch?" he asked.

"Langevin's still working on it. He says it won't be ready until the end of the day, at the earliest."

Lessard sighed. Artists! It was like they lived on another planet.

"As soon as you get the sketch, fax copies to Véronique Poirier and all the stations on the island."

"Aye-aye, sir!"

He hadn't realized how peremptory he was being.

"I'm sorry, Nadja. I really appreciate your help."

The young cop couldn't help smiling. Lessard was an outwardly grumpy guy with the heart of a Mother Teresa.

"By the way," he asked, "did you get back in touch with the owner of the BMW?"

"Éric Leclerc? No. I thought you were taking care of it. He won't be too happy. I asked him not to leave his room until he heard from us."

"It completely slipped my mind. Do you have his number?"

Fernandez leafed through her notebook. The call was answered on the first ring.

"Is Éric Leclerc there, please?"

"Speaking," a gruff voice answered.

"This is Victor Lessard of the Montreal Police."

"You certainly took your time getting back to me."

Lessard resisted the temptation to tell the guy to go to hell.

"Just a few questions, and you can get on with your day. When did you park your car at the airport?"

"When? The day my flight left!"

"What date was that?"

"March 12th."

"At what time?"

"Seven in the morning."

"Was anyone with you?"

"My wife. And another couple. I really don't see why —"

The detective sergeant was wasting his time. This idiot wasn't going to give him anything useful.

"Mr. Leclerc," Lessard said sharply, "we're investigating a murder. Just answer my questions."

Leclerc fell silent.

"Was your car locked?"

"Of course."

"Did anyone have a duplicate key?"

"My wife. Nobody else."

"Do you have all the keys with you now?"

"Yes, they're both here."

"Did you hide a key anywhere on the vehicle?"

There was an embarrassed silence.

Jackass.

"I kept one hidden in a magnetized pouch near the exhaust pipe. But I was the only person who knew —"

"Thieves are familiar with that trick," Lessard said, cutting him off. "Were there any valuable items in the car?"

"No."

"Photography equipment?"

"No."

"A hockey bag?"

Leclerc sighed disdainfully.

"Definitely not."

"A slip of paper was found in the car with '4100 CN' written on it. Does that hold any significance for you?"

"None that I can think of."

"Okay. We're done. Thanks for your time, Mr. Leclerc. Enjoy the rest of your stay in Florida."

"Hang on a second. What about my car? I'll send my daughter to pick it up today."

"The vehicle is still being analyzed as part of an ongoing investigation. You can call our office when you get back."

"I demand that the car be handed over to my daughter as soon as she arrives. Do you know who you're dealing with? My brother-in-law is a deputy minister!"

"I'm very happy for you," Lessard couldn't help answering. "But you're still going to have to wait for your car."

"I intend to lodge a complaint. Your attitude is unacceptable. I want my car back, and I have friends in high places."

Lessard's ears began to ring. He lost his temper.

"I don't care if you're on a first-name basis with God. You'll get your car when we're done with it!"

He hung up. He lacked the restraint to put up with the man any longer. He was in the midst of one of the hardest cases of his career, an investigation that might cause problems for some very influential people. He had just learned that his son was a car thief. And this blowhard was threatening him with a complaint?

Fernandez put a hand on his forearm.

"You okay, Victor? Maybe you should get some rest …"

"No, no. The guy was just pissing me off."

"We're all under stress. It's natural."

"We need to catch a break today, Nadja."

"I have trouble buying into this whole blackmail-photograph theory."

"People have killed for less. And who knows, there may be other explosive material in the safe."

"Maybe so, but in a milieu where appearances matter so much, the killer's methods seem pretty incongruous."

Lessard's phone started dancing on the table.

"Sorry. It's Pearson. Yeah?"

"You'd better get over here. I have a witness. He says he talked to a man who was searching for a BMW at noon on Friday."

"Where are you?"

"A pharmacy at the corner of Côte-des-Neiges and Forest Hill."

"I'll be there in fifteen minutes."

He turned to Fernandez.

"I've got to go. Tell Langevin we need the composite sketch now."

He was putting on his leather jacket when he remembered that Tanguay had tried to reach him three times that morning. He pulled his phone back out.

You have three messages.

First message.

"Lessard, it's Tanguay. Call me back. I want a complete rundown in the next hour."

The detective sergeant took a bite of his sandwich and felt a twinge in his stomach. He'd have to buy a fresh bottle of Pepto-Bismol when he got to the pharmacy.

Second message.

"Don't play games with me, Lessard, or I'll have you on traffic duty at the corner of Berri and Sherbrooke."

Tanguay's tone was harsh and uncompromising.

Third message.

"Lessard, you … hole, if I don't hear from … next ten min … I'll transfer the case … Maj … Crimes Unit."

Judging from the breakups, Tanguay's last message had come from his cellphone. Lessard called the commander back on his office line. As he had hoped, the call went to voice mail after five rings.

"Commander Tanguay, it's Lessard. I just tried your cellphone, but it wasn't working. I'm out of town at the moment. I think we have a serious lead. My battery's almost dead, but I'll call you back as soon as …"

He ended the call. Fernandez looked worried.

"Is it bad?"

"Very. I'm going to see Pearson. He may have a witness. Call Tanguay for me. Tell him I've been trying to reach him all morning. And tell him to get his cellphone checked, because it's not receiving calls."

"He's never going to fall for that."

"I don't give a shit. I just need you to buy me some time."

"Where are you if Tanguay asks?"

"Didn't you hear me just now? I'm out of town, following up on a major lead. I'll get back to him as soon as I can."

Fernandez sighed. Lessard gave her a kiss on the cheek.

"I love you, Nadja. You're the best."

"Yeah, right."

As he drove, Lessard thought about the slip of paper Adams had discovered.

4100 CN.

Pearson hadn't found any error messages bearing that number. Fernandez had gone over all of CN's train schedules. No luck.

Ariane got up early.

The first order of business was making breakfast for Mathilde, who'd been awake since dawn. Then Ariane had to get the child ready for ballet class.

She laid out Mathilde's leotard and tutu on the couch.

"Get dressed!" she called from the kitchen, where she was making coffee.

Hypnotized by the TV, the little girl didn't react.

"Am I going to have to give you a time out, sweetie?"

"I'm getting dressed," Mathilde said, hurriedly pulling on the tights.

Ariane came into the living room, cup in hand.

"Are you drinking coffee, Mom?"

"Yes, sweetie."

"It tastes bad."

"How would you know?" Ariane asked, smiling.

"Axelle told me. She tried it."

"I think you'll learn to love coffee when you're a big girl."

"Yuck! And I'm already a big girl."

"Good point. Okay, let's go. We don't want to be late."

Pearson was standing in front of the pharmacy, sipping coffee.

Lessard had to slam the Corolla's rusty door twice to get it to stay closed. The car squeaked like the box spring on which he'd lost his virginity.

"What have you got?"

"Let's go inside," Pearson said.

The place looked more like an overstuffed general store than a pharmacy. The range of available items was startlingly vast.

Lessard made his way down an aisle jammed with cleaning

products, a freezer full of prepared meals, and a bin overflowing with brightly coloured balls. He tried without success to spot a prescription counter. Pearson headed toward the cash register, which stood behind a neon-lit Plexiglas display case full of cigars.

Lessard looked over the cigars, which were wrapped in cellophane. They must really have thought their customers were fools. In the old days, he'd been in the habit of stopping off at the Casa del Habano to enjoy an occasional smoke with the manager. He'd sink into one of the leather armchairs and puff on his Cuban cigar while, all around him, businessmen in sharp suits discussed money matters.

On such occasions, the manager would serve him a strong cup of coffee, to which Lessard would add a shot of cognac when the manager's back was turned. And his back was turned a lot. Lessard would also drink straight from the flask on his (too) frequent trips to the men's room.

He hadn't been back for a cigar since starting AA.

The cigar-alcohol association was so deeply rooted in him that the mere act of lighting up would have knocked him off the wagon.

Pearson walked up to an Asian man in a lab coat. This was clearly the pharmacist.

"You talked to an unusual customer yesterday, didn't you?" Pearson asked him.

"Yes," the pharmacist said, "quite unusual."

"Would you please tell my colleague what you told me a few minutes ago?"

"I step outside every so often for a cigarette. I saw a man walk past the pharmacy a few times. He seemed to be searching for something."

"What made you think that?" Lessard asked.

"I couldn't say, exactly. It was an impression I got. The guy was weird."

The detective sergeant tried to get the pharmacist to be more precise, but he remained vague.

"What happened next?"

"I asked if he needed help. He hesitated, then said he thought his car had been stolen."

"Did he describe the car?"

"He said it was a black BMW, and he'd parked it across the street from the pharmacy."

Pearson looked pleased with himself.

"And then?"

"He asked if I'd seen a tow truck on the street."

"And had you noticed anything?"

"Unless I'm on a cigarette break, I'm much too busy to pay attention to what goes on outside."

Lessard remembered the hypothesis that Fernandez had thrown out earlier, that the killer had parked the BMW with the intention of coming back for it. The pharmacist was now confirming that Fernandez had been right.

"What time did this happen?"

"Between noon and one o'clock. I know because I cover for the cashier during the lunch hour, and she was on her break when it happened."

Lessard frowned.

"Who fills prescriptions if you're at the register?"

"I do. But over the past few years, more and more of my revenue has come from merchandise sales. The truth is, I spend most of my time restocking shelves. The cashier starts work at ten-thirty every morning, and I have a stock clerk who comes in early on Saturdays."

"What do you remember about the man?"

"He was wearing a hat and sunglasses."

"Was he white, black, Asian?"

"White."

"Did he speak with an accent?"

"No."

"Tall? Short?"

"On the short side. I'd say he was about five foot seven."

"Was he wearing a jacket?"

"Yes, black or navy blue. Anyway, it was dark."

Lessard was scribbling in his notebook. "Did you notice anything else?"

"He was carrying a knapsack."

"How old was he?"

"Hard to say, because of the hat and glasses. Fifty, maybe."

The pharmacist's description was roughly consistent with the one given by Mongeau's secretary regarding height, ethnicity, and age. Unfortunately, the pharmacist couldn't confirm the man's hair or eye colour. Lessard knew from experience that those were the two details that were easiest to alter. Hair could be dyed. Eyes could be changed with contact lenses. Or they could simply be hidden, as in this case, under a hat and sunglasses. The composite sketch would be a useful aid in cross-checking each witness's description.

Damn Langevin! Why couldn't he work faster?

"What did he say to you, specifically? Can you remember his exact words?"

"It was something like 'I think my car's been stolen.'"

"How was he? Upset? Angry?"

"No, he seemed calm."

"What happened next?"

"I offered to call the police. He said he already had."

"That's all?"

"He said his antidepressants were in the car. He asked if I could replace them. He didn't have a prescription."

"Did he mention the name of the medication?"

"Amytal."

Lessard frowned. "What's that?"

"It's a barbiturate used to treat insomnia and anxiety."

"What did you do?"

"I offered to look him up in the system, but he said he lived in Ontario."

"So?"

"Since I don't have access to prescription databases in other provinces, I couldn't help him. I suggested that he speak to his doctor."

"Then what happened?"

"He walked away, and I went back inside."

Lessard glanced sharply at Pearson, who was looking triumphant.

"This medication, Amytal — does it get prescribed a lot?"

"Not anymore. For anxiety and sleep problems, benzodiazepines, better known as tranquilizers, have almost completely replaced barbiturates. Benzodiazepines are also used to treat alcoholism."

"Why aren't barbiturates used anymore?"

"Because tranquilizers don't carry the same risk of a lethal overdose."

"Is the use of barbiturates rare enough that we could pinpoint who was prescribing them?"

"No. Amytal remains a valid treatment option. Psychiatrists will still prescribe it when the circumstances are right."

Having finished the interrogation, Lessard bought three jumbo bottles of Pepto-Bismol. Stepping onto the sidewalk, he gave Pearson the same summary of the situation that he'd given Fernandez a few minutes earlier. They agreed that Pearson would have the pharmacist look at the composite sketch as soon as it became available.

"What do you make of the information he gave us?" Pearson asked.

"Fernandez was right. The killer didn't abandon the car. He came back for it, only to discover that it had been stolen out from under him." He paused. "There's something I don't understand, Chris." Lessard rarely addressed his younger colleague by his first name. "Why would the killer risk leaving the car unattended with a body in the trunk?"

"Because he was supposed to meet someone in the neighbour-hood?"

"Maybe. But let's not forget that Simone Fortin was run over just a few blocks from where he parked the car."

"So what? We can't be certain it was the killer who ran her over."

"We can't be certain, but it's a fair guess."

Pearson looked at him. Lessard continued.

"We know she was struck at ten-thirty in the morning. The BMW was stolen around noon. What was he doing during that time?"

"Okay, let's say you're right. Maybe he panicked afterward. Maybe he pulled over and got out of the car to settle his nerves. When he went back, the car was gone."

"Did he hit her deliberately?"

"He killed the other two victims with a hunting knife," Pearson replied without hesitation. "If he wanted to get her, too, why would he use a different method? No, if the killer did run her over, it was definitely by accident."

Lessard didn't know what to think. He had a nagging sense that Simone Fortin was somehow involved in all this, but he couldn't figure out where the intuition was coming from.

"What bothers me," Pearson said, "is the barbiturate thing. Should we be looking for someone who's depressed? Suicidal?"

Lessard, who had been given a prescription for antidepressants the previous year, was aware of the prejudices that many people had on the subject.

"Even if the killer were under treatment for depression, that wouldn't narrow the field a whole lot. Half of Quebec's adult popu-lation is depressed. We'd be looking for a needle in a haystack."

They were silent for a long while.

"There's also the question of residency," Pearson said. "Do you think he really lives in Ontario?"

"If it was the killer, I'd be surprised if he was reckless enough to reveal where he came from."

"So what's our next move? Is it worth drawing up a list of people who are using barbiturates?"

"That would take too long, especially if the killer doesn't live in Quebec. And we'd run into confidentiality issues in a hurry."

"Do you have a better idea?"

"If the killer really lost his medication because of the car theft, he might try to replace it some other way. Check to see if there have been any pharmacy thefts in the last forty-eight hours. That way we'll be sure we haven't overlooked anything."

"Then what?" Pearson asked. "Should I continue questioning people in the neighbourhood?"

"Might as well. You never know."

Lessard's cellphone started humming in his pocket as he was rolling along Victoria Avenue.

"Lessard."

"This is Véronique Poirier. You told me to get in touch if I remembered anything. It's probably not important, but a reporter came around a few months ago, wanting to ask me some questions."

"About Mongeau and his soirées?"

"Especially the soirées. He was well informed. He mentioned the names of people I'd met at a few of the events. I pretended not to know what he was talking about."

"Did he ask about the photographs?"

"No, he never brought them up. Naturally, I informed Jacques right away. He didn't seem too surprised, but he called me back a few hours later and asked me to let him know if anyone else came looking for information about the subject. I did a little checking and discovered that the person who had visited me wasn't a real reporter."

"Do you know who he was?"

"No. Jacques told me not to worry, he knew what it was about, and it wouldn't happen again. But I could tell that it bothered him."

"Would you recognize this person if you saw him now?"

"It's been quite a while, but I think so. He was tall, dark-haired, in his midforties."

Lessard pondered for a moment. What did this mean? Could the fake reporter have been a hitman hired to get rid of Mongeau? If so, they would need to find out who had hired him.

Véronique Poirier's description didn't match the ones furnished by Mongeau's secretary and the pharmacist. It occurred to Lessard that Tanguay was fairly tall, dark-haired, and in his midforties.

He had a feeling that something was out of place. But what?

"I can hear the wheels turning."

"Sorry," Lessard said. "Do you remember when this person came to see you?"

"It was last summer. Before my vacation, I think. Sometime in late June or early July 2004."

More than eight months had passed since then. Was there a link between this incident and the murder?

A sudden sensation of defeat washed over him. He wasn't going to make it. He longed to buy a bottle of Jack Daniel's and drink himself into oblivion.

"Victor?"

His heart jumped. Had she just called him by his first name?

"I know you're in the middle of a difficult case, but when it's over, we should go out for dinner sometime. Do you enjoy open-air whirlpools and saunas? This is the ideal season to go to a spa."

Lessard felt light-headed. He'd never been to a spa, but he knew people wore swimsuits there.

"It would be a pleasure," he heard himself say.

"Great. See you soon."

She hung up.

It would be a pleasure.

Had he really said that in the smooth, confident tone of a man of the world? Had he, Victor Lessard, pronounced those words? Was it conceivable that an exquisite woman like Véronique Poirier was actually interested in a loser like him?

He glanced around. Surely, somebody was about to emerge from an unseen corner and point to a hidden camera.

25

Trois-Pistoles

I got up, taking care not to wake Kurt Waldorf.

I regretted not having offered to share the bed with him. He had slept fully clothed in the sagging armchair, and he would certainly feel the painful effects when he woke up.

How had I ended up here?

It was quite simple, really.

After approaching me in the parking lot, Waldorf offered to drive me to the only local motel that was open at that hour. It was four in the morning. I was bone-tired, I didn't know Trois-Pistoles, and frankly, how could things get any worse? Ignoring the instinct that urged me to be suspicious of the man, I followed Waldorf to his car.

While he drove, I checked my messages. Ariane had tried to reach me while my phone was off. I was hesitant to bother her at this hour, but I knew she always turned off her cellphone at night. My call went directly to voice mail. I left her a message saying I'd gone on a short trip to the Lower Saint Lawrence region, and I wasn't sure when I'd get back, but I'd tell her all about it when we saw each other. I asked her please not to worry, and also, if it wasn't too much trouble, to stop in at my place and feed the cat.

As I was turning the key in the lock of my motel-room door, the anxious voice in my head got louder.

Why are you letting this man come in with you? Because he wants to talk about Miles, and I need to understand what's going on!

Waldorf pulled the table into the middle of the room and drew up two chairs. Then, like a magician, he produced a bottle of vodka from the folds of his coat and placed it on the table. I took two plastic glasses from the edge of the sink and removed their cellophane wrapping. He half filled them and dropped in some ice cubes that he'd gotten from the reception clerk.

As I brought the glass to my lips, I felt myself getting woozy again. He caught me before I fell off the chair and helped me to the bed.

"Let me examine you."

"I'm okay."

I looked at him warily. Who did he think he was, wanting to examine me?

"I insist."

Without putting on his coat, he walked out to his car and came back with a medical bag.

I sat up, ready to fight him off.

"Relax," he said. "I'm a neurosurgeon. Or was, anyway."

He looked about as much like a neurosurgeon as I looked like a belly dancer. But I didn't resist. His voice was so warm, so sincere. A man with a voice like that couldn't possibly have evil intentions.

Waldorf shone a bright light in my eyes and checked my blood pressure.

"You've sustained a head injury," he said, unwrapping the cuff from my arm. "Your pressure's a little on the high side, but on the whole, you seem okay."

"I don't —"

"When did you come out of your coma?"

The conversation had just taken a very weird turn. In my astonishment, I could think of nothing better to tell him than the truth.

"Yesterday afternoon at two-thirty. But how did you —"

He interrupted me once more. "You didn't waste any time. It took me several weeks to work up the nerve to come looking for Miles."

I didn't blink at this further revelation.

"You're the second person in less than twelve hours who's tried to convince me that you saw him. Is this a conspiracy?"

"So you've met Gustave, have you?"

Two glasses of vodka were enough to batter down the last of my defences. Dazed by alcohol and fatigue, I wanted to learn more about Gustave, but Waldorf, who was seated with his legs crossed on the sagging armchair, stopped me short.

"You need to rest. I'll wake you up in a few hours."

I had so many unanswered questions.

Under normal conditions, I'd have fought tooth and nail to extract every shred of information he possessed. But at that moment, his voice had seemed to be coming from far away, and the mattress was as soft and yielding as the creamy foam on a café au lait. Even so, I tried to press him, if only out of pride. "How did you find me?"

"I asked to be notified if anyone came to visit Miles."

I was drifting off. Waldorf spoke again.

"Did Miles speak to you about his son, Laurent?"

"Yes."

My eyelids were heavy. My speech was slurred. Waldorf hesitated.

"He's here in Trois-Pistoles. We'll go see him tomorrow."

As he said those words, I fell asleep.

And that was how I ended up in this room.

Though it might have seemed like an impossible feat, the motel dining area managed to be even uglier than the room. Waldorf ordered orange juice and a plate of bacon and eggs. I settled for a cup of sour coffee and a limp croissant.

The waitress brought our meals to the table and we ate in silence. After a few minutes, Waldorf pushed his empty plate aside.

I clearly remembered that he and I had discussed Miles, his son, and Gustave before I'd fallen asleep. I was desperate to know more.

"Kurt, I —"

Perhaps anticipating my question, he cut me off gently, as though reluctant to hurt the feelings of an old friend.

"I know, Simone. I owe you an explanation."

He took a few seconds to gather his thoughts. I took a sip of coffee and grimaced. Through the window, I saw a car go by on the wet asphalt.

"Not so long ago, I thought I had the perfect life. I'd been married for sixteen years to an extraordinary woman. I worked as a neurosurgeon at the Cité de la Santé Hospital in Laval. I was a successful professional, respected by my colleagues. I had money, a country house, ample opportunities to travel …"

His features grew sombre, and I couldn't help thinking that I, too, had once aspired to a successful and prosperous life.

"That perfect life continued until one chilly evening in October of 2004. I was driving home after a day of surgery. I can't even remember if I felt tired. Should I have been worried about falling asleep at the wheel? In any case, that's what happened. I woke up twelve days later in the intensive care unit, having sustained a cranial trauma and multiple fractures to my legs and pelvis. My car had plowed into the back of a tractor-trailer. By some miracle, I wasn't permanently disabled. In the first few hours after I regained consciousness, I had trouble recognizing my wife. But my condition improved rapidly. Within twenty-four hours, my neurological signs were back to normal. Everything was fine, except that a memory was haunting me, a memory so strange that I didn't dare mention it to anyone. While I was in a coma, I had met a man named Miles."

I felt myself grow tense in my chair, my fingertips whitening as I clutched the armrests. I looked at Waldorf with an expression of incredulity, even though I knew he was telling the truth.

"I'm not religious or spiritually inclined. Being a physician, I had to get past some serious doubts. I was assailed by the same questions that have surely been eating at you. Was it a dream? Was I crazy?"

Listening to Waldorf describe his uncertainty, I felt simultaneously relieved and terribly woozy, as though realizing for the first time the full implications of what I'd been through.

"You can well imagine that for someone like me, someone who prides himself on his knowledge of the brain and its functions, the level of disbelief was very high. Could my coma really have brought me into contact with another comatose person? Naturally, the idea struck me as absolutely inconceivable. After a few days in the hospital, I went home. I spent hours on the internet, searching medical databases for reports of similar cases, but I came up empty-handed. As the weeks went by, I resumed my day-to-day life, trying to convince myself that nothing had happened. I didn't want to talk to my wife about it, because I felt afflicted by a shameful deficiency. Eventually, unable to stand it anymore, I decided to consult a trusted colleague, a man I knew to be more open-minded than I was when it came to spiritual matters. After hearing me describe my experience, he put me through a battery of tests, more for the purpose of calming my fears, I now realize, than of figuring out what was going on. The tests came back perfectly normal, and my colleague tried to convince me that I was simply suffering from the post-traumatic effects of my head injury. All of which led to one inescapable conclusion: if this man refused to entertain the possibility that something unaccountable had happened, then no one else would, either."

Remembering my own brief conversation with Ariane, I knew the hopelessness he'd felt as he realized that the whole world might start questioning his grasp on reality.

Waldorf went on. "I tried to put the matter behind me, but I couldn't. It had become an obsession. I finally opened up to my wife and close friends. If you insist on speaking frankly about uncanny experiences, people are quick to let you know they don't appreciate it. When you walk into a room, you can see them whispering, 'Poor Kurt, he hasn't been the same since the accident. He's not all there.'"

"Your wife didn't believe you?"

He lowered his gaze. "That was the hardest part. The accident left me with a permanent impairment of my fine motor skills. When it comes to everyday tasks, I'm okay, but as far as surgery's concerned, my career is over. So a big part of my world came tumbling down after the accident. Surgery had been my life." He gazed vacantly into space for a moment. "I think my wife came to believe that I'd invented the story to avoid having to face reality." He stared at the wall for a long time, as though scenes from his past were being projected there. "But there was more to it than that. The accident opened other wounds. Over the weeks that followed, my wife became a stranger to me." His expression clouded over. "We separated more than two months ago. That was when I started trying to locate Miles."

"I'm very sorry," I said.

"Don't be," he answered. "It's in times of hardship that we learn the truth about those closest to us." He paused. "I haven't yet succeeded in grasping the phenomenon, let alone explaining it. But after torturing myself for weeks, I've realized that I have two choices: I can believe or I can deny. I choose to believe. I choose to accept that these things really happened."

"You mentioned Gustave earlier. How do you know him?"

"He approached me when he saw me hanging around Miles's hospital room. It's not easy to have a rational conversation with Gustave, but from what I could gather, he spent more than a week in a coma as a result of a snowboarding accident. He had an experience similar to yours and mine. But he decided to deny what had happened ... or rather, he settled on an explanation of his own."

"The men from the other world."

"Exactly."

At least two other people had been through the same thing as
me. One of them, Kurt Waldorf, was a trained neurosurgeon and a
highly articulate man.

"Why has this happened to us?" I asked. "Are we the only ones?"

"Those are some of the questions I've been trying to find
answers to. Simone, I don't know whether you've come to any conclusions about all this, but you can rest assured that I understand
what you're going through."

The waitress placed the bill on the table. Though I objected for
form's sake, Kurt handed her a credit card and she went away.

Now that my curiosity had been satisfied, I could tell from the
intensity of his gaze that he was waiting for me to describe my own
experience. It took me a little more than fifteen minutes to give
him the details of my accident, my visit to the cemetery in Miles's
company, and my encounters with George and Jamal. I wrapped up
with an account of how I had regained consciousness in the hospital and set off in an effort to track down Miles.

As I spoke, I saw an expression of surprise on Kurt's face.

"Did Miles give you some kind of message for Laurent?" he
asked.

"No. Did he give you one?"

"I … uhh … yes," he said at last.

"Would you care to explain?"

Waldorf jumped to his feet.

"Not now. Come on."

Laurent didn't know what to think.

Waldorf had stayed with him through the night. The young
man had come to find his presence reassuring, especially in the
worst phase of withdrawal, when the longing for alcohol had been
unbearable. The guy hadn't said much, but there had been great
empathy in his gaze.

Maybe Laurent had been wrong about him. Then a phone call had come in the middle of the night. Waldorf had stepped away to take it, so Laurent hadn't heard the conversation.

When Waldorf had returned to the bedroom, he had freed Laurent from his restraints and helped him walk to the kitchen.

What he had done next was mystifying.

Waldorf had declared that he'd be gone for a few hours, and when he returned, he'd be able to offer corroboration for his claims.

"I'll give you tangible evidence that I'm telling the truth," he had said.

Then Waldorf had given him a choice. He could handcuff him to a chair or set him free to move around as he wished. After a few seconds' hesitation, Laurent had asked for the handcuffs.

He was lucid enough to know he couldn't trust himself.

Waldorf was driving skillfully along a foggy road. The temperature was hovering near the freezing point, and wet snow was falling, making the road slippery.

"What was the message you were supposed to give Laurent?" I asked.

Waldorf paused, as though unsure whether he should answer.

"I don't know why, but it seems like Miles didn't want to use you as a messenger. Maybe he changed his mind."

"Could you be a little more vague?" I asked sarcastically.

"Look, I'm honestly not sure how much I should be telling you."

"About what?"

He took his eyes off the road for an instant.

"Miles didn't discuss his condition with you?"

"What do you mean?"

"His feelings about being in a coma."

"Of course not."

Waldorf shook his head.

"I had assumed that he'd talk to others the way he talked to Gustave and me. I must admit, I'm not sure what's going on."

"That makes two of us. I have no idea what you're getting at. What's so important or so awful that you're not sure whether you can talk to me about it?"

"I don't want to hide anything from you. But I'm realizing that Miles may have had something special in mind for you."

26

Lessard bought himself a cup of coffee and found an armchair in a quiet corner. He enjoyed the tranquil charm of the Westmount Municipal Library, where he sometimes came to clear his mind when he was in the midst of an investigation. This time, though, his primary objective was to avoid running into Tanguay at the station.

His brain was teeming. He needed to get his thoughts in order. The details of the case were so numerous and disjointed that he was having trouble keeping track of them.

What had he learned since this morning?

First, there was Adams's examination of the BMW, which had yielded some interesting leads. Then there was the information supplied by Véronique Poirier and the pharmacist. What conclusions could Lessard draw from this motley assortment of facts?

He allowed his mind to stray, trying to fit the puzzle pieces into a coherent whole. But he had a nagging sense that he was neglecting significant details. There were moments when he felt like he was getting close to something important, only to have the insight slip out of his grasp.

He made a mental effort to get back on solid ground, focusing on the facts. He opened his notebook and began to write.

- Friday, 10:30 a.m.: A BMW carrying the first victim's body probably runs over Simone Fortin.

- Noon: Martin steals the BMW. Shortly afterward, the killer asks the pharmacist about the missing car and tries to get barbiturates without a prescription.

- 3:30 p.m.: Jacques Mongeau is killed.

- Question: What was the killer doing between 10:30 and Mongeau's murder?

Lessard reread his notes. He scratched out the word *probably* and replaced it with *possibly*.

His instincts were telling him that the barbiturates didn't fit with the rest of the pattern, but he couldn't figure out why.

He got up and walked to the computer terminal that the library made available to users. After several unsuccessful attempts, he managed to get an internet connection. He typed *Amytal* into the Google search bar and skimmed through the various pages that came up. They largely confirmed what the pharmacist had told him. Lessard also read a technical summary of the barbiturate's effects. At low doses, Amytal reduced the tension caused by anxiety or insomnia. Higher doses could cause visual problems, slurred speech, impaired perception of time and distance, and a slowing of reflexes and respiration.

An overdose could lead to coma and death.

He paused to consider this.

The pharmacist had said that the killer seemed calm. Was he using the drug to control his anxiety or insomnia?

Lessard printed the page and stuffed it in his leather jacket pocket. Then he sent a message to Berger. Had he found traces of Amytal or other barbiturates in his autopsies of the two victims?

Returning to his armchair, the detective sergeant opened his notebook and drew up a list of unanswered questions.

- Q1: Who was the first victim?

- Q2: Why did the killer modify his modus operandi (severed finger, CD)?

- Q3: Did Mongeau hide his photographs in a safe protected by biometrics?

- Q4: Who might have wanted to kill him?

- Q5: What was the significance of the number printed on the disc? And 4100 CN?

Lessard couldn't help thinking about the commander, who was doing everything he could to keep Lessard from investigating the kinky photographs.

Was Tanguay protecting someone?

As he reread everything he'd just written down, an idea struck him. Adams had said that the photography equipment found in the BMW was professional grade. Had the pictures in Mongeau's computer been taken with that camera?

The question was a good one. He sent a message to Adams.

The signs of impact on the car body, along with Hilaire Gagnon's confirmation, seemed to suggest that Simone Fortin had been struck by the BMW, which was carrying a corpse at the time. Was it a simple accident, or had she been targeted? If she'd been targeted, was there any link between her and Mongeau's erotic soirées?

Lessard slammed a fist onto the armrest of his chair. He was getting nowhere. And he still hadn't found a motive. He needed an opening. The detective sergeant looked out the window. A smiling mother was leading three small children along the sidewalk. The father was following behind, pushing a stroller. They seemed happy. He missed his family. What were his wife and kids doing while he was here, struggling to unravel the twisted actions of a killer? Was it too late? Could he still hope to have a positive influence on the lives of Martin and Charlotte?

After this investigation was over, he'd have to do some thinking. He needed to decide whether he wanted to stay on in this stress-filled job.

He descended to the ground floor and tried to buy a fresh cup of coffee from the vending machine, which swallowed his coins but failed to supply the desired nectar. Frustrated, Lessard kicked the machine violently. An elderly lady gave him a frightened look as she went by. He needed to get a grip on himself. As a police officer, he was supposed to be helping people feel safe, not scaring them.

He thought about calling his mentor, Ted Rutherford. But Rutherford hadn't been the same man since his devastating stroke five years ago. Whenever Lessard visited him these days, he came away badly shaken.

Ted, what would you do in a case like this?

The truth was, he knew very well what Ted would do. Using the available facts, he'd try to work out a plausible hypothesis. He would then confirm or rule out his theory as the investigation progressed.

Lessard pondered. What was the most logical hypothesis at this point? Someone had murdered Mongeau because he was in possession of compromising photographs. Maybe Mongeau had blackmailed this person, or applied pressure to extract benefits.

A nebulous image began to take shape in Lessard's mind.

In a way, this person is running his own investigation. He must have considerable resources at his disposal. He sends a fake reporter to obtain information from Véronique Poirier. Mongeau gets wind of it, but the person still learns about the existence of the safe.

Where did the first victim fit into this theory?

Was he an associate of Mongeau's who had to be eliminated?

In any case, a hitman is hired. He kills the first victim, then Mongeau. He cuts off his index finger to get into the safe.

Did it all make sense?

Suddenly, Lessard had an idea.

He left Sirois a phone message asking him to look and see whether the first victim appeared in any of the photographs found in Mongeau's computer. As he ended the call, he saw that

Fernandez had tried to reach him. He returned her call, but got her voice mail. He checked his messages and saw that she had just left one. Tanguay was on the warpath. And she still hadn't heard back from Simone Fortin.

Through the window, the detective sergeant saw snowflakes falling from a colourless sky. He loved the first flakes of November, all white and innocent, giving you faith in a better tomorrow. But he hated the flakes that fell in April, desecrating the springtime before it had even shown its face.

Goddamn winter …

Lessard was neglecting important elements. He was sure of it. He thought back to his conversation with Fernandez at Shäika Café. She had said something that now seemed enormously significant. But what?

He tried to reach her, but his call went to voice mail once again. He didn't leave a message. As he pocketed the phone, he knocked over the cup containing the cold remains of his coffee.

Emitting a stream of profanities, he wiped up the mess with sheets torn from his notebook. His memory was on overload. He yawned.

He woke up and looked at his watch. He had slept eleven minutes. He shook himself to get rid of the lingering cobwebs. There was a sharp pain in his back.

He decided to go back to the beginning, but this time from the killer's point of view. He needed to establish a chronological order for the murderer's actions. He grabbed his notebook.

- Thursday: The killer steals the BMW at the airport and murders his first victim.

- Friday, 10:30 a.m.: The killer runs over Simone Fortin. The first victim is in the trunk. The killer parks the car two blocks away.

- Friday, noon: Martin steals the BMW.

- Friday, between 12:00 and 1:00 p.m.: The killer stops outside the pharmacy. He asks the pharmacist about the missing BMW. He tries to get barbiturates without a prescription.

- 3:30 p.m.: Jacques Mongeau is killed.

As Lessard mulled over these facts, he kept coming back to the same two questions.

- Why does the killer park the car in the first place?

- What is he up to between 10:30 a.m. and 12:00 noon?

He tried to come up with a credible hypothesis.

Maybe Pearson was right: the killer was supposed to meet someone. Or maybe he was supposed to deliver the car to an accomplice, who would then get rid of the body. But if that were the case, the rendezvous would have been planned ahead of time. The accomplice would have been waiting, and stealing the car would have been practically impossible.

It didn't make sense. Something didn't fit. Furiously, Lessard scratched out what he'd just written. The killer had taken the risk of parking the BMW two blocks from the scene of the accident, leaving the car and its contents unattended. There was no way he could have expected the vehicle to get stolen, but he had to know that someone who had witnessed the hit and run might recognize the BMW and call the police. Even so, he had walked away. With a corpse in the trunk, that surely wasn't a risk he'd taken lightly. Unless he was totally oblivious, he had to have a serious reason for doing what he did. The bags of ice were further proof that he wanted to preserve the body as long as possible.

Another hypothesis suddenly occurred to him.

Could the killer have returned to the scene to finish off Simone Fortin? He leaned back in his chair and pondered for several seconds. He wasn't convinced.

Was the idea too simple or too absurd?

He tried to replay the scene in his head. The killer waited until Simone Fortin came out of her office building, then gunned the engine and ran her over. Afterward, he walked back to the scene to be sure she was dead. He saw that she wasn't, but the crowd of onlookers prevented him from finishing the job.

Lessard frowned. Conceivable, yes. But was it likely?

He rubbed his neck. His thinking was clearer now. This theory had the advantage of providing a logical explanation for the killer's actions. On the other hand, it raised new questions, and it had weaknesses of its own.

For instance, the killer had stabbed two of his victims to death, yet he had tried to kill Simone Fortin by running her over.

Why? What was his motive for killing her? Had she participated in Mongeau's soirées? Did someone want to silence her, too?

Lessard stood up and put on his leather jacket. Was he on the right track? Should he have the investigation team follow up and see where this led?

As he walked to his car, he shivered.

What kind of dehumanized world were we living in? For most people, violence was simply part of everyday life. Two men stabbed, a woman run over — it was the kind of thing we all saw every day on the news, in the papers, and at the movies. How could anyone be upset by such things when genocide, war, and bombings were routinely included in the continuous flow of barbarism coming from our TV screens?

Atrocity leaves us desensitized.

Even so, Victor Lessard shivered.

Not from cold, but from disquiet. He shivered because, in his efforts to navigate this ocean of violence, he couldn't remain indifferent to the fates of the two murdered men.

As he got behind the wheel of his Corolla, he realized that he was crying. He was crying for those two dead strangers.

He was crying for everyone who stops caring.

He was crying for everyone who turns off the nightly news, gets into bed, and forgets.

He wished he could forget, too.

27

Lessard drove west on Côte-Saint-Antoine, turned right on Marcil, and rolled through Monkland Village, the trendiest neigbourhood in Notre-Dame-de-Grâce. Spotting a gas station, he pulled in to fill his tank.

After some small talk with the attendant, he took a few steps to stretch his legs. The gas station was close to an Italian restaurant where Lessard regularly bought fresh pasta and homemade sauce. He waved to the owner, who was cleaning the four digits of his address plaque with a sponge and a bucket of water.

As he watched the man, an idea came to him.

4100 CN.

Was it too simple to think it was a street address?

4100 Côte-des-Neiges.

He sped away from the gas station and went straight back to the office. If he wasn't mistaken, that address was very near the spot where the young woman had been struck. Where had she said she worked? An advertising agency.

He patted his pockets, found his notebook, and leafed through it. Damn! He knew he had scribbled it down somewhere. He promised himself to write more legibly from now on.

He was about to give up when he found what he was looking for.

Simone Fortin (33)
Dinar Communications

Lessard typed *dinarcommunications.com* into his search engine. The website opened with an animated sequence, but he skipped the introduction and went straight to the home page. After searching for a few seconds, he saw *Contact Us* and clicked on the tab. A new page appeared.

Dinar Communications
4100 Côte-des-Neiges Road, Montreal, QC

This isn't just a coincidence.

A slip of paper with Simone Fortin's office address on it had been found in the BMW. Lessard's intuition was telling him the situation was urgent. He had to assemble the team immediately. The killer had returned to finish off his victim.

But what if he was wrong? What if he was steering the investigation up a blind alley?

He dialed Fernandez's number.

Simone Fortin was in danger. He could feel it.

Lessard started off the meeting by summarizing the situation for his fellow investigators. Then he outlined his hypothesis. It was simple. Simone Fortin had been the victim of a murder attempt that linked her to the two dead men.

Had she participated in Mongeau's intimate soirées?

Had she become a problem that needed to be eliminated?

Starting now, the team would have to concentrate its efforts on the young woman. She was the missing piece that would enable them to solve the puzzle.

Pearson objected that Lessard was jumping to conclusions.

"What proof do we have that the BMW was the car that struck Simone Fortin?"

"We have an eyewitness. We have the impact damage on the hood of the BMW. We have the piece of denim that was caught in the bumper. And we know the car was in the neighbourhood after the hit and run occurred. What more do you want?"

"Okay," said Pearson, not giving up, "let's say it's the same car. What proof do we have that it wasn't just an accident? What proof do we have that Simone Fortin is in danger?"

"This is what I'm trying to explain to you! The slip of paper marked 4100 Côte-des-Neiges. The killer was waiting for her, Pearson! First he runs her over. Then he parks the car, intending to finish her off, but the crowd of onlookers gets in his way. In the meantime, the car is stolen."

"Nice theory, Victor, but it doesn't explain why the killer keeps changing his modus operandi. He murders the first victim with a knife and sticks the body in the trunk of the BMW. He cuts a finger off the second and tries to kill the third in a hit and run. And let's not forget the disc we found in Mongeau's office, or the blog. Do you see a pattern in all this?"

The feeling that he might be mistaken weighed on Lessard once more. Was he leading the team in the wrong direction?

"It's just a hypothesis, but I'd be willing to bet that there's a connection between Mongeau's murder, the body in the BMW, and the hit and run involving Simone Fortin. We need to look into her past, dig up every scrap of available information, and find the missing link."

"Maybe I've been watching the wrong science shows," Sirois said, laughing, "but I thought the best place to find the missing link was Africa."

Lessard glared at him. This was no time for jokes.

"Should we drop everything else?" Fernandez asked.

Lessard hesitated.

"Let's make this our focus for the next few hours. By the way, have you heard from Simone Fortin?"

"No."

"We need to track her down in a hurry. Do you think she left the hospital under her own steam? I wouldn't have thought that was possible after being in a coma."

"Good point. I'll talk to the nurse who was on duty. We need to know what condition she's in."

"I'll call Ariane Bélanger." He reddened, but no one noticed. "She may be able to help us."

"Unless Simone Fortin is already dead," Sirois said.

Lessard's response was sharp and instantaneous.

"Keep the helpful comments to yourself, Sirois."

He looked around at the group. "I want her description sent to all patrol units. Let's go!"

Not another death. Please. It would be more than he could bear.

Lessard poured himself a cup of coffee and retreated into his office. His chair creaked under his weight. When he reached for the phone, he realized that his hand was trembling. He took some time to compose himself before dialing the number. Once again, his call went to voice mail.

"Hello, Ariane, it's Victor Lessard." His voice was cool and professional. "I need to talk to you right away about Simone Fortin. It's urgent." His voice softened a little. "Uh ... I also want to apologize about last night. I had to leave in a hurry. I'll explain later." Then he turned professional again. "Please call me as soon as you get this message."

He left his cell number and hung up. Only after cutting the connection did he realize that he'd forgotten to say goodbye.

Why must he always be so awkward?

Ariane had managed to do the impossible. She had prevailed on Mathilde to get dressed.

Then she had taken a lightning-quick shower.

The challenge now was to find a parking space on Sherbrooke

Street. After searching for a while, she gave up and left the car in a no-parking zone.

She took a sip of coffee as she watched Mathilde bouncing around on the dance floor. When the class was over, they'd stop off at Simone's place to feed the cat. Ariane had been relieved to get a message from her, but she'd also been concerned to hear that she was so far away. What was Simone doing way out there?

She thought affectionately of Victor Lessard. She had enjoyed their evening together, but he seemed so shy. He'd crept away without a word. Ariane was certain that she'd scared him.

Would he call today?

Lessard had considered going home for a nap, but he decided to stretch out on his office rug for a few minutes instead.

He had just rolled his jacket into a ball to serve as a pillow when he heard a commotion in the corridor. Voices were being raised, though he couldn't make out what they were saying.

Please, please … not another dead body.

He opened the door and found himself nose to nose with a crimson-faced Tanguay. There were flecks of foam at the corners of the commander's mouth.

"Do you think I'm a complete idiot, Lessard?"

"I was just going to call you, Commander. We have an important lead —"

"Save it for Major Crimes. I'm taking you off the case."

Lessard didn't have time to reflect on the fact that he was putting his career on the line with what he was about to say. His reply came out like an arrow, swift and true, and hit the bull's eye.

"No, you're not."

Tanguay stared at him. "Excuse me?"

Lessard swallowed. "You heard me, sir."

"You don't have a say in the matter, Lessard!"

Tanguay was glaring at him. The detective sergeant took a moment to steady himself. Everything hinged on the words that were about to come out of his mouth.

"If you want to transfer the file to the Major Crimes Unit, that's up to you, Commander. But if you do, there's a fair chance that certain photographs will come out — photographs I would have thought you preferred to keep private."

Tanguay's face went white. The bluff had worked.

"I don't know what you're talking about, Lessard. Is that a threat?"

"Let's just call it a friendly warning."

For a few seconds, the two men looked at each other. Then Tanguay lowered his eyes.

"You have no conception of the shitstorm you're walking into, Lessard."

He turned and marched away down the corridor. Before going around the corner, he punched the wall hard, leaving a crater in the plaster. Tanguay had powerful friends. Lessard was certain that his career as a cop had just ended.

He was a dead man walking.

28

Waldorf pulled the car over on a dirt road beside a chalet. Thick white smoke was rising from the chimney. As we crossed the threshold, I recoiled. A young man was sitting in the kitchen, handcuffed to a chair.

"I forgot to tell you, Simone. Our friend Laurent has agreed to go cold turkey."

The young man turned away, humiliated.

The resemblance between father and son was striking. They had the same fine features and magnetic eyes. Laurent's build was more athletic and imposing than his father's.

"I know," Waldorf said, noticing my reaction. "They really do look alike. Did you have a good night, Laurent?"

"Fabulous," he grumbled. "Don't ever go into the hotel business. You'll lose your shirt."

The scarred man prepared a syringe and injected its contents into Laurent, who didn't flinch. I watched in shocked silence.

"It's to help him get through the initial phase of withdrawal," Waldorf said.

"Unlock the cuffs, Waldorf! I want to take a shower."

When Laurent came out of the bathroom, he was freshly shaven. His damp hair had been swept back from his forehead. He had put on clean blue jeans and a black shirt. Waldorf, who was pouring coffee, let out a low whistle.

"You look like a new man."

"Give it a rest, Waldorf. Like I said, you're not my type."

Laurent looked me over.

"Is she the tangible evidence?" he asked.

"She is indeed," Waldorf answered. He turned to me. "Simone, would you excuse us for a moment?"

I was seated at the table with a cup of coffee in front of me. Without understanding what was going on, I nodded. Waldorf led Laurent into the bedroom. When they re-emerged, Waldorf was wearing his coat and holding a sports bag. I reacted without thinking.

"Are you leaving, Kurt?"

He cleared his throat.

"Yes."

I got up. I didn't want him to leave without explaining what he'd said earlier about messengers. There were dozens of other details I hadn't yet asked him about. I glared at him resentfully. He raised a hand to placate me.

"Laurent will fill in the gaps. At this point, he knows as much as I do."

My mind was teeming with questions. I couldn't just stand there like an idiot while Waldorf escaped. There was no way I'd let him run out on me.

"You said you received a message. Why didn't Miles give me one?"

It wasn't just a question. It was an expression of bitter disappointment.

"Simone, I've kept the promise I made to Miles. As far as everything else is concerned, I'm going to trust his judgment. I don't think your being here is simply a coincidence."

I became agitated.

"Kurt, you can't leave now!" I said, making a pathetic effort to block his path.

Gently, he moved me aside.

I wanted to hold him back by force. I wanted to punch him in the face. Laurent's gaze was fixed on the wood grain of the table.

But as Kurt was leaving, he called out.

"Hey, Waldorf!"

Kurt stopped. Wringing his hands, Laurent spoke in a voice that was barely audible.

"Thank you."

The former neurosurgeon waved before vanishing into the morning light. His departure left me drained. My strength was gone.

Laurent and I looked at each other for a few seconds.

He was staring at me, expressionless. The silence was unsettling, but I held his gaze.

"I'd like an explanation," I said at last, to dispel the awkwardness.

"There's nothing to explain."

He stood up and went to the window. I waited for him to speak again.

"I don't know what Waldorf told you about me," he said at last.

"Not much," I answered uncertainly.

"I guess you've figured out that I have a drinking problem."

What was I supposed to say to that?

I decided to say nothing. Was it my silence that won his trust?

At Laurent's suggestion, we went for a walk on the pristine snow that covered the beach. I was wearing boots and an immense down coat that I'd found in a closet.

"Waldorf told me earlier that you met Miles," he said.

He sighed and looked out across the water. A freighter was making its way through the ice floes.

"That's right," I said.

"It was very nice of you to come all the way out here, but I really don't feel like having someone else try to convince me that my father is living in a parallel reality."

"Is that what Kurt told you?"

"Yes. It all started a few weeks ago. He sent me a letter claiming that while he was in a coma, he'd been in contact with Miles. At first, I thought he was just some nut job. I didn't reply. But not long afterward, a second letter came, along with documents proving that he'd had an accident and been hospitalized. The envelope also contained newspaper clippings about his career."

"You still didn't believe him, though, did you?"

"What did that stuff prove? That he was a successful guy who'd spent some time in a coma, and now he'd lost his mind. As far as I was concerned, it was just another hard-luck story. But then he started harassing me. I lost my temper. I wanted him to leave me alone."

"So why did you agree to see him? What changed your mind?"

"I didn't agree. He just showed up."

Laurent started walking again, his hands thrust in his pockets. I looked into the distance. The sky was full of low, cottony clouds.

"And are you convinced now?"

"I don't know anymore. To tell you the truth, he troubled me. He was nothing like the raving lunatic I'd expected him to be. He told me things that only my father and I ever knew about. But I have to say, even now, I have trouble believing that Miles is living somewhere else."

"I agree, it's a hard thing to accept."

"Did Miles also give you a message?"

"What is all this stuff about messages, Laurent? I don't understand."

He studied my face, gauging my sincerity.

"Miles told Gustave and Kurt to let me know."

"To let you know what?"

He'd been shadowing Ariane Bélanger all morning.

Discreetly, through the front window of the building, he had observed the child's dance class while keeping a constant eye on her mother. Ariane's attention had been focused on a fashion mag-azine. As far as he could tell, she hadn't received any phone calls. But he wasn't discouraged.

Sooner or later, Simone Fortin would turn up.

The little girl was adorable. A tiny flower in a heartless world.

He knew a thing or two about children. They were incontro-vertibly the most precious treasure of all. Yet society scarcely lifted a finger to protect them.

Daycare workers and teachers were underpaid. Intent on preserving a few crummy private-sector jobs, the government pre-ferred to give tax breaks to multinational corporations whose only goal was to increase their profits.

How could we hope to create a better world if we didn't invest in our children?

Ariane Bélanger and the little girl stepped out onto the sidewalk. The child was skipping along, holding her mother's hand. Her tutu was visible under her coat.

He followed at a distance, never losing sight of them.

"Miles wants me to take out his feeding tube. He wants to die."

I stared, astonished.

"Do you know why I've gone all these years without having it removed?"

Laurent fixed his gaze on me. I contemplated my boots, which looked like dark spots on the snow. His heartache was touching me to the very core.

"People think it's all about religious convictions, but it's not. I understand the diagnosis. I know my father is in a neurovegetative state. What I don't know is whether that state is irreversible. What if the doctors are wrong? What if, a few years from now, science figures out a way to give him his life back? And who's to say he won't wake up all by himself someday?"

"I'm not judging you, Laurent. Euthanasia is a huge step."

He let out a long sigh.

"And if he's living in a parallel reality, that complicates everything. How can I be sure he really wants to die? How can I be sure I won't be cutting short his long struggle to stay alive?"

I didn't speak. What he needed right now was to be listened to.

"If I knew for certain that he was ready to end it, I'd do whatever it took to honour his wish, even if that meant committing a crime. But who am I supposed to believe? Gustave and Waldorf, who tell me he wants to die? Or you, who didn't hear him say anything about his intentions?"

Laurent was about to say something else, but he changed his mind. We were approaching the top of a rise. He helped me climb the last few metres. From the summit, we had a spectacular view of the river and l'île aux Pommes, a narrow, rocky island a few kilometres in length.

"The day it happened, we'd gone sailing. We had stopped for a picnic lunch on that island over there. The sun was shining in a clear sky. Since my mom's death, he had always urged me to live every moment to the fullest. He was never sad, never defeated."

Laurent told me that after arriving at the wharf, Miles had asked him to tie up the boat. He described the accident and explained how the coroner had reached the conclusion that an improperly fastened rope was the cause of Miles's catastrophic fall.

"The people of the town never said anything. No one pointed a finger at me." He wiped away a tear with his thumb. "If only I'd taken a few extra seconds to tie up the boat securely. But I was on autopilot, doing something I'd done hundreds of times before."

"It was an accident," I said.

"How is a person supposed to go on living after something like that? What's left? I mean, can you even understand what it feels like to be responsible for such a serious accident, for its terrible consequences?"

I saw Étienne Beauregard-Delorme standing a few steps away, motionless, staring at me. The pallor of his face accentuated his blood-red lips. He was simply standing there, without emotion, without reproach, mute and disembodied. I reached out with one hand, convinced that I could touch him. As suddenly as the vision had appeared, it was gone.

Our paths had been identical. Guilt had flayed us alive. We both bore the crushing burden of our past actions. Would there be time enough in Laurent's life to find redemption after the error for which he had condemned himself? And what about me? After so many years spent fleeing my past, would I ever achieve grace?

"You're wrong, Laurent. I do know how it feels to be responsible for someone's death."

We stood on that hilltop for a long time as I told him my story. When I was done, we went on standing there for an even longer time, gazing at the river in silence.

29

The breakthrough that Lessard had been hoping for came short-ly after 10:00 a.m. He had nodded off when Fernandez and Sirois burst into his office. In fact, he'd been dreaming. The two caribou heads he'd seen at Baron Sports were moving their lips, trying to talk to him, but he couldn't understand their gurgles.

"I think we've found a connection between Fortin and Mongeau," Fernandez said eagerly.

Lessard sat up in his chair. His teeth were hurting. "I talked to the nurse at the hospital. She said Simone Fortin seemed to know a lot about health care. In fact, she suspected that Fortin might be a nurse herself."

"So?"

"That surprised me. You had said she worked in IT. I checked the members' directory of the Order of Nurses and found nothing. But that gave me another idea."

"Get to the point, Nadja," Lessard said impatiently.

"I checked the membership of the College of Physicians. And that's where things get interesting."

"Don't tell me she's a doctor!" Lessard exclaimed.

"She's a doctor who doesn't practise anymore," Fernandez said. "I spoke to the administrator at the hospital where she worked. He confirmed that she was a resident in the emergency department until June 1998."

"Why did she leave?"

"I don't know yet. The administrator I spoke to wasn't working there when it happened. But he gave me a number for a Dr. Stefan Gustaffson, who was Fortin's department head. I left him a message."

"You said there was a connection with Mongeau. I don't see how that's possible, unless Simone Fortin was working at the Montreal General Hospital."

"No, she was at the Enfant-Jésus Hospital in Quebec City. Remember I told you Mongeau's wife pressured him to leave Quebec City and come back to Montreal?"

"So Mongeau was executive director of the Enfant-Jésus before moving to the Montreal General?"

"Bingo. They worked in the same hospital at the same time."

Lessard felt his excitement rising, but he was still puzzled.

"She was an emergency doctor in Quebec City until 1998, and now she's working as an IT specialist in Montreal? That's kind of unusual, isn't it? Are you sure we're talking about the same Simone Fortin?"

Sirois dropped a stack of wrinkled documents on the desk in front of Lessard.

"The administrator at the Enfant-Jésus gave us her social insurance number. I searched several databases and cross-checked the results with the information we already had. Debit and credit cards issued to Simone Fortin were cancelled and bank accounts held in that name were emptied in June 1998. The grand total is pretty impressive — fifty-four thousand dollars. Her driver's licence, health insurance card, and passport were never renewed. Basically, she dropped off the grid. Then I checked the information that she gave you at the hospital. The address is right, she does live there. But when I checked with the owner of the building, I learned that the lease was signed in the name of Simone Ouellet. Strange coincidence, Ouellet is the maiden name of Simone Fortin's mother. The phone number she gave you is valid, but it's unlisted. She doesn't have a landline. The social insurance number given to me by Dinar's head of HR is the same as the number I got from the administrator at the Enfant-Jésus. The HR person told me Simone Fortin receives a salary cheque twice a month. She takes it to a cheque-cashing service and they give her the money in banknotes. No account or ID required."

"So you're telling me it's the same person, and she's doing her best to stay below the radar."

"It's the same person, all right. The social insurance number proves it. She's tried to muddy the waters, but confirming her identity was pretty straightforward."

Lessard smacked a fist into his palm. Were the pieces finally falling into place? What was lurking in Simone Fortin's past? Why was she hiding from the world?

The detective sergeant turned to Sirois.

"I think we're on to something. Keep digging. If Mongeau and Fortin were co-workers, she may have been a guest at his kinky parties."

Sirois picked up the stack of papers and went out.

"Nadja, we can't wait for Stefan Gustaffson to call us back. We need to speak to someone at the Enfant-Jésus Hospital."

"I figured you'd say that. The administrator gave me the number of someone who worked with Fortin back then. Her name is Suzanne Schmidt."

Lessard put the phone on speaker so that Fernandez could listen in. They needed to catch a break and speak to a human being, not another voice mail. Miraculously, someone answered. To Fernandez's surprise, Lessard whooped joyfully.

"Hello?" said a little girl's voice.

"Is your mommy there?"

They heard a bang as the handset was dropped onto a hard surface. Then they heard footsteps, followed by whispers.

"Remember what we talked about, sweetheart? You have to say, 'Just a minute, please.' Hello?"

"Suzanne Schmidt?"

"Speaking."

Lessard introduced himself. There was a surprised silence at the other end of the line.

"Has something happened to my husband?"

"No, no, nothing like that. I'm calling about Simone Fortin."

Without going into details, he said that Simone Fortin's name had come up in the course of an investigation, and he needed to confirm a few facts.

"Is this about the man in the coma?"

"Pardon me?"

"Does it concern Miles Green? I had a feeling something strange was going on."

Now it was Lessard's turn to be surprised.

"Would you mind telling me what you're talking about, Ms. Schmidt?"

She described the previous day's phone conversation she'd had with Simone.

"So the last time you spoke to her was around six p.m. yesterday?"

"Yes."

"Do you know whether she went to Trois-Pistoles to visit this man?"

"I have no idea. It's been years since we were in touch." She hesitated. "Has Simone done something wrong?"

"Not at all. On the contrary."

This seemed to reassure the woman. Fernandez was looking puzzled. What connection did this man, Miles Green, have with the case? Was he a former patient? Lessard made an effort to stay focused.

"Ms. Schmidt, this is very important. I need to know the circumstances surrounding Simone Fortin's departure from the Enfant-Jésus Hospital."

He could sense her discomfort.

"It's … it's a sensitive subject, Detective. You should really talk to Stefan. He'd be in a better position to —"

"Stefan Gustaffson?"

"Yes. You know, it was hard for everyone when they split up. It was so sudden."

Lessard and Fernandez exchanged startled looks.

"They were married?"

"No, but they'd been a loving couple."

"We've been trying to reach Dr. Gustaffson without success. I must insist that you tell us what you know."

"Did you try his pager?"

Fernandez spoke up. "I left him a message over forty minutes ago."

"I'm surprised he hasn't gotten back to you. You'll probably hear from him in the next few minutes. He always returns his calls promptly. He's on vacation until the middle of next week, but as head of the emergency department, he's always on call."

Lessard had to suppress his impatience. "We appreciate the explanation, ma'am, but we really need to know about Simone Fortin."

"Stefan is the only person who can tell you exactly what happened. Simone and I weren't close enough for her to confide in me."

"You must have an idea of what happened."

Lessard could hear her hesitating.

"I think she had some kind of breakdown. She went through a rough patch at work. An ethics complaint was lodged against her. From what I gathered, her relationship with Stefan was going downhill at the same time, but I couldn't tell you exactly what went on between them."

Lessard was searching for a crack in the wall, an opening of some kind. He decided to try a different approach.

"Does the name Jacques Mongeau mean anything to you?"

"Of course. His picture has been in all the papers. I know he was our executive director while all this was happening, but I never had any direct contact with him. Why? What does he have to do with Simone?"

"That's what we're trying to determine, ma'am. Do you think she knew him?"

"By name, probably, same as me."

"Not personally?"

"Not that I'm aware of."

Lessard was thinking hard. What would cause a loving couple to split up so quickly?

"Ms. Schmidt, I'm going to put you on hold for a moment."

He turned to Fernandez. "Let's say Simone Fortin is participating in Mongeau's soirées. Gustaffson finds out. He gets jealous, even enraged. Who knows? He could be our guy …"

"After all this time? I doubt it. But maybe he was a participant. It's worth checking to see if he fits the descriptions given by Mongeau's secretary and the pharmacist."

Lessard put Suzanne Schmidt back on the line. "Ma'am, can you describe Stefan Gustaffson for me?"

"Early forties, tall, blond hair, fair skin. Stefan is an international chess master. There are pictures of him on his website if you want to have a look."

Her description didn't sound much like the killer, but Lessard wrote down the web address that Suzanne Schmidt gave him.

He asked a few more questions, then ended the conversation. Once again, he had a sinking feeling that he was driving the investigation into a dead end.

"Where does this leave us, Victor?" Fernandez asked.

Simone Fortin had suddenly abandoned the medical profession and ended her relationship with Gustaffson. Why? Lessard sighed wearily.

"I don't know," he said, opening his browser to have a look at Gustaffson's website. He pecked at the keyboard for a few seconds, hit ENTER, and waited for the home page to appear on the screen.

Suddenly, he stiffened in his chair.

"What is it?" Fernandez asked. From where she was standing, she couldn't see what he was looking at.

Lessard had recognized the man instantly. Under the photograph, the caption read: *Stefan Gustaffson, 3rd Place, 2004 Nantes
Open.*

"What's the matter, Victor?"

"We just identified our first victim, Nadja."

He turned the screen so that Fernandez could look at the picture.

A blond man was smiling at the camera, little suspecting that he
would end up in the trunk of a BMW with his throat slashed.

30

Laurent filled the stove with logs.

I gave him a detailed account of my encounter with Miles. He was affected by the description of their old apartment.

"I went back a few years ago," he said wistfully. "There's an elderly couple living there now. They let me look around the place."

Of course! Laurent was the young man the old lady had told me about.

"The wife lives alone now," I said. "Her husband died last year."

Infernal heat was filling the room, which seemed to be closing in on itself. Laurent got up, his face sweating, and opened the window. An icy wind blew in.

Laurent questioned me on specific points, demanding precise descriptions of certain details and asking me to repeat some parts of the story. I didn't try to convince him of the truth of my account. I simply answered his questions, knowing how important this was to him.

I understood his anguish. On the one hand, he wanted to believe that Miles was alive and well in some hypothetical elsewhere.

On the other, common sense was telling him to be skeptical.

At one point, I mentioned the treasure chest that he and Miles had planned to dig up in the year 2000. Seeing how emotional Laurent was, I put an arm around his shoulders.

A strange sensation came over me. It was as though I knew him intimately. Some people can cross your path every day for years without having any effect, while others blaze though your life like a meteor, changing your existence forever.

Laurent got up and went to the window. "Everything you've told me about Miles is true, down to the smallest detail. There's just one thing that doesn't fit. He asked Gustave and Waldorf to let me know he wanted to die, but he didn't ask the same of you."

Why hadn't Miles used me as a messenger? That was the question tormenting Laurent.

What should he believe?

Was it possible that Miles had changed his mind?

"Maybe," he mused, "he *did* give you a message, but not in a form you could decipher by yourself. Maybe he said something that didn't strike you as important when you heard it."

Hearing him use the word "decipher" reminded me of the word games that he and Miles had played when he was a boy.

"He told me you often communicated in anagrams."

Laurent stepped closer to me. There was a sudden eager light in his eyes. "Yes. And?"

"And nothing. I just remembered, that's all."

He started pacing back and forth across the room, his steps as precise and regular as if they'd been mapped out on the floor. "Could he have given you a series of words for me …?"

"If he did, I wasn't aware of it."

Laurent couldn't conceal his disappointment.

He rubbed his temples for a moment, then picked up his coat. "Come on," he said. "I have a treasure chest to dig up. And I'm five years overdue."

•　•　•

We drove along the Chemin du Havre and parked next to a house with decrepit shingled walls. There was a FOR SALE sign standing half-buried in the snow. Laurent took a shovel from the trunk of the car and went up the walk.

When he saw me hesitating, he said, "Don't worry. Nobody lives here." We went around to the backyard, which overlooked the river.

"This is the place."

Before starting to dig, he sighed like a condemned man.

"You okay?" I asked.

He gave me a look.

"Yeah."

Despite the frozen ground, it only took him a few minutes to dig up the chest.

"Do you want to open it here?"

Laurent gazed at it. His face was haggard. "I was just a kid when we buried this thing. The year 2000 seemed so far away …"

"Do you remember what you put in it?"

"Not really." For a moment, he was lost in thought. "There's a quiet restaurant near the church where we can go for a cup of coffee."

Laurent started the car.

I held the treasure chest in my lap, moved by the knowledge that I was holding fragments of Miles's past, and touched by the thought that his love for his son had prompted him to bury objects so that when the boy became a man, he would have things that reminded him of his youth. The chest made me painfully aware of the deep void my own father had left in my cardboard existence.

As we approached the church with its multiple towers, I thought about how the gift of life comes with a pair of parents. There's no choice involved. It's just luck of the draw. Maybe fortune will smile on you. Or maybe not, in which case — assuming you believe in reincarnation — better luck next time.

Were all my memories of my father painful?

Would I ever forgive him for starting a new life with a woman barely older than myself? Would I ever get past the sense of betrayal that I felt when he showered all his attention on the child he'd had with his second wife?

As Laurent had predicted, there were only a few customers in the restaurant. We took a table in the back and ordered two bowls of café au lait. The waitress knew Laurent by name and offered to liven up our coffees with some cognac. He declined, looking embarrassed.

"This is it," he said brightly, trying to mask his emotions. "The moment of truth."

He reached for the chest, but I stopped him. "Wait. Try to remember what's inside."

Laurent made an effort to concentrate. "I think there's a picture of Miles and me in a cornfield. I had one heck of a scare that day."

"What else?"

"A marble, maybe. I can't remember anymore."

He started to lift the lid, then paused.

"I don't have the nerve. You do it for me."

Why should I have the nerve, if he didn't? I felt about as brave as a damsel in distress. Even so, I drew my chair closer and did as he asked.

The chest contained four kraft paper envelopes. I opened the first and withdrew a little pile of yellowed newspaper clippings from 1986. We looked through them together.

February 25th, Cory Aquino is elected president of the Philippines, restoring democracy and putting an end to the dictatorship of Ferdinand Marcos; February 28th, Swedish prime minister Olof Palme is assassinated; March 29th, Falco's "Rock Me Amadeus" becomes the first German-language song to hit number one in the United States; April 3rd, *Out of Africa*, directed by Sydney Pollack, wins the Academy Award for Best Picture; April 26th, the nuclear power station at Chernobyl explodes; May 24th, the Montreal Canadiens defeat the Calgary Flames four games to one to win the Stanley Cup; September 5th, in Pakistan, four hijackers seize control of a Pan Am Boeing 747, leading to an army assault that kills twenty-one people and injures over one hundred; September 17th, a bomb explodes on the Rue de Rennes in Paris, causing seven deaths and fifty-one injuries; October 11th, Ronald Reagan and Mikhail Gorbachev meet at a summit in Reykjavik; November 17th, Georges Besse, chief executive officer of Renault, is assassinated by the Action directe terrorist group; November 28th, the Nobel Peace Prize is awarded to Elie Wiesel; November 29th, actor Cary Grant dies.

The second envelope contained two drawings by Laurent.

In the third envelope, we found a dozen photographs, including a picture of Laurent as a baby in his mother's arms, a snapshot of the family in front of a sailboat, and the photo in the cornfield that Laurent had mentioned.

The fourth envelope contained a note in Miles's handwriting.

November 29th, 1986

Laurent,

In a little while, we'll bury our treasure chest. The plan is to open it together in 2000. For a boy your age, that seems like a lifetime from now. But that's not how it feels to me. As I write these words, I know something you'll only learn years from now — that once you reach the age of twenty, time begins to race by. You find yourself wishing you could stop the clock to enjoy life more fully. I'll admit, the very idea of stopping the clock is selfish. It's a notion that adults have come up with out of nostalgia, which is something kids don't suffer from. As I watch you grow up, I wish this period in our lives would never end. I'm already dreading the *moment when you start to separate yourself from me. But at the same time, I'm so proud of you, so proud of the progress you're making. And now, rereading my words, I see that the impulse was too strong to resist. I've written this note to the boy sleeping in the next room rather than to the man he will become. If you have children of your own when you read this, perhaps you'll understand some of what I'm feeling right now.*

Ivy cloy eve humour run late

(Will you remember how to decipher that?)

Miles

Laurent wiped away a couple of tears with his thumb and handed me the note. As I read it, I had to fight back sobs of my own. But I stopped short when I saw the words "run late."

"That list of words — it's an anagram, right?"

"Right."

"What does 'run late' mean?"

"It's my name, with the letters rearranged. 'Ivy cloy eve humour run late' is an anagram for 'I love you very much, Laurent.'"

I thought about the painting tacked to the wall in Miles's bedroom and the words that appeared on it: *Run, late, elapse, lid, me, tee.*

I tried to tell myself that it was simply a coincidence.

Come on, Simone! It's staring you in the face. That's the message you've been looking for.

"Do you recall the picture that your father painted, the one that showed a stone wall covered with graffiti?"

Laurent frowned. "What are you talking about? My father wasn't a painter."

"Are you sure?" I hesitated. "There was a painting in his bedroom. I remember very clearly that he said he'd created it."

"I'm positive. My father didn't paint. Why do you ask?"

"Because there were six words written on it in red letters."

"So?"

"Two of the words were 'run' and 'late.'"

Laurent's face flushed.

"What were the others? Hang on. Write them out."

He handed me a pen. Hastily, I wrote the words on my paper napkin and gave it to him. He scribbled briefly, his lower lip twitching involuntarily.

"Waldorf was right. You *have* brought me a message."

His face had grown pale. He slid the napkin over to me.

Under the six words I'd written, he had deciphered the anagram.

Ariane paid the bill and they stepped out onto the sidewalk.

"Did you enjoy your lunch, sweetie?"

The child put a hand on her stomach.

"Yes. That was good. What are we going to do now, Mom?"

"We're going to run some errands."

"Like buying food for dinner?"

"That's right, my love. We're also going to stop off at the pharmacy, and we'll drop by the video store to return the movie you watched last night."

"Then what?"

"Then we'll go to Simone's place. Can you walk a little faster, honey?"

"Why are we going to Simone's place? Is she home from the hospital?"

"She did leave the hospital, but she's not home right now. That's why we're going. She asked me to feed her cat."

Mathilde's face lit up. "We're going to feed Mozart? Can I do it, Mom? Please? Can I feed Mozart?"

"Of course, sweetie. Hold my hand, we're going to cross the street now."

"Yay!"

Ariane Bélanger smiled. She'd had a troubled adolescence. She had struggled with issues of physical self-acceptance. She'd fallen into all the classic traps — alcohol, drugs, tattoos, piercings, unbridled sexuality. She had intended to spend a month backpacking in Central America. In the end, she'd stayed three years.

It was while working as a volunteer with underprivileged children that she'd taken control of her life. Bringing Mathilde back to Canada had completed a process of transformation that had begun long before.

Ariane liked to have fun now and then, and she occasionally allowed herself to go overboard. Her fling with Diego had been particularly entertaining, but she defined herself first and foremost as a mother, with all the responsibilities that entailed.

Ariane Bélanger had reached a point in her life where she wanted to share her happiness with a man who wasn't afraid of commitment, a man who wanted to devote time to his family.

She had found her path in life when she'd realized that children are the embodiment of hope.

She thought of Victor Lessard. She was convinced that her best days were still to come. Had Victor called? She was suddenly eager to go home and check the messages on her phone, which she had plugged into the charger before leaving the house.

Laurent, please let me die.

Nothing else existed beyond these words. It was as though the world had come to a standstill. I took the letters of the message and reinserted them, one by one, into the six words that I'd seen on the painting. There could be no doubt. Even so, I turned to Laurent.

"Are you sure you haven't made a mistake? Maybe the letters could be put together in some other order, creating a different message."

"Do you honestly think this is just a coincidence?"

I looked at him without answering.

"I didn't want to believe that my father was living in a parallel reality," Laurent said, "let alone that he was ready to die. But that was the message that Gustave and Waldorf brought. And now you."

"I never got the impression that Miles was ready to die," I said.

Why hadn't he confided in me? I wasn't sure I had grasped all the implications of what I'd just learned. Laurent was looking distressed, his breath coming in short, sharp gasps.

"Is something wrong?" I asked.

"I have to get out of here. I can't breathe."

He jumped to his feet, dropped some money on the table, and rushed out of the restaurant. I quickly put the envelopes back in the chest and caught up to him on the sidewalk.

"Take it easy, Laurent, you're having a panic attack."

But he darted into the street, weaving between the cars.

He ran into the church parking lot, followed by a chorus of honking horns, and disappeared out of sight.

31

Thinking back on the investigation afterward, Lessard kept second-guessing himself, unable to dispel his doubts or erase his feelings of guilt. Could he and the team have responded sooner? Could they have found the killer's trail more quickly? Whatever the case, from the moment the first victim's identity was known, the detective sergeant became feverishly active.

He started giving orders in a disconnected rush as they came into his mind. His only concern was not to forget anything.

"I want officers sent to Stefan Gustaffson's home. They need to establish a crime scene, check for signs of forced entry or a struggle, search for bloodstains, dust for prints, the whole nine yards."

Fernandez was writing in her notebook. Sirois was already on the phone.

"I also want Berger to look at the photographs on the website and give us his opinion. Is our first victim really Gustaffson?"

"Do you have any doubts?"

"No, but I want to cover all the bases. Someone should get in touch with the Quebec Provincial Police. They'll need to find out whether Simone Fortin visited Miles Green at the Trois-Pistoles Hospital. If she did, the provincial cops should be given her description. She may still be in the area. Also, I want a background check on this Green character. Who is he? How does he fit into the case?"

"Slow down, Victor, you're going too fast."

BLOOD301

Fernandez was scribbling furiously.

"Somebody find a picture of the young woman and make sure it goes out to the onboard computers of all our patrol units. And I want an officer posted in front of her home to intercept her if she turns up."

What are you hiding from me, Simone Fortin? What's the connection that I'm not seeing? What were you up to with Mongeau?

He had a sudden intuition.

Because of the kinky photographs, they'd been trying to find some kind of personal link between Fortin and Mongeau. But what if the link was professional?

Lessard regretted not having dug deeper into the question when he had Suzanne Schmidt on the line.

"We'll need to do some more digging into the ethics complaint," he said to Fernandez. "Call Suzanne Schmidt. I assume there's some kind of council or committee that oversees ethics issues. Let's talk to someone who was on the committee at the time. I want to know if Mongeau was mixed up in the complaint. There'll be a case file. Let's find it. And someone track down Pearson. I want him back here as soon as possible. Simone Fortin is at the heart of this thing. We need to find her before the killer does."

He called Ariane's number and got her voice mail for the twentieth time.

"It's Victor. Call me as soon as you get this message. It's urgent."

His cellphone buzzed as he was putting it down. Ariane? No. It was his ex-wife.

"We should talk, Victor. I really respect what you did this morning. But I'm worried about our son."

"So am I, Marie, but can I call you back a little later?"

"Is this a bad time?"

"It's just —"

The old resentment welled up.

"It's always the same old story, isn't it, Victor? Putting your work ahead of your family."

Marie hung up.

Lessard threw the phone across the room.

Laurent was sitting under a tree beside the rectory.

I approached quietly. I was hesitant to touch his shoulder. I've always felt that pain creates a deeply private space around a person, a space that shouldn't be intruded upon, unless it's with infinite care.

I sat down next to him without a word and let him weep in silence. A man walked by, smoking a pipe. He stared at us for a moment. In the man's eyes, I saw the conviction that he was looking at a couple of quarrelling lovers. I had a sudden urge to shout, "Mind your own business!" People can be so insensitive. Even so, it was true that we looked pitiful. Wearing a faint smile, the man continued on his way, leaving in his wake a long trail of vanilla-scented smoke.

"When Waldorf and Gustave told me that Miles wanted to die," Laurent said, "I didn't really believe them. But the message I just deciphered has hit me like a gut-punch."

We walked back to the car without talking.

As I opened the door, I asked, "What will you do now?"

Had he heard the question?

I put the treasure chest in the back seat and we drove to his house in silence.

Hurriedly, I tossed a few items in a bag.

I can't remember what was said, or who suggested what, but within minutes, we were speeding along Highway 20.

I didn't know what Laurent was planning.

Only that he'd be dropping me off at my apartment.

While Fernandez was making calls from her office, Lessard and Sirois went over the file from the beginning. They compared notes but were unable to come up with any fresh insights.

Pearson arrived, hair uncombed, wrinkled shirttails hanging out of his pants. His excitement brought a brief burst of fresh energy to the team.

"A pharmacy on Saint-Jacques Street was broken into the night before Mongeau's murder. And guess what was stolen? Some vials of Amytal and a syringe."

Lessard turned over the information in his head. Something didn't fit.

"We're looking for a professional who planned the murders with care. Yet the night before committing a major crime, he does this crude smash-and-grab job to steal some barbiturates? That's one hell of a risk."

"Not if he absolutely needs the stuff to steady himself," Pearson said.

"It doesn't make sense," Lessard said. "Why ask a pharmacist to give him the same drug the very next day? Without a prescription."

"Maybe he was telling the truth when he said the medication had been taken at the same time as the vehicle."

"In that case, we'd have found the vials in the BMW." Lessard swore to himself. "Unless Martin and ..."

He stopped himself.

"What?" Pearson asked. "What does Martin have to do with —"

Lessard pretended to be thinking hard.

"No, nothing. I have to go to the men's room."

He got up and hurried out as Pearson stared after him, astonished.

· · ·

In the men's room, Lessard called his son's number.

"If you didn't take them, is it possible that your friend Jimbo did? Write down the name. *A-M-Y-T-A-L*. This is very important. Call me as soon as you talk to him."

As he ended the call, Lessard heard a toilet flush. He stepped out of the cubicle and saw Sirois.

"Hey, Victor. Are we getting somewhere?"

Lessard froze, convinced that his colleague had overheard the conversation.

"Mmm."

Sirois was soaping his hands compulsively, washing them with as much care as a surgeon about to enter an operating room. "Judging from appearances, I'd say the Fortin woman is trying to hide something," he said, breaking the awkward silence. "Why else would she go to so much trouble to cover her tracks?"

"Let's keep digging," Lessard muttered, splashing cold water on his face.

A vague recollection came back to him. Fernandez had said something this morning, something that had made an impression on him. But what? Why did his memory fail him so cruelly in critical situations? In the state he was in, remembering his own address would have been a fifty-fifty proposition.

"Sirois, would you ask Fernandez to come to the conference room?"

The young woman arrived in her stocking feet, looking groggy, with a red patch on one side of her face. She had fallen asleep at her desk.

"Nadja, while we were talking at Shäika Café, before I left to meet Pearson, you said something. It had to do with appearances. Do you remember?"

"Vaguely."

"Can you try to repeat what you said, word for word?"

"Hang on …" She thought for a moment. "As I recall, I said the killer's methods were pretty strange, considering Mongeau's professional milieu — I mean, a milieu where appearances matter so much."

Lessard's idea was becoming clearer.

The crime scene had been marked by a brutality that was at odds with everything else.

"Does that help?" Fernandez asked.

"I think so." He hesitated, unsure of which way to steer the discussion from here. "Let's think about the killer's methods. We've been assuming that he was a professional, and that the murders were related to Mongeau's secret activities."

The other members of the team said nothing, waiting for him to continue.

"But would a professional have left the BMW unattended, knowing there was a body in the trunk? Would he have taken the risk of being noticed as he was trying to get his hands on barbiturates without a prescription?"

"Where are you going with this?" Sirois asked.

"I'm not sure. We still don't have enough facts to put together a clear picture, but there may be holes in our theory. Were the murders really committed in response to a blackmail attempt by Mongeau? Should we be searching for a professional, or for an individual whose actions were driven by some other motive?"

Lessard didn't elaborate on his doubts. But inwardly, he was torturing himself. Had he been wrong to place so much importance on the photographs?

Had he led the investigation into a blind alley?

Kilometre 88

The whole thing was beyond me. I wished I could have talked it over with Laurent, questioned him about it, but I respected his silence.

I regretted not having gone back to see Miles one last time to make up for my uncontrolled weeping the previous night. But under the circumstances, I hadn't dared to ask.

I felt tired and empty. I had a distinct sensation of being disembodied, somewhere between reality and perception, as though my mind had been shut up in a box, which in turn had been shut up in another box, and so on, like a succession of Russian dolls.

Had I become a stranger inhabiting myself?

The team went on floundering for a while, unable to come up with any new ideas. The cops' faces were sallow, distorted by fatigue. Lessard was making them work at an impossible pace, and he knew it. The table in the conference room was cluttered with disordered files and coffee cups. Sirois had given up trying to obey the no-smoking rule. An empty soda can served as his ashtray. They needed to keep working, whatever the cost. Even the smallest step forward might turn out to be decisive.

Lessard called Constable Nguyen, who had been instructed to take up a position outside Simone Fortin's apartment.

"Any developments?"

"I was held up. I'll call as soon as I get there."

Moving in slow motion, Fernandez came into the room with a crumpled piece of paper. She handed it to Lessard.

"I called Suzanne Schmidt. She gave me a number for Marcel Loranger, who's been a member of the ethics committee at the Enfant-Jésus Hospital since 1996. I have him on hold."

"What did you tell him?"

"The bare minimum."

Lessard hit the speaker button.

"Mr. Loranger?"

"Hello, Detective Lessard. What can I do for you?"

The man's tone was frank and direct.

"I need some information about a former employee of your hospital, Simone Fortin. Specifically, I'd like to know about the case that brought her before the ethics committee in 1998."

"I don't have the file in front of me, but I remember the facts pretty clearly. It was a somewhat unusual case."

"Can you summarize it for me?"

"Let's see ..." Loranger had a sudden coughing fit. Lessard recognized the signs. The man was a smoker. "Dr. Fortin had to deal with two patients simultaneously — a young boy and his grandfather. They'd been in a car wreck. First she stabilized the child, who only had a fractured leg. Then she turned her attention to the grandfather, whose condition seemed to be critical. While she was dealing with the grandfather, the boy went into respiratory distress. Despite Dr. Fortin's attempts to resuscitate him, he died. The parents filed a complaint, alleging medical malpractice. After an administrative inquiry, we organized a conciliation meeting with the parents. That's standard practice. Dr. Fortin and her department head, Stefan Gustaffson, were also present." At the mention of Gustaffson's name, Lessard looked over at Fernandez. "Based on the facts, the committee concluded that correct procedures had been followed and that the child's death, though unfortunate, couldn't reasonably have been foreseen."

"So Simone Fortin did nothing wrong?"

"Correct. But the parents didn't see it that way. Their reaction was ... well, let's just say it was extremely hostile. That's why I remember the file so clearly. During the hearing, the boy's father tried to assault Dr. Fortin physically. He even uttered death threats. I had to intervene with another colleague to remove him from the room."

"Did Dr. Fortin file criminal charges?"

"No, she decided not to pursue the matter."

"What about Jacques Mongeau? Was he on the committee?"

"Jacques! What terrible news! We're all just heartsick about it."

"Mr. Loranger, please answer the question. Was Mongeau on the committee?"

"No. Although parents would occasionally go to the executive director hoping to overturn a decision. I couldn't tell you if that happened in this case. In any event, committee decisions are non-reviewable. The executive director has no power to change the outcome."

Lessard found himself thinking he'd been on the wrong track the whole time. Loranger had just confirmed that the killings were unrelated to Mongeau's erotic pictures. The solution to the crimes was much simpler.

And much more terrible.

"If what you're telling me is correct, I need to know the father's identity. And his home address. I understand that this is confidential information, but there's a life at stake. I'll send a patrol unit to pick you up."

"That won't be necessary. I can jump in my car and be at my office in ten minutes. Our files have been stored at an external facility since 2002, but I keep computer records with a summary of each case, as well as the names and addresses of the parties. Finding this particular one may take a little time. I didn't index my files back then."

"Please hurry." Lessard gave him his number. "I'll stay where I am until I hear from you."

"Detective Lessard? You've piqued my curiosity. Does this have to do with the investigation into Jacques's murder?"

"I can't answer that for now, but you'll know soon enough."

The detective sergeant sat there in shock for a few seconds, then banged the table with his fist. Fernandez approached him. He knew they were on the right track at last. Until this moment, he'd been steering the investigation in the wrong direction.

"I screwed up."

"We don't know that yet, Victor."

He stood up and kicked the wastebasket, which tumbled across the room, scattering papers everywhere. Why hadn't he figured it out earlier? Why? He hoped with all his heart that Simone Fortin was still alive.

Kilometre 142
"Are you asleep?" Laurent asked.
"Mmm?"

Kilometre 175
The car stopped. I opened my eyes. We had pulled up at a service station. Laurent had stepped out of the car. I closed my eyes again. The door opened.

"I got you a sandwich. Do you like mayonnaise?"

I sat up in the seat. I had dozed off. "Yes, thanks."

"I came *this* close to buying a few beers," he said, looking at me nervously.

He started the car. We ate in silence.

32

Lessard picked up on the first ring.

"Do you have a pen and paper?" Loranger asked. The detective sergeant wrote down the information that Loranger gave him.

"This is a Montreal address," Lessard said. "I thought the boy had been treated in Quebec City."

"As I recall, the accident happened during a family visit. Do you want me to fax you the file?" Lessard gave him the number, thanked him, and hung up.

He handed Fernandez a piece of paper covered with his illegible handwriting.

"Have the tactical squad get ready. We'll go in as soon as you confirm that the address is still good."

Kilometre 226

"Do you miss helping people get well?"

That morning, on the icy rise overlooking the river, I had opened up to Laurent. I had explained that I'd formerly been a physician, and that I held myself responsible for the death of a young boy.

"Sometimes," I answered.

"Why did you become a doctor?"

"Because of my mother, I think. I was completing my bachelor's degree in computer science when she died of a ruptured aneurysm."

"You think her death influenced your decision?"

"My father had left us for one of his mistresses when I was twelve. My mom had a particular gift for making me feel special. I was devastated when she died. I guess going into medicine was my way of giving some kind of meaning to her death."

"What about your father? Are you still in touch with him?"

What was he getting at? Did he want me to admit that my father was a complete asshole?

"Mom's death brought us a little closer. He helped me financially while I was a student. I reached out in distress the night I lost that young patient. I needed his support. True to form, he only called back a week later, between meetings. I haven't spoken to him since."

Pearson was on the phone, talking to his wife in a low voice. Sirois was smoking a cigarette.

Lessard had almost succumbed to temptation a couple of times, but he had promised himself he wouldn't smoke, which put him in a terrible mood.

"Stop jiggling your leg, Sirois, you're driving me nuts."

"Sorry, Victor."

Just then, Fernandez burst into the conference room, out of breath.

"We had the wrong address. They moved to Quebec City in 1999, less than a year after the death of their son."

She handed Lessard a sheet with the updated address written on it in block letters. He swore. He had been hoping that they'd be able to surround the killer's home in the next few minutes and, with a little luck, arrest him. This new information changed all that.

"We've got to contact the Quebec City Police and have them send units to this address immediately. If we assume that our suspect is after Simone Fortin, he won't be at home. But they should be cautious. There's no way to know whether the place is a crime scene …"

He turned to the team.

"Someone will have to go to Quebec City to coordinate with local police. Any element that can help us locate the killer needs to be analyzed."

Sirois jumped to his feet and grabbed his jacket.

"I'm on it."

"Take a service car," Lessard said.

But Sirois was already gone.

Ariane parked her car less than two hundred metres from Simone's apartment. She turned to Mathilde, who was sitting in the back seat.

"You can take off your seat belt, sweetie."

The child gave her mother a sly look. "Will you let me hold Mozart, Mom?"

"Of course, my love."

Ariane unfastened her seat belt and got out of the car. As she was stepping onto the sidewalk, a Buick Regal pulled up behind her car.

She took Mathilde's hand and they headed for the apartment. The little girl was dragging her booted feet as she went along.

"Do ballerinas make noise when they walk, sweetie?"

"No, Mom."

"Show me how they walk."

The child began to tiptoe.

"Much better."

Ariane helped Mathilde climb the stairs. She took out her key ring and unlocked the door. They stepped into the apartment. Mathilde ran up the hallway.

"Here, kitty, kitty."

"Mathilde, come and take off your boots!"

He waited for a minute, then went up the stairs. The door swung open when he pushed. He closed it noiselessly behind him.

Quebec City

Guy Simoneau was the first officer to arrive on the scene, accompanied by his partner, François Béland.

Simoneau was forty-one, a native of the Charlesbourg district of Quebec City. An experienced, competent officer who knew nothing about the Mongeau case.

With his hand on his service weapon, he got out of the patrol car and walked toward the modest brick bungalow. The shabby, poorly maintained house was conspicuous among the neat little homes that lined the street. Followed by his partner, Simoneau knocked several times on the front door. There was no answer.

"We're going in," he said.

He drove his shoulder into the aging door, which gave way with a feeble crack. Before stepping inside, he unholstered his Glock.

"Police! If anyone is here, identify yourself."

"It stinks," Béland said.

Simoneau looked around. The kitchen was littered with dirty dishes and rotting food.

"The place is disgusting," he said.

The two cops waited a few seconds, then started advancing slowly. There was no one in the kitchen or living room. They started moving along the hallway that led to the bedrooms.

A door at the end of the hallway was closed. Simoneau heard a rustle and felt his heart begin to race.

"Police! If anyone is here, identify yourself."

The officers looked at each other. On a signal from Simoneau, Béland broke through the door.

The room was lit by numerous votive candles. A thin woman lay half-naked on the floor. A syringe was still planted in her arm.

Simoneau approached cautiously.

"She's strung out. Call an ambulance."

The woman stirred. Her fist was clenched. Fearing that she might have a weapon, Simoneau pried her fingers open and took the object she'd been clutching. It was a photograph of a little boy, his face dotted with freckles.

Cute kid, he thought.

Ariane was opening a can of cat food when she became aware that someone was standing behind her.

A tingle of fear ran down her spine, but before she could react, a hand was pressed to her mouth, drawing her backward. She felt the cold metal of a blade on her throat.

Before she knew what was happening, her assailant began to pull her toward the bedroom.

She tried to scream, but her voice was muffled by the hand over her mouth. Her greatest fear was for Mathilde. She wanted to yell a warning to flee.

A voice murmured in her ear.

"Calm down, Ariane. If you co-operate, I won't hurt you or your child."

A man. How did he know her name?

They had reached the bedroom when Mathilde appeared at the other end of the hallway, near the front door.

The child froze. It took her a few seconds to process what she was seeing. A bad man was threatening her mother with a big knife.

But he was looking at her in a nice way. "Come here, sweetheart. I'm not going to hurt you. It's just a game. I'm a friend of your mom's."

Mathilde hesitated. Her mother's eyes were sending her a message that she didn't understand.

At school, she'd been taught to look for houses with a Block Parent sign. She decided the best thing to do would be to go outside and try to get help. She hoped her mother wouldn't be mad at her.

She started to back away, keeping her eyes on the man.

"No, Mathilde," the man said. "Don't move!"

For a fraction of a second, his grip loosened. Ariane managed to free herself. "Run!"

Ariane felt a cold stroke cut through her carotid artery.

She tried to yell again, but all that came out was a bubbling noise. Her legs went weak and she fell to the floor.

She put her hands to her throat. Stunned, she saw thick blood running between her fingers. The room became blurry. Very gently, it started to fade. She was slipping away.

She realized that she would never see Mathilde grow up. She wouldn't drive her to school when she started a new grade in the fall, wouldn't help her with lessons and homework, wouldn't see her first ballet recital, wouldn't take her in her arms when she went through her first heartbreak, wouldn't be there to watch as she received her diplomas, wouldn't meet the people who mattered in her life, wouldn't see her children, wouldn't offer wise advice on how to avoid the innumerable pitfalls of life. She would eventually be nothing but a distant memory.

Why?

What had she done to deserve this?

She only had the strength to breathe a single word.

"Mathilde."

Then she was silent.

It had taken a few seconds for her life to be cut short.

There was a knock at the door.

Constable Nguyen had no idea of what had just happened inside the apartment when he heard the lock slide open.

Lessard was alternating sips of coffee with swigs of Pepto-Bismol when Fernandez informed him that the police officers dispatched to Stefan Gustaffson's home had just found a disc dated March 31st, 2005, bearing the same label as the one discovered in Mongeau's office. *Error message: 10161416.*

The disc contained photographs of Stefan Gustaffson's body.

Lessard should have been pleased. The disc confirmed that the two killings were linked, and it helped pin down the time of death. But the wait was eating away at him.

He headed for the men's room, planning to plunge his face into a sink full of cold water. Just then, his cellphone buzzed in his pocket.

"Lessard."

"This is Guy Simoneau of the Quebec City Police. I'm at the suspect's house. We found his wife, Isabelle Beauregard, in the home. She's high as a kite, and the ambulance guys are saying it'll be hours before she comes down. Clearly an addict. No sign of Pierre Delorme."

"Shit!" Lessard said.

"They live in a quiet suburb where everybody knows everybody. According to the neighbours, the two of them have been on hard drugs for a few years now."

"Does anyone know where the husband might have gone?"

"Nobody's seen him in a few days. Every so often, he's admitted to the Robert-Giffard Hospital for psychiatric treatment. One neighbour thinks that's where he is. I'm on my way over there now. My partner's searching the house. I'll get back to you as soon as I have more information."

It occurred to Lessard that psychiatric treatment might be compatible with the profile they had put together for the killer. Amytal was used for the management of anxiety disorders.

"Tell your partner and the technicians to treat the house as a potential crime scene. And have him fax us a photograph of the suspect as soon as he finds one."

He was about to hang up when he remembered the dream he'd had earlier that morning: the two caribou heads. He didn't know why, but that image was haunting him.

What had the sales clerk at Baron Sports said about the knife?

"Hunters love them."

"Simoneau? Be careful. We may be dealing with a hunter."

"I know. I saw a stuffed moose head in the basement."

Did that confirm Lessard's intuition? Did they have the right man? He'd have given anything to be in that patrol car instead of Simoneau. He felt like a bystander at his own investigation, helpless as a child.

Kilometre 336

"Human beings are weird creatures. We're the only species in the animal kingdom that prolongs suffering, that extends the lives of cells after they've stopped functioning. To tell you the truth, Simone, I ask myself every single day why I haven't had the feeding tube removed. Is it my own death I'm trying to postpone? Maybe I just need to maintain some connection with the land of the living. Apart from Miles, I have no one in the world."

"You're not the only person who faces those questions," I said. "Everybody in a situation like yours has to confront the same doubts."

Kilometre 375

"I need to think. I'm going to go for a walk through the cemetery where my father worked."

"And then?"

"I don't know."

Pearson came in and handed Lessard a couple of sheets of paper.

"This is all we've got at the moment."

Pierre Delorme had been born in Montreal on March 7th, 1964. He had worked as a firefighter for the City of Montreal from February 1984 until December 1999. A few parking tickets, one speeding ticket. No criminal record. In March 2000, he had secured a transfer to the Quebec City Fire Department.

Lessard dialed the number of Delorme's fire station in Quebec City and asked to speak to the senior officer on duty. His call was transferred to Captain Bolduc. He introduced himself. There was no time for tact or formalities.

"We're trying to find Pierre Delorme. We think he may have committed a serious crime. Murder."

"Pierre? Impossible!"

"Why do you say that? Doesn't he turn violent occasionally?"

"No. He's gentle, a shy person, very reserved by nature. He may have been different before the death of his son, but believe me, these days it's almost as though he isn't there at all."

"You know about Étienne?"

"Everyone at the station knows. He put in for a transfer a few months after the boy died. We're like a family here. My wife and I have done everything we could to be supportive. Étienne was a miracle in their lives. His death shattered them."

"And the drugs?"

Bolduc hesitated.

"It came on gradually," he said at last. "About two years ago, we started to realize that something was wrong. We covered for him for a while, but the problem was deep-seated. I finally convinced him to see a psychologist. He's been on sick leave for the last fifteen months. He called here one time, in really bad shape. With some help from another member of the team, I went and got him. He was delirious. Hallucinating. We brought him to the Robert-Giffard Hospital, where he was admitted right away. The doctor explained to us that he was seriously depressed. When he's in treatment, he manages to function normally. But as soon as he's discharged, he goes home, stops taking his medication, and gets back into the heroin with Isabelle."

"But you say he's never violent?"

"That's right. The medication calms him down. And when he relapses, he's only a danger to himself."

It was a sad situation. Lessard almost pitied the guy. Then he remembered the bodies of the two victims, and his compassion evaporated.

"When was the last time you saw him?"

"A couple of weeks ago. Madeleine and I brought them some food. We didn't know what else to do for them. They're wasting away."

"How was he?"

"Totally drugged out. He didn't even recognize me."

"Does he have family? Friends?"

"I think his father's still alive. He may have a sister. But we never see them."

"Was Delorme a hunter?"

"Pierre? No. Hockey's his sport. He's one of the only Canadiens fans at the station. You have to understand that since the Nordiques left town, things haven't been the same."

"Do you have any idea where he might be?"

"If he isn't at home, try the shopping centre near the psychiatric hospital. That's where I picked him up last time."

Lessard saw on his phone screen that Simoneau was trying to reach him. He hung up abruptly, without saying goodbye to Captain Bolduc.

"I just spoke to one of his doctors," Simoneau said.

"Is he in the hospital at the moment?"

"No. They haven't seen him in two weeks. Every now and then, he's admitted for a short stay, especially when he's having a breakdown. They've been treating him for severe depression. The doctor also confirms that he's a heroin addict, which makes for an explosive cocktail. The heroin can exacerbate the effects of his medication, and vice versa."

"Does he have violent tendencies?"

"The doctor says yes, but they're only directed at himself."

"Is he suicidal?"

"And prone to self-mutilation, from what they told me."

"Is it conceivable that he committed the acts we suspect him of?"

"The doctor seemed surprised at first. He said those crimes didn't fit with the profile. But then he added that in psychiatry, anything's possible."

Lessard slammed a fist down on the table. They weren't making any progress.

"Put out a search alert. Check the shopping centre near the psychiatric hospital. I just spoke to one of his former colleagues. Apparently he hangs out there."

"That's always one of the first places we look."

"By the way, do you know what they've prescribed for him?"

"You mean the name of the medication?"

"Yes."

"I didn't ask. Is it important?"

"It could be. Ask the doctor if he has a prescription for Amytal. *A-m-y-t-a-l.*"

"Got it. I'll call you back."

Kilometre 412

"The little boy you lost …"

"Yes?"

"Can you tell me what happened?"

I dove back into my memory and saw Étienne lying on the gurney.

"I said three cc's?"

"Yes, Doctor."

"Are you sure?"

The nurse nods.

"He's in respiratory depression. Put him on oxygen."

"Yes, Doctor," the nurse says calmly.

"Did you call Stefan?"

"I left a message on his pager."

The monitor suddenly emits a strident, continuous alarm. There's a dull roaring in my ears. My hands are damp. A drop of sweat runs off my eyebrow, stinging my eye. The light is harsh, blinding. The nurse looks at me. What is she saying? Count. One, two, one, two. Count. Keep counting. Come on, Simone. Pick up the defibrillator.

"Clear!"

A white flash. Again, Simone. Do it again. A second white flash. Another injection of adrenalin. Done. My hands are shaking. Cardiac massage. Count. Keep counting. Come on, little guy, hang in there. Don't give up on me! Breathe, Étienne. Breathe! The nurse is looking at me. She puts a hand on my shoulder. Her voice is gentle.

"It's over. There's no pulse."

"There had been a car accident. When the grandfather came in, he was in cardiac arrest. The boy was conscious. He had an open fracture of the right femur. His blood pressure was falling, so I told the nurse to administer intravenous medication while I stabilized the grandfather. I got the dosage wrong. The nurse didn't double-check. It wasn't a huge mistake, but serious enough to be lethal. The child went into respiratory depression. I couldn't resuscitate him. Stefan, the head of my department, showed up five minutes later. By then it was all over."

"Did the grandfather die, too?"

"No. His pelvis was fractured. He pulled through after spending a few days in intensive care. I tried to keep working afterward, but as the weeks went by, I couldn't get a grip on myself. Every time I saw a child ... Étienne was five years old. He had a mop of tousled hair and freckles on his nose, and there was a heart drawn in ballpoint on his right hand." I stopped to wipe away my tears. "Stefan made sure I wasn't bothered by the hospital administration, and he saw to it that the death was ruled accidental. Was he simply covering his own ass because we were a couple? The boy's parents never believed it, especially not the father. There were some death threats. My relationship with Stefan began to go downhill. I couldn't forgive him for getting on with his life as though nothing had happened. And at a deeper level, I suppose I was angry that he hadn't been there to help me. I've always thought, rightly or wrongly, that those five minutes would have changed everything, that he'd have caught my mistake, that the little boy's life would have been saved."

"So you left?"

"'Fled' would be a better word. Quebec City was suddenly too small. I had sworn to myself that I'd never talk to my father or Stefan again."

We were silent for a moment.

"There were days when I wanted to end it all, to inject myself with the vials of morphine that I kept in a drawer of my bedside table."

Laurent nodded.

"I still think about the boy every day. He'd be twelve years old today."

To keep his anxiety at bay, Lessard tried to stay busy.

Why hadn't Langevin delivered that damn composite sketch? It should have been done hours ago. The detective sergeant searched the Montreal Police directory and found his cell number. Langevin was in his twenties. A tall, gangly kid with bleached hair.

"Hello?" said a female voice.

"Xavier Langevin?" Lessard growled.

He heard whispers and muffled laughter at the other end of the line.

"Uhh … he's kind of busy right now. Can I take a message?"

"Tell him it's Victor Lessard, and if he doesn't get on the line right now, I'm going to shove my gun so far down his throat it'll come out his asshole."

He heard more whispers.

"Detective Lessard, I —"

"Shut up and listen. Fifteen minutes. That's how much time you have to get your dick back in your pants and bring me that composite sketch."

He hung up, steaming, then called Adams.

"We haven't identified any prints yet, Victor. Nothing."

"What about the kinky photographs?"

"They weren't taken with the camera found in the BMW. I'm still looking for the retailer who sold the equipment. I have five or six possibilities left. It's just a matter of time."

"Hang in there, Doug."

Next, Lessard tried to reach Berger. He got his voice mail. He was in such a foul humour that he left an offensive message, then instantly regretted it. He was calling back to apologize when Berger answered.

"How's it going?" Lessard said, embarrassed. "I'm just getting in touch, uh … to find out if you've come up with anything."

"I was about to call you. The toxicology reports have come in. No trace of Amytal, or any other drug, for that matter. As for the identity of the first victim, I think you're right. It's the man whose photographs are on that website, Stefan Gustaffson. But I can't give you an official opinion until a relative formally identifies him. I'm also waiting for the results of the dental comparison."

"I understand. Uh …" He wanted to put this delicately. "I just left you a message. Do me a favour and delete it without listening to it. I'm under a lot of stress. Thanks, Jacob."

What next? Why hadn't Simoneau called back?

Lessard picked up his leather jacket and stepped outside. He crossed the street and went to the convenience store in the building facing the police station. On an impulse, he bought a pack of

Camels and, even though he had quit five years ago, smoked two of them before stepping back into the station.

Simoneau called twenty minutes later.

"I talked to the doctor again. Delorme isn't on Amytal or any other barbiturate."

"You're sure?"

"Absolutely. He opened the file in front of me."

Simoneau promised to call back in an hour.

What did this mean? Had the barbiturate been used for some other purpose? Lessard went back to his office and picked up the sheet he'd printed at the library. As he reread it, one passage caught his attention.

> Higher doses can cause visual problems, slurred speech,
> impaired perception of time and distance, as well as a slow-
> ing of reflexes and respiration. An overdose can lead to
> coma and death.

Lessard pondered. Impaired perception of time, slowed reflexes. Coma.

What were you planning to do with the stuff? You didn't drug your first two victims. Who were you going to give it to? Simone Fortin?

They had to find her, whatever it took.

Lessard called Ariane's number and got her voice mail again. It was nearly five o'clock. Where the hell was she?

33

Lessard picked up the sheets that the fax machine had spat out. The ethics committee file that Marcel Loranger had sent was fifteen pages long. The detective sergeant returned to his office and looked over the document. It was much more detailed than he'd expected. It had been dictated by Loranger himself. The first thing that caught Lessard's eye was the file number on the complaint.

No. 10161416.

Why was that number so familiar?

Lessard was about to consult his notes when he remembered the discs. The file number was the same as the number printed on the discs found at Gustaffson's home and Mongeau's office. If there had been any doubts about whether the investigative team was on the right track, this put them to rest.

A photocopied press clipping dated March 28th, 1998, accompanied the file. Lessard looked at it.

The headline said it all: BLUNDER AT ENFANT-JÉSUS HOSPITAL? The accident had taken place around 11:00 a.m.

Lessard scanned the first paragraph.

The grandfather, Robert Delorme, had brought the boy to visit the forestry school in Duchesnay, where he had formerly been an instructor. They were driving home on Route 143, about forty-five kilometres from Quebec City, when a tractor-trailer swerved and rammed their vehicle.

The story went on to describe how it had taken an ambulance thirty minutes to reach them and another thirty to get them to the hospital. When the EMTs arrived, local volunteer firefighters had already stabilized the injured man and boy. As for the driver of the tractor-trailer, he'd been treated for shock.

The article then lapsed into sensationalism, raising doubts about the quality of the medical care the two had received without citing specific facts. But it ended with a troubling question: "How is it possible that a little boy in perfect health was admitted with a simple fracture, only to die a short time later?"

A second page was devoted to an interview with a grieving neighbour who said she had known the little boy and his mother very well.

There was also a brief article that quoted a hospital spokesman as saying there would be no comment "before the facts are clearly established."

Lessard set aside the clipping and began to read the official report. Loranger's account opened with a clinical description of the victims' medical conditions when they were brought in.

This description was so technical that Lessard had trouble understanding it. But from what he could gather, the boy had been put on intravenous medication while his grandfather was being attended to. The child had subsequently lost consciousness and died.

There was a detailed description of the measures Simone Fortin had taken. Once again, the technical language was hard to follow. Lessard skipped to the conclusions. The committee members were unanimous in finding that adequate treatment had been administered. As a result, the parents' complaint was rejected and the case was closed.

In an addendum to the main report, Loranger described the unpleasant incident that had occurred during the hearing. Whereas the report itself was highly detailed and precise, Loranger's language in the addendum was strikingly vague. He simply observed that "Mr. Delorme, the patient's father, made statements that were offensive, disturbing, and liable to cause Dr. Fortin to fear for her safety."

Lessard put down the document.

He could understand the father's distress. Losing a child must have been unbearable. But it didn't justify murder. Without knowing why, Lessard felt uneasy. Once again, he had a feeling that he was overlooking something. He reread the file carefully, but he still couldn't put his finger on what was bothering him.

Pearson appeared in the doorway. There was a large brown coffee stain on his shirt.

"I'm going home to change. I should be back in three quarters of an hour."

"No rush. Spend some time with the baby. It's pointless for all of us to be here twiddling our thumbs. I'll call you if anything comes up."

Pearson's expression darkened. He resented what he saw as Lessard's attempt to sideline him.

"I'll be back in forty-five minutes. No more."

Unable to sit still, Lessard got up and went to Fernandez's office. He sank into the visitor's chair and let out a sigh.

"I'll be gone after this investigation ends."

Fernandez frowned.

"You're quitting?"

He told her about the confrontation with Tanguay.

"He can't fire you for that. The union will back you up."

"He'd be doing me a favour if he threw me out. I'm not worthy of this job."

"Don't say that. You know it's not true."

Lessard hesitated.

"Do you remember the informant who told me about the stolen BMW?"

"The anonymous call?"

"I lied."

"What do you mean?"

"It was Martin."

Fernandez stared.

"Your son? What are you talking about?"

Lessard took a deep breath. His lungs ached.

"He's mixed up in that car-theft ring we've been after. He and an accomplice were the ones who stole the BMW. My son is a common criminal, and I hid that fact from the investigation team."

The young woman sat in silence for a moment as a tear rolled down Lessard's cheek.

"What you did was stupid," she said at last, "but I would have done the same thing."

He looked at her, surprised. "Really?"

"Of course. He's your son. What else could you do?"

Fernandez put her hand on his for a moment. Feeling awkward, Lessard pulled away.

"We need a pick-me-up," she said. "I'm going out for pizza. You want some?"

"I'm not hungry."

"Ah, come on, Lessard. Sparkling water with that?"

"Thanks, Nadja. You're sweet."

She gave him a significant look that caught him by surprise.

"I'm more than just sweet, Victor."

She put on her coat and went out.

Lessard pondered that last remark. What did she mean?

He needed to keep busy, or he'd lose his mind.

He picked up his notebook, intending to go over the notes he'd taken since the beginning of the investigation, but he couldn't concentrate. He went out to the parking lot and smoked three cigarettes in quick succession.

He couldn't help thinking that with each passing minute, Simone Fortin's chances of survival went down. The killer on her trail would show no mercy.

He dialed Ariane's number, but hung up when the call went to voice mail. Maybe she didn't want to talk to him. After all, he had crept away without even bothering to leave a note. He also tried to reach Nguyen, but once again, the call went to voice mail. He left a message. What a maddening day. Nothing was moving.

What else could he do, but wait?

He decided to call his sister. She answered after two rings.

"Hey, it's Victor."

"I know," she said coldly. "Your name's on the caller ID."

"Am I disturbing you?"

She didn't answer the question.

"I … uhh … I'm sorry about the way I behaved at Christmas dinner. I was drunk, and … I was an idiot. I've stopped drinking. I'm going to AA."

His sister began to sob. Lessard felt his own throat tighten.

"Don't cry, Valérie. I'm totally to blame. I apologize."

"It's not that." She sniffled. "It's Paul. The bastard's having an affair. With one of his students."

Lessard had to fight down an impulse to let out a whoop. He had never liked his brother-in-law. The guy was a literature professor who'd spent the last fifteen years telling everyone that he was about to finish a novel.

"Are you going to leave him?"

"I was ready to wipe the slate clean, but he's the one who's decided to leave. The girl is twenty-two, Victor! She has breasts like Monica Bellucci. A body that's never been through pregnancy!" She was weeping. "He could almost be her grandfather."

Lessard took care not to say anything tactless, aware of his own propensity for spouting clichés.

"I know how hard it is, Valérie. You just need to be patient. You'll get over it eventually."

He was lying through his teeth. What he really believed was that there are some things you never get over. But he kept that to himself.

"It's good to hear your voice, Victor. When the phone rang, I was cutting up his underwear with scissors." She laughed. "Come by anytime."

"I will. I promise."

And he meant it. But almost a year would go by before he kept his promise.

Lessard had gotten up to go pour himself another cup of coffee when the phone rang.

"It's Simoneau. We've found him."

Lessard's heart skipped a beat.

"Where? When?"

"Actually, it's my partner who found him. While he was searching the house, he came across a cellphone bill. He decided to try calling the number, and ..."

"And the guy answered?" Lessard asked excitedly.

"Not exactly. The phone was answered by a priest who was looking after the guy's phone."

"A priest? What the hell are you talking about, Simoneau?"

"No joke. A priest at the Quebec City Seminary. That's where Pierre Delorme has been living for the past week."

Lessard was baffled.

"Hang on. I'm not following you ..."

"I know it sounds weird, but according to this priest, Pierre Delorme was given permission to stay at the François-de-Laval Residence. It's a midlife vocation centre for older men who want to enter the priesthood or who are looking for spiritual refuge. Delorme left his phone with the priest in case his wife called."

"Is he there now? Have you talked to him?"

"Not yet. Since he's on a closed retreat, I ..."

Lessard blew up. "I don't give a shit about his closed retreat, Simoneau! This is a criminal investigation, and we need to talk to the guy right away!"

"That's what I told them, but they insisted that I come in person. I'm driving over now. I should be there in fifteen minutes."

"Are you telling me the guy's been on a closed retreat this whole time, while the murders were being committed?"

"Sure seems like it."

"Would he have been able to leave for a few hours without anyone noticing?"

"The priest said the men do get some free time. But he didn't know anything about Delorme's comings and goings."

"Could he have slipped away at night?"

"I don't know. I'm guessing he could."

"That would give the guy a perfect alibi! Call me as soon as you're with him, Simoneau. I want to be the first person to question him."

"Will do."

Lessard unleashed a string of swears.

Over the past few hours, childhood memories that Laurent thought were lost forever had been flooding back. Driving had turned out to be beneficial. It helped him think clearly. He hadn't wanted a drink since their stop at the service station.

He knew he wouldn't need to drive for days to reach a decision.

He couldn't go against his father's wishes. It was true that for years, in an effort to make the situation more bearable, he'd been clinging to theoretical arguments. He'd been giving himself excuses — such as the possibility of a scientific breakthrough — for postponing the decision to end Miles's life.

But did he really hold out hope that science might someday cure his father, or was he just being selfish? Was he simply afraid to cut the last thread that bound him to his family?

Even if the man on that hospital bed was a pale shadow of what Miles had once been, Laurent loved him no less.

By now they were within thirty kilometres of Montreal.

Every so often, he would glance at the rear-view mirror and see Simone fast asleep in the back seat.

Lessard called Sirois, who had gotten as far as Saint-Hyacinthe on the road to Quebec City, updated him on recent developments, and ordered him to proceed directly to the seminary. He hadn't stopped thinking about his conversation with Simoneau.

Was the whole thing too far-fetched? Even if Pierre Delorme had some free time at the residence, how could he possibly have committed a murder in Montreal and gotten back to Quebec City, a drive of more than two hours, without anyone noticing?

By doing it at night?

But Mongeau had been killed in the middle of the day.

A sudden feeling of anxiety came over Lessard, an extreme level of urgency that he hadn't felt before. Something was seriously out of place. He could feel it.

He reread his notes. What was he overlooking? What was it that had eluded him?

The image of the two caribou heads came back into his mind, along with the stuffed moose head on the wall of Pierre Delorme's home.

Why was he thinking about these things?

What had Simoneau said? Lessard couldn't remember the exact words, but he'd been talking about a hunting trophy.

As simple and gruesome as the theory seemed, Lessard wondered if the severed finger might simply be a trophy.

But that was beside the point. Something else was nagging at him. *What, damn it? What?* He thought of Valérie again. What had she said about her husband?

He could almost be her grandfather.

The grandfather. What had Loranger's report said about him?

The solution was there somewhere, he knew it. He had read a phrase that had caught his eye, but he hadn't made the connection. What was it? He scanned the loose sheets on his desk.

The newspaper clipping.

He reread the first paragraph. Without really knowing why, he underlined a passage. "The grandfather, Robert Delorme, had brought the boy to visit the forestry school in Duchesnay, where he had formerly been an instructor ..."

He caught his breath and felt the space around him begin to contract. He lingered over one word and considered it, letter by letter.

Forestry.

The mental images were colliding. It was a matter of intuition rather than knowledge. In the forest, an unsuspecting deer moves among the trees. Behind it, close by, a hunter shoulders his rifle in the early morning light.

Lessard tried to open his browser, but his trembling hands made it difficult. After several painstaking attempts, he found the website for the Duchesnay School of Forestry and Woodland Technology.

He scanned the home page without finding what he was looking for. Under the Study Programs tab, he clicked on Protection and Exploitation of Wildlife Reserves.

He felt faint.

At the bottom of the page, a harmless-looking line of text was assaulting his retinas. *Principal job openings: wildlife protection officer; hunting, fishing, and trapping guide.*

It took Lessard a few seconds to process the information.

The grandfather had taught at the forestry school in Duchesnay — a school where people were trained to be hunting guides.

The detective sergeant froze.

Now he saw clearly what he had only sensed intuitively a moment ago. There would be no need to check on Pierre Delorme's comings and goings. He wasn't the killer.

Lessard shuddered.

He was now convinced that somewhere in the streets of Montreal, a grandfather was tracking his prey, waiting for the right moment to move in for the kill.

A hunter.

What was the best place to lie in wait? Lessard felt the bile rise in his throat.

A few weeks ago, on the National Geographic channel, he'd watched footage of a hibernating polar bear. A member of the production team had talked about how rare it was to film the animal in its natural habitat.

They had tracked it to its den.

With trembling hands, he checked his voice mail. He called Constable Nguyen three times.

No answer.

He grabbed his leather jacket and ran to his car.

What if he was wrong again? No. Not this time.

As he pulled out, he almost ran over a pedestrian. He honked his horn. The pedestrian jumped aside, and Lessard sped away.

He didn't register that the pedestrian was Langevin, coming to deliver the composite sketch.

Nor did Langevin recognize the detective sergeant, whose face had gone deathly pale and whose bulging eyes seemed to be staring in all directions at once.

Lessard's cellphone rang, but he didn't answer. He needed all his concentration to drive. Officer Simoneau left a message that

Lessard would only hear hours later, after it was all over. The Quebec City cop was with Pierre Delorme.

Lessard raced through the snowy streets. He never glanced in his rear-view mirror long enough to notice that an unmarked car was following him.

34

Sine sanguine non fit redemptio.
(Without blood there is no redemption.)

— Saint Paul, Epistle to the Hebrews

When I woke up, Laurent and I were rolling across the Jacques Cartier Bridge into the city. We only exchanged a few words, as though each of us understood that the important thing now was to process our emotions, not to share them.

We had agreed that we'd get together for a bite to eat later that evening. And I had offered to let Laurent sleep on my couch. Worn out, he had accepted my invitation. But first, he intended to visit the Notre-Dame-des-Neiges Cemetery. I had a feeling it was a symbolic act. Did he want to walk in the footsteps of his father's ghost one last time before removing the feeding tube?

He stopped the car in front of my building.

"There's a curry place not far from here," I said. "We can bring our own wine."

I only realized the blunder after it was out of my mouth. Wine was out of the question.

"I'm sorry, I wasn't thinking —"

"It's okay. Curry would be great."

I got out of the car and closed the door. He rolled down the window.

"Simone!"

I turned around.

"Do you really think Miles wants me to let him go?"

I nodded.

He drove away.
Blowing snow had begun to fall.

I put the key in the lock, opened the door, and locked it behind me.

The first thing I would do was get undressed and take a hot bath. Though I didn't want to admit it to myself, I was hoping my old nemesis the cat had come in. I groped for the light switch and pressed it. Nothing happened.

The fuse box was acting up again. This was one of the drawbacks of living in an old apartment — an antediluvian electrical system. But I was pretty sure there were some spare fuses in the kitchen.

I took off my coat and boots. I walked up the hallway and tried another light switch.

Nothing.

I looked out the living-room window. Maybe there had been a local blackout. No, the lights were on in the building across the street. Damn system. This time, the owner would have to renovate. Otherwise, I'd complain to the Rental Board.

I edged forward along the dark hallway. Suddenly, I felt something wet under my feet.

Were the pipes leaking?

That was all I needed!

I bent down and touched the liquid. It was viscous. Oil? I couldn't see a thing. I'd deal with it later.

In the kitchen, I tried another switch. The light came on instantly.

I screamed. What I saw would mark me for life.

A police officer was lying dead in a puddle of blood, and … oh, my God. Ariane!

I rushed over to my friend, knelt down, and turned her over.

Her throat had been cut.

Our picnics at Beaver Lake, our cross-country ski excursions on Mount Royal, our sushi dinners at home, our afternoons spent drawing pictures with Mathilde, our bike rides along the Lachine

Canal, our weekend camping trips to Vermont, our evenings spent sipping wine and ogling waiters at outdoor restaurants; my confidant, my friend, my sister, my twin, my guide, the four points of my compass … shattered.

Before I could get my bearings, a voice spoke behind me, cold and hard.

"Hello, Simone."

For a moment I was unable to move, paralyzed by fear.

Overcoming my terror, I turned slowly.

A man was staring at me. Short, with unremarkable features and a few wrinkles. Midfifties? Early sixties? Younger? He was holding a bloody knife.

From his calm expression, I knew I was going to die.

Why? Who was he?

"Don't you remember me?" the man asked.

I shook my head, unable to speak.

He pulled a piece of paper from his pocket. No, it was a photograph. He handed it to me.

"What about him?"

I looked at the photograph. A face dotted with freckles.

It was him. Little Étienne. A knot in my throat made it difficult to speak.

"Étienne," I said weakly.

"Very good, Simone. Your memory isn't so bad, after all."

He stepped closer, grabbed me by the hair, and dragged me along the floor to the bedroom.

The pain was so great, I couldn't even cry out.

When he opened the door, I saw Mathilde on the bed, bound and gagged. A chair had been drawn up to the bedside. A book lay on the chair.

"Don't worry, Mathilde. Everything's going to be fine."

I tried to get up, tried to hit him with my feet and fists, but he grabbed me by the throat and cut the skin under my right eye, releasing a trickle of blood.

He leaned in close and murmured in my ear. His fetid breath reeked of coffee. "We were reading Andersen's fairy tales when you came in. A book I gave Étienne for his fifth birthday. If you co-operate, her life will be safe, you have my word. If you try anything, I'll kill her."

He ran the knife blade along the curves of my face. Then he closed the door softly.

"Who are you? What do you want?"

"Try to remember, Simone. Who was in the car with Étienne? Who did you look after first, neglecting to check on the boy's condition?"

"The grandfather! You're his grandfather."

I glanced around, panic-stricken. There was a baseball bat in the broom closet. I had to find a way to distract him. After what he'd done to Ariane, I knew he wouldn't hesitate to kill Mathilde and me.

I struggled to calm down. Panicking wouldn't help. I needed to make him talk, to lower his guard.

"I remember. I treated you. You had multiple fractures."

"That's right. You did a first-rate job." Yanking on my hair, he pulled me to my feet. "See? I'm fit as a fiddle. Too bad you weren't so skillful when it came to Étienne."

"Medicine isn't an exact science. I did my best to save him. But I made a mistake. That can happen to anyone."

"Now we're getting somewhere," he said, his voice rising. "Mistake. A forgotten word in our society. Why does nobody talk about fault anymore, Simone? Everyone is always going on and on about probability, statistics, risk evaluation, unfulfilled commitments. It's not the losing driver who blundered, it's the race car that had a glitch. It's not the politician who lied to the public, it's the estimates that were thrown off by the previous administration's budget gap. Yes, Simone, mistakes can happen to anyone. The trouble is, no one takes responsibility for them anymore. Who raises a hand to say, 'I messed up, I'm sorry, I'm prepared to face the consequences'? The worst error of all, Simone, is denying the existence of error. Lying. Continuing to live as though nothing had happened. So what if some corporation is spying on its employees? Or if some multinational is turning out products that harm people's health? Even if the evidence is overwhelming, the executives will deny, deny, deny. They'll appear on TV and lie through their teeth. And we, as a society, keep putting up with it. Integrity, Simone. There just isn't enough of it anymore."

"What about murder? Is that any better?"

He laughed heartily.

"Murder in itself isn't necessarily a mistake. As long as he's willing to face the consequences, why shouldn't the father of a sexually abused child punish the abuser who gets off with a laughable fourteen-month sentence, of which he'll actually serve a third?"

Could I somehow get to the phone and dial 911?

I needed to play for time, to keep him talking.

"If everyone took the law into his own hands, we'd collapse into anarchy."

"At first, yes. But the deterrent effect would settle things down in a hurry."

"And what about killing innocent human beings? How does that fit into your scheme?"

"I grant you, it was wrong of me to kill the police officer and that lovely young woman. I'll have to live with the consequences of my actions. But sometimes, collateral damage can't be avoided."

A wave of nausea suddenly washed over me. Ariane ... what had this monster done to my friend?

"I've admitted to you that I made a mistake in Étienne's case. And believe me, I've regretted it every day of my life since it happened. It's why I don't practise medicine anymore."

"What do you want me to do about that?" He raged. "Are you expecting me to show mercy? Do you think maybe you're the victim in all this?" He composed himself. "Why didn't you come clean when you had the chance? You deceived and manipulated the ethics

committee by conspiring with Stefan Gustaffson to hide your mistake. You could have told the truth to a family that was shattered
by grief. You could have looked them in the eye and told them *why*
their son had died. They just wanted a little compassion. A little
dignity. To be treated like human beings. But no, you decided to lie
so you could save your career. And the system protected you. The
hospital's executive director, Jacques Mongeau, refused to review
the committee's decision. But then, like I said, that's how things
work. Nobody acknowledges mistakes in our society. Above all, no
one faces the consequences. As long as someone out there is doing
worse things than you are, you can just point fingers and tell yourself you're not to blame."

I began to cry. The man was deranged, but he was right about
one thing. Instead of facing the consequences, I had hidden away.
And I was ashamed.

"Did you ever stop for a few minutes to think about the parents?
About what they were going through? Do you know what became
of them? My son is a mental patient, Simone. He drifts from one
depressive breakdown to the next. My flesh and blood. As for my
daughter-in-law, she spends her time in a drugged-out haze. She's a
heroin addict. Their lives have been destroyed, obliterated by your
falsehoods. And for that, Simone, you will now pay. You will face
the consequences of your mistakes. You will be punished."

Still brandishing his knife, he pulled a syringe from his pocket.

"What's that?"

"A barbiturate. At high doses, it acts as a paralytic. In a few
minutes, you'll be conscious, but incapable of moving. You'll
witness your own death in real time, without being able to do
anything about it. Just like Étienne. If I've got the dosage wrong,
the drug will plunge you into a coma, or kill you. Which would
be a shame."

I knew that if he injected me with the drug, I'd die without any
chance of saving Mathilde. I tried to wrestle free, but he tight-
ened his grip and dragged me by the hair into one of the empty

bedrooms. In the middle of the room, he had created a circle of votive candles.

I was on my knees. His intention was to make me stretch out inside the circle. All I could see was one thing: the syringe. As the man began to press downward, I made my move. It felt like everything was happening in slow motion. Channelling all my strength, I straightened my legs and pushed upward, knocking him off balance. He reacted by pulling harder on my hair, but I kept rising. I was resolved not to stop, whatever happened.

I felt the hair lifting from its roots, and then the skin itself stretching, separating, and finally tearing away altogether as a lightning bolt of pain shot through me. But I was on my feet, with my attention entirely focused on the syringe. For a moment, the man stared in surprise at the piece of scalp in his hand. Taking advantage of his brief distraction, I seized his wrist with both hands, held it tightly, and sank my teeth into the base of the thumb, biting down with all my strength. I saw his fingers release their grip one by one. The syringe seemed to hang in the air for an instant before it fell. The needle broke when it hit the floor.

At the same moment, I felt a cold stroke in my flesh. I turned and saw the man pulling his blood-soaked knife out of my right shoulder. The sensation was bizarre. I don't remember feeling any pain. A shudder went through me, similar to the spasm that incapacitates you when you're suffering from a fever. Unable to stand, I fell onto my back. I could barely hear what the man was saying.

"You should have let me inject you, Simone. I'm going to take my time. I want you to appreciate the show."

He started by slicing up my face. Each time the tip of the blade touched my cheekbone, an electric jolt went through me, reminding me that I was alive. Then he cut open my blouse and bra, exposing my chest. By now, I felt like I was outside myself, observing the scene. The man bending over me had withdrawn as well, leaving only a predator crouched atop its prey.

He grazed the knife across my chest; he pierced my bicep and shoulder. Each new wound he inflicted wasn't meant to kill, only to cause additional damage as I sank deeper into numbness. Finally, the man raised the blade, aiming for my heart.

I was looking at what I believed was the last thing I would ever see: a blurred image of the vein throbbing in the man's temple, his body and his weapon merging into a single, unified whole as the votive candles glinted in the blade that was poised to end my life.

A deafening explosion filled the room. The man stopped in mid-movement. Like a puppet whose strings had been cut, he sank to his knees and fell backward to the floor, blood spreading across his shirt.

Night falls, black and moonless. He's scared, but the old man will be proud of him. He moves forward, compass in hand. Suddenly, he sees two staring yellow eyes through the trees. Lights! As he advances, he realizes that the truck's headlights have been turned on. He makes an effort not to walk too fast. The old man gets mad if you run with a rifle. "Dad! Dad! I got him!" The yell bursts out of him. He's too excited to hold it in. No answer. Now he understands. The old man has gone out looking for him, leaving the headlights on to help him find his way. The truck is only a few paces off. Its headlight beams are blinding him. The driver's door is open, and he can make out a silhouette inside. "Dad?" He steps closer. The interior is splattered with brains. His father is covered in blood. Half his skull has been blown away. His finger is still curled around the trigger.

Victor Lessard reholstered his weapon and bent over Simone to check her pulse. She was alive. He called 911.

Her lips moved.

He told her not to speak, to save her strength. But her eyelids fluttered and she murmured something. He leaned closer to hear.

"Mat ... ild ... in ... edroom ..."

"In the bedroom? I'll be right back."

Lessard went up the hallway toward the other bedroom. Its door was closed. That was when he saw the bodies in the kitchen. Nguyen and Ariane. Yes, it was her. He wasn't dreaming.

Rage swept through him. This time, he didn't vomit. He walked straight up to the man lying on the floor. He cocked his pistol and aimed at the forehead.

He was about to fire when a voice rang out behind him.

"No, Lessard! Lower your weapon."

He turned.

Commander Tanguay, who had followed him from the station in an unmarked vehicle, was walking slowly toward him. Lessard holstered his gun.

Simone Fortin staggered toward the murderer and sank to her knees beside his motionless body. Where had she found the strength to move? It didn't matter. There was no way Lessard would stop her from finishing the man off.

She began to administer cardiac massage. Was he dreaming, or was she giving orders to Tanguay?

"You! Grab a towel and apply pressure to the wound. If the ambulance comes quickly, we may be able to save him."

"Emergency units are on their way," Tanguay said, obeying her commands.

Lessard went back to the bedroom and held the little girl in his arms. He rocked her, whispering soothing words in her ear, until help arrived. When the EMTs tried to take Mathilde from him, he became so agitated that everyone backed off. It was only when Fernandez arrived that he agreed to follow her out of the apartment and into a patrol car.

Outside the building, a local TV news team captured close-up footage of a weeping Lessard clinging to the child as tightly as a shipwrecked sailor might cling to a lifebuoy.

Long after the police car had rolled away, the reporter, deeply affected, ordered the cameraman to erase the footage he'd shot.

It was a gesture of respect that no one would ever hear about. If the station's news director had learned of it, there would have been hell to pay. But the reporter didn't regret it for a moment.

Maybe there's a shred of decency left in me, he thought, as light snow swept along the street.

VICTOR LESSARD

On Sunday, May 1st, 2005, Victor Lessard walked to a convenience store on Monkland Avenue and bought a bouquet of red roses.

From there he headed up to Terrebonne Street, went west as far as Grand Boulevard, then north to Somerled. The sun was glinting off the cars. Passersby were dressed in light clothes, and the trees were budding. Spring had come knocking at the door like a mischievous kid.

He arrived at Station 11 around noon. Stopping in the kitchenette to pour himself a cup of coffee, he greeted Constable Chagnon, who was in conversation with the team's latest recruit, Macha Garneau. Youthful and slender, Garneau was a recent graduate of police college. She had been hired to replace Nguyen, who had died in the line of duty.

Lessard hoped she'd survive the jungle of Montreal's streets.

He closed his office door softly behind him.

The official funeral had taken place a few weeks previously. Officers had come from all over the country, and even from the United States, to pay their last respects to a fallen comrade. But despite an offer of help from Fernandez and Sirois — who knew writing wasn't his strong suit — Lessard had insisted on drafting and delivering his own speech. On the morning of the funeral, he still hadn't managed to string together two sentences.

Squeezed into his dress uniform, he had stepped to the lectern not knowing what he was going to say. He'd started off a little shakily, but eventually he had hit his stride, using simple words to describe their late colleague's human qualities, his contribution to the team, and the gaping hole he was leaving behind in their lives and their community.

Returning to his seat, Lessard was surprised to see that he'd spoken for over ten minutes. He couldn't even remember exactly what he'd said, but Pearson had looked over with tears in his eyes and nodded his approval.

Nguyen had been a father of two little girls. When Lessard had approached his widow, whom he knew from Christmas parties, there was nothing he could do but take her in his arms.

He placed the bouquet on a chair and sat at his desk. The last few weeks had been long and difficult. He wanted to tidy up his papers before leaving.

The events of early April came back to him. Though he had tried to forget, the painful memories were still desperately vivid.

Thanks to Simone Fortin's timely intervention, doctors had succeeded in saving Robert Delorme's life. But the bullet had struck his spinal cord. He would never walk again.

Lessard had questioned Delorme several times. He had expected to feel animosity toward the man, but he'd felt a kind of void instead, a deep and overwhelming sense of weariness.

He slipped a few sheets into a cardboard folder. Beneath them, he found a transcript of one of the interrogations. He began to read.

April 14, 2005

Re: Robert Delorme Interrogation
Interrogator: Victor Lessard
Witness: Nadja Fernandez

Witness: Mr. Delorme, have you been informed of your constitutional rights?
Suspect: Yes.

Witness: Do you wish to have a lawyer present?

Suspect: No.

Witness: The interrogation can begin.

Q: Why did you want to kill Simone Fortin?

A: To make her face the consequences of her actions.

Q: What actions in particular do you blame her for?

A: She killed my grandson.

Q: She may have made a mistake, but she also saved your life. Don't you ever make mistakes?

A: It wasn't the mistake I wanted to punish. It was her refusal to acknowledge it.

Q: Why did you wait so long? Étienne died in 1998.

A: She had dropped out of sight. I only found out where she was this year, in early March.

Q: How?

A: An article appeared in the newspaper, along with a photograph. She had created a piece of software that was sold at a charity auction.

Q: Why did you kill Stefan Gustaffson and Jacques Mongeau?

A: I had no choice. They needed to face the consequences of their mistakes.

Q: What did Gustaffson do that made him guilty in your eyes?

A: He lied to help his girlfriend cover up her mistake.

Q: And Jacques Mongeau?

A: He could have contested the decision of the ethics committee, but he didn't, because he was a coward.

Q: Why did you take the risk of transporting Stefan Gustaffson's body to Montreal?

A: (Inaudible.) I don't know.

Q: You wanted her to see him, didn't you?

A: I think so, yes.

Q: You think so? You should know. You planned the whole thing. We found your notes in your laptop.

A: I wanted her to understand that she was responsible for their deaths. I wanted her to go through what my son had gone through, even if it was just for a fraction of a second before she died herself.

Q: What were you planning to do with the blog? Post photographs of the victims?

A: (Stenographer's note: Suspect does not answer.)

Q: And why did you leave the discs at the crime scenes?

A: I wanted to set an example. These days people try to minimize their guilt by pointing fingers at others who have done worse things than themselves. I wanted the world to see what happens to those who try to dodge their responsibilities.

Q: Tell me about the chains that you bolted to the walls of your hunting lodge at Mont-Laurier. Were you planning to confine Simone Fortin there before killing her?

A: I wanted to destabilize her mind.

Q: How? By torturing her?

A: You don't understand.

Q: By showing her the bodies of Gustaffson and Mongeau? That's what the two freezers were for, right? To preserve the bodies?

A: (Stenographer's note: Suspect does not answer.)

Q: You were planning to transport the bodies of Gustaffson and Mongeau to the hunting lodge. That's also in your notes.

A: She needed to see.

Q: See what? Your insanity?

A: I'm not insane. I wanted her to see what happens when you don't take responsibility for your mistakes.

Q: And what about the projection system in your torture chamber? What was that for?

A: I had put together a video about Étienne, from his birth to his death.

Q: If you had prepared everything so she could see, why didn't you follow your plan? Why did you run her over with your car?

A: She was walking along so cheerfully. She seemed so happy, while my son ... (Inaudible.) I ... seeing her smile ... I couldn't bear it.

Q: And afterward? Why didn't you stick to your plan regarding Jacques Mongeau? You still could have killed him and transported his body to the hunting lodge.

A: I hadn't foreseen that the car might get stolen. I didn't know how much time I had. And I needed to be sure I could finish the job. I didn't want to run the risk of getting arrested before I was done.

Q: What about the photographs? Why did you take them?

A: So I wouldn't forget.

Q: Wouldn't forget what?

A: Why I'd killed them.

Q: When you cut off Jacques Mongeau's finger, that was also to help you remember, wasn't it? A hunting trophy?

A: I just wanted a reminder.

Q: A reminder of what?

A: That justice had been done.

Q: Do you really think justice was done? Did Étienne's death really need to be avenged with blood? And what about the killing of Ariane Bélanger? And Constable Nguyen? Was justice done for them? Wasn't it wrong for you to kill two people who had nothing to do with any of this?

A: I sincerely regret their deaths, but sometimes collateral damage is unavoidable. I had to finish what I'd started. But I readily admit that I did something wrong, and I'll face the consequences.

Q: You'll face the consequences? What does that mean? Are you aware that your madness has ruined the lives of numerous people? Jacques Mongeau had a family. Constable Nguyen had two kids. Ariane Bélanger was the mother of a little girl.

A: I'm not insane. I knew what I was doing, and I intend to face the consequences of my actions.

Q: Those are just words. But I hope with all my heart that the psychiatrists share your opinion about your mental health. (Inaudible.) In any case, I hope you realize that if you're alive today, it's because Simone Fortin saved your life a second time.

A: (Stenographer's note: Suspect does not answer.)

END OF INTERROGATION.

Lessard put down the document and sat for a while, lost in thought. Officially, Robert Delorme had killed four people. But Lessard knew the number of lives he had shattered was much higher. Little Mathilde had lost a mother; the Nguyen family had lost a father, a husband, a brother. Lessard himself had been deprived of a colleague and a woman who had briefly touched his life.

On top of all that, Fernandez had informed him last week that the killer's son had died of an overdose.

Was that just a coincidence? Or was it a direct consequence of his father's arrest and the shocking realization that he was the son of a monster? And in the end, what difference did it make? Pierre Delorme's death was yet another terrible waste.

Robert Delorme had decided to represent himself in court. There would be a trial. Justice would take its course. And so would injustice. When would the destructive madness that burned in human hearts finally be extinguished? Lessard was about to turn off the lights when Fernandez walked in.

"What are you doing here?" she asked. "I thought you'd left."

"I had some papers to file. I'm leaving this afternoon."

"How's Martin?"

"He's doing well. I've convinced him to enrol in a sound-engineering program. He's really excited about it. By the way, did you finish questioning Tool, the guy who was running the operation?"

"Yeah. With the information Martin gave us, it was a slam dunk. The ringleaders have all been rounded up. Tanguay's pleased."

The car-theft ring had been dismantled with ease on the strength of anonymous information provided by Lessard's son.

"Thank you for not telling anyone about Martin."

She seemed too moved to acknowledge his thanks. She stepped close and gave Lessard a hug. When she pulled away, she kissed him lightly on the lips.

"We're going to miss you, Victor. Stay in touch."

She hurried out, not wanting to cry.

Carrying the bouquet, Lessard arrived at the Notre-Dame-des-Neiges Cemetery around three. The grass was starting to turn green. Petunias were blooming around some of the gravestones. He hadn't walked this far in one day since he was a teenager.

He passed the chapel and went up the cemetery's main avenue. Birds were singing lustily, and two grey squirrels were chasing each other among the trees. Life was returning to the city after a long, hard winter.

Lessard remained in front of Ariane Bélanger's grave for a long while. She had died a month ago, almost to the day. Cut down in her prime. He had never believed in an afterlife. There was nothing he wanted to say. He didn't believe in heaven, either. But the connection he'd shared with Ariane, brief though it was, had stayed with him. It would help him on the road ahead.

He looked at the grave one last time before turning around and going back the way he had come.

Without noticing it, he walked past a grey granite headstone that stood over a fresh grave.

Miles Green
1956–2005

He went back along the main avenue to the chapel. The others hadn't arrived yet. He sat down on a bench to wait.

Tanguay hadn't demanded any explanations. The commander had even congratulated him for preventing Robert Delorme from committing another murder. Lessard would be awarded a service medal. Tanguay had also refrained from bringing up Lessard's failure to inform him about Stefan Gustaffson's murder.

In return, Lessard had taken no further action regarding the kinky photographs in Jacques Mongeau's computer, and had decided not to do any more digging into the "intimate soirées."

What role had Tanguay played in the whole affair? Was he personally implicated? Protecting someone? Had he been taking bribes from Mongeau in return for his protection? Had anyone blackmailed him? Was he the man who had posed as a journalist?

Lessard would never know. The truth was, he didn't care. The only thing that mattered was striking a deal and ending hostilities.

Tanguay had granted him the six-month leave of absence he'd requested, half of which would be paid.

Lessard had left the commander's office without shaking his hand. There was no longer any respect between the two men, only a working relationship based on a shared understanding of their respective interests.

He saw the car coming up the avenue.

Marie had agreed in principle to the idea of shared custody. Within a month, Lessard would be able to keep the kids for three consecutive days each week. If everything went well during that trial period, he'd be able to take them for seven days at a stretch, alternating with Marie.

Charlotte was the first one out of the car. She threw her arms around him. Martin came after her. As always, the boy had headphones over his ears, but he was grinning from ear to ear. Marie, leaning against the car, was smiling, too.

He had already bought a tent, a camping stove, and sleeping bags. The kids were thrilled at the idea of crossing the country by train. If everything went according to plan, they'd be gone for six weeks.

Victor Lessard lifted a tear-streaked face to the sun.

He didn't know what the future held. He didn't know whether he'd go back to police work when he returned. But with his daughter hugging him for all she was worth, he couldn't help thinking that life was a beautiful thing.

At times.

SIMONE FORTIN

The sun's glare is intense on this unseasonably warm September day, but a caressing wind helps keep the heat at bay.

I stretch lazily.

Beyond the wharf, the river has extended a couple of liquid tentacles between the few boats that lie on their sides like beached shellfish. At low tide, the salty tang of seaweed fills the air.

I look at my watch. It's almost one o'clock. Lunch break will be over soon. The nurses who came outside with me are putting on their shoes, getting ready to go back to work. I wrap up the uneaten half of my sandwich and do likewise.

Through the trees, I can make out the outline of the Trois-Pistoles Hospital. If we walk at a decent pace, we'll be back well before one-thirty. As I do every time I come here, I glance at the spot on the wharf marked with a cross, where Miles fractured his skull that summer day in 1998. I'm not sad or emotional. I simply walk with the others in silence.

After multiple requests to the College of Physicians, several interviews, and a few written examinations, I was given permission to practise medicine again on the condition that I redo my residency. I chose the Trois-Pistoles Hospital not out of nostalgia, but because I wanted to settle down in the area.

By pooling our savings, Laurent and I were able to buy the house on the Chemin du Havre where he had spent his childhood summers with Miles. Laurent has poured all his energy into restoring the place. Every evening, when I come home, his hair is full of plaster dust. But he never complains. He's been working on the house for several weeks now, and we'll soon be able to move in. I'll occupy the ground floor with Mathilde; Laurent will live upstairs. For the moment, we've agreed that the only shared space will be the kitchen.

Coming to the town's main street, the nurses and I walk past the church and then the rectory. A young priest is standing outside in his shirtsleeves, enjoying the sunshine. He waves at us, and I give him a big smile.

When I brought Mathilde to school this morning, her teacher pulled me aside. She showed me a drawing that the child had made. In it, Ariane was sitting in a blue sky beside a sun that shone down on three smiling people: Laurent, Mathilde, and me. "I think she's on the right track," the teacher said in a low voice. She was right. Mathilde has been through a lot, but time is slowly healing the wounds.

I continue to walk. The nurses in their white uniforms giggle when we pass a group of young men. I can sense them stealing glances at my face, but I hardly care.

The scars that Robert Delorme's knife etched into my flesh are still very visible, and they're certainly not attractive. The ones criss-crossing my body are easier to conceal.

The stab wound in my back punctured one of my lungs, but it didn't cause any permanent damage.

It took considerable effort for a medical specialist to reconstruct my torn scalp. The result isn't perfect, but the damage is hardly noticeable to an untrained eye.

We come to the hospital parking lot where I met Kurt Waldorf a few months ago. I keep walking, unfazed by the young men's reactions.

To me, these scars mean nothing. They're part of me, just like all my other imperfections. Ariane is dead, and I have no right to feel self-pity over such trivial considerations. And if I still cry when I remember her, or when I think of Stefan, I only do it late at night, when Mathilde is asleep. One sad irony: the cat I loved to hate never came back after Ariane's death.

I'm not angry at Robert Delorme. How could I be? As far as I'm concerned, he doesn't exist.

With the passage of time and Laurent's support, I've begun to forgive myself, both for Étienne Beauregard-Delorme's death (case in point: I've stopped referring to it as a "mistake") and for Ariane's. As Miles said, the line between a good decision and a bad one is sometimes very thin. I've even made peace with my father. He's supposed to come and visit us next month.

Will we get to know each other again?

I've stood by Laurent as he faced difficult challenges. I was at his side when Miles's feeding tube was removed, and again at the moment of his death. We buried Miles together in the cemetery he loved so much.

Sometimes, I accompany Laurent to his AA meetings. I feel so proud of him. We're learning to help and support each other.

A few days ago, he kissed me for the first time. It was a strange feeling, and we both laughed about it for a long time afterward. For now, all I feel toward him is boundless tenderness.

I have no expectations.

Many questions remain unanswered.

How could Miles have known about my past and little Étienne's death? How could I have spent twenty-four hours in his company when I was only in a coma for a few hours? Why, instead of giving me a clear message, did he send me back with that crazy anagram? Why did Miles's apartment and the jazz bar appear so different from reality?

As far as my past is concerned, I've reached the conclusion that Miles didn't know about it. All he did was create the conditions in which I could confront my own demons. As for all those other questions, I've learned to accept uncertainty. At the same time, I've rediscovered faith. Faith in those I cherish. Faith in myself.

Now, don't go thinking I've turned religious. But the fact remains — and it's a fact we're all too willing to overlook — that in life, as in death, there's an element of mystery. If we can only accept that mystery, it will bring a thrill to our existence.

Sadly, we human beings are all the same. We want answers. We don't even know what the questions are. But we still want answers.

As for me, I know that from now on, my redemption will lie in the hands of a stranger who holds a door open for me, in the fleeting smile of a passerby, in the gentle gaze of a woman carrying a child. Sometimes you find love where you least expect it. These days, there's redemption in an afternoon spent at the park with Mathilde, or in an hour sanding a wall with Laurent at my side.

Someday, perhaps someday soon, I'll visit George Griffin and Jamal Cherraf in their hospital rooms. And I'll call Kurt Waldorf. Just like that. To say hello.

You have to make time for the things that matter.

For now, though, I'm riding the elevator up to the third floor, where my shift will resume and I'll go back to my duties: treating patients, writing reports, giving instructions, leading meetings.

The nurses riding up with me are chattering and laughing. I'm keeping quiet, as usual, because of that rule I mentioned before:

Never talk in an elevator.

All the same, I'm humming a tune to myself, too low to be heard, with perhaps a little note of triumph in my voice. It's a song by Björk that's been going through my head ever since I saved Robert Delorme's life a second time:

"All Is Full of Love."

I'm alive.

RUN LATE

On the morning of October 3rd, at the Sainte-Justine Hospital in Montreal, thirteen-year-old Juan Ramos emerged from the coma in which he'd lain since April 15th, 2005. He'd been horsing around with friends at a dump when a stack of heavy planks collapsed onto him.

That morning, the duty nurse, who'd gotten into the habit of humming songs to Juan while she checked his vital signs, saw that his eyes were open and he was smiling at her.

"Welcome back," she said, her voice breaking with emotion.

The boy responded by asking for something to write on. The nurse handed him her pen and notepad, then watched carefully as he filled a sheet with fine, deliberate handwriting, as though he were trying to transcribe a message that he knew by heart.

When he was done, he gave her the sheet.

"What's this?" she asked.

"It's a message for Simone Fortin and Laurent Green. We need to find them and give it to them. It's very important. I promised Miles that I'd pass this along."

"Who's Miles?"

"He's a man I met while I was in a coma."

Juan saw the skeptical look on her face.

"Miles was in a coma, too," the boy said, "but he's gone now."

The nurse looked at the sheet, but she could make no sense of the strange text the boy had written down. It was just a series of words without any logical connection.

. . . .

A few minutes later, the treating physician walked in happily and examined Juan. Having lost a young patient the previous night, he was pleased by this unexpected reawakening.

Juan seemed to be in good condition, with no apparent loss of neurological function. As the doctor emerged from the room, he saw the nurse holding a piece of paper, wearing a concerned expression. He approached her.

"It could be transient confusion," he mused, after hearing the nurse's account of the message.

"He's convinced that he met someone while he was in a coma."

The doctor let out a long sigh.

"Another one. To hear them tell it, you'd think there was a whole other world out there."

The nurse smiled, but she was pensive for a long time after the doctor walked away.

One Saturday morning in November, Juan Ramos and his mother, Encarnacion, knocked at the door of a house on the Chemin du Havre in Trois-Pistoles.

The young woman who came to the door welcomed them warmly, offering a bowl of café au lait to Encarnacion and a glass of orange juice to Juan. Awkwardly, Encarnacion explained the reason for their visit: her son had insisted on coming here to deliver a nonsensical message. To her astonishment, the young woman took the matter very seriously and spent several long minutes talking to the boy. Encarnacion never really understood what passed between the two, but from that moment onward, she stopped doubting Juan's claims.

When Laurent brought Mathilde home from her skating lesson, Encarnacion and Juan Ramos had left. Simone had placed the message on a corner of the table, without even trying to decipher it.

• • •

After pouring himself a cup of coffee, Laurent read the message. It took him a couple of minutes to solve the anagram. He wrote down the solution for Simone's benefit.

She kept busy with various chores until late that evening. Then she made up her mind. Before looking at the words that Juan Ramos had written down, she took a deep breath.

She put the message back on the table.

Outside, the first snow of the season was falling in cottony squalls that drew long white streaks against the opaque sky. Another winter was beginning.

Simone Fortin stayed at the window for a long time, watching the white maelstrom. When she stepped outside tomorrow morning with Mathilde and Laurent, the virgin ground would be untouched, immaculate.

They would trace a path across it.

Their path.

AUTHOR'S NOTE: CONFESSION

Forgive me, dear readers, for I have sinned. I've taken some liberties in this novel. For plot purposes, I've reconfigured Côte-des-Neiges Road, creating buildings and businesses that don't exist in the real world. On the other hand, the walk that Miles and Simone take through the cemetery is rigorously accurate. The cemetery is worth visiting at any time of the year. It's an oasis of peace and beauty. If you'd like to share your impressions, or if you're interested in learning more about Lessard, come find me on Facebook at MartinMichaudAuteur.

ACKNOWLEDGEMENTS

To the friendly, collaborative, and enthusiastic team at Dundurn. It is an honour for me to be part of the family.

To Arthur Holden for understanding and respecting my characters and style in a very subtle way. When I read my book in English, I hear my voice. And that is because of your talent and sensitivity, my friend! You are the artist.

To my dear agent, Abigail Koons, for putting in the hard work and her faith in me at the start of this new journey, and for her ongoing guidance, passionate support, and ability to make me laugh. You are a gift.

I wish to thank my editor, Ingrid Remazeilles, and the whole Goélette team. It's a privilege to work with you. Heartfelt thanks to Marc-André Audet, who provided the initial impulse. Thanks, as well, to Louise Daoust for helping me to understand comas, and to the gardener at the Notre-Dame-des-Neiges Cemetery, who answered my questions when this novel was still just an idea.

I'd like to offer particular thanks to Geneviève, my parents, my sister Mélanie, and all those who offered their support as time went by (in no particular order): Marc, Hélène, Mireille, Pierre-Yves, Jacques, Nathalie, and Christophe.

Finally, special thanks to Sandrine and Stéphane, who were my first readers, and to Igor, who encouraged me to write this novel, saying that "the coma story" I had described to him sounded pretty cool.

Mystery and Crime Fiction from Dundurn Press

Victor Lessard Thrillers
by Martin Michaud
(QUEBEC THRILLER, POLICE PROCEDURAL)
Never Forget
Without Blood

The Day She Died
by S.M. Freedman
(DOMESTIC THRILLER, PSYCHOLOGICAL)

Amanda Doucette Mysteries
by Barbara Fradkin
(FEMALE SLEUTH, WILDERNESS)
Fire in the Stars
The Trickster's Lullaby
Prisoners of Hope
The Ancient Dead

The Candace Starr Series
by C.S. O'Cinneide
(NOIR, HITWOMAN, DARK HUMOUR)
The Starr Sting Scale
Starr Sign

Stonechild & Rouleau Mysteries
by Brenda Chapman
(INDIGENOUS SLEUTH, KINGSTON, POLICE PROCEDURAL)
Cold Mourning
Butterfly Kills
Tumbled Graves
Shallow End
Bleeding Darkness
Turning Secrets
Closing Time

Tell Me My Name
by Erin Ruddy
(DOMESTIC THRILLER, DARK SECRETS)

The Walking Shadows
by Brenden Carlson
(ALTERNATE HISTORY, ROBOTS)
Night Call
Coming soon: *Midnight*

Creature X Mysteries
by J.J. Dupuis
(CRYPTOZOOLOGY, FEMALE SLEUTH)
Roanoke Ridge
Coming soon: *Lake Crescent*

Birder Murder Mysteries
by Steve Burrows
(BIRDING, BRITISH COASTAL TOWN)
A Siege of Bitterns
A Pitying of Doves
A Cast of Falcons
A Shimmer of Hummingbirds
A Tiding of Magpies
A Dance of Cranes

B.C. Blues Crime
by R.M. Greenaway
(BRITISH COLUMBIA, POLICE PROCEDURAL)
Cold Girl
Undertow
Creep
Flights and Falls
River of Lies
Five Ways to Disappear

Jenny Willson Mysteries
by Dave Butler
(NATIONAL PARKS, ANIMAL PROTECTION)
Full Curl
No Place for Wolverines
In Rhino We Trust

Jack Palace Series
by A.G. Pasquella
(NOIR, TORONTO, MOB)
Yard Dog
Carve the Heart
Season of Smoke

The Falls Mysteries
by J.E. Barnard
(RURAL ALBERTA, FEMALE SLEUTH)
When the Flood Falls